ESCAPADE

DOLCE

Published by
DREAMSPINNER PRESS

5032 Capital Circle SW, Suite 2, PMB# 279, Tallahassee, FL 32305-7886 USA
www.dreamspinnerpress.com

This is a work of fiction. Names, characters, places, and incidents either are the product of author imagination or are used fictitiously, and any resemblance to actual persons, living or dead, business establishments, events, or locales is entirely coincidental.

ISBN: 978-1-63477-057-6
Digital ISBN: 978-1-63477-058-3
Library of Congress Control Number: 2015918972
Published April 2016
v. 1.0

Printed in the United States of America

This paper meets the requirements of
ANSI/NISO Z39.48-1992 (Permanence of Paper).

This work is dedicated to all the people who have helped me grow as a writer and given me the confidence to be myself.

To my family and friends, especially my parents, my hilarious brother, and my best friend, who were always supportive and believed in me, even when I was not yet comfortable sharing the writer side of myself with them. I especially want to thank my father, who passed away suddenly weeks before this book was published.

To English teachers and drama directors, who taught me to embrace creativity and run with it.

To patient, brilliant readers from lovely fandoms, who have supported me for years without asking for anything in return.

Acknowledgments

AN ENORMOUS thank-you to Jess, who was with me every step of the *Escapade* journey and has been both cheerleader and dear friend, someone who was always in my corner. I can't imagine writing *Escapade* without her support and am so, so thankful for her generosity. Thank you to Lina for the push I never knew I needed, along with Cass and Alice for their support. Thank you to my dear friends D, B, Kat, and H, who have been with me from the beginning. Thank you to local cafés who have strong coffee and even stronger Wi-Fi. Thank you to Dreamspinner Press and the entire staff. Finally, thank you to musicians around the world for all that they do and all the people they inspire.

Chapter ONE

Wednesday, April 8

LUCAS THOMPSON rose from a long table, pressing the tips of his fingers on top of the smooth glass. Sunlight beamed around his body from the floor-to-ceiling windows behind him. He pinched the bottom seam of his tailored navy blue suit jacket and tugged once, surveying the row of older men staring up at him. Their expressions ranged from furious to terrified. They were a study in scrunched eyebrows, huffed breaths, and flushed cheeks.

"Anyone need a stretch?" Lucas flattened his hand on his lower back and pushed his hips forward. "Long negotiations make my legs cramp." His query was met with steely silence, save for the quiet hiss of air being circulated into the conference room. The corners of Lucas's mouth quirked. "Would anyone else care for more water, perhaps?" He ran his fingers over the trinity knot of his black tie and laid his other hand flat on the silky material. "I'm feeling parched."

"No," Acker said, the word snapping out of his mouth before Lucas finished speaking. "No, we don't want any of your sodding water. Just as we don't want anything to do with your scam of a deal."

Beside Acker, another older gentleman, called Jones, bounced in his seat. His bushy white eyebrows twitched.

"You're stalling, Thompson. It's a load of rubbish." Jones's words sounded like burps being propelled out of his cracked lips while his pudgy arms crossed over his chest. "Pure rubbish. Wasting all of our time."

Lucas turned away from the group while lifting his curled fingers near his face in a gesture of casual surrender. "As you wish."

He walked ten paces to the sleek bar resting against the wall. A sweating glass pitcher sat on top of the bar. Delicate slices of cucumber mingled with the perfectly square ice cubes. He gripped a tall glass and began to fill it. Cucumbers vibrated against the ice cubes in an effort to escape out the mouth of the pitcher.

He took a slow sip, letting the cool water slide down his throat. He stared out the window, and his heart pounded in his ears as he watched cars speed by on the street below. There was something hypnotizing about watching others go about their day without a care in the world as to what was happening above them. From forty floors up, central London resembled a Seurat painting, people and cars blending into colorful, moving dots.

If he stared long enough, he would see his own reflection in the polished glass. He could already see the people sitting at the table behind him and feel their eyes burning holes in the back of his head.

On one side of the table sat his boss, and CEO of Covington Associates, Peter Covington II. Covington sat comfortably in his high-back leather chair. A small smile curled his lips, and his dark blond hair was combed into a stylish, but responsible, swoop.

Their client, Maxwell Schilling, relaxed in the seat beside Lucas's. Schilling was a collector of small businesses that posed any sort of threat to his own construction firm, Schilling Builders, the Walmart of corporate construction. He appeared to be even more comfortable as he lounged in his chair with his crossed legs propped on the corner of the table and a constant glass of scotch in his hand.

On the other side of the table was a group of men who looked out of place in every way possible. The owners of Acker-Jones Construction were built for work sites, for spending long days in the sun, elbow-deep in cement and dirt. They were better suited for inhaling sawdust than for breathing filtered air and sipping cucumber water.

Lucas's side of the table wore custom-tailored suits, fine silk ties, Italian leather shoes cobbled to fit the specific shapes of their feet, and had standing appointments with barbers to ensure not even a single hair was ever out of place.

Acker-Jones wore suits made of cheap fabrics bought off the rack. Their trousers were a touch too short, their jacket sleeves an inch too long, their hair matted into permanent helmet shapes from hours spent on work sites. Their dress shoes were still squeaky and not yet broken in, even though their wives probably purchased the shoes for them to attend a wedding years ago. Even Acker-Jones's duo of lawyers seemed out of place and fidgety. Their budget for legal advice was a fraction of Schilling's monthly food budget for one of his dogs.

Lucas refilled his glass to an inch from the rim. "I know this has not been an easy process for you, Mr. Acker." He pitched his voice low and his tone gentle. "Nor you, Mr. Jones."

"You don't know shit, Thompson," Jones barked. "You're nothing more than a vulture!" He coughed, punching himself in the center of his chest. "A leech on society!"

"Gentlemen," Covington chuckled. His leather chair creaked as he reclined farther back. "Such language."

Lucas took another sip of water. He could practically smell the blood bubbling in their veins, could feel the stress sweat seeping into their scratchy, overstarched collars. His body replied in kind—his blood raced faster, and a pleasant, burning heat settled beneath his skin as he turned back with one hand tucked in his trouser pocket. Victory sizzled in his bones as he brought his eyes from left to right. Acker-Jones was so on edge, their bodies so tight, that a tiny tap of an archaeologist's hammer to their shoulders would cause the room to fill with dust.

"We're here to help you." Lucas licked his bottom lip. "This entire time, I've tried my best to help you. To ensure you're taken care of."

Jones's face reddened like a tomato. "You're a liar and a cheat. Why should we believe a damn word that comes out of your mouth? You work for"—his eyes darted to Schilling, his voice dropping to a rasp—"him." Jones coughed violently and Acker held his hand out toward his partner. Their lawyers shuffled papers on the table.

Lucas took two steps forward. "I know how you feel. Both of you." He pointed the top of his glass at both men, swaying it side to side. "I understand more than you know."

"What's that supposed to mean?" Acker asked with his lips in a snarl.

Lucas blinked at him, then tilted his head. "May I tell you a story?" he asked softly.

Covington's eyes crinkled at the edges, but he remained facing forward. His gaze was trained on Acker and Jones, who remained silent and stony. Schilling refilled his glass; scotch glugged in the silent room.

Lucas offered Jones and Acker a small smile. He locked eyes with Acker, and Lucas's brows arched. A beat passed, and Acker shrugged one noncommittal shoulder. Jones glared at him with a hand bunched in the center of his wrinkled white button-down.

"When I was a little boy, my father and his brother went into business together," Lucas said as he walked closer to the table. He glanced at Jones's tie, forest green with small blue fish stitched into the material. "They opened a shop that sold fishing supplies." He looked back to Acker. "Bait, tackle boxes, poles, those little floaty things. Uh…" He snapped his fingers near his face. "Floaty things. What are they called?"

"Bobbers," Jones grunted.

"Bobbers!" Lucas held his hand out toward Jones. "Yes! Thank you. How silly of me to forget. Bobbers, hooks, the whole bit. If you needed it to fish, they sold it."

Acker shifted in his seat and asked, "What's your point?"

"It was a very, very small shop," Lucas said, staring out the glass wall of the conference room. His shoulders rose. "That was all my family could afford." He sipped his water and swallowed quickly, furrowing his brow and shaking his head. "Nothing like the size or importance of your company, by a long shot. But they loved it." He flattened his hand on his chest. "I loved it, and I knew I wanted to run it when I grew up."

Lucas studied a spot above Acker and Jones's heads. A far-off warmth softened his features. "I spent hours in the shop hiding under the counter. Spent my summers staring at my father's shins as he rang people up and told them what pole was best. I listened to him give the pros and cons of which bait would catch which fish. He even let me pretend the worms were my pets. I was heartbroken when I found out where my pets were going each day." He chuckled. "I wasn't the brightest kid, I suppose."

A flicker of amusement ran through Acker's eyes as Jones's serious expression wavered ever so slightly. Lucas brought himself within touching distance of the table and took a long sip of water. Even with his face directed at the ceiling, he could feel every eye in the room on him.

"And then my father passed away." He paused to let his voice linger. "Heart attack."

Acker-Jones's side of the table was motionless. Lucas nodded his head forward for three long beats.

"And my uncle," Lucas continued, "who had expressed no desire to sell our family's shop, was swooped up in a moment of tragedy by someone who convinced him to sell. To let another larger, more established business management company take over, under the guise of allowing my uncle to maintain ownership and a portion of the earnings. I don't think I have to tell you the entire end of the story. As you can see—" Lucas held his hands out. "—I'm not behind the register of a tackle shop. There is no tackle shop. The deal was bad for everyone besides the broker, and my family was left with nothing. My father was dead, his business was gone, and we had nothing."

Lucas took the last sip of water out of his glass and placed it on the table. He leaned over the tabletop, tilting his head toward Schilling.

"This is not that. This is not a bad deal for you and your company. On the contrary." He spun their contract back toward them. "This is a good deal, one that rewards you for your years and years of hard work."

He watched Jones and Acker study the contract they had been hemming and hawing over for weeks.

Acker crossed his arms over his chest. "You'll chop up our company," he said. "Take away everything that makes it ours. Choose cheap quantity over good quality, something we never wanted to do."

"Max has no desire to do that," Lucas said, shaking his head. Covington shook his head along with Lucas, and steepled his fingers in his lap. "There would likely be some changes in management, which is completely normal for this type of acquisition, but Schilling Builders desires a smooth transition. Who better to ease that transition than the Acker-Jones employees who know your company best?"

"But why do you even care about our company?" Jones asked, his hands turning to fists. "Why us?"

The answer was that a house Acker-Jones built for a celebrity, full of custom carpentry and exquisite detail, had been so well received in design magazines that Acker-Jones became the most sought-after construction group in England. The small company had begun to encroach on Schilling's bids for clients. Schilling did not enjoy competition, especially from a company with such a spotless reputation, ever-growing fanbase, and potentially enormous yearly profit.

Lucas slid into his leather chair. "Schilling Builders has been searching for a company to bring a personal touch, a family mentality, to their structures. Your work is exquisite. You have both poured yourselves into your work for countless years." He spread his arms. "Why not let someone else do the heavy lifting?"

"Because it's our legacy." Acker gently pushed the contract back across the table. "Because we want our sons and daughters, our families, to have something to inherit. Because this company is us, and to put it in the hands of another would risk throwing away a lifetime of work."

"I completely understand. You're very right." Lucas nodded as he closed the folder holding their contract and pulled it back to his side of the table. He tapped his fingers three times on top of the file. "I apologize for wasting your time with my"—he blew air out of his nose—"silly fishing story."

"No need to apologize." Jones cleared his throat. "It... it was a fine story."

"Thank you, sir. That's very kind of you to say. You only get one dad, you know?" Lucas let out a small chuckle while shaking his head. "I wish someone would have told me that when I was a kid. Would have spent less time on the pitch and more time with him."

The stiff files clicked against the glass as Lucas stacked them.

Lucas continued, “If he hadn’t passed away, I probably would have slept in the shop to be near him all the time. To learn from him. I completely understand where you’re coming from. I would have fought tooth and nail to keep the shop for myself, simply so he could retire comfortably and enjoy his time with his kids. With his grandkids. Even if we were just as poor as when he ran the shop.”

He dropped the folder pile in front of himself, prompting a soft whoosh to brush over the table.

“You only have one life—one chance to live the best life you can. I know I’d spend it with my loved ones, if given a choice.”

Lucas glanced at his boss, who had not moved once during his story. The right side of Covington’s lips lifted. Lucas’s eyes fluttered shut for a split second. With his face still toward Covington, Lucas started to say, “Gentlemen, I’ll walk you—”

“Wait.”

Jones broke first. He held on to the closed folder. Schilling chuckled into his scotch, and the other side of Covington’s lips rose. Both Covington and Lucas smiled across the table.

Five minutes later, Lucas stacked the same bunch of folders, complete with signed contracts. Acker-Jones and their lawyers were still packing their documents as Covington lined up champagne flutes in the center of the conference table.

Acker-Jones declined their champagne. Both men were green in the face, a vast difference to their formerly tomato-red cheeks. Lucas went in for the required final handshake, but Jones pulled him closer, squeezing both of his shoulders. Jones smelled of sunlight and aftershave.

“Thompson.” Jones’s voice was still a bark, but it sounded less angry and more grandfatherly when compared to his earlier words. “If you ever want to go fishing, you have my card. Give me a ring, son. You’re about the same age as my son, Gregory. We go fishing all the time.” He patted Lucas’s arms. “We’d love to have you on board.”

Lucas forced a smile and nodded. It felt as if his lips were slithering off his face, his cheeks fighting to keep the corners of his mouth up.

“Thank you, sir. That’s very generous of you.”

Acker-Jones and their team left the conference room. The glass door clicked shut. Lucas watched the group walk down the hallway and disappear near the lifts.

A champagne bottle popped.

“Would it be cliché for me to make a hook, line, and sinker remark so soon?”

Schilling howled at Covington's comment. Lucas stared at his reflection in the glass wall.

"You are a genius, my boy," Schilling said, slapping Lucas between the shoulder blades. "A fucking genius! Worth every penny. You've won yourself a client for life." He pulled Lucas sideways into his muscled chest and walked them back to the table as he laughed a hot breath of scotch over Lucas's face. "Pete wasn't kidding when he said you were the best, though I must remind you, keeping their employees or policies is not in my plan for their company, which is now *my* company."

"I'm well aware." Lucas swallowed dryly. He wondered how long it would take for their current employees to receive news about the future of their jobs. "They'll be rich, though," he said, almost as an afterthought. "Very, very rich."

"Not nearly as rich as me, once I give their company a bit of a remodel. Shit, they gave up a goldmine and they don't even realize it." Schilling downed his scotch and slammed the glass on the table. He blew air through his clenched teeth. "I love it when that happens."

Covington came up to them with two flutes of champagne. He held one out toward Lucas. "Fisherman father, hm?" He did a quick scan of Lucas's face, smirking. "Must have missed that on your CV."

Lucas accepted his glass. "I wouldn't recognize my father if I ran into him on the street tomorrow." He sipped once, then traced his tingling bottom lip with his tongue. "Never been fishing, either. Watched a documentary on a flight last week about fly fishing." He buffed his fingernails over his jacket. "Felt inspired."

Schilling sprayed champagne out of his mouth. "Fucking wunderkind!" he cried. "You deserve an Oscar for that performance. I'd say you should go to acting school if I didn't want to keep you in the boardroom all for myself."

"He's good. Very, very good," Covington said slowly. He pinched Lucas's cheek. "It's that sweet face and those baby blues. No one can resist." His eyes narrowed in thought as his fingers loosened their hold. He gave his cheek a gentle slap. "No wonder I pay you so well."

Lucas clinked their glasses together.

"Cheers to that."

The cheerful ping did not match the resigned fog that settled over Lucas's body. He set his mouth in a straight line.

Once he wrapped up with Schilling and Covington, Lucas excused himself to return to work. Employees scurried around the office in tailored suits, the highest of high heels, and chic pencil skirts. All of their clothing was hued from black to white. There was no visible color besides the red accent flowers perched on the receptionist's glass desk.

The lift doors slid shut and Lucas exhaled a long breath, letting his head drop forward. He adjusted the knot of his tie and moved his head side to side as he pulled his mobile out of his pocket. A number of texts, e-mails, and voice mails waited for him, some personal and some professional. He flicked through the notifications while a stress headache built at the base of his neck, then pressed the bottom button and held the phone up.

"Phone Mum within next three days," he said into the speaker.

His phone beeped, and a calendar alert popped up on the screen. He approved it as a new call came in. Zamir, his best friend, was calling. Lucas's jawline tightened, his thumb swaying over the screen before sending the call straight to voice mail.

His assistant, Albert Green, had called a number of times during his meeting, along with leaving even more text messages and e-mails. It was normal behavior for Albert, who panicked if he was unsure about whether Lucas had watered the fern in his office sitting area. The answer was always a resounding no. Lucas never remembered to water the fern Albert had insisted on purchasing to increase brain circulation or oxygen flow, or some other thing related to brains and oxygen that he lectured him about.

While his excessive calling would be annoying to some, Lucas didn't mind. Albert served as the perfect, polite filter to keep unwanted calls and people away while also managing his insane schedule and putting up with excessive client demands. Albert did all of that with a smile on his face and a hop in his step.

Since Albert became his assistant, Lucas had not missed any meetings, flights, or required work events. He often received compliments about his lovely assistant's e-mail etiquette, and his family had practically adopted Albert, despite Lucas's wishes to keep his work and personal life separate. Albert had yet to master Lucas's preferred method of how he took his tea, but he was only human. His strength was in the office, not the kitchen.

Lucas walked out of the lift on the main level, where the polished marble floor caused his shiny black shoes to click. He dialed Albert and brought his phone to his ear.

Albert picked up halfway through the first ring. "Hello, sir! How is your day?"

"Hi. Fine, thanks." Lucas dodged a crowd of businessmen in all black, marching forward with their heads down and their eyes glued to their phones. "What's up?"

"All went well with Acker-Jones?"

"I got them." Lucas pushed through a revolving door. "It's done."

"Well done, sir!"

Lucas could hear genuine excitement ringing in Albert's voice. When Lucas did well, Albert's salary usually followed.

"What do you need?" Lucas stepped outside, and chilly air slapped him in the face. He tightened his charcoal-gray scarf. "Lay off the sirs, mate. You're starting to sound like Jarvis from *Iron Man*."

"Are you nearly at Branson's?"

Lucas's heart dropped to his stomach. He stopped walking. People flooded around him on the sidewalk. "What?"

"Ray Branson? You have a lunch meeting with him today?" Albert's voice pitched half a tone higher. "I know I put it in your schedule." Frantic typing carried through the phone. "Hold one moment, please. I'll straighten this out."

"Shit," Lucas said, drawing out the word and rubbing his wrinkled forehead. "Yes, you did. I got the alert this morning and completely lost track of time. This is all my fault. The meeting took longer than I thought and…." He checked his watch, then walked quickly to the end of the street. "I'll have to get a cab. I'll never make it in time if I take the train."

"I could reschedule for you, sir."

"No, no way." Lucas shook his head, eyes darting over the cabs flying by. "I've been trying for months to wrangle a lunch with him. He's sitting on the biggest tech merger in this city's history, and I'll be damned if I lose him to Yarnwood Corp."

"Mr. Branson is quite busy."

"I know."

"Shall I tell him you're running late?"

"No, no, he's cranky and old. Traditional. He won't like that." Lucas rubbed his palm in a circle over his nose, squeezing the cartilage out of shape. "Ugh, and the day was going moderately well."

More keyboard clicks sounded through the phone as Albert spoke, brisk and professional.

"Based on current traffic reported approximately three minutes ago, I'd say you could make it to Quo Vadis in eight minutes if you catch a cab within the next thirty seconds, bringing you there with one and a half minutes to spare."

"Yeah, working on the whole cab thing." Lucas lifted his arm and his tan wool trench coat stretched open. His eyes lit up. A black car slowed and pulled over to the curb. "Got one. I'll touch base when I'm at lunch."

"Enjoy, sir. Try the lamb tongue. I've heard it's lovely."

Lucas snorted and hung up. His phone started to vibrate in his palm. He swiped his thumb to silence the call without checking who was calling. Then his phone buzzed again, indicating yet another call. He opened the cab door and slid across the seat. His arse collided in the center of the backseat with someone sliding in from the other side.

"Excuse me." Lucas shoved himself against the person's firm body. His phone started to ring in the closed space. "I believe I was here first," he said, his tone more pointed.

Both doors slammed shut and both men settled in their seats.

"Excuse me," a deep voice replied beside him. The man drew out each word. "I believe *I* was inside first." Lucas could see only his back covered in expensive black material and his wavy chestnut hair cascading to his shoulders as he leaned forward to say to the driver, "Old Compton and Wardour, please."

"I'm not really in the mood for this," Lucas huffed and wiggled his arse into his seat, "but we're both heading to Soho. We might as well share." He pushed his way in front of the man, who dropped back to the seat, and made eye contact with the driver in his mirror. "Quo Vadis, please. It's a restaurant on Dean Street. Dean and Bateman should be fine. I need to be dropped first."

"Awfully bossy, aren't we?"

Lucas looked over his shoulder at the deep drawl. His eyes traced over the lounging stranger.

The man's long legs were crossed at the knee. His voice and posture both reflected his boredom as his thumb flicked over his iPhone screen. Large black sunglasses shielded his eyes. A small cross earring swayed from his left ear. His black trench coat wilted open over his muscled torso in the most couture way. He wore all black, from his leather trousers to his half-open, sheer button-up. His nipples were visible beneath the draped shirt.

Lucas flexed his jaw. "I'm late for a very important meeting and need to be first."

The man snorted. "Like I care."

Lucas studied the top of the man's head. Rings glimmered on each of his long fingers as he scrolled through his phone—tiny reflections of light bounced around the cab's interior. Lucas's eyes dropped, then rose back to the man's face. High cheekbones and a noble nose were visible amid his hair, which was held back by a long, tasseled headscarf.

"Not sure what you're late for, besides perhaps a Rolling Stones role-play convention, but my actual meeting takes precedence." Lucas turned back to the driver to quickly say, "Please start driving and drop me first. I cannot be late."

"Don't be rude," the deep voice purred. His pointed-toe black boot swayed as he bobbed his leg. "It's not his fault you have poor time management."

Lucas sat back with his mouth agape. The man lifted his face, staring at Lucas for a long beat, from eyes shielded by black sunglasses.

"Yes?"

Lucas rolled his eyes, crossing his leg and pulling out his phone. He saw three more missed calls from his mother, plus a voice mail from Zamir. He gritted his teeth behind his closed lips and angled himself away from the stranger, lowering his phone's volume. He clicked on the voice mail and pressed his phone to his ear.

"Mate—Luke—Lucas," Zamir's voice, raspy and quiet, said through the phone. He sounded out of breath. "I—Luke—Cillian proposed!" There was a booming cheer over Zamir's words. "We're getting married!"

Cillian's voice sang, "We're getting married!" through the phone in his cheerful, Irish lilt, and sunshine practically beamed out of the tiny speaker holes. Lucas watched the street rush by out the window, forcing his face to remain still in the reflection.

"Call me when you can, man," Zamir said, quiet but sounding even more excited. "I can't wait to tell you all about it. We're gonna get married soon. Really soon. Within a month. Within weeks! A destination wedding. Cillian had this whole thing planned, he's gonna pay for everything, and it's just—B-babe—"

Zamir was interrupted by sucking sounds. His raspy chuckles mixed in with Cillian's ecstatic donkey laugh, and their words became so garbled that it sounded like two babies babbling into the phone. Lucas gritted his teeth tighter and squeezed his fist against the outside of his thigh.

"It's going to be amazing," Zamir insisted. "Call me when you can. We can talk about everything. I'll e-mail you some details we've got figured out already. Can't wait to see you in paradise, bro. Have missed you so much."

Cillian's voice popped into the voice mail to sing, "And now you'll be my bro too! Yay!" Their loud chatter caused the speaker to overload and crackle before the voice mail cut off.

Lucas swallowed. His fist clenched tighter for a moment before he released it, wiggling his fingers against his outer thigh. He turned away from the window and thumbed a reminder to himself to call Zamir within the next twenty-four hours. An e-mail from Zamir popped up on his screen before Lucas could save the alert. His phone rang yet again. He sighed and accepted the call from his mother.

"Not a good time," he murmured into the phone. "Can I call you—"

"Oh, *Lukeybear*! Have you heard the wonderful news?"

Lucas closed his eyes, pressing the pads of his fingers to his temple. He could hear the man beside him cracking his gum; his black boot bobbed in Lucas's peripheral vision.

"Yes," he said, keeping his voice low. "I'm in a car on the way to a meeting. I'll call you later."

His mother continued to babble. "Can you believe it? We're all over the moon. What a sweet boy that Cillian is. Tracy is beyond words! The whole family is! And the Bahamas, how lovely! We'll have a proper family holiday and then the wedding. I'm sure it'll be lovely, just lovely!"

"I really do have to go," Lucas said, tension twingeing the back of his neck. He squeezed the tight muscles. "I'll phone you later, all right?"

"Oh, fine, fine." She exhaled a loud sigh and muttered, "Christ, could you forget work for one bloody minute to be excited for your best friend getting married? The Matins are like family! Zamir is like your brother!"

Lucas's mouth went dry as he stared straight ahead at the back of the driver's seat.

"I've very happy for him. And Cillian." His voice sounded as robotic in his ears as it felt coming out of his throat. "I'll phone you later, I promise. Love you, bye."

He ended the call before her reply and pocketed his mobile. He exhaled slowly, focusing on the dull buzz of the driver's radio.

"Well? What's the good news?"

Lucas gasped and startled at the slow, held-out words while jumping sideways into his door, remaining only half on the seat. The stranger smirked at him with little mirth. His leg continued to bob and his gum kept on cracking.

"Nothing." Lucas removed his hand from the center of his chest and straightened his posture, adjusting his cufflinks. "None of your business."

"Forgot I was here?"

"I'm sure it happens often."

The stranger grinned wider; a dimple deepened on his cheek. "Ooh. You're a feisty one."

He pushed his sunglasses up to rest on top of his hair, his feline green eyes practically ablaze as he smiled and held Lucas's stare. He did an open scan of Lucas, from his neatly constructed quiff of light brown hair to his close shave, his fitted blue suit trousers to his glimmering gold Rolex.

The man bobbed his leg even slower, and pressed his tongue against the inside of his cheek, bulging the skin outward. "And a pretty little slice of pie, as well." The man's voice and growing smile matched the slow, lethargic pace of his body. He held his hand out. "I'm Jack. Jack McQueen."

Lucas snorted and glanced out the window. Everything about the man seemed too large and too unique. His boots. His legs. His fingers. His eyes. His grin. Even his white teeth were unfairly straight.

Lucas checked his watch. He tapped his thumb three times against the top of his thigh.

"Worrying about traffic will only make you more on edge. You'll get there when you get there."

"Yes, thank you for your Zen advice," Lucas said, turning back to the man. He crossed his leg away from Jack and folded his hands on his knee. "I'm ever so glad we got stuck together this afternoon. Do you give life lesson seminars?"

"You could say that."

Lucas arched his brows as a chuckle escaped him. "Are you serious?"

Jack procured a black business card from nowhere, balancing it between two fingers. He leaned closer to Lucas and his shirt flopped open. One dark nipple peeked out from the sheer fabric. His body gave off gushing waves of heat, even with plenty of space between them.

Jack's scent was masculine and raw with a touch of metallic sweat, like a coin left too long in the sun. His smooth, hypnotic, slightly sweet cologne, which Lucas identified as Tom Ford's Tobacco Vanille (he was a Tom Ford Tuscan Leather man, himself), lingered almost enough to hide the fact that he was wearing last night's clothing and could probably use a shower. The dusty patches on the knees of his trousers and his wrinkled shirt clued Lucas in as to why this man had stumbled into a cab at noon, looking like the moon, lost on his trip back into space.

Lucas studied the card for "Jack McQueen, Personal Consultant."

Jack's low voice murmured, "I'm more of a one-on-one type of consultant."

Lucas pulled himself away from the rolling heat and light brushes of air over his ear. "Excuse me?"

Jack dropped his gaze to Lucas's mouth, his tongue tracing over the lower ridge of his teeth. "You seem like a bright enough chap. I'm sure you'll get it eventually. If you do, give me a call." He met Lucas's gaze. "I'd be happy to help in any way."

"Ohh," Lucas said, nodding. "I get it." Jack arched his brows and slid his sunglasses back on the bridge of his nose. "You're a rent boy."

Jack's face tilted toward the driver, who cleared his throat and accelerated the car. "I prefer personal consultant, but"—he shrugged—"you say po-tay-toh, I say po-tah-toh." He fluffed his shirt over his chest. "I'm not fussed."

Lucas cackled. "Wow. And I thought I was good at spinning shit."

"What do you do?"

"Doesn't matter, now, does it?"

Jack extended his arm along the back seat. His fingers rested inches from Lucas's shoulder. "Simply making conversation."

"It that what you're paid for? To make conversation?"

Jack grinned, unbothered. "At times, yes."

Lucas chuckled, the sound breathy and light. "I'm sure you're quite the conversationalist."

"I might have some room in my schedule next week, if you're interested in having a chat."

"Are you joking? I have no need, nor desire, for a rent—" Lucas licked his lips, then tilted his face to paste on a bland smile. "My apologies. For a personal consultant."

"Seems like there's a need, mate. You're wound up tight, like a guitar string about to snap."

"Is poetry included in your consultations?"

Jack laughed a loud, throaty honk, his fingers tapping the seat beside Lucas's neck. "At times. I'm better at getting others to spout poetry for me, but I've been known to craft a stanza or two when the mood strikes."

"Ugh, who are you?" Lucas sighed, crossing his leg away from Jack. He took his phone out of his pocket. "You're like a clichéd television character. Don't tell me… you're a hooker with a heart of gold?"

"Sort of. It looks gold, but is actually filled with chocolate."

A genuine grin fought its way onto Lucas's face as he gazed out the window. He could see Jack smiling to himself in the reflection. Jack's face was down as he scanned through his phone.

"I'm an excellent escort, as well as poet, if all a client needs is company," Jack said after a beat. He sounded bored, but his words pinged with a higher frequency racing between them. "Corporate events, birthday parties, *weddings*, and so on."

Lucas's eyes froze on the e-mail from Zamir, featuring a rough draft of the schedule for his surprise wedding trip in a few weeks' time. He pocketed his phone and sat up straighter, then gripped the door handle. "I'm fine, mate, but thank you for the generous offer."

"Whatever you say."

The car came to a halt in front of the white building that housed Quo Vadis. Lucas opened the door and placed one foot on the ground. He reached into his pocket for his wallet, but Jack's warm palm landed on his wrist. Lucas looked at his own reflection in Jack's sunglasses.

"No worries, mate," Jack said, giving the *t* an extra pop on his hard palate. He pulled a wad of cash out of his jacket pocket. Long, nimble fingers plucked a couple of bills off the top. "It's on me."

Lucas held his gaze for a moment, cars whizzing by outside the cab. "Nice, long chat last night?"

Jack's smoothness faltered for a split second. The slight droop of his mouth would be unnoticeable to most, and he recovered before his eyes even finished blinking. One blink later and he was smirking again. "Long? Yes." His tongue darted out to wet the corner of his mouth. "Nice? Not particularly."

Lucas caught sight of Ray Branson hobbling into Quo Vadis, leaning heavily on a pale wooden cane. "Old bugger is late too," Lucas muttered to himself, chuckling and exiting the cab. He directed his attention back at Jack, who looked up at him from his phone. "Well." Lucas tucked his hands in his pockets. "Best of luck with your poetry."

"Best of luck at your wedding."

Lucas's nostrils flared. "It's not my wedding."

"No, I didn't think so," Jack breezed, moving to pull the door shut. He winked over the top edge of his sunglasses. "Better hurry. Don't want to be late for your important meeting."

The door slammed shut and the car sped away.

Chapter TWO

ALBERT STARED at his desk with his fingers clasped over his chin and his brows furrowed. He reached toward a metal cup on the upper right corner of his desk and switched the position of a sharpened pencil with a black pen.

He stepped back and tilted his head. His weight shifted from leg to leg. Albert added a blue pen to the writing implement mix and switched it all around until the pencil stood in the front, with the blue-and-black pens resting behind it.

His eyes were narrow and serious as he nodded in rhythm with the song quietly playing through his computer speakers. He maintained his work-safe Spotify station with as much care as his desk's pen and pencil placement.

He reached out and rotated the metal cup one inch to the left. He pulled his hand back, then rotated the cup half an inch right. He nodded once.

"There. Perfect."

He glanced around the modern office that occupied one of the many floors Covington owned in the building. Other assistants hurried from desk to desk. Papers fluttered around the copy machines, and phones rang off the hook, though their ringtones were set as low, vibrating buzzes instead of a normal ringing phone. He looked over his shoulder at Lucas's open office door, then looked to the silent phone.

An assistant named Jane ran by. She had a tray of scones and steaming cups of tea clasped in her small hands. Jane gave Albert a harried sigh. "Busy day!"

Albert nodded at her, friendly yet professional, and widened his eyes while loosening the knot of his tie. "You're telling me!"

"See you at happy hour?"

"Sounds good," he said, holding his thumb up. "Wouldn't miss it."

He watched her go, craning his neck to be sure no other assistants were around. He fixed his black tie to its proper place and smoothed the material down his chest. He pinched the corners of his pale blue shirt collar, giving that a shift, as well.

His boss never left stacks of busywork whenever he knew Albert would be alone for an afternoon. As long as his schedule was organized (Albert would rather die a fiery death than bumble even a single event) and all tasks were completed on time (On time? Please. Most tasks were done with at least twenty-four hours to spare on their deadline), Albert was left to his own devices.

His boss never requested that he call him "sir," or "Mr. Thompson," as most of the other assistants were required to call their superiors. Lucas preferred to be called Lucas. Albert was working on cutting out his "sir" habit.

The executive he'd assisted prior to Lucas at a company three buildings down the street was a tyrant. He required Albert to be on call twenty-four hours a day, seven days a week. If he could have added a day to the calendar, he would have, simply to make Albert work extra overtime. He ordered all employees to avoid eye contact with him and often whispered commands in Albert's ear for Albert to voice, resulting in Albert having to notify staff of all sorts of unsavory business, with his boss sitting silent and smug at his side.

While he waited for his interview at Covington Associates, he had watched applicants flee the designated interview room in tears. When he'd walked through the door and found only Lucas sitting on the other side of the table, he was confused. This young man was the beast people were sobbing about to their friends in the lobby?

Albert would soon find that Lucas was no beast. He was simply blunt. He had never been happier to correctly answer "No, sir" to the single question Lucas asked in their interview: "Are you incompetent?"

Lucas never set a required start and end time for Albert's daily hours. He was more than generous with whatever time off Albert desired, let him come in late or leave early for personal appointments without question, and instituted a three o'clock end time for summer Fridays from the end of May through September. Lucas himself often stayed behind once Albert had left.

Albert diligently monitored his hours to be sure he was putting in an average of at least eight point five hours per day, but it was nice to know that his boss would not mind him leaving early for a doctor's appointment or taking a long lunch if a friend was in town.

The most outlandish task asked of him was the occasional midday dog walking when Lucas was out of town on business and his normal dog walker was unavailable. Who could complain about getting paid to take hour-long breaks to play with the cuddliest pug he had ever met?

Albert tapped his fingers against his chin, phones buzzing around him. He stared at the phone on his desk. The screen was dark, the speaker silent.

He ran his palm over the top of his computer screen and stared at his palm. A small breath left his nostrils. He touched his pointer finger to the top of the screen and pushed harder. A tiny speck of dirt lingered on the center of his fingertip.

"Aha!" He pointed at the screen. "You could use a dusting."

He crouched to retrieve a bottle of cleanser from beneath his desk. Legs in an expensive blue suit whooshed beside his body.

"Hi," Lucas said. Something covered in paper landed on top of Albert's desk. "Lunch."

Albert went to stand up, forgetting he was under the desk. "Ow," he blurted out, clutching the back of his head. He huffed and righted his feet on the floor. "I mean, hello!"

He popped up straight with his hands clasped behind his back, then looked at the space where Lucas had been.

"Sorry, sir." Albert spun and power walked into his office. He found Lucas behind his desk, sorting through envelopes with his hip quirked to the left. "Good meeting?" Albert's eyes followed each envelope Lucas tossed on top of his desk. "Shall I do that for you?" He stepped closer. "Allow me to do that for you, please. Don't waste your time with silly envelopes."

"It was fine." Lucas tossed the entire bunch of envelopes on his desk. He peered at Albert over the rim of his black aviators with an amused smirk. "Envelopes can be silly?"

Albert gaped. "I—I—"

Lucas started to chuckle quietly, pushing his glasses up to rest in his hair. "Relax." He shrugged off his trench. "I'm kidding. Meeting was good, though. Very informative. I made him laugh a few times, so I think he liked me. He was also quite drunk." Lucas tapped his fingers on his desk. "That might have had something to do with the amusement."

"I've read that if you can make someone laugh, you can make them do anything."

"Thank you, Marilyn Monroe."

"Would you like anything?" Albert hurried to Lucas's side of the desk and took his coat, floating around the office to hang it on a rack near the door. "Tea? Kale smoothie?"

Lucas sat heavily in his leather chair, blowing out a breath. He tossed his sunglasses on the desk and rubbed his hands over his face. "Tea would be lovely, thanks. It's been a strange day."

Albert grinned and nodded. "Yes, sir!"

LUCAS WATCHED Albert power walk out of his office. He placed his mobile on his desk, double-clicking his computer's space bar. The computer came back to life, and he entered his log-in information. His e-mail popped up. Lucas cracked the knuckles of his left hand with his thumb. His thank-you e-mail to

Branson needed to be sent within the hour if he wanted Branson to remember whom he had actually eaten lunch with.

His mobile vibrated, making it slide across his desk. He glanced at it. Zamir's name popped up on the lock screen. The small slide revealed a sliver of Jack McQueen's black business card stuck beneath the basic white case on Lucas's phone.

"Shall I put your leftovers in the break room refrigerator?"

Lucas blinked up at the sound of Albert's cheerful voice as a cup of tea was placed in front of him. "That's yours to eat."

Albert gave him a look of pure joy and adoration. "You brought me leftovers?" Albert flattened his hand over his heart. "Oh, thank you!"

"No, you silly envelope. It's that nasty lamb's tongue you mentioned. I had the chicken, but I managed to order you a tongue takeaway during one of Branson's many toilet trips."

Albert clutched his hands beneath his chin. "Thank you so, so much," he whispered. "Sir. Lucas. Thank you, Lucas."

Lucas snorted and started to click his mouse around his computer screen. "It's a lamb's tongue, Al. I wouldn't plan our honeymoon yet."

Albert resumed standing at attention. "Oh! Speaking of honeymoons, well, weddings in general. I received the notification of Zamir and Cillian's upcoming nuptials and added the dates to your schedule, though I'm still waiting for the detailed itinerary. When would you like to travel to the resort? I can take care of your booking. It seems most guests are spending ten days total, Saturday to the following Monday."

"Ten days? Jesus. Don't these people have jobs?"

"I suppose guests would use holiday time, or only go for part of the week. From the e-mail you received from the couple-to-be, they seem to want you there the entire time. They also queried as to whether you'll be bringing a date."

Lucas narrowed his eyes. "Why on earth do they need that much time with guests? Weddings are dreadful when it's only half a day's commitment." Quieter, he whined, "Ten days?"

"The invite said they wanted guests to feel as relaxed, pampered, and rejuvenated as possible before they participated in the joining of two free spirits into one."

"Did it really say that?" Lucas bobbed backward in his chair, listening to the quiet squeak of the metal joint. He felt like he had something sour in his mouth. "Two free spirits into one?"

"Yes."

"You memorized the invite already?"

"It—" Albert cleared his throat. "—made me think of the Spice Girls."

Lucas cackled. "I'm so glad you're my assistant."

Albert clasped his fingers in front of his stomach. "They also sent me a personal 'save the date,' which was very, very generous of them. I wasn't sure what your thoughts are on me attending the wedding."

Another text from Zamir came in and Lucas stifled a groan, flipping his phone upside down. He cracked the knuckles on his right hand with his thumb.

"Of course you can go, if you'd like. You've probably spoken to Zamir more in the past year than I have. I'll be there anyway, so it's not like much will be happening here."

Albert's brows pinched together. "But, sir, usually when the executive is gone, the assistant must stay to hold down the ship."

"Hold down the ship?" Lucas repeated amusedly. "Is that in a handbook somewhere? *Executive Assistants 101*?"

"I would assume it appears in some publication, somewhere."

Lucas fiddled with his sunglasses, swaying them in a circle on the desk. "It's up to you." He held his palm out. "Whatever you'd like to do, I'm fine with it."

"Excellent," Albert said, a touch too quickly. Lucas raised his eyebrows with a hint of a smile. Albert rubbed his hand over the back of his neck. "I'd, um, been meaning to plan a trip back home for a few days to see my family and Anna, and could probably work it out to do the first half of the week at home, then fly to the Bahamas for the long wedding weekend." Bashfulness colored Albert's face. "Since Cillian's paying for everything, this is sort of a fantasy holiday. Anna nearly died when I told her."

Lucas snorted and picked up Jack's card. "Yeah, right." He thumbed the raised letters. "Some fantasy."

Chapter THREE

IN AN airy one-bedroom flat in Soho, water hot enough to scald skin beat down on the back of a man with his head dropped forward. His dark hair was matted to his face, and smaller drops of water dripped off the ends to race down his chest. Suds of shampoo swirled down the drain. His oddly shaped toes dipped into the foamy mix.

Jack took a deep breath and tilted his head back. Water pounded over his face. He opened his mouth and let the spray bounce off his teeth. A mouthful of water gathered under his tongue until he closed his lips. He held his breath for a moment before he exhaled hard enough to blow water against the white tiles.

His routine after work was less involved than his prep before work, but often included staying in the shower for as much as forty-five minutes. He felt that he'd require at least an hour that day.

He grabbed bodywash and squeezed it on a white loofah, running it over every inch of his long body. He squeezed even more bodywash onto the loofah, and he followed the same path. A double scrub after work was never a bad idea.

Jack switched to an exfoliating brush and swirled a creamier bodywash over every inch of himself. His feet were the most difficult part, and he wobbled each time he had to stand on one leg. Not even bristles scratching the spaces between his toes could lift the cloud of exhaustion weighing him down.

Body hair came next. Before he could remove it, he had to make sure every strand was well cared for. He lathered up his body hair with shampoo, then conditioner, and finally with deep conditioner. He let the shower pound over his back as the deep conditioner set under his arms and on his groin.

He rinsed and stepped out of the shower with the water still on. He took a tube of hydrating mask out of his mirror cabinet from among his other products that had been lined up in color order. He slathered it on his face and neck until the smell of kiwi and grapes filled the air. A collection of darkened bites along his collarbones stood out on his creamy skin. They received an extra-thick glob of mask.

The mask started to tighten as he stretched side to side in front of the mirror. He gently gripped his arsecheeks to spread them as he bent over. His fingertips ghosted over the hairless, dark rose-colored skin of his entrance. He spun around to face the mirror. He stroked the downy brown hair at the base of his cock with one hand as he opened a drawer in his vanity.

He stepped into the shower with a small pair of silver scissors and ran his fingertips through the hair under his navel until he gently tugged the hair away from his skin. The scissors snipped diagonally through the hair, traveling over his groin and trimming the hair to a soft dusting. He rinsed the area and ran his palm over the patch of hair, tilting his hips forward and back a few times.

The scissors made a similar journey to graze through the hair that barely grew under his lifted arm. He repeated the trim under the other arm and rinsed the scissors of any leftover body hair.

Stretching both of his arms to the ceiling, he arched his back while letting the shower spray his upper body. He squirted a dollop of gentle exfoliant into his palm and placed his face under the stream of the shower, using easy presses of his fingertips in an upward motion to rid himself of the mask.

He retrieved yet another bottle of deep conditioner off the top shelf of the shower and finger-combed it through his hair. Once out of the shower, he wrapped his head in a towel, then fluffed another towel over the closed toilet seat. He sat down with a pair of tweezers and a magnifying mirror, yawning and relaxing his brows with the tweezers poised.

When he was done plucking, moisturizing, and washing out his deep conditioner, he stood in front of the foggy shower. His phone rang in the bedroom, and he glanced in the direction of the sound. From the Radiate ringtone, he knew it was his separate work phone. His work phone, and the version of himself associated with it, often received much more attention than his regular phone.

He walked out of his en-suite naked, save for the white towel looped around his head. His phone was on the bedside table, buzzing away until he picked it up. The number on the screen was unknown. Blue eyes and a sharp tongue flashed in his head, starting tingles swirling in his lower belly.

He exhaled a slow breath and placed the phone at his ear, swallowing once. "Hello?" he said, his voice a deep purr.

There was a short gap of no talking—nothing but choppy breaths carrying through the phone. Finally, the other person worked up enough courage to speak.

"Y-yes, hello, I…." Flop sweat practically dripped through the phone. "I'm looking to speak with Jack? Jack McQueen?"

Nope. The bumbling voice was not Mr. Blue Eyes from the taxi, unless he had lost his wit and sarcasm in the last two hours.

"Hi there. This is Jack," he said, soothing the purr in his voice to a gentler, calmer tone. He walked to his chest of drawers and started rifling around. "What would you like for me to call you?"

"Paul. Shit, I mean," Paul huffed, "should I—Do most people use a fake name? I've never—I'm—"

"Paul is just fine." Jack chuckled. Paul's low whine carried through the phone. "It's lovely to meet you, Paul. How may I help you?"

"I… I'm in need of a-a date. A companion. Overnight, if possible."

"My apologies, Paul. I don't do overnights with a first-time client."

"All right, well…. Half the night? Even just—" Paul cleared his throat. "A few hours, even. I'm… I'm in need."

Jack kept his voice conversational while pulling a pair of dark gray briefs out of the top drawer. "Maybe we can work something out, Paul. May I ask who referred you?"

There was a pause.

"I'd rather not say."

Jack's voice hardened ever so slightly. "I won't proceed without a referral."

His client list was built exclusively upon referrals. His clients were all so wealthy, and in such positions of power, that a prostitution scandal was not on their agenda. He found that men behaved better in the bedroom when they were aware that he knew one of their friends. A network of high profile, incredibly private clients was the best insurance he could hope for.

"I…. Guh…. Erm…."

While Paul made a variety of stressed noises, Jack observed his pert arse in the mirror on the back of his bedroom door. The skin of his arse was only a touch rosy. He ran his fingers over a lingering duo of prominent slap marks, one a bit too high on his back while another mark sat too low on his thigh. That skin felt extra warm and was reddened, even after his shower.

He enjoyed a good spanking as much as the next person, but sometimes clients became a touch too involved or a touch too power high when caught up in the moment. One slap too low on his thighs could be brushed off as a mistake in the heat of a session. When a second slap landed almost on his spine, even after a verbal warning, he was off the bed in an instant.

He had gripped his client by the cock, pulled him off the bed, and pinned him up against the wall. He set him straight with a severe tongue-lashing about respect, boundaries, and the proper way to include power play and aftercare in sex. His warning was so severe that it resulted in the client cowering naked in the corner and begging for forgiveness.

Begging seemed to turn the man on even more, and Jack received double his normal rate for the entire night. What could he say? His versatility was among his best features, though that particular client would never get to experience his versatility again.

He frowned at his reflection and dropped the briefs back into the drawer.

"Paul?" he asked, keeping his voice quiet. He pulled out a pair of baggy black sweats. "Are you still there, love?"

"Y-yes. I… I'm here."

He lifted his legs one by one to slide into the soft, thin material. The waistband sagged off his flat stomach and his abs flexed as he arched side to side.

"And your referral?"

"Marlow. William Marlow."

"William Marlow. Wonderful," Jack drawled. William was one of his easiest clients—a billionaire widower in his late sixties who preferred the sweet boyfriend routine with more cuddling and talking than actual sex. "And do you have much in common with Mr. Marlow?"

"No, I… I have a bit of a… a preference."

"A fetish?"

"I—I don't know if you'd call it that."

"Paul, I hold no judgment. I'm simply checking to see if I'm the right guy for you. If not, I have some excellent, discreet friends in the fetish industry who would be happy to help you."

"You *are* the right guy. I know it."

"How's that?"

"William… William said you have a beautiful smile. And… a cute laugh. And dimples."

Jack grinned at that comment, rubbing his hand over a pec. He thumbed his right nipple and stifled a shiver; the small bit of skin was puffy and stood away from his chest.

"That's awfully nice of him to say all that about little old me."

"I… I like a man who can smile. And…" Paul's voice dropped to a secretive whisper. "Laugh."

There it was.

Humans were unique creatures when it came to sexuality. Some never wanted to put a name to their kink for fear of judgment or mocking. Even while on a private phone call with the person hired to play along with whatever fetish he had, Paul could not verbalize exactly what he wanted.

"I understand, Paul," Jack said slowly, drawing out Paul's name. He threw in a small giggle and heard the same sharp intake of breath through the phone. "Sounds like we could have some fun together. A few laughs."

He balanced the phone between his ear and shoulder. He lifted both arms over his head and twisted his tattooed torso. His muscles and bones flexed beneath his skin, and his soft brown hair barely dusted a few select parts and was darkened by shower water.

"Do you have a preference for my body hair?" He brushed his fingers under his right arm, tracing around a black wire birdcage inked a few inches lower on his side. "I'm not waxed completely bare, but I'm pretty smooth, otherwise. Other clients with your interest have never seemed to mind."

"P-please, leave it all. I'm sure it's perfect. William said you're perfect."

"You'll have to call me more often, Paulie, you're making me blush." Paul's breathy, grunted sound of happiness was whimpered through the phone. "Just to be sure we're both on the same page, I will *not* do bondage at our first meeting. I will not incorporate light bondage until we have had three successful sessions." Jack lowered his arms and placed the call on speaker. "You'll have to make me laugh all on your own without restraints."

"Perfect. Whatever you say. Tonight? Please?"

Jack pulled up his schedule. "I'm afraid my nights are booked solid the next two weeks."

"Are you free now?"

Jack glanced at the red marks on his lower back, his arse smarting beneath the baggy sweats. He looked to his bed, white and rumpled and unmade. His laptop was open on the center with a paused episode of *Bob's Burgers* waiting for him.

"I'm not, sorry." He pulled the towel off his head, running his fingers through his wet hair. "Today is not available."

"Do you do lunch meetings?"

"I'd love a lunch meeting with you."

Paul's excitement grew in his voice. "Tomorrow?"

"Unavailable. I can do—" Jack mentally scrolled through his week. "—a Friday lunch? I'm free from noon until three. You have to host at a hotel, no less than four-star, and I'll need private access to the shower once we've finished. I don't do house calls for first-time clients."

"Perfect!"

Jack picked up the towel and hung it over his doorknob. "I'll need your e-mail and a working mobile number."

"Of course, whatever you need."

Jack walked to his bed and knelt on the edge. He started to rattle off details. "By the end of the day, you'll receive a contract, which includes a pricing breakdown, my preferences for food and drink on overnights, a form to consent to a background check, a nondisclosure agreement, and a liability waiver." He swung his legs under the duvet. "I will need to have all forms signed, scanned, and sent back to me before I make your reservation in my schedule."

He pulled his laptop onto his thighs and opened his calendar, making half his screen Netflix with the other half an empty client intake form.

"You will need to provide a credit card number as a deposit to hold your time. Please be sure your card number is accurate, as I will check to run your deposit. Any false numbers will result in you losing your reservation, and you will be blacklisted for any future services."

"I would never do that to you," Paul said, hushed. Jack propped a white pillow behind his lower back. "Money is no issue. I can give you my number right now, if that works for you? Whatever you need."

Jack tilted the phone away from his mouth to yawn and rewound his *Bob's Burgers* episode, dragging his finger over the track pad. "You're fast becoming my new favorite, Paulie."

Paul blustered a mix of chuckles and words in reply.

"You may pay with a credit card," Jack said, "but cash is also acceptable. All payment is due in full before our session begins. Any cancellation less than forty-eight hours in advance will result in forfeiting half of your deposit. All of this will be explained in the contract, and I'm always available if you have questions."

"Wow, Will was right!" Paul laughed gruffly. "You're a real pro! I wish my divorce lawyer had been as serious as you are. Or the kids in my office. You're a sharp one!"

Jack nibbled his bottom lip, staring down at his white sheets. He shifted his hips and a sharp spark of pain shot up from his arse. He brought his hand to his mouth and bit on the meat of his palm as he turned onto his stomach. "Thanks," he murmured. He let his head fall limp on the pillow. He forced a boyish laugh to ask, "You ready with that credit card number, love?"

Chapter FOUR

Friday, April 10

"DO YOU need anything else before I head home to get ready?"

"No, I'm fine, thanks." Lucas shrugged on his khaki trench and offered Albert a quick smile. "Thanks for picking up my tux. That was a huge help."

"Anytime," Albert said as he rolled up on the balls of his feet. "I'll see you later, then?"

Lucas nodded. "You will see me later."

Albert left his office in a whirl of paper-scented air. Lucas walked to the door and lifted his black garment bag from the hook on the back.

It wasn't that he hated the occasional company gala, per se. Galas could be fun, with lots of food and alcohol and the chance to see other executives sloshed enough to do the macarena.

After three wedding calls with Zamir and Cillian within the last forty-eight hours, plus a Skype session dedicated to asking Lucas about his love life, where the connection mercifully kept dying, the last thing he wanted was to squeeze into a tux and stand around in uncomfortable shoes all night. Alone.

Lucas did not have an issue attending events alone. He did it all the time. He preferred to be alone, rather than drag someone to an event that he'd have to introduce and make nice with, only to have to repeat the process at the next event with the next person he took out.

For some reason, all the talk of two spirits joining made him more curious than usual as to why he never seemed to find anyone to hold his attention for more than a night. A night in with his dog, enough curry to feed an army, and something mindless on television sounded like heaven at that moment, not a luxurious gala with a pretty face on his arm.

Hours later, Lucas walked into the ballroom Covington Associates had rented for the evening. It was as picturesque and sterile as he had expected it to be. His sofa and a spicy curry had never looked better than when he glanced over the menu of tiny, unpronounceable foods he'd dine on that night.

"Thompson! Get over here!" Covington cried out to him.

Each time he tried to get to the bar, he was pulled aside by some executive or other. News of his Acker-Jones performance had spread, and every employee he ran into wanted to congratulate him on his success.

"No date tonight?" a woman from HR queried.

With every congratulation came the confused question of his relationship status. His lack of a date, more specifically. How could he not want to drag a date to an event full of sharks, wolves, and monsters in tuxedos and gowns?

Even Albert could not rescue him from being sober and single. Albert's lovely Italian girlfriend, Anna, had surprised him for the weekend, and both were lost in their own little bubble of love on the dance floor. For a person who listened to more up-tempo dance pop than anyone Lucas knew, Albert seemed to love slow dancing.

Lucas finally made it to the bar in the farthest corner of the room. He lifted himself up on the balls of his feet and craned his neck, peering at the beers on tap.

"What can I get you, sir?"

He looked at the bartender, who was a middle-aged woman with short auburn hair. She momentarily seemed to have the face of Albert. He blinked once.

"Pale ale, please."

He downed his first beer almost as soon as she placed it on a coaster. She wordlessly started to prepare him a fresh glass. There was a sympathetic softness in her brown eyes. She most definitely was starting to resemble Albert.

Lucas turned to rest his back on the bar. He stretched his elbows a few inches from his sides and crossed his ankles in front of himself. Another bartender handed over a round of appletinis to a group of people standing to his right, prompting the loud group to teeter toward the dance floor.

Their shift revealed a tall man in a perfectly tailored black tux. His long waves were styled back off his forehead while maintaining their natural curl at the ends. His skin was tan and glowing, his expression the picture of bored relaxation. The coloring of his features, vibrant green eyes and deep rose lips, were even more radiant in the soft lighting of the ballroom, no longer hidden by black sunglasses or a cape of uncombed hair.

Lucas found himself blinking again, his brows furrowed. As if he could feel eyes on him, the man turned his head as a gin and tonic was placed on the bar.

"You," Jack said, his lips curving upward.

"You," Lucas repeated. His mouth mirrored Jack's and a wry smile appeared without his control. Jack moved closer to him. A foot of air remained between them but they faced each other. "Would it be too cliché for me to ask if you come here often?"

Jack grinned and leaned his elbow against the bar. "I had to stifle myself from asking the same question."

"You look…." Lucas squinted slightly, swirling his glass in a small circle in front of himself. "Cleaner."

Jack stirred his drink with his red straw, making his ice cubes clink in the glass. "Yes, well, even filthy hustlers enjoy a wash every now and again. Shocking as that may seem."

Lucas licked beer foam off his top lip. "I didn't call you a filthy hustler."

Jack's eyes rolled toward him. "You didn't have to." His gaze flickered from Lucas's shoes up to his face, clean-shaven and smooth. "I never did get your name in the car."

"No. You didn't. You look…."

Jack angled his body toward Lucas, crossed his ankles, and propped the toe of his black shoe on the ground. "I look?"

Lucas sipped his beer, keeping his face forward. "Different. You look more"—he swayed his hand up and down in Jack's direction—"normal like this. I'd think you would shoot for this aesthetic all the time."

"Not every client wants clean-cut. Some want a bit more sleaze, makes it feel more authentic, I suppose." Lucas felt as if his tux had been incinerated to reveal he'd opted not to wear pants as Jack's eyes roamed over his body. "We all play our own characters. I'm no different."

"What are you doing here?"

"I was invited."

"By who?"

Jack nudged his chin forward, smiling at someone across the dance floor. He waggled his long fingers. "Mr. Carson."

"You—You're dating Mr. Carson?" Lucas looked across the floor and stared at the ancient executive, quickly masking his shock with a blank expression. "He's one thousand years old."

"We're not dating. I'm his date. That's all."

"Why?"

"Some people seem to enjoy companionship, even the nonsexual kind, though that seems like a memo you never received. You should alert your assistant."

"Don't joke about that. Albert would leave the gala to search through every bin in the office."

"Which one is Albert?"

Lucas tilted the top of his beer glass toward a spot on the left side of the dance floor. "The bloke surgically attached to the gorgeous brunette."

"He's hot. Very military-slash-puppy dog."

"Could you please try to control yourself? You're like a feral cat."

"Personal assistant?"

"Executive assistant."

"Ooh la la. I'm speaking with an *executive*."

"Wouldn't want to encroach on your *personal consultant* territory."

"And where's your date, then?" Jack flattened his hand and pressed his pointer finger to his brow, making a show of scanning the room as if he was a pirate on a ship. Too bad he'd left his earring home. "Where are they hiding out?"

"No date."

"Pity."

"I'm quite fine, thanks."

"Are you, though?" Jack clicked his back teeth in a wince. "Glued to the bar. Constipated face. Lonely eyes. I've seen it all before."

"I do not have a constipated face. Or lonely eyes. Don't be ridiculous. Besides, what are you even doing over here? Shouldn't you be over there with Mr. Carson? Administering a vat of Viagra?"

Jack's lips quirked and he blinked slowly. "Like I said, not all companionship has to do with sex. He brings me to these things because he's a nice man who likes to share the wealth. He likes it when I socialize and enjoy myself." His gaze hardened. "You could learn something from someone like him."

"How's business been? Well, I hope?"

"Business is good." Jack's nose wrinkled. "A bit tiring but, otherwise, fine."

"Tiring? Business must be booming, then."

Jack's green eyes moved with hypnotic slowness as he glanced around the room before landing on Lucas's face. "I started early today. I had a client who, among other things, tickled me on and off for around three hours straight." He smoothed his hand over his hair. "It was exhausting."

"Wh-what?" Lucas laughed, a genuine, belly-shaking laugh. "Three hours of tickling? No sex?"

"No sex. Well, actually"—Jack swayed his head side to side—"I wanked him off afterward, but he was pretty worked up so it took about ten seconds. Painless."

Lucas's hand cradled his ribs, his mouth in a pained grimace. "Three hours of just tickling? What the hell did you do the entire time?"

"It was mostly chatting and laughing and touching, with bursts of tickling thrown in if he felt like it. Some little games. Lots of regular foot attention too, which I'll never turn down. Can't complain about getting paid to get an hour-long foot rub, even if my stomach aches a bit." He rubbed his stomach. "At least I won't have to do abs tomorrow."

"How much do you charge per hour?"

Jack raised one eyebrow. "Interested?"

"You wish. I'm just curious how much this poor sod threw away worshipping at your filthy hustler feet."

Jack's eyes crinkled as he sipped his drink; his scent floated to Lucas. Instead of Tom Ford, this fragrance smelled older, almost like the women's perfume Chanel No. 5. Jack's full lips popped off his straw, looking wet and slightly swollen. "I charge in ten-minute increments."

Lucas hummed amusedly. "Fancy yourself a lawyer?"

Their eyes locked.

"I fancy myself a businessman. I like punctuality," Jack said, letting each syllable sing in his deep voice. "Keeping my increments low makes sure I'm never anywhere I don't want to be for longer than I need to be there. Money seems to be the only way to get people to stick to a schedule."

"I respect that. What's your rate?"

Jack grinned around his straw, biting on the plastic for one long beat. He rolled his eyes toward Lucas. "That's an industry secret for clients only."

"Bullshit," Lucas chuckled. He mimed locking his lips and throwing away the key. "C'mon, I'll never tell another soul. I'm curious." Lucas's eyes shimmered. "I've never met anyone like you before."

Jack shook his head. "You're not even subtle about it. I expected better from you," he said, amused and smirking crookedly. "You're playing me."

"Am not."

"You can't hustle a hustler, love."

Lucas sighed and leaned his hip against the bar. He took a big gulp of beer, then gestured to the dance floor with his glass.

"This gala is hell. You could at least entertain me. Unless you require payment?" He patted his jacket pocket. "It's been a few minutes. Wouldn't want to upset your bookkeeping."

"Ha. Ha."

"Still laughing after your strenuous afternoon?"

Jack's eyelashes fluttered. "You're so amusing. I can't help myself."

"My executive assistant informed me that if you can make someone laugh, you can get them to do anything."

"I thought you said your executive assistant was called Albert, not Marilyn Monroe?"

Lucas paused in their banter and traced his tongue over the back of his top teeth. "C'mon, please? I'm really curious." He held one flat palm toward Jack. "No game playing, I'm being truthful."

Their eyes met. Jack nibbled the corner of his mouth while Lucas sipped his beer, big blue eyes peering at him over the rim of his glass. Jack sighed through his nose.

"One full hour of my time is six hundred, which breaks down one hundred pounds per ten minutes, though I have a thirty-minute minimum. Most clients don't bother with thirty or forty minutes. They go for at least an hour. My rate goes up for an overnight or multiple days, and anything over three hours receives an additional fee. All travel and accommodations are paid for, obviously, and—"

"Wait. Excuse me. Six hundred? Six-zero-zero?" Lucas blinked at him, the motion of his eyelids stuttering. "Six hundred pounds?"

"Yes."

"And people actually pay you that much money?"

"They do. Happily."

"When people enter you, does God himself come down to whisper the meaning of life in their ear?"

"Dunno about that, but most of my clients seem to be religious. They're usually calling out to God for most of our sessions."

"I can't believe it." Lucas shook his head faster, insisting, "I cannot believe people would pay that much money just to have sex with you, no matter how good you think you are. That can't be right."

"Believe it, love. I've got bookings lined up for at least a year. Most weeks are fully booked unless I opt to take a break. I'm discreet, professional, and flexible. I've never had trouble filling my schedule."

Lucas chuckled, taking a sip of his beer. "If I paid you six hundred pounds, I'd do more than tickle you for the hour."

"Is that so?" Jack's eyes crinkled at the edges, his voice dropping lower. His gaze left paths of heat as he studied Lucas's profile. "And what would you do to me for the hour, hm?"

Lucas smirked and turned his head. Their eyes locked. "Wouldn't you like to know?"

Jack looked toward the dance floor, shaking his head, a small smile on his face. "You have no interest in becoming a client. Why do you care about my rates?"

"Just wondering how your operation works, is all. Seems dangerous. And stressful. Not worth it, even with your outrageous hourly rate."

"I have rules." Jack sipped his drink. "Lots of them, actually."

"Like what?"

"All sorts of rules about safety and privacy. I vet my clients before adding them to my list. Safe sex is an absolute requirement. Everyone signs an NDA—a nondisclosure agreement—which protects both me and my clients."

"NDA?" Lucas giggled, delighted. "Do you fingerprint them, as well? Take a blood sample?"

"Not quite, but I do run background checks. I also work off of referrals only, no strangers unless I invite them in, which is next to never. I've found people behave better when they know I know one of their friends or colleagues."

Lucas could imagine Jack's business card burning a hole through his wallet. "And they're all right with that?"

Jack sipped his drink. "At first, me doing everything above board turned some clients off." His right shoulder rose. "Who wants a paper trail for their rent boy habit? The thought of an escort running background checks and using NDAs was unheard of. Eventually, I was able to build a client list that didn't care about money and had nothing to hide, which is when things got easier."

"So, let me get this straight." Lucas squared himself to Jack, ticking off his list on his fingers. "You charge these men up the arse, make them fill out *paperwork*, ugh, and refuse to give them anonymity, yet you still are fully booked?"

"Yes."

"I don't believe it."

"I require a lot of my clients, but they also receive a lot in return. It's an even balance."

"I'm sure."

Jack's eyes bored into his face, friendly and calm but with razor-sharp concentration.

"For the sake of clarity, my hourly rate may seem high, but I'm a solo operation. That's what keeps it legal. I pay for all of my own security, my online memberships to run background checks, my scheduling software, fees for credit cards, tips for hotel desk staff that I'm friendly with, and who keep an eye out for me when I'm working, plus an abundance of personal expenses I absorb to maintain my image."

"Your image," Lucas repeated.

"I'm all about the full experience for my clients, which includes maintaining my image to the best of my abilities. Clothing, skin care, hair removal, gym membership."

"I see, I see." Lucas took a drink of beer as Jack sipped through his straw. "You have a security guard?"

"No. I have this."

Jack lifted his right wrist and pulled his white sleeve down, revealing a thin black leather bracelet with a simple black button in the center and a red symbol painted on the inside of the button.

"You—" Lucas's eyes narrowed and his words slowed. "—believe having diabetes will keep your clients from mistreating you?"

"I don't have diabetes. This is my security. If I press this for more than five seconds, the police are notified, along with a security company I pay to monitor my location. I wear it when I work. I also keep the company updated as to my schedule, and if I don't check in at a designated time, they will alert the authorities. Costs me a pretty penny each month, but it makes me feel safer. I'm lucky I can afford this. Many in my field cannot."

"What if you fall asleep on it?"

"I have to really press it. It's okay if it's under a pillow or something."

"What if you're tied up?" Lucas's mouth twitched closed, his brain sizzling inside his skull. That question had come out faster than he anticipated.

Jack seemed unbothered, continuing to chat casually. "I never allow my clients to tie me up in such a way that I can't get out and won't even consider it unless we've had at least three appointments prior. I only agree to light bondage and I always provide the restraints. More for the look than for the actual restraints. If they want heavy, I refer them to a professional Dom or sub."

Lucas wiped the back of his hand over his forehead and took a gulp of beer. It had gone warm in his glass, and his hand was sweating.

"But what if someone drugs you? Or attacks you?"

Jack shrugged, sipping his drink through its straw. "Someone could drug or attack you at any time, whether you meet them on OkCupid, in a pub, or in the supermarket. I hope that people seeking companionship have good intentions. So far, I've been fine. It's rare, but that's been my experience."

"Have you ever used it? Your button, I mean."

"Nope. I'm bigger than a lot of my clients, and usually much younger. The most I'll have to do is give them a lecture about boundaries, and then they behave like polite little schoolboys. Once I blacklist someone, there's no going back. They don't want to risk landing on that list, small as it is."

Lucas placed his empty glass on the bar top. Another beer was pressed into his hand before he could signal the female bartender who possessed Albert's face. He nodded at her, then sipped his new beer. "And your rules?"

"So many questions," Jack purred. His eyes danced with light. "Are you sure you work here and are not undercover for the *Sun*? Sorry, love, I don't kiss and tell."

"Maybe I'm a cop."

Jack's lashes fluttered with an amused chuckle. "You'd look precious in a copper's uniform, I'm sure, but everything I do is legal, just as if I was selling handmade pottery or knitting sweaters for a living."

"Yes, because pottery, sweaters, and sex all go in the same work bracket."

Jack's eyes followed a tray of spring rolls. "Judge all you want, but I run a clean operation."

"All right. Next rule?"

"No photos."

"No photos?"

"None. It's one of my policies."

Lucas stared at him, thumbing the rim of his glass. "How is that possible in this day and age?"

"It's possible."

"What if your client wants you in a photo?"

"I don't care," Jack lilted, shrugging his right shoulder. "I don't do photos. I don't film anything. I want absolutely no record of me at work in any form of media." He swirled his straw in his glass; perfect cubes of ice clinked against the sides. "It's all made very clear before I enter into any sort of arrangement. If I found out a client filmed me without my consent, my lawyer would come into play. That's another expense I absorb, Mr. Numbers, though I've never had to use him."

"You mean you don't leave tart cards in phone booths? I bet you'd look fetching in red lace and lippy."

"Oh, darling. You don't even know who you're dealing with, do you?"

"And I'm not talking about naked photos." Lucas sipped his beer, then scoffed. "Get your head out of the gutter." Lucas kept his head forward, but heard what could have been a muffled chuckle from beside him. He was unsure about why he was engaging Jack in conversation, but a small puff of satisfaction warmed his chest at the thought of making Jack's controlled, calculated demeanor break. "What if you had a client who wanted to take a picture with you at a function?" Lucas slowly circled his pint glass in the air, outlining the shape of the crowded dance floor. "Like this sort of function. What then?"

"My answer would be no, and they'd know it before we even entered the function. If they tried to engage me for a photo, I'd leave and they would pay a heavy penalty. It's never been an issue."

"I find that very hard to believe."

"Really?"

"Yes."

"Why?"

"When you do an overnight with a client, how do you know they don't photograph you in your sleep?"

"So," Jack said as he widened his eyes, "you're that type of creepy. I figured you were more of a used underwear collector or a clingy—"

"Excuse me, I've never done that in my life." Lucas fought a laugh. Playfulness illuminated Jack's face, washing away some of his bored indifference. "But I'd think it's a valid concern in your line of work."

"I rarely sleep on overnights. And before you assume, I'd say at least three-quarters of my overnights include little to no sex."

Lucas caught sight of Mr. Carson's thinning white comb-over and severe hunchback across the room. Toilet paper had stuck to the bottom of his black dress shoe. "Pity." Another soft sound was exhaled beside him, muffled by a sip of gin and tonic. Lucas fanned his fingers out toward the dance floor, speaking quietly to Jack. "At corporate events like this, there are hired photographers all over the place, hired specifically to catch guests at awkward moments when they're eating too much prawn cocktail or fake laughing at something to please their boss."

"Speaking from experience?"

"Please," Lucas snorted. "Everyone flocks to the prawns. They're the star of appetizers. What I'm trying to say is that it's almost impossible to escape an event like tonight without being at least in the background of a photo or two. It's impossible. The poor wait staff even gets roped into photos."

Jack's neutral, handsome-without-trying expression was back, staring across the room as if there were an ocean between the walls of the ballroom. The ice in his glass shifted; his thumb rubbed the condensation building on the outside. "I'm good at making myself invisible for self-preservation purposes," he eventually said, his voice quiet. "Very good."

Lucas watched Jack sip his gin and tonic through the tiny red straw meant to be a stirrer. "I don't believe it."

Jack shrugged and widened his elbows on the bar. The simple motion was somehow graceful when expressed by his lithe limbs. His broad chest arched upward beneath his white tux shirt.

Jack's green eyes slid smoothly to Lucas's face. They made a slow, discerning journey from his eyes down to his chin, then back up to meet his gaze. The right side of Jack's lips rose ever so slowly. "Find a date to the wedding yet?"

Lucas remained perfectly still for a moment. The colorful lights that had been flickering over the dance floor changed to subdued white, the size of the lights fattening to dreamy spotlights instead of lasers.

"No," Lucas said.

"Interesting."

"I don't need a date. I've gone to plenty of weddings and functions alone. The world continued to rotate."

Jack smiled properly with all of his perfect teeth. His dimples deepened and the tip of his tongue, even pinker than his lips, peeked out to lick the corner of his mouth. "Is that so?"

"Yes, it is." When Jack said nothing, simply smirking and letting his long eyelashes bat up and down, Lucas's jawline set and his eyes narrowed. "What?"

"Nothing," Jack said, almost on a giggle.

"Why is it a requirement to bring someone to a wedding?"

"S'not a requirement," Jack shrugged. "It seems to make things more pleasant, is all."

"I'm not going to start seeing someone new, have one date, then ask them to go to a destination wedding with me for over a week. I'd look insane. I move fast in business, but not in relationships."

"You do move fast in business." Jack sucked the end of the stirrer. A small drop of bubbly tonic water glistened on the center of his lips. His eyes made another lazy sweep of Lucas, this time dipping down to his shiny black pointed-toe shoes before landing on his face. "I read all about you."

Lucas snorted. "What?"

"I, of course, knew where my client worked. I looked into Mr. Carson long ago when our arrangement first started. But, out of sheer curiosity, I paid your company website another visit, just to brush up on people I might bump into tonight. I'm very thorough." Jack barely nudged the top of his glass at the dance floor toward Mr. Carson. "Researching him and the company meant running into details about you. It was unavoidable."

"Whatever."

Jack lowered his voice, dropping it to a deep, raspy tone more suited to announcing bands on the stage of a punk rock club. "Commandeering his field of corporate mergers and acquisitions, Lucas Thompson began his illustrious career at the top of his business class at the University of St. Andrews, later completing his graduate studies in business at Cambridge. Not yet thirty—"

"All right, all right," Lucas said, waving his hand. He lifted his beer in Jack's direction. "You can read. Congratulations."

Lucas took a swig as Jack sipped his drink, smirking around the straw.

"Quite a pedigree for someone from somewhere north." Jack's eyes narrowed, and he tilted his chin to the left. "Sheffield?"

Lucas blinked at him, curious and a touch concerned. "That is not in my bio."

"I'm good with accents. You meet a lot of different people in my line of work."

"Hey, I hold no judgment. You do what you do and that's it. There's nothing wrong with working to make a living."

"Then why the reluctance to pay me for my time? Surely it's chump change for you."

Lucas's gentle curiosity changed to a shuttered stare and tight, straightened jawline. The air in the room felt a few degrees cooler. Slowly, he explained, "Because I would rather go alone to every event for the rest of my life than pay the ghost of Mick Jagger's youth to pretend to tolerate me."

"Is that so?"

"It is."

"For the rest of your life?"

"The rest of my life," Lucas said. His expression didn't flicker once.

"A life is a long time to be alone."

"And a life built on lies is no life at all."

"Strong words coming from someone who plays a character almost as well as I do."

"You don't know shit about me."

"I know you because you're like me. Like dissolves like. I can tell."

"You don't know shit about me," Lucas repeated, enunciating each word. "And we're not alike at all."

"No?" Jack's eyes ran over Lucas's face. His voice was quiet and gentle, drawling, "Do you not lie to people every day? Do you not pretend to be someone else to make a living?"

"I don't give my body away to put food on the table."

Jack tutted his tongue. "Oh, darling, you disappoint me. Such judgment from someone who proclaimed 'no judgment' mere moments ago. And this is not given away." Jack gestured to himself. "Far from it."

"No, I suppose it's not. Not when you prey on senile old men—"

"Prey?" Jack laughed over him.

"—who are lonely and looking for so-called companionship. If you're such a saint for the elderly, volunteer at a nursing home."

"I never said I was a saint. Do I sense that I've struck a nerve?" Jack stirred the remaining inch of liquid in his glass. The ice cubes clinked. "Lonely young men turn into lonely old men much faster than you may think, both searching for companionship no matter what age."

"Aren't we wise," Lucas said, running his thumb around the rim of his glass. "The Buddha of hookers."

Jack downed his drink and placed it on the bar. He dusted his hands together. "I'm being beckoned." He smiled warmly across the dance floor, looking far younger than seconds earlier in their rapid-fire conversation. He pushed off the bar and stood to his full height. The expensive material of his tux clung to the deep curve of his lower back. He glanced at Lucas over his shoulder. "Lovely conversation, as always, Mr. Numbers."

Lucas tipped his head back to finish his beer. "Enjoy the rest of your evening with your date."

Jack batted his eyes extra slow. "Enjoy watching other people slow dance in paradise while you sit alone in the corner, contemplating the meaning of life and your right hand."

He sauntered toward Mr. Carson.

"JACK," LUCAS said from behind him.

Jack's long strides slowed; the thick carpet slid under the smooth soles of his shoes. He stifled a grin, instead exhaling a deep breath. He could practically taste the piña coladas he'd be drinking on his paid holiday. He could use some sun and sand.

He angled himself sideways and stretched his long neck enough to see Lucas. "Yes?"

Lucas came up next to him with his hands dug in his pockets. He did not lay a finger on Jack, but his body seemed to produce vibrations of energy, a force field of heated power spilling onto the sleeve of Jack's jacket and slowly spreading across his body.

"What did you want to be?"

Jack blinked at him, his head tilting without his control. He kept his face toward Mr. Carson, who was waving him over in a way all too reminiscent of a grandfather rooting a child on at a football game.

"Pardon?" Jack asked.

"Before this." Lucas's breath brushed over Jack's neck, and Jack felt goose bumps popping up on his skin. "What did you want to be?"

Jack swallowed. The back of his throat was thick. He pushed the thickness down to his belly, mentally picturing the journey through his veins and bones until it melted out of his feet. "A photographer," he said, maintaining the even tone of his voice.

Lucas chuckled low and quiet. There was little humor in the sound. Jack could feel cool eyes tracing the sharp curve of his jawline, the flabby bit of his earlobe. The shadow of a hickey, he knew, was peeking over the collar of his shirt—it was a day away from fading completely.

Lucas whispered, "A lover of photographs spends his life skulking around events he wasn't invited to, scared of cameras like a little boy."

Jack's jawline tightened. He turned ever so slightly with his face still toward Mr. Carson. "I have my date to attend to."

"Of course, of course." Lucas ghosted his hand over the back of Jack's shoulders, though he still did not touch him. "I apologize for taking up your valuable, *valuable* time."

Jack held up one finger toward Mr. Carson while pretending to chuckle at Lucas's last statement. "I wondered how you managed to climb the corporate ladder so fast." Jack turned his face toward Lucas and looked him dead-on with vicious, furious eyes, though his calm expression never faltered. "Now it makes sense. You're the most cliché of wolves in sheep's clothing."

Lucas mimicked Jack's fake amusement, slapping his thigh and bending slightly forward. "Oh, you're a funny one. A funny personal consultant. Do your clients pay per laugh or per orifice?"

Jack said nothing, turning away from him and gliding across the dance floor.

LUCAS WATCHED him walk up to Mr. Carson and bow. His goofy gesture delighted the older gentleman to the point of clapping his bony hands together. Jack placed his hand on Mr. Carson's hip and lifted their joined hands up as far as Mr. Carson could manage. He started to gently lead a waltz. Mr. Carson grinned from ear to ear as they spun around the dance floor.

Lucas walked back to the bar.

The bartender asked, "Another, sir?"

"Yes, please."

Lucas heard the beer tap's smooth, scooped sound as it poured beer into a fresh pint glass. Jack and Mr. Carson danced, their bodies flitting between other couples swaying to the string-heavy classical music. It was like watching a time machine whirling on a pole, every spin exposing him to either Jack's fresh-faced youth or Mr. Carson's near-crippled seniority.

"Here you are, sir."

Lucas nodded his thanks to the bartender and took his fresh pint. When he looked back to the dance floor, he was hit by Jack's eyes boring into him, blazing, intense green even from meters away. Lucas held his gaze while drinking a long draught of his beer. He finished drinking and licked his lips, then spread his elbows across the bar. Jack's gaze was still glued to his face.

Chapter FIVE

Monday, April 13

ALBERT POPPED his head into Lucas's office.

"Anything else before I leave, sir? Everything is prepped for the remainder of the day."

"Hm?" Lucas looked from his watch to Albert's face. "What's today?"

"Today is my appointment at the dentist." Albert pointed at his mouth as if to demonstrate that dentists deal with teeth. "I e-mailed you and put it in your schedule. Is that still all right?"

"Yes, yes. Enjoy your afternoon of getting your teeth poked at." Lucas shuddered and looked back down to his paperwork. "I hope you have a nice, long lunch planned for afterward with lots of sweets. Have a nice rest of the day."

"You too, sir. Let me know if you need any help with your travel arrangements. Cillian left me a message asking if you'd taken care of it yet. He said he'd reimburse you as soon as you do."

"It's not necessary for him to do that, but thank you for relaying the message."

Albert went to leave but swung his upper body back inside the office, while gripping the doorframe. "Oh! I forgot to ask if you read over the updated schedule yet."

"No, not yet." Lucas ran his hand through his quiff. "I've been swamped with this Bingsby nightmare all day."

"When you get a chance, give it a look. Zamir and Cillian really outdid themselves planning fun activities all week. Anna is so excited we'll be there in time for ballroom dance lessons."

Lucas stared at him for a beat while holding a stapled packet of paper open. For that moment, he was frozen. "Buh—" He tilted his chin. "Ballroom dancing?"

"Thursday afternoon." Albert's mobile rang in his pocket. "Sorry, I need to get going. I mean—" He straightened up. "May I—"

"Yes, yes. Please." Lucas waved his hand forward. "Get going."

Albert called a cheerful, "Bye, sir!" over his shoulder as he flew out of the quiet office.

Lucas steeled his expression and loosened his hold on the paper packet to grip his mouse. He opened his personal inbox and double-clicked on the newest e-mail from Zamir.

> *Hello loved ones!*
> *Here is the schedule for our magical time together. Obviously each activity is optional, but we hope to see you at as many events as you can attend! If you'd rather sit one out, be sure to bring lots of sun cream and your bathing suit! The beaches are beyond beautiful!! So excited to see you all!!*
> *Namaste and love!*
> *Zamir and Cillian! xoxoxo*

"Namaste and love," Lucas whispered to himself, double-clicking the attached PDF. "Namaste, love, and exclamation points."

The multipage schedule opened. Even though Flamingo Cove, the resort they'd chosen for the trip, was definitely on the more sophisticated, elite side of all-inclusive tropical resorts, Cillian and Zamir had managed to wrangle multiple large rooms and beach settings for their week of events.

A wedding-bell-and-seashell border lined the itinerary's pages. Beach photos were interspersed between paragraphs. Each day on the schedule was bolded and given a trip-related title, plus a small symbol to match the title and an obligatory array of excited punctuation.

Seashell Sunday!
Toucan Tuesday!!
Flamingo Friday!!!
The Happiest Day of Our Lives Saturday!!!!

Lucas's eyes widened as he read. Each day was jam-packed with group meals and activities. If you attended each activity, you would be with other guests from sunup to sundown.

He loosened his tie and exhaled, then turned to look out his floor-to-ceiling office window. Among the hustle and bustle of London, a smoky gray fog covered the street scene. An old woman walked a miniature Yorkie. The dog pulled at the leash despite the woman's slow and deliberate steps.

"All right, let's see," he whispered to himself, refocusing on the schedule. He scrolled back to the top and nodded. "I can do this."

BBQ Lunch on the Beach!
Bocci and Shuffleboard!
Bike Riding Adventure!

"Okay," he said, continuing to read. "Totally fine."

Beach Volleyball Tournament!
Zumbaaaa!
Pottery with Zamir!!

His nose twitched.

Island Scavenger Hunt!! Bring your partner and get ready to run!
Family Movie Breakfast Extravaganza! (Tissues suggested!!!)
Crafting and Jewelry Making with Cillian!

His mouth tightened.

The First Annual Zill Beach Olympics! *The ZILL-YMPICS*! Bring your A Game!
Beach Tote Painting and Beading!!

His throat went dry, and he'd barely made it two days into the schedule.

Couples' Horseback Riding and Chocolate Tasting on the Beach!
MIDNIGHT KARAOKE!!!

He stared at the screen. Copy machines and printers whirled outside his door. A phone rang once, twice, three times before it was picked up. The person who answered the phone was far enough from his office that he could not hear their words, only low murmurs of combined voices.

He swallowed, reached forward, and picked up his office phone.

"YOU'RE ALMOST there, almost there! Give me five… four… three… two… and one. Done! Relax."

Jack fell onto his stomach, his torso drenched with sweat and squelching on his yoga mat.

"Breathe," the fitness instructor's chipper voice said through his television. "Great job, everyone. Let's breathe together. Bring our heart rate down. Time for the cooldown."

"Okay, mate, whatever you say," Jack panted, rolling onto his back. His chest heaved up and down and he sprawled his arms over his head. He gasped out, "Fucking plyometrics," and shut his eyes, sweat stinging in the corners of his eyes and gushing down from his hairline. "Fucking power yoga."

"Now we stretch!"

He rolled onto his side, his muscles screaming and his hands shaking. Though he wanted to melt into a puddle of sweat and flesh goo for the next day or so, he listened to the instructor's voice and stretched.

Once the guided cooldown was complete, he followed through with his plan to melt into a puddle of sweat, collapsing on his back on the yoga mat and listening to the DVD menu music play. His phone vibrated on the white coffee table. He slowly opened his eyes to blink at the sound of his work ringtone, then groaned as he peeled himself off the mat.

Any other time, he would let the call go to voice mail, but the next couple of weeks were turning out to be rather slow. One of his regulars had booked him for a weeklong trip to Acapulco, but had to cancel due to a work emergency. Before Jack could inform his client that he would be responsible for half of his deposit, since Jack had held the long slot in his schedule, his client e-mailed him to apologize profusely and insist that Jack keep the whole deposit (half of the entire week's fee).

He managed to schedule an overnight with a regular client, but it was unlikely that he would book another long gig, or even a few random one-nighters, for the next couple of weeks. Spring break meant a lot of his clients were out of town or on holiday. He didn't need the money, and wouldn't mind a few days off, but was unsure what he'd do with so much time to himself. Maybe he'd finally get around to replacing the backsplash in his kitchen.

He crawled over to the table and glanced at the phone screen. It was an unknown number, as usual. He accepted the call. His voice was a touch out of breath when he said, "Hello?"

"Am I interrupting you at work? I was unsure what your hours of operation are." Jack's eyes widened at the raspy voice, and his mouth popped open. A tutting tongue carried through the phone. "Quite rude of you to take a call with a paying client there, especially given your strict fee schedule."

Jack exhaled hot air out of his nostrils. "What do you want, Thompson?"

"To talk."

Jack brought himself to his feet and walked to his tall living room windows. He crossed his arms over his sweaty chest. "I've given you enough of my time for free. No more freebies. Hanging up now."

"Please, don't. Please?"

Something in Lucas's voice, something quiet and shockingly gentle, made Jack stop walking. "Why shouldn't I?"

"Because I treated you so poorly," Lucas said, his tone softer. "So, so poorly, and I'm embarrassed by my behavior. You have every reason to hang up. I don't blame you. If you hang up, I won't ring you again. I promise."

Jack pulled the phone away from his face and peered at it, then brought it back to his ear. "You're embarrassed?"

"I am. And I'm sorry, truly sorry."

"Oh." Jack thumbed his knuckles, hugging himself tighter across the chest. He listened to Lucas breathe for a moment. "So, why are you calling, then?"

"I have a proposition for you."

"Like I haven't heard that one before."

"I just want to talk to you. Businessman to businessman."

A slow grin spread over Jack's face as he studied his reflection in the window. He flexed his right bicep; the fine hair under his arm was darkened with sweat.

"You're calling about that wedding, aren't you?"

"Yes."

"I see," Jack said, glee sneaking into his voice. He checked out his left bicep, turning to study the curve of his lower back. He did an easy twerk of his plump arse. "Finally giving in?"

"No. I want to negotiate."

"I don't negotiate. You're aware of my strict fee schedule," he said, giving his words extra clipped diction. "You're a numbers man. Do the maths and pony up, or don't call me again."

"I refuse to pay for your services."

Jack snorted. "Then why the call? You get off on talking to sex workers without actually having sex?"

"I'll take care of your expenses for the trip," Lucas said calmly. The all-white decor of Jack's flat faded away to a conference room. A visual flashed in his mind of Lucas sitting with his fingers steepled at the end of a long mahogany table. "Food, hotel, flight, security, everything. Whatever you need to enjoy yourself and feel comfortable. All you have to do is accompany me to group events and pretend to be my boyfriend."

"And my fee?"

"Your fee is ten days in the Bahamas. We're not having sex, so I don't feel an hourly rate is needed. When money is exchanged, there's an implication that goods will also be exchanged. I don't want there to be any awkwardness or discomfort on either of our parts, but especially yours."

Jack snickered softly. "Luke, love, I don't do charity. You follow my rules, or you're not one of my clients. It's as simple as that." He stepped on his left foot with his right neon yellow Nike. "Besides, I'm not even available that week—"

"Yes, you are," Lucas said over him, slow and quiet.

Jack sucked his tongue into his mouth, listening to Lucas hum amusedly on the other end of the phone. His nipples prickled on his damp chest. "How do you know that?"

"Why do you think Mr. Carson gave you a ring a couple of hours ago? Asking for your availability, which," Lucas deepened his voice and slowed his words to mimic Jack's speech, "recently opened up a bit due to a change in plans, love."

Jack's mouth pursed even tighter, his blood boiling hotter than during the peak of his P90X workout. "That doesn't mean I'm free the entire week. I have someone booked for Friday to Saturday."

"Reschedule them."

"I don't appreciate you using my clients against me or poking around my schedule." Jack gritted the words through his teeth. "At all."

"You yourself said I was a wolf. I'm simply playing my part. That's what we do best, isn't it? Play our parts. Besides," Lucas snorted quietly, "do you really think you're the only person who does their research? If anything, I'm following your rules. My referral is Mr. Francis Carson. He had the loveliest things to say about his old friend Jack. Such a sweet, sweet boy."

As Lucas's tongue caressed each softly spoken word, Jack's boiling blood rushed to his cheeks. Bursts of fresh sweat itched on top of his already drenched skin.

"I'm not discussing my client any further."

"Fine with me. I'm aware of your rules. Are you interested in talking about this or not? I've got work to do."

"I'm not accepting anything over the phone, are you mad? And you call yourself a businessman."

"Fair enough. Let me take you out for lunch tomorrow and we can talk details."

"Don't tell me what to do. Besides, I'm busy."

"Dinner, then? Or is tomorrow afternoon Mr. Tickles, and you'll need a night to recover?"

"I'm busy," Jack repeated, slower, fighting a laugh.

"Wednesday lunch?"

Jack nudged the toe of his trainer against the bottom of the window seat. A mug of cold tea sat abandoned on top of the cream-colored cushion. "Fine. Wednesday."

"Don't sound so excited."

Jack's head snapped up. "This doesn't mean I'm accepting the offer. Why should I cancel two nights with a paying client to do you a favor?"

"As a numbers man, let me remind you that the cost of ten days at this resort is worth a touch more than two nights with your client, despite your ridiculously inflated prices. Why are you playing hardball with me? I'm offering you a free holiday."

"Nothing in life is free, and people who say things like that are usually liars. You could be a complete psychopath."

"Look," Lucas said, letting the word marinate for a moment. "You are more than welcome to stay in rainy, gray, cold London. Twiddle your thumbs, go shopping for more pirate clothes, catch up on *Big Brother*. Whatever. I don't care."

Jack's phone vibrated against his face. He placed Lucas on speaker and checked the screen, scanning over a new text.

Babe, my ex broke ankle skiing & i need to take the kids next wknd. will have to reschedule. so so sorry love :((, was so looking forward to it xxx can you run my cc on file for cancellation fee? not sure if time to drop £ busy wk. thx love xx call u soon.

"Or," Lucas continued, "you can come with me on an all-expenses-paid trip to paradise and relax. No hustling necessary. You can sleep on the beach, for all I care. We barely even have to talk to each other, as long as we're convincing enough in public and limit our bickering to when we're alone."

Jack licked his lips. A pigeon took off from his window ledge. Sunlight beamed over his face as he tilted his head back to follow the rising path of the bird. He tapped the toe of his trainer against the wall and took Lucas off speaker, bringing the phone to balance between his ear and shoulder.

Lucas cleared his throat, quietly asking, "Jack?"

"We can talk details at lunch on Wednesday."

A small rush of air carried through the phone. "Good. Very good," Lucas said. Jack walked into his kitchen and took out a slice of wheat bread from the breadbox beside his white toaster. "Have you ever been to J+A Café?"

Jack walked back to the living room while pinching off small pieces of bread, cradling the bits in his palm. "Yes."

"Noon?"

"Works for me."

"I'll see you then."

"Fine."

"Th—" Another brush of air came through the phone.

When no words followed, Jack sighed, tapping his middle finger against the edge of his iPhone.

"Are we done?" Jack asked. He was starting to smell himself, sharp sweat drying sticky on his skin. He cracked a window and tossed the bread pieces onto the window ledge. He brushed his hands together. "I've got things to do."

"I was going to say thank you."

Jack's brushes slowed, his eyes following the flight pattern of two pale white birds weaving between buildings. They landed outside his windowsill, pecking at the bread bits.

"Thank you for taking the time to speak with me," Lucas said, quieter. There was less drive than usual behind his tone. "And thank you for agreeing to meet with me. We… I haven't been very polite to you in our interactions. I apologize for that. Thank you for giving me a chance."

Jack bit his bottom lip, and stared at his reflection in the window. Lucas might have a direct way of speaking, but he felt no nerves or fear with him. Years of meeting strangers had refined his gut reactions as to who was good and who was bad. He didn't feel like Lucas was a bad one.

"What can I say?" Jack ran his fingers through his hair and squeezed his high bun. "I'm a sucker for a big arse and a free lunch."

Lucas's laughter crackled through the phone, and Jack smiled wider as he watched the white birds stumble around on his landing. He traced their outlines through the thin pane of glass; condensation fogged the space around his fingertip.

"I'll see you Wednesday, Jack."

There was that gentle tone again. Jack lifted his finger from the glass and the two white birds took off into the foggy sky.

Chapter SIX

Wednesday, April 15

IT WAS raining when Lucas ran into J+A Café with his coat tucked over his head. He pulled the door open and bumped into someone standing in the front of the crowded cafe.

"You know, there's this thing called an umbrella," Jack said, steadying Lucas with an arm on each shoulder. They walked farther inside together, Lucas stepping forward and Jack walking backward. "It was invented a long, long time ago, but is still very handy in this day and age."

Lucas dropped his leather briefcase to the floor and shrugged his wet coat off. Jack took it from him and hung it on the coat rack.

"Cheers," Lucas said, finger-combing his hair back.

Jack pushed his black Ray-Bans up like a headband. Politeness radiated out of his warm voice. "Two for lunch, please," he said to the hostess.

"I left my umbrella in my office," Lucas said as he flicked water off his hands. "It's only down the road from here so I thought I could leg it." He wiped his palms on his trousers, bending to pick up his briefcase. "The weather had other plans."

"Busy day?"

"Erm, sort of. My assistant's girlfriend bought him a basketball hoop to put on a wastebasket as a gag gift. He was horrified and told me he thought it was an immature distraction—he's quite professional, you see—until I said we should try it." He gave up on his hair, resulting in a small section on the very top of his head sticking straight up. "Three hours later, I've gotten no work done, we wasted an entire pack of printer paper, and he's revealed himself as the Michael Jordan of throwing rubbish."

Jack's dimples popped as he laughed, the rough, deep sound barked suddenly out of him. Lucas's brows arched with his own small smile, surprise lightening the sound of his soft chuckle. Jack quickly schooled his features.

"I've got your table ready, guys." The hostess held her arm out with two menus in hand. "This way, please."

They followed her down the aisle of white tables. They were seated next to a window, where rain pounded against the glass in a soothing, dull drone.

Lucas pulled Jack's chair away from the table and held his arm out. Jack sank into his seat with his eyes trained on Lucas.

"Too bad it's raining." Lucas sat and scooted his own seat closer to the table. "I like their outdoor tables when the weather's nice."

Jack nodded, reading over the menu. "Me too."

"You've eaten here?"

"I have. Their bar is good too."

"Do you live in the area?"

"I don't."

Lucas waited for the rest of Jack's sentence, but it never came as Jack's eyes scanned over the menu. "Okay," Lucas said slowly, picking up his menu.

Two lines of starters into the menu and his eyes were pulled away from the list of food. He peered over the edge of the white card stock. Jack seemed to have gone for a more relaxed, fresh rock-star look as opposed to his greasy, sheer shirt aesthetic. He wore a fitted black blazer, dark jeans that clung to his thighs, and a loose white button-down that appeared to have motorcycles on it, all somehow tied together by a pair of mustard brown Chelsea boots.

"Was a pleasant surprise when you suggested this place."

Lucas looked up from Jack's full lips. "Sorry?" The small upward tilt of the left side of Jack's mouth made the back of Lucas's neck burn.

"I said it was nice that you picked this place. I like it here." Jack took his sunglasses off his head and hung them from the deep vee of his shirt. His right hand ruffled through the front of his long locks. "It's comfortable."

"Where do you usually have lunches like this?"

Jack's mouth pursed, his head bobbing side to side. "Food is the last thing on a lot of my clients' minds, but I've found that men who want to bother with meals together want to show off a bit. The whole wine and dine thing. I never thought I'd get sick of foie gras and lobster and champagne, but sometimes you just want a sandwich for lunch, you know?"

"Understood. This morning some investor or another decided to cater a huge breakfast for the office. God knows why. I'm still pretty full."

"Too much prawn cocktail?"

"For breakfast? No, thank you. Disgusting."

"Rubbish-ball didn't spark an appetite?"

"No," Lucas chuckled, placing his menu on the table. "All I'm going to get is tea, but you can order whatever you want. Food, drinks, whatever."

The waitress appeared at their table and placed a carafe of water on top, along with two glasses. "Have you two decided?" She looked from Jack to Lucas. "Do you have any questions about our menu?"

Lucas opened his mouth, but before he could ask about their tea selection, Jack said, "I'd like a glass of the Clarendelle, please."

Unsure how a lunch meeting had turned into an event for red wine, Lucas glanced at the wine list. His eyes landed on the expensive Bordeaux Rouge at the same time as Jack tutted his tongue and tapped his forehead.

"Silly me," Jack chuckled, his face flushed pretty pink. "You only offer that one by the bottle." He glanced at Lucas for one slow bat of his eyelashes. "We'll take a bottle." His brows arched, delicate and innocent. "That works for you, right, babe?"

The waitress's eyes lit up. Her pen flew over her pad. "Excellent choice of wine, sir."

Lucas murmured, "Yes," and tilted his head. Jack's foot banged rhythmically against Lucas's shin under the table. "Excellent choice, *babe*."

"Then," Jack continued in his standard low drawl, "we'll start with the crab on irish soda bread, split the quiche of the day, and I'd like the steak sandwich, please." He handed her his menu, flashing a winning grin. "Thanks so much, love."

The waitress flushed under his attention, fumbling the menu and sputtering, "Yes, okay, great choices."

Lucas rolled his eyes so hard he nearly blinded himself. He kicked at Jack's irritating boot, which only continued to bang against his shins. Jack stifled a laugh with his fist pressed to his mouth. He perched his elbow on the table.

"Oh," the waitress said, looking baffled at Lucas. "Sorry, sir." She straightened her posture. "What can I get for you?"

"Tea, please," he said, handing her his menu. "Yorkshire, if you have it."

"We have Irish Breakfast tea?" Lucas nodded and she scribbled on her pad. "No food for you?"

Lucas pasted a sunny smile on his face, reaching across the table to place his hand over Jack's free hand. "Oh, don't you worry about me. I'll share with my better half." His voice rose to coo, "My sweet little honey bunch."

Jack's grin faltered. Horror flashed in his eyes, and his nose scrunched as if a sewer had opened beside their table. He recovered within seconds and turned his hand over, lacing their fingers together.

"Aw, my silly fluffy-bum, don't be shy." Jack giggled, the sound so cutesy and coupled with such a boyish wiggle that Lucas's stomach turned. "I can hear your wee little tum-tum rumbling from all the way over here." He gripped Lucas tightly to keep their joined hands on the table, aiming a sickly sweet grin at the waitress. "He'll have the irish stew and a big piece of the chocolate Guinness cake for dessert." He thumbed toward Lucas and exhaled, amusedly exasperated. "Such a sweet tooth, this one."

Lucas crunched his hand in an iron grip, their fake expressions of joy bordering on manic. The waitress didn't seem to notice, chuckling lightly and pocketing her pad. "Lovely. I'll put your order in right away and be back with your drinks."

She left them to check on the table behind theirs. They maintained their position until she moved out of earshot. Their hands sprung apart, Jack cackling while Lucas scowled.

"Fuck," Lucas said, rubbing his reddened hand. "You must be a shit escort if you're hustling me for quiche. Is that what this is? I'm not paying you, so you're going to order six hundred pounds worth of food to spite me? We should have picked a more expensive restaurant to save time."

Jack started pouring water into his glass. "I'm excellent at my job. Not that you'll ever know that, but into every life a little rain must fall." His face twitched as if he wanted to snort. "I usually keep a pretty strict low-carb, low-sugar diet, but am feeling rather ravenous today."

Lucas squinted at him, shaking his head and still cradling his hand. "You're insane."

Jack placed the carafe on the table without filling Lucas's glass. "You're the one who called me."

"I'm on a time crunch."

Jack narrowed his eyes and gave a tiny nod. "Just keep telling yourself that."

"If you were hungry, all you had to say was that you were hungry. I'm not so much of a barbarian that I wouldn't treat you to lunch." Lucas thought for a moment as he filled his water glass. "I'm not even in the mood for stew."

"You're a disgrace. They make delicious stew here and"—Jack's hand flexed toward the window—"it's perfect stew weather."

"I told you I'm not hungry."

"Ugh." Jack sat back in his chair, shaking his hair backward. "You're killing my hunger buzz."

"Look, I get what you're doing," Lucas said, crossing his arms over his chest. "You're sore because I made that photography comment at the gala. And the orifice comment. That was also not right for me to say. And kind of gross." He winced, gritting his teeth. "Kind of really gross."

Jack looked to the side and sipped his water, his fingers prim as a prince. "I'm not sore."

"It was a low blow and I'm sorry," Lucas continued. "I shouldn't have said it, and you shouldn't be spoken to like that. Not by me and not by anyone."

Jack sipped again. He curled his hand around the glass, his gaze glued to a spot on the table. He licked his lips. "Whatever."

"I don't know you. I don't know your history. I didn't mean to judge you. I was… I was just—"

"Being rude."

"I suppose."

Their eyes locked.

"Rude. And a prick," Jack said, giving each word a pop of diction.

Lucas tilted his head side to side as Jack's bright green eyes pinned him in place. "I was going to say drunk and cranky, but, yes. You're right. I was rude and a prick. And I'm sorry."

Jack placed his water glass on the table. "A bit rare for a man like you to know how to say the words, 'I'm sorry,' and sound sincere."

"I'm being sincere. I am sincere."

"Fair enough." Jack stared at Lucas. "I… shouldn't have said what I said about you climbing the ladder. Or about the right hand thing. That was rude, as well." His attention was so focused on Lucas that it felt like heat waves radiating into Lucas's skull. "I'm sorry."

Lucas nodded and crossed his legs, leaning his shoulder against the windowpane. Under the rainy light, a pale glow illuminated the right side of his face. "Apology accepted."

"Apology accepted," Jack repeated.

"I wonder, though, how would you know what a man like me would say or do? You don't know me at all. You have a clichéd view of me based on my profession, the same way I have a clichéd view of you. That's not who I am, and I reckon that's not who you are either."

Jack's face bloomed with a smile, his eyes sparkling. "Oh, you're good," he said, purring the words. Lucas smirked, an equal amount of heat simmering behind his stare. The toe of Jack's boot brushed softer against Lucas's shin. "You could be blowing complete smoke up my arse right now, but I can't bring myself to care. It's that good."

"Aren't you a bright one? You've nailed it. My secret fetish isn't collecting used underwear." Jack tossed his head back and started laughing throatily before Lucas could even say, "It's blowing things up arses. Well done, Jack Sparrow, well done."

Jack kept laughing with his hands on his shaking stomach and his eyes scrunched shut. His tongue stuck slightly out of his mouth.

"Oh my God, you're a goofy laugher," Lucas said. He couldn't seem to look away from Jack's boyishly amused face. "That's amazing."

Jack dabbed the top of his hand under his eyelid as he calmed. "I'm not a goofy laugher," he groused, though his rumpled smile indicated he knew exactly what Lucas was talking about. "You're being ridiculous."

"But you are. It's refreshing."

"Refreshing? Why?"

"It wouldn't be fair if you looked how you look all the time without a wrinkle in there somewhere."

Jack lowered his arm to rest it on the table; his fingertips fluttered, from pinky to thumb, on the smooth surface. "And how would that be?" His fingertips did another round of flutters. "How do I look?"

Lucas made a shooing motion. "Oh, shut up. You know you're gorgeous. It's a fact, not a compliment."

Jack's boot was back on Lucas's shin, prodding at his ankle. He grinned, his dimples on full blast, his hair cascading in soft ringlets around his high cheekbones.

"Aw, babe, you think I'm gorgeous?"

"I'm going to send you my dry-cleaning bill," Lucas muttered, kicking his foot away. "Most people take their shoes off to play footsie. Is that not in the Hustler Handbook?"

They both chuckled for a moment. Their smiles were easy, their bodies relaxed in their seats. The realization that they had not viciously bickered within the past few minutes, and had actually exchanged adult apologies, dawned on both at the same time.

The waitress came back to their table. She placed Lucas's tea, a small pitcher of milk, and a selection of sweeteners in front of him. Another server dropped off two wine glasses. The waitress pulled a corkscrew out of her black apron pocket.

"You two seem to be enjoying yourselves. I think you'll really enjoy this wine."

As her corkscrew neared the bottle, Jack said, "Oh, before you open it, would it be possible for me to switch to tea, actually? Not in the mood for red anymore. I'm terribly sorry for the inconvenience."

Lucas's brows furrowed. "I thought you wanted wine?" He nudged Jack's ankle under the table. "It'll go great with your steak sandwich. I'll help you with the bottle."

"I could bring you a cup of tea in addition to the wine," the waitress suggested with corkscrew poised.

"Um, all right, thanks," Jack said, nodding across the table at Lucas. His eyes lit up, his attention back at their waitress. "Oh! And for the stew I ordered for him, I meant to—"

"Ask if that comes with the crusty bread?" Lucas said as he reached across the table and rested his hand on Jack's knuckles. Jack's flexor muscle flickered on the top of his arm. "I love the bread it comes with." He tilted his head at the window. "It's perfect stew weather."

The waitress chuckled as her arm worked the corkscrew. "Yes, crusty bread is on the way. Fresh out of the oven."

Lucas looked to Jack, who stared wide-eyed at him. The cork popped, and deep red wine drizzled into the glass in front of Jack. Lucas's thumb ran over his knuckles.

"Go on, love." He nodded gently. "Try it."

JACK'S EYES narrowed, his hand tensing under Lucas's palm.

It felt to Jack as if alarm bells were wailing and flashing in the quaint cafe—as if the other patrons were standing on their tables and spraying the room with fire extinguishers while screaming at the top of their lungs. He had the sudden sensation of trying to wake up from a dream where he was stumbling down a flight of stairs but couldn't get himself to wake up and was stuck in limbo, with his legs trapped and kicking weakly against the blankets.

Jack blinked once and all the alarm bells quieted to the dull chatter surrounding them. "Sure." He lifted the glass and sipped, then nodded at the waitress and replaced his glass on the table. "It's perfect, thanks."

He watched her pour wine into both glasses. It could have been children's grape juice, for all he knew; his mouth had gone numb. He eyed Lucas as if he were a viper sitting upright, while Lucas chatted with the waitress about bread making being done in-house.

"I'll be back with your starters in just a moment." She placed the wine on their table. "Enjoy your wine, and please let me know if you need anything else."

Jack's eyes followed her back as she wove through the tables. Lucas shifted in his seat in Jack's peripheral vision. Jack looked to Lucas, who tilted his glass across the table.

"Well, here's to going back to work with purple teeth. Can't say it'll be my first time."

Jack lifted his glass and took a sip. Some of the warm notes in the wine brought feeling back into his tongue. He took another small sip, then placed his glass on the table.

"We should figure out our backstory," Jack said.

Lucas thumbed wine off the corner of his mouth. "I don't think that's necessary, do you?"

"I've done this before and I think it's necessary. People love to ask questions, especially if they're caught off guard by a new relationship. We should settle on a story for how we met. Even if it's simple, we should be on the same page."

"Anything we plan in advance will sound stilted when we say it in person. I'm better at improvising."

Jack sighed and poured himself more wine. "Improvising is fine when you're alone, but when you're with your boyfriend it will be a different story." He touched the center of his chest. "Your *boyfriend* would appreciate a heads-up as to what he should be telling complete strangers. Our story is that we met on Valentine's Day in a cab."

"Gross. Why Valentine's Day?"

"It's a holiday. You're more likely to remember it in the moment," Jack said as he swirled his glass. "And we did meet in a cab, so that's actually true. The best lies stick close to the truth."

Lucas blinked at him. "That rolled off the tongue rather easily."

Jack sipped his wine, shrugging one lazy shoulder.

Lucas's face scrunched. "But if we were a real couple, our anniversary would be Valentine's Day. I'd hate it if that was our anniversary. I'd want our anniversary to be unattached to any holiday, that way we can celebrate it just us, not have to deal with every other couple on earth trying to get restaurant reservations and flowers."

"Who knew you'd be so stubborn about a fake anniversary?"

"I'm only asking questions and expressing my opinion."

Jack's smile emerged, quickly hidden by a long drink of wine. He ran his hand through his hair, and Lucas's gaze followed the motion. "It's easier to pick a holiday instead of a random day of a random month because we'll both remember it under pressure. Would you prefer New Year's? Christmas?"

"No. No, thank you. My birthday is the day before Christmas, and that's stressful enough for me to remember."

Jack started to chuckle. "Halloween, maybe?"

Lucas nodded, his eyes brightening. "Oh, yes. I'd prefer Halloween, please."

"Are you serious?" Jack cradled his chin on his palm. "Halloween?"

"Yes. Can Halloween be our meeting date? I promise I'll remember it."

Jack's mouth opened and closed. "You'd rather have Halloween as our anniversary instead of Valentine's Day? Is our wedding going to be a costume party that involves jack-o'-lanterns and bobbing for apples? Is our song 'The Monster Mash'?" His eyes widened with bewilderment. "I have so many questions about our future. I'll have to completely change the color scheme for our floral arrangements to black and orange."

"I have a love-hate relationship with scary movies. Plus, Valentine's Day is the worst of the fake holidays."

"If we say Halloween, that's, like…" Jack's eyes rolled backward. "Six months we've been together."

"So?"

"That's a long time. Half a year. You'd really keep a relationship from your friends for that long?"

Lucas's mouth twitched, his thumb tapping the stem of his wine glass. "Yes. I would."

After a beat, Jack nodded. "All right. If you say so."

"Here we are," the waitress said, appearing beside their table. She gave them each a small white plate, while another waitress handed over two larger plates. "Crab on irish soda bread and our quiche of the day: artichoke and goat cheese."

"Thanks so much." Jack smoothed his napkin on his lap. "Looks lovely."

"Shall I freshen your drinks?" she asked, going for the wine bottle.

Jack rested his hand over the top of his glass. "I'm fine, thanks. Maybe once I get some food in me."

"Same," Lucas said, pulling his glass to himself. "It's a really good red."

She nodded and left them alone.

LUCAS CUT into the quiche. He poked his tongue out the corner of his mouth. "You were right to order enough for both of us." He put a small slice on his plate. "I'm hungrier than I thought. Do you want me to cut a piece for you? You can have the rest of it, if you'd like."

"Let's set the terms."

"Oh." Lucas froze with his arms at odd angles, his fork and knife still piercing the quiche. "Okay." He pulled his flatware back to his side of the table. "What do you usually do in this situation? Like, a long overnight trip sort of thing?"

"I've traveled with clients for a month straight. Two months straight. This will be nothing. It all usually depends on the client's needs and wants."

"All right," Lucas said.

A beat passed.

Jack gestured toward him with one hand. "What are your needs and wants?"

"I… don't have any," Lucas said, confused. "What should they be?"

"Impossible."

"Why impossible?"

Jack shifted in his seat. "If you can't verbalize what you're looking for, this isn't going to work. I can't read your mind."

Lucas gently karate-chopped the table. "I want someone who can go to the wedding-week events with me." He karate-chopped again. "And the wedding, obviously. You're not an idiot. I trust you can behave yourself in public without me telling you to behave."

"Such kind words. No wonder you're single."

Lucas rolled his eyes, continuing, "The only rules I can think of is no drug use, as I'd rather not bail you out of a Bahamian jail, and don't see any other clients while we're there, as it might confuse the wedding guests if you're seen with someone else."

"Why?"

"Why don't I want you to go to jail? I'd think that's an easy answer."

Jack chuckled. "No, your rules make sense. I'm drug-free and I'd never see a client while with another client." Insult dampened his features, his fingers fanning on his chest. "I'm a professional. Give me some credit." He leaned across the table, his movement sending a wave of soap-scented air in Lucas's direction. "I meant why are you doing this in the first place? Why bring a fake boyfriend as a date? You don't seem like the type to care what other people think."

Lucas cleared his throat and sat up in his chair. He shifted, moving one side first, then the other. He picked up his fork.

"I don't care what other people think of me. I'm doing this because my family and friends don't seem to understand that I'm doing perfectly fine without a serious boyfriend, no matter how many years I've tried to get them to understand." He used the side of the fork to cut off the tip of his quiche slice. "It would be exhausting to explain that for ten straight days, and to be honest, for the sheer sake of my sanity I'd rather not go to thousands of group events alone."

"Why me?"

"You're used to being with big groups of people you don't know, you're discreet, you seem to be able to keep up with me, and I find you mildly amusing." He lifted his bite of quiche. "I think I can manage with you as my boyfriend for the week."

Jack held his gaze for a moment, then looked down to cut into his crab starter. He felt his cheeks flush. He placed half of the crab and soda bread on Lucas's small plate. "What kind of events are we talking about?"

"Ah." Lucas reached down, unbuckled his briefcase, and withdrew a crisp packet of paper. "Here's the mighty itinerary."

Jack accepted the packet. He glanced over the schedule as he chewed a mouthful of crab and soda bread. The corners of his lips curved up. He turned two pages, his eyes moving from side to side.

"A-ha!" he said out of the corner of his mouth. He swallowed. "No wonder you want a date. There are far too many karaoke events to stomach it alone. And what's with the craft obsession?"

"I've already checked, and there will be plenty of alcohol available at all times."

"Speaking of alcohol, my policy is that all meals and travel expenses are covered by the client."

"Yes, of course. Everything will be paid for. Meals, travel, everything. I can even pay for an international security company, if your bracelet is out of range or something."

"That's kind of you to offer, but I'll figure something out, thanks."

"And while we're there, if you need anything, just let me know and I'm sure we can work it out. Whatever you need to feel comfortable. Whatever you want."

"In return for sex, you mean?"

"What? No. Not sex. I meant if you wanted to buy a magnet or something." Jack started to giggle, his face brightening with the bubbly sound. "Oi, what do I know what your souvenir taste is? Lots of people like magnets. They're a classic souvenir."

"I'm going to need this in writing, especially the sex part." Jack brought a bite up to his open lips. "I don't quite believe it."

"No sex." Lucas watched Jack stick his tongue out before placing the bite on top. "This is a companion sort of thing. Like you said the other night with Mr. Carson. But, of course, if you'd feel more comfortable with it in writing, I'd be happy to draw up whatever document you'd like. You eat like a cat, you know."

Jack nodded, forking quiche into his mouth. "I'll draw up the contract and e-mail it to you tonight. I have my own forms. I'll book my own travel. You can reimburse me." He dabbed his mouth with his napkin. Quieter, he muttered, "And I do not eat like a cat. What are you on about?"

"Oh, I…." Lucas spun his wine glass. "I figured we'd fly together. I'd rather not arrive separately. I think that would make people suspicious."

Jack fluffed his napkin onto his lap. "We can travel together, but I do my own bookings. It's for my privacy."

"All right. Sure. If that's what you prefer."

"It is."

"Fine. Anything else?"

"What do you want me to wear?"

"Jack," Lucas chuckled on an exhale, running his hand through his hair. "This is not a normal job. This is you coming to an island with me for a few days. As long as you have something nice enough for the beach wedding, which I'm guessing is pretty casual, you can pack whatever you want. Wear swim trunks all week. I don't care."

"I need to know if there's a dress code or if I need to prep for anything special. Didn't you research the resort? The restaurants at high-end, all-inclusive resorts usually have dress codes."

"You dress well on your own. Why do I need to tell you what to wear?" Lucas's eyes crinkled. "Oh, I get it."

"What?"

"You're used to dressing for your clients. Like, what turns them on."

"What turns you on?"

"Nice try."

Jack grinned and snapped his fingers. "Drat. I was so close to finding out about your obsession with men in thigh highs and heels."

Lucas's hand flew to his mouth to block soda bread from flying out. They munched for a moment.

"What did you mean by prep?" Lucas asked.

Jack pressed his napkin to his lips before swallowing and saying, "I usually prep for a holiday."

"Prep what?"

"My body."

There was a pause. Jack sipped his wine, and Lucas blinked at him over a forkful of crab.

"Prep… your body?"

"Yes. I'm very meticulous with planning. Waxing, tanning, enemas, that sort of thing. Are there going to be any nude pool parties?"

Lucas slowly said, "Uh, no. It's safe to assume you will not have to attend any nude events. I think there will be more kids than adults at the wedding. Swim trunks should be fine. You can leave your"—he looked around and lowered his voice—"enemas at home."

Jack shrugged. "Suit yourself. I'll look over the schedule and pack accordingly."

"Sounds good."

"We should kiss and touch a few times."

Lucas scratched the front of his neck. "Why? We're not having sex, and it's all just for companionship."

"Because we're going to a wedding, where people kiss and dance and hold hands. We need to practice all that to make it believable that we've been together half a year."

"That seems unnecessary."

Jack's eyes sparkled. "Are you afraid to kiss me?"

"Absolutely not," Lucas said over him. "I just…." He tried to remember the last person he kissed just for the sake of kissing, with no sex involved. Make-out sessions were never his forte—he got bored too easily. Somehow, he didn't see himself getting bored with Jack, which only caused a different sort of nervousness to prickle sweat on the back of his neck. "I don't think it's necessary. I have a very tight schedule leading up to the trip, and I don't have time to set up a pretend date with my pretend boyfriend to pretend to snog."

A boot nudged Lucas's ankle. "How many times do I have to tell you that I've done this before? It will make things a lot less awkward if we pop a few cherries—that way it looks normal if we kiss in front of other people. No matter how good you are at improv, the first time we kiss you're going to get an adrenaline spike. That's not bragging—it's science. It's better to do it in private than look like a freak in front of other people who are already going to be paying close attention to us."

"Fine, fine. You're the expert. Where and when are we practicing?"

"I'm not showing you where I live, but I'd be happy to join you at yours sometime in the next few days. I can even bring my laptop and we can book our flights together."

Lucas took his phone out and unlocked it, scanning over the screen. "Erm…." He scrolled, then tapped the screen once. "Tomorrow night? I think I understand Albert's schedule notes. It seems I've got a late day but should be home and ready for guests at around nine."

"Perfect."

"Lovely." Lucas typed a quick text. "I just sent you my address. I'll leave your name with the doorman."

"Great. I'll e-mail you the contract tonight. I'd appreciate it if you could return it, signed, in the next twenty-four hours."

"Sure." Lucas bent over and lifted his leather briefcase. He snapped it open and searched through a few stacks of paper before pulling out a packet. He offered it to Jack. "I brought this for you, as well."

"So much to read," Jack sighed, taking it from him. "And you made fun of my paperwork requirements." He scanned over the neatly prepared document with photos, names, and short blurbs. "What is this?"

"I made it for Albert when he first started working for me to help him become acquainted with my family and friends."

Jack peered over the paper. "Is that a normal executive-to-assistant thing?"

"No, but my family has never seemed to understand that they aren't supposed to rely on my professional assistant to get to me, and they feel it's appropriate to call my office at all hours. It was only human to warn him of the cast of characters in my life. They can be… a lot."

Jack frowned as he flipped to the second page. "Maybe they want to stay in touch with you. You only get one family, you know?"

Lucas said nothing, and sipped his wine. He watched Jack read for a moment, mouthing along for certain unidentifiable words.

"Either way," Lucas said, shifting in his seat, "I thought it would help you get up to speed with some of the people who will be at the resort with us. I don't have everyone on there, like Zamir's and Cillian's extended families, but the main people are all there."

Jack brushed the corner of the packet with his thumb. "So…." He flipped the packet around and pointed at a page of small faces. "Kids are going to be there?"

"Yeah. Zamir and Cillian are into big families. My mum and sisters are going. My family and Zamir's family are tight, which expanded to Cillian's family too, once he and Zamir got together. Cillian's Irish and has a billion aunts and uncles and cousins. Zamir's family is fairly large, as well."

"I…." Jack wet his lips, flattening the papers on the table. "I don't usually interact with kids on the job."

"Oh. Do you have a problem with kids?"

"No, not a problem. Just…." His eyes darted to the side. "It's not usually who I mix with on work trips."

Lucas crossed his arms over his chest. "Is this going to be an issue?"

Jack shook his head quickly. "No, not a problem. It's fine. I'll make it work."

"Fair enough." Lucas finished his glass of wine, resting the back of his hand on his mouth as he swallowed. He nudged his chin toward the itinerary. "As you saw from the schedule, there are a lot of kid-friendly activities. If you don't want to do an activity, please feel free to tell me. I'd love nothing more than to skip the Zill-ympics to nap on the beach."

"No way," Jack said with an enthusiastic bounce to his voice. "We're gonna win the Zill-ympics. No doubt."

Lucas flipped the packet back to the first page. "This is my family, who you will likely interact the most with. If they're being too much, you can, I dunno, make a birdcall or something, and I'll get them off your back. This document has their names, nicknames, ages, and some random details. You don't have to memorize it. I'll have to introduce you to everyone anyway. I just thought it might be helpful."

Jack read aloud, "Joelle Mackey. Goes by Jo. Mum. Fifty-one. Does not work. Enjoys wine, handmade candles, and other generally overpriced rubbish." He nodded and studied the photo of an attractive brunette with the same twinkling blue eyes as Lucas. "She's so pretty. Looks young."

"Be sure to tell her that. You'll be her new favorite."

"Married to John Mackey," Jack said as his eye landed on the red face of a jolly looking man with salt-and-pepper hair. "Age: Sixty-five. Venture capitalist. Enjoys money, cigars, and American football. Huh. I could talk American football with him all day."

"Yeah? He's a Cowboys fan."

"Ugh, the Cowboys," Jack groaned, rolling his eyes. "That's like finding out someone's a Yankees fan. Packers are where it's at. A team with heart."

"I don't know what any of that means."

Jack snorted, looking down at the paper. "Is he your dad?"

"No."

Lucas said nothing else. Much like Lucas not pressing Jack for information about where he lived, Jack could take a hint. He simply nodded and touched a photo of a woman with blue eyes and long, straight brown hair. She looked very similar to Lucas, especially around the eyes.

"Elena Matthews. Goes by Lane. Sister. Age: Twenty-eight. Works for a nonprofit that helps victims of natural disasters. Enjoys wine, hmm…." He narrowed his eyes at Lucas. "I'm noticing a pattern. Wine, competitive sports, and refinishing furniture by hand. Married to Dean and mother to Margaret."

Jack moved on to a photo of a grinning, burly man with a backward red baseball cap and dirty blond hair sticking out of his hat.

"Dean Matthews. Brother-in-law. Age: Thirty. Mechanical engineer. Does great impersonations. Likes cars, craft beer, and *The Fast and the Furious* film series. Father of Margaret."

Jack smiled to himself. He thumbed a photo of a pudgy-faced, bright-eyed girl with curly brown hair. Her toothy grin was infectious.

"Margaret Matthews. Goes by Maggie. Niece. Age: Four. Loves piggyback rides, flowers, coloring, and ponies." He glanced at Lucas. "She doesn't look like a Margaret, but I could see her as a Maggie."

"Margaret was some family name from the past. Some favorite great-aunt of my mother's. I think Lane did it to calm our mum when she got pregnant before she got married."

Jack let the papers flutter to the table. "Did your mum seriously think you and Lane were both waiting for marriage in this day and age?"

"I think my mum was horrified Lane didn't tie down some poor bloke before she got pregnant. She has a weird view of marriage. Lucky for us all, Dean is great. I like him more than some of my actual family. Maggie is even better."

"I can see Dean and Lane being our biggest competition for the Zillympics. And Maggie is so, so cute."

An uncontrollable grin spread over Lucas's face. "Don't let the cute face fool you. She is brilliant and will talk her way into, or out of, anything."

"Huh, wonder where she got that from," Jack drawled, his eyes boring into Lucas's face. The right side of his mouth rose. "Cute face and a fast tongue? Must be a Thompson genetic trait."

Lucas's entire body heated. He tapped a photo of a younger woman with chocolate-brown waves. "My youngest sister, Marcy, well, Marcelline, is probably going to come in halfway through the week. She has a friend's wedding the first weekend of the trip, if you can believe it. She's a journalism student at NYU."

Marcy did not share Jo's, Lucas's, and Lane's blue eyes. Her eyes were warm chocolate-brown and round, with envy-inducing long eyelashes.

"She's beautiful."

"She is." Lucas turned to the next page. "This is Zamir and Cillian. Zamir's my best friend. Cillian's his boyfriend. Fiancé. Sorry. Fiancé."

Jack read over Zamir's paragraph. He tapped the darker-haired person in the photo, with almond-shaped eyes and a delicate bone structure to rival even the most famous of supermodels.

"Zamir Matin. Best friend from birth. Artist. Age: Twenty-nine. Hm. Pretty eyes." He glanced up at Lucas and found him to be staring at his fingernails. "Are you twenty-nine, as well?"

"I am. How old are you?"

"Twenty-seven."

"Ah."

"Enjoys meditation, striving for peace on earth, creativity in all forms, and meditative retreats in volcanoes." Jack checked the next page, his brows furrowed. "He doesn't have a job besides art?"

"No. He always said he needed complete freedom of mind to express the truest channel of his soul." Jack's eyes bulged as he read. "He does a lot of sculpture and pottery."

"Oh, nice. I do pottery."

"You do pottery." Lucas repeated, stating it rather than questioning.

"I do. I take a class twice a week. It's very relaxing." Jack let his head fall to the side as he turned the page. "What, you thought I'd be so busy taking a dick every night that I don't have time for hobbies?"

"I didn't say that," Lucas said.

Jack smirked and went back to the list. "A work-life balance is very important no matter the field, Mr. Thompson."

"You really do have a knack for being a personal consultant. So many gems pop out of that pretty mouth of yours." Lucas's mouth immediately snapped shut.

"Pretty mouth, hm?" Jack murmured, deliberately licking the corner of his lips and thumbing over the spot. He turned the page with his thumb. His tongue flickered quicker to trace the inside of his bottom lip, and he chose that moment to make eye contact. "Is that so?"

"Ugh, stop." Lucas waved his hand weakly. "You truly are an overgrown tomcat. You're about two seconds away from licking your own arsehole in the middle of this lovely cafe."

Jack leaned across the table, dropping his voice. "I can do that, you know." His eyes widened. "Hustler powers."

Lucas gaped at him; his features slackened. Jack waited three seconds before he burst out laughing. Lucas exhaled and pushed his small plate to the end of the table.

"I'm kidding, I'm kidding," Jack said with sparkling eyes. He wiggled his eyebrows. "But I think you were into the idea."

"I was not."

"All right, Grumpy, whatever you say. So, let me get this straight." He turned the packet toward Lucas. He pointed at Cillian's biography and accompanying photo, where Cillian was smiling so wide the photo was nearly all teeth. "This guy."

"Cillian."

"The groom. Well, the other groom."

"Yeah. What about him?"

"His family is the owner of Moran Sausages?"

"Yes."

"And that's why he's filthy rich?"

"They make some special sausage that's sold in every baseball stadium in America, many football stadiums all over the world, and even in arenas for American football."

"Yeah, I've definitely eaten a few at games. It's, like, a spicy sausage and pepper sandwich. They're huge. Not only in size, but, wow. He must be, like, really, really rich. They've been around forever."

"He is. Really, really rich."

"Question," Jack said, placing the packet on the table. He steepled his fingers. "Does he tolerate sausage jokes?"

Lucas's serious expression cracked. "Tolerate? Encourages. Loves." He pointed at the packet. "Didn't you read his bio?"

"So, he's totally fine with us joking about how the wedding of two gay men is being paid for by sausages? Like a legitimate sausagefest?"

Lucas's shoulders shook as he laughed. Jack grinned. "He'll love it. He's fun. You'll like him. Do you golf?"

"I fuck old men for a living. Of course I golf."

The deadpanned joke slipped out easily. Lucas's answering laugh showed no sign of pity or disgust. He glanced across the table and found Jack flushed, with his eyes directed at the ceiling, his arms shifting at his sides, and his neck glistening.

"Cillian will like that," Lucas said, stacking their dishes at the end of the table. "I'm pretty shit at it, but since I usually don't have a partner to make four, I can escape his golf outings." He refilled Jack's wine glass, offering him a dry smile. "I suppose I won't be able to escape this time. Are you hot or something? You're sweating."

"I'm fine, thanks."

Jack directed his attention back to the packet just as the waitress returned with their lunch.

"Everything good over here?" she asked, sliding a steak sandwich in front of Jack. Jack nodded, folding his papers and pushing them aside. "Need anything?" She picked up the carafe and refilled their waters. "I'll bring you more water."

"Thank you." Lucas held his bread poised at his steaming bowl of stew.

Jack lifted his sandwich to mouth level, and rolled his tongue out before he bit into it. Muffled snickers came from across the table, and he squinted at Lucas as he chewed.

Jack's throat bobbed to swallow. "What?"

"Nothing."

Lucas lifted another spoonful of stew and stuck his tongue all the way out before sticking his spoon in his mouth.

Jack rolled his eyes, his cheeks puffing as he chewed. "You're ridiculous," he said out of the corner of his mouth.

"All right. Okay, kitten. Whatever you say."

"I think I prefer honey bunch to kitten, fluffy-bum."

"You are *not* calling me fluffy-bum in front of my family."

Jack slowly extended his tongue to bite his sandwich with an innocent expression.

Lucas looked at the ceiling and whispered, "Dear God, what am I getting myself into?"

"You're not getting into anything or anyone, remember?" Jack bit his sandwich. "Contract and all."

Lucas let his head roll forward to stare at him. Jack smirked with his lips shut, a dab of juice from his steak lingering on the corner of his mouth. His long lashes bobbed ever so slowly as his pink tongue darted out to grab the juice. Lucas's hand clenched around his spoon, and Jack's smile widened.

Chapter SEVEN

Thursday, April 16

"Name?"

"Jack McQueen. I'm here to see Lucas Thompson in 30A."

The bald security guard stared at him long and hard. Jack blinked at him and maintained his stance. Their staring contest went on for nearly half a minute. The guard lifted a telephone from his desk and punched in three digits.

"A Mr. Jack McQueen is here to see you, sir. Shall I send him up?"

Jack waited with his breath held for the five seconds of silence between the guard's question and Lucas's reply. He knew Lucas would let him up, but his heart still pounded with stuttered beats under the stern gaze of the guard. He smoothed his hand over the front of his thin button-down. The shirt was cream-colored with tiny black stars; its first four buttons had been left undone.

"Very well, sir," the guard said. He hung up the phone and stared at Jack. The lobby was silent. The guard's nostrils crinkled to sniffle in a quick breath. "You're not his usual type."

Jack's eyes narrowed. "Excuse me?"

The guard said nothing but pressed a button on his desk. The clear plastic half doors that led to the lifts swayed open.

"First lift. Top floor."

Jack nodded and said, "Thank you," while adjusting the strap of his brown leather messenger bag.

He went to the bank of lifts and stepped into the first one. He pressed the top button for the thirtieth floor. The doors shut and the lift started to rise quickly. Jack watched the numbers light and fade, light and fade, light and fade, until he reached the top. The doors pinged open.

He stepped out and found that he was not in a hallway with multiple doors, but what seemed to be a foyer. There was only one black metal door labeled 30A. He rang the doorbell.

"Sorry, one second," Lucas said from inside. Footsteps came closer until the door swung open. "Hi." Lucas stepped back on bare feet and held the door open. "C'mon in. Sorry." He rubbed a red towel over his damp hair. He had on black sweats that bunched at his narrow ankles, and a long-sleeved white

Henley. “My meeting ran late, then I was late to meet my trainer, then my taxi home was caught in traffic, and here we are now.”

Jack stepped inside and schooled his expression. He’d been in many luxury penthouses, hotels, and mansions in his life. He’d ridden on expensive yachts with rooms larger than any house he could hope to ever own, and flown on private jets to every corner of the world.

Lucas’s penthouse was impressive, but not surprising. It looked much like most other apartments owned by men with a similar profession and income. It was an open-plan with expensive electronics tastefully hidden among the modern, dark decor. Floor-to-ceiling windows ran around the entire length of the space.

The fact that Lucas didn’t have a platformed grand piano under a spotlight or a glass cabinet full of awards and photos with dignitaries made Jack’s nerves calm. The place was spotless, so clean he assumed Lucas hired a daily cleaning person, but it still felt lived in. The flat-screen was quietly playing footie highlights in the background.

“You want a drink?” Lucas asked, padding into the enormous kitchen. He opened the stainless steel refrigerator, still toweling his hair. Jack studied the rows of prepared meals in neat plastic containers, each container labeled with the meal name and date of preparation. “Water?”

“No, thank you.”

Lucas glanced over his shoulder for a moment then looked back to the refrigerator. He pulled out a bottle for himself and walked back to Jack. Lucas arched his brows. “What?”

Jack looked away from the pile of colorful stuffed toys and rubber bones on the floor beside the leather couch. “Nothing.”

“You don’t like my place?”

“It’s fine.” Jack looped his thumbs in the pockets of his black skinnies. “It’s exactly what I thought it would look like.”

“And what does your flat look like, then, hm? The aftermath of a bender with Captain Jack Sparrow and Stevie Nicks?”

Jack snorted at that, rubbing his fingers over one eyebrow. “Not quite.”

“I’m imagining lots of scarves and tapestries,” Lucas said, creating a scene in the air with his fluttering fingers. “A pottery wheel in the center of the room. Constant candles and incense. Body oil galore. And a treasure chest overflowing with earrings.”

That pulled a throaty laugh from Jack. Lucas smiled at the sound.

“Do you want me to take off my shoes?”

Lucas blinked at him. “Why?”

"Didn't know if you were one of those clean freaks paranoid of bacteria carried in on the bottoms of shoes."

"I wasn't, but now I'm rethinking my stance."

Jack toed his boots off, then carried them to the front door. He noticed a long blue leash hanging off a hook beside the door at the same time Lucas said, "Jesus, George, relax!"

Jack turned in time to see a round khaki-and-black blur of fur flying at him on frantic, short legs, its tiny toenails clicking on the hardwood.

"Sorry!" Lucas called, running after the blur. He tried to grab the dog, but George darted sideways. "Are you okay with dogs?"

Jack stared at the wiggling bundle of energy as it rammed repeatedly into his shins. George panted, his tongue hanging out of his mouth, his breathy, oinking sounds huffing out of his flat nose with each head-butt.

"Yeah, I'm fine," he said softly. He knelt down and held his hand out for George to sniff; his other hand scratched the tiny rolls of fat that covered George's neck. "Hello, George."

"He's harmless, I promise. He's a blob in dog form."

Jack chuckled, using both hands to massage his fur. "He's really cute. A pug?"

"Mm-hmm."

George stood up on his back legs and grasped Jack's leg with his front paws. He rapidly humped his hips forward.

Jack laughed. "O-oh."

Lucas's jaw dropped. "Oh my God, I'm so sorry," he blurted out, bending and lifting George. "What the fuck? He's never done that before." He gaped at his dog, who was still wiggling and leering at Jack. "What's the matter with you, mate?" He looked back to Jack. "I'm so, so sorry. I gave him a bath tonight and sometimes he gets all hyped up afterward."

"It's all right, happens to the best of us." Jack stepped up to Lucas and held his arms out, George jumping away from his owner to burrow against Jack's chest. Jack's coy gaze landed on Lucas's face. "At least someone in this household has a healthy sex drive."

"Ha. Ha." He nodded toward a hallway beside the kitchen. "Wanna go to my bedroom?"

"Sure."

Jack carried George in his arms, and George went to town licking his neck. Jack bit his bottom lip, shifting his head side to side. Lucas turned off the television in passing.

"Guest room." Lucas held his arm out toward a closed door on the right. They walked a few more steps. He pointed to the left. "Second guest room." They passed yet another closed door on the right. "Office."

"Riveting."

"C'mon in." Lucas glanced over his shoulder. They both stepped into his bedroom. He tossed his water bottle on the king-sized bed. A black duvet covered the wide surface. "Make yourself comfortable."

His bedroom was decorated much like the rest of the flat. Lots of dark colors and luxury fabrics were incorporated into the modern design. Warm lights were scattered around the room. The space was large enough for his bed, a built-in custom chest of drawers, and a seating area off to the left side, next to the floor-to-ceiling window. The seating area included a sleek sofa and armchair positioned around a small rectangular table.

Jack sat on the end of the bed and dropped his laptop bag on the floor. He crossed his legs on the bed, placing George in the space between his stomach and ankles.

"Why George?" Jack rubbed George's soft belly. George's tongue hung out of his mouth and his eyes were delirious. "That's a rather serious name for a pug who smells like candy canes."

LUCAS CHUCKLED from inside the en-suite. "You caught him on a good night." He tossed his wet towel into a stainless steel laundry basket. "He usually smells like tacos."

As Lucas rubbed lotion on his face, he could hear Jack's deep voice quietly crooning a familiar tune to George. Jack paused for a moment; his voice was softer and more tentative as he sang the rest of the melody on the neutral syllable "la" as if he'd forgotten the rest of the words.

Lucas caught sight of himself in the mirror and froze. A fond smile was softening his eyes. He scowled and rubbed his cheeks harder. Even his strongest scowl was no match for the nonsense words sung in a low baritone as George was making what Lucas thought of as his *happy pant*.

He returned to the bedroom and glanced at the duo lounging on his bed. He walked close enough to scratch the top of George's head.

"When I brought him home from the shelter, 'Here Comes the Sun' was playing on the car radio," Lucas said, thumbing around George's soft ear. "He was kind of whimpering, but it was to the words. It sounded like he was singing." He watched Jack's eyes soften as he stared at the pup; his hand was gentle on George's round belly. "When I would try to change the song, thinking he didn't like it, he'd whimper more, until he finally fell asleep right at the end of the song. George was always my favorite Beatle. It seemed meant to be." Lucas cupped George's chubby cheeks and the pug panted a doggie grin at him. "From that moment, George Harrison Thompson was born."

"That's so sweet," Jack said, lifting George carefully. "The sweetest dog story ever." He held the dog up, Simba style, and cooed, "Isn't that sweet, Georgie?"

Lucas put his hands on his hips. "His name is George."

Jack squinted from George to Lucas and back to George, swaying his head side to side with each look. "Nah." He cuddled George to his chest and put a bit of growl in his voice to say, "I think he's a Georgie."

Lucas watched him bring the pup closer to his face and nuzzle into his fur, George's tiny tongue attempting to lick his nose.

"You're not a *Geooorge*." Jack deepened his voice for the droned name and shook his head, looking from George to Lucas. "You're a Georgie boy!" He nodded with wide, excited eyes, and when he spoke, his voice was full of even more hushed excitement. "Right, Georgie?"

George made a pleased little yelp, only prompting Jack to mimic the sound, starting a back-and-forth doggy conversation. Lucas picked up his water bottle from the bed and unscrewed the cap, taking a long drink. He sighed, "Traitor," and rubbed his hand over his mouth.

Jack stretched on his side. His arm draped over George in a semispoon. George mouthed at the front of his shirt, mumbling puppy sounds into the thin fabric.

"Is his eye all right?" Jack asked, scratching behind his ears. "The left looks different than the right."

Lucas swallowed another mouthful of water. His trainer had been merciless that evening. "He's blind in his left eye. His vet said it could have been abuse by his breeder, or maybe another dog got too rough with him when he was a puppy, the poor guy."

Jack frowned, cradling George against his chest. "That's terrible."

"It is. Wanna book your flight?"

"I suppose." Jack smoothed his hand over George's fuzzy head. "C'mon, Georgie. Time to work."

JACK SPRAWLED on his stomach on the center of Lucas's bed, his laptop in front of him. His long, socked feet swayed in the air. George snoozed on his lower back in a coil of vibrating, warm blubber.

Booking his flight was easy. He managed to snag the seat next to Lucas for both legs of the trip and was happy to learn they'd be flying business class—he would have accepted no less. Lucas had enough cash in-house to reimburse him on the spot, which was always a pleasure.

Once Jack was done making travel arrangements, he transitioned into surfing the Internet while watching Lucas move about his bedroom. Lucas had an enormous walk-in closet. Light spilled out from the all-white space. Rows of perfectly pressed suits and shined shoes formed a rainbow around the perimeter of the room. There was a collection of luggage in front of the closet, and Lucas hopped between rooms with clothes and accessories in hand.

"Official hustler business?"

Jack's eyes snapped from the closet to Lucas's amused face. Lucas jutted his chin toward his laptop. Jack minimized the open window from www.pugfanclub.com.

"I told you. I'm very thorough."

"Why do you have two browsers open?"

Jack blinked at him. "What?"

Lucas pointed at his laptop screen.

"You've got both Safari and Chrome open. Doesn't that make it lag? Why not use one?"

After a beat, Jack said, "I like to keep business and personal separate."

"Ah. Makes sense." Lucas placed a stack of white undershirts in one suitcase. "I take it you received my signed agreement?"

"I did." Jack pulled up his inbox and clicked on the Sent folder. "I messaged you back to confirm."

"Ah, sorry. My bad. I always forget to check my personal account. My phone goes off with all these beeps." Lucas opened the top of his chest of drawers, one hand flitting in the air. "I probably missed it."

"You mean you didn't want Albert to know about our arrangement?"

Lucas closed the drawer with his elbow, holding two boxes of cufflinks in hand. "Ha. I'm sure he'd love to be in the loop to update my schedule, but no." He glanced at Jack and tossed the cufflink boxes into one suitcase. "I'd prefer to keep it between us."

Jack touched his big toes in the air. "All was fine in the contract? I'm shocked you didn't want to negotiate."

"I negotiate enough at work." Lucas offered him a tired smile, sinking to his knees in front of his luggage. "The agreement was fair."

"Good." A sizzle of pride zipped through Jack's body. "I'm glad you think so."

Lucas unzipped an inner pocket, and slid his hand around inside in search of something. "I noticed you usually offer a multiday discount to paying clients." He pulled out a crumpled boarding pass, tossing it to the floor. "Very generous of you."

Jack's feet swayed as he typed. "Even I can acknowledge that charging someone my hourly rate for twenty-four-hour days over an entire week is excessive. Billing twelve hours per day when people book seven or more days is a bit easier for people to handle, plus it gives me twelve hours to sleep or be by myself to recharge."

"You write well, but your NDA could use some tightening up." Lucas stood up straight with his back to Jack. He rubbed his hand on the top of his fluffy hair. "Just a bit of professional advice."

Jack's thumb froze on his trackpad and his eyes darted to Lucas's back. Lucas's white Henley hung off his sharp shoulder blades but clung to the small of his back before flaring out over his round arse.

"What?"

Lucas tossed three leather belts into one suitcase. "Your NDA," he said from inside the closet. "It's fine. It's a standard nondisclosure agreement. But if someone really wanted to find loopholes, they could. The loopholes are there if you look hard enough."

"What loopholes?"

Lucas walked out of the closet with a stack of colorful polo shirts in his arms. He dropped half the stack in one suitcase and the remaining half in the other suitcase.

"You allow your clients to speak to each other about you because you use a referral program, which is fine, but the language gets murky when it comes to just how much they should disclose. They could say something about you under the guise of a referral to someone who might not ever contact you, yet that stranger, not covered by the NDA, would know details about you. It leaves you vulnerable."

"I… will have my lawyer look into it," Jack said, his words slow and confused. "Thank you for the advice."

"You're welcome. I can look over it too, if you'd like. I'm no lawyer, but the bed you're on right now was bought with loopholes."

Jack propped his chin up on his left hand, his socked toes prodding at his calf. "Are you packing for the wedding already?"

Lucas came out of his closet and tossed a stack of white Oxford shirts into one suitcase, followed by a bunch of balled black socks. "I've got to go to Manchester for work from Sunday to Tuesday evening. I'll be back in the office

Wednesday, but from Thursday to Friday we're finishing merger negotiations with this tech giant that's been a huge pain in my arse." He went back inside his closet. "I'll be pretty swamped all week to prep for the time I'll be gone. If I don't do it now, I'll be so out of it by Friday night that I'll pack nothing but Q-tips." He tossed a pair of black swim trunks into one suitcase. "And flip-flops."

"Oh." Jack minimized the Wikipedia article for pugs. Lucas tossed five identical pairs of black boxer briefs into one suitcase. "So, you'll be busy all next week?"

"Yes. I won't see you until the flight." Lucas brought out a pale gray suit, holding it up next to a royal blue tie. "Why?" His eyes shimmered at Jack. "You gonna miss me, honey bunch?"

"Of course. I simply don't know what I'll do without you." Lucas snorted, switching the blue tie for a black tie. Jack's brows furrowed. "Is that for the business trip or the wedding?"

"The wedding," Lucas said, reaching into the closet and pulling out a deep green tie. "What do you think?" He weighed each tie in his hands. "Blue or black? Green, maybe? Green's tropical, yeah?"

"Neither. None of it. Didn't you read the schedule?"

A tiny wrinkle formed on Lucas's forehead. "About what?"

Jack eased George off his back, rolling onto his side.

"They want everyone to wear white for the wedding." He swung his legs to the edge of the bed. "All white."

Lucas's arms fell to his sides, his ties wilting to the floor.

"Are we joining a cult? Posing for a Gap ad? What's with the all-white trend?"

"Babe, it's not like you're going to get your period. Just throw on some white and you'll be fine. It's for one day. You'll survive."

"I don't know if I even have white trousers. I'm not an ice cream man. Who owns white trousers?"

Jack got to his feet, then tiptoed around Lucas's barrier of open suitcases. He went into the organized closet and pushed hangers aside with quick, short motions, metal sliding on metal.

"Here we are! You have white trousers, you liar." He pulled a pair of white jeans off their hanger and ran his hand over the fabric. The material was soft and thin, holding none of the normal stiffness of denim. "Pair these with a comfortable white shirt and you'll be set."

Lucas fingered a belt loop. "I haven't worn those in years. I don't know if they'll even fit."

"Try them on." Jack smirked, popping his dimple and batting his lashes. "Please?"

Lucas sighed and took the jeans. He walked out of the closet, and Jack started to poke around.

There were built-in shelves with stacks of more casual clothes, T-shirts and sweats, and another built-in chest of drawers, which held more underwear than he had ever seen in one person's home. There was a vanity built into the farthest closet wall, complete with lights around the mirror. Cologne bottles, a pair of cufflinks, and two watches rested on top of the white vanity table.

He lifted each cologne bottle, taking quiet sniffs of the tops. He sprayed Tom Ford's Tuscan Leather on his wrists and dabbed cologne below his jawline, then pulled his shirt away from his torso and spritzed his lower belly. After replacing the bottle on the vanity, he strolled toward the front of the closet, where he picked up a pair of long black-and-white board shorts.

"Are these your only swim trunks?" Jack called, turning them over in his hands. He whispered, "Yikes."

Lucas zipped up. "Yeah. Why?"

Jack's nose scrunched as he searched farther back on the shelf. "What a waste of that bum." Lucas's quiet laughter came back into the closet. Jack looked away from his T-shirt collection and gasped. "Speaking of that bum," he practically crowed, reaching out. He spun Lucas in place and lifted his Henley from his lower back. "Hello there!"

"You're nuts," Lucas said, huffing chuckles through his words.

The white material of his jeans clung to his round arse and thick thighs. A peek of black Ralph Lauren boxer briefs stuck out of the waistband; his feet were bare at the ends of the tapered jeans.

"They look amazing!"

Lucas dropped his gaze to the floor, letting out another soft chuckle. He turned to face Jack, who was rapidly sliding metal hangers over the closet rod.

"I guess these will work," Lucas admitted.

"This will look perfect with the jeans," Jack said, offering a short-sleeved white button-down. "It'll probably be hot on the beach, plus this shirt will show off the guns."

"The guns," Lucas said, holding the shirt up to his chest. "All right, then. That's settled."

"What else are you bringing?"

"I dunno. Like—" Lucas flicked his hand at the dressier side of his closet. "—clothes?"

"No way, you can't bring this stuff." Jack ran his hand across Lucas's wall of ties. "Too corporate. It's a beachside resort. You probably don't even have to bring a tie. Maybe one."

"I need to bring at least two ties."

"Why? Planning on tying anyone to a bed?"

Lucas's face flamed bright red, his hands faltering with a pair of khaki trousers. He swallowed and folded the trousers over his arm, padding away from Jack's snickers. "Can you grab me some T-shirts, please?" Lucas asked. George's collar clinked in the bedroom, jeans unzipped, and Jack could have sworn he heard Lucas whisper, "Hello, my Georgie."

When Jack walked out of the closet, Lucas was back in his sweats.

"What's your relationship with Zamir and Cillian like?" Jack asked, offering an armful of T-shirts. "Do you hang out with them a lot? Do they live near here?"

Lucas took the stack of shirts from him and started to divide them into both suitcases. "Don't know if I'd say we hang out a lot, but at least a few times a year. Holidays and such, or if they come to London for a visit. They live in Ireland, but they travel all the time. I've known Zamir my whole life. Our families go way back. He and Cillian got together about two years ago. They met at a yoga detox thing in Bali."

Jack sat on the bed, leaning back on his elbows and crossing his legs.

"They were detoxing from yoga? Isn't the point of yoga to detox?"

Lucas shrugged. George scurried around his bare ankles. "Who knows. They're both on that whole, erm"—he waved his hand in the air—"Zen wavelength."

"And you're not?"

Lucas snorted. "Shocking, I'm sure, but no. I'm not." George climbed into a suitcase. His wiggling tail stuck in the air. "That's the main reason we didn't work out. We're better as friends."

Jack's head tilted to the right, his blinks slowing. "What?"

"Zamir and I dated when we were much younger."

"Um…." Jack held out the word, sitting up straight. "That was not in the materials I was provided with. Of all the details you included, you leave out that you dated the groom? No wonder you're so skittish about the whole thing."

"It's not a big deal and I'm not skittish." Lucas took a patterned tee out of one suitcase and dropped it in the other. George followed the shirt's path and jumped into the other suitcase. "It was a million years ago."

"Please elaborate."

"There's nothing really to elaborate on. We were best friends for years before anything happened. We were each other's first boyfriend. Neither of us wanted to end the friendship, just the relationship aspect."

Jack bent over the edge of the bed and whispered, "Georgie." George climbed out of the suitcase and ran toward him. Jack scooped him onto the bed and resumed their spoon. "Why did the relationship end?"

Lucas placed a black blazer in a suit bag, his motions smooth and easy. "I proposed. He said no, thank you. He didn't believe in marriage, though he still loved me like a brother." He zipped the bag. "Then we had a beer, watched the football, and that was that."

Jack pressed his chin into George's pudge. "You would have married him?"

Lucas exhaled slowly, his hands on his hips. "I thought so at the time. Twenty-year-old foolishness. I guess when he said he wasn't the marrying type, he meant he wasn't the marrying type if I was to be his husband." He turned away to tend to a leather carry-on bag, mumbling, "He always said I was too serious for him. Makes sense."

"Hey."

"What?"

"C'mere."

Lucas glanced over his shoulder. "Why?"

"It's getting late. We should practice."

Lucas looked at the floor, his throat bobbing. He opened his mouth as if to speak, then closed it, his feet taking two steps forward. Jack got to his knees on the bed, gently placing Georgie on a pile of pillows.

"Pretend we're in front of your mum," Jack said, smoothing his hands over the tops of his thighs. "How would you kiss me then?"

"I wouldn't kiss you at all in front of my mum. Or anyone."

"You would if you were love-drunk with your gorgeous boyfriend of half a year," Jack sang in his low, purring voice. He held his arms out. "C'mon. Just a little. It'll be painless, I swear. Maybe even pleasurable."

Lucas stepped up to him, gripped his hips, and pecked his right cheek. "There you go."

Jack grinned and tilted his head, his lips landing on Lucas's jawline. He whispered, "What a gentleman."

Lucas huffed and gently squeezed his hips, then stepped back. "This is ridiculous. I feel like we're twelve. We might as well play spin the bottle."

Jack tugged the cord of his sweats and pulled him closer. "We can if that will loosen you up. Or…." Jack sat back on his heels. "You could get on the bed with me." He patted the mattress. "It's a very good bed."

"Is that the voice you use while working?"

"Depends on the client." Lucas placed a hand on Jack's jawline, his other on his outer bicep. "You should be thanking your lucky stars right now instead of bellyaching. Most men pay thousands to—"

Lucas tilted his head and firmly pressed his lips to Jack's mouth. Their gazes locked, their eyes unblinking. Lucas pulled back with a smacking sound. He squeezed Jack's bicep and pecked him once more, then was gone before Jack realized what was happening.

Lucas declared, "There. Done. We've kissed. Happy?"

They stared at each other for a beat. Lucas's left eye twitched and his cheeks were tinted pink; Jack's mouth was a perfect circle with saliva shimmering on his top lip.

"All right," Jack said slowly, licking his lips. A thoughtful wrinkle appeared on his forehead. "Well, that was great if we are actually twelve and in a summer camp production of *Guys and Dolls*, but that ain't gonna cut it if we're convincing people we're involved."

Lucas's nostrils flared, his mouth tightening. "If I had a boyfriend, I wouldn't kiss him in front of other people, and he'd respect that, or else he wouldn't be my boyfriend."

Jack folded his hands on top of his thighs. "I'm not talking about full-blown tongue in front of friends and family. That's not my cup of tea, either. I'm simply saying that real couples, even ones who avoid PDA, slip up once in a while and get caught kissing or being flirty. People eat that shit up, especially at weddings where everyone is drunk and hopped-up on love."

Jack held his palms out. "If you're not comfortable and don't want to do this, that's fine. Absolutely fine. I don't ever want to make you uncomfortable. We can go through the trip without touching, if that's what you want. It's no bronzer off my abs." He lowered his hands to his thighs, buffing his fingernails against his jeans. "I'm simply offering you a bit of professional advice, much like you did with my NDA, to make this easier for you."

Lucas stared at him. He placed his hands on his hips and his left leg quirked. His tongue pushed against the inside of his cheek. He blew air out of his mouth and rolled his eyes to the ceiling.

"I believe you. You're right." Lucas nodded while worrying his bottom lip, relief softening Jack's smile. "You're right. I'm being difficult. I'm…." Lucas ran his fingers through his damp hair, and his shirt rode up on his stomach, revealing a sliver of honey-hued skin. "It's been a long time since I—"

Jack gently curled his hands around Lucas's hips and Lucas jerked away.

"Don't, please." He met Jack's shocked stare. "I… I've got sensitive hips."

"Noted," Jack said with a small nod. He kept his hands flat to pull Lucas closer by his lower back. Lucas's knees bumped the mattress. "Do you want to tell me more of your sensitive spots not to touch?" His right hand lifted the bottom of Lucas's Henley. Their lips brushed. "I'd love to learn."

When Lucas said nothing, Jack arched his eyebrows.

"No? Not talking? All right, then." He slid his fingers up the dip of Lucas's spine, whispering, "C'mere." He kissed beside Lucas's mouth, exhaling before softly pecking him, almost too soft to be felt. "Can I kiss you, Lucas?"

Lucas's throat bobbed to swallow. "I suppose," he sighed. "If you must."

Jack brought his lips close enough for Lucas to feel his warm breaths, to smell the mint gum he had tucked under his tongue. Lucas slowly slid his gaze from Jack's eyes to his wet mouth, his body swaying.

Jack pulled back an inch and Lucas's mouth met air. Lucas narrowed his eyes as the right corner of Jack's mouth lifted, his face coming close enough for Lucas to lean forward again. Jack tightened his grip on the bottom of Lucas's shirt, his other hand flat on the very top of his arse.

Lucas gripped Jack's hips and pulled him against his body. The pull was hard enough for their lips to connect, but not so hard as to force Jack off the bed.

"All right," Jack murmured, massaging his lower back and kissing him firmer. "I think we're progressing to around age fifteen. Nearly there."

He felt Lucas's lips plump under his own and Lucas exhaled quick stutters of air. He watched Lucas's eyes drift half shut as he brought their lips together again, innocent and easy.

"You taste so good, lovely." Jack licked his own lips, leaning in for a kiss. "Sweet like candy."

Lucas's mouth froze as Jack kissed him. He pulled back and flattened his hand on Jack's chest. "Don't use that voice on me."

Jack's playful stare sent bolts of prickly heat through Lucas's body. "You don't like it?" Jack asked, his voice taking on a breathy, boyish innocence. He batted his eyelashes, brushing a kiss to Lucas's pulse point. "Shame." He opened his teeth on the spot. "Most people love my voice."

Lucas held his face in both hands and guided him up. "I don't like to be teased, and I'm not most people."

Jack's tongue flickered over Lucas's bottom lip with their eyes locked. Jack's openmouthed smirk turned into a laugh. "No, you're not." Jack used his teeth to pinch the fullest bit of Lucas's bottom lip. Lucas's fingernails dug into his lower back. "Now," he whispered, his voice at its usual husky depth, "less talking." He sucked a kiss to his mouth and Lucas's head tilted to follow the motion. "More practicing."

Jack lowered himself to sit on the bed and spread his long legs, pressing his inner thighs to Lucas's hips. He lay back and used his legs to pull Lucas down, but Lucas planted his hands into the bed, planking above Jack's body.

"What are you doing?"

"It'll be more fun horizontal."

"Is that on your business card?"

"Of course. Along with a money-back satisfaction guarantee."

LUCAS SPUTTERED and Jack grinned, his legs hugging tighter. Jack caught him around the shoulders as he fell onto him. Jack's socked feet rubbed against the backs of Lucas's knees. Lucas attempted to right himself and get some of his weight off of Jack's middle, but Jack wound his long arms around Lucas's back, lacing one hand in the back of his hair.

"Jack—"

Invisible, inexplicable heat, like the shock of an electrical fire or the remnants of a lightning storm in humidity jolted between Lucas's ears. Jack's wet, confident tongue pried his mouth open.

Their mouths broke apart for a split second. Before Lucas could inhale fully, Jack's mouth sucked a searing kiss to his lips. Another tiny lightning storm blitzed Lucas's brain, and the storm built each time Jack sucked or bit at his lips.

Lucas's eyes trembled to remain open, his teeth clashing with Jack's, and his nose sucking in air until his eyes fell shut. His muscles gave out on top of Jack's body. Waves of heat transferred through Jack's gauzy shirt. Jack hitched Lucas's shirt up his lower back, his palm burning with each press to Lucas's skin and causing Lucas's shirt to ride up on his stomach.

Lucas pulled back to breathe. "Just what do you think you're doing?" Their lips tangled together. Lucas cupped Jack's cheek while Jack's hand ghosted over his arse. "I'd never do this in front of anyone."

They were inches away from another kiss when Jack flipped Lucas onto his back, straddling him as if in a choreographed movie scene. Lucas stared up at him with his mouth agape.

"And yet you're doing it, which is a good thing," Jack said. "You need to get comfortable with me. Physically. And you said you don't like to be teased." Jack's mouth had begun to puff and darken. He smoothed his hands up Lucas's stomach to curl around the fronts of his shoulders. "I won't tease you, unless you want me to." Jack's eyes flashed before he shifted lower to suck wetly on Lucas's bottom lip. "I want to please you."

"That stupid voice of yours," Lucas said, sounding suspiciously like growling. He rolled Jack onto his back as Jack cackled in his face. "Fuck. You're so frustrating." He sealed their lips together and Jack arched under him.

When Lucas tried to pull back, tried to break their marathon kisses, his body would not move, save for an involuntary grind against Jack's firm weight. His brain sent signals to his limbs to shift, to get away before he memorized what Jack's sweet saliva tasted like, to escape before he became obsessed with the exact heat of the inside of his mouth and the soft breaths Jack exhaled through his nose when their lips were connected.

Those signals were lost among the light storm flashing behind his closed eyes. His brain's messages were drowned out by the quiet, soft, almost pleading moans Jack made against his mouth as they kissed. The sure motions of his kisses and touches made Lucas feel like they were the only people on a shrinking planet. Every sound he wrenched from Jack's body was a lifeline, a gallon of oxygen injected into his lungs or the buzz of electricity in his veins.

"I get it now," Lucas whispered between kisses, a hot tongue teasing his own. "I get it."

"Get what?"

"Why men pay you thousands to play pretend."

"Oh yeah?" He bit and sucked at Lucas's neck with quick nips of his teeth, and Lucas's hips stuttered against his groin. Jack smiled wider and suckled on the spot, whispering, "Tell me." Jack cradled the back of his head and guided his neck to stretch sideways, sinking his teeth into his bodywash-scented skin. "Tell me, Lucas. Please?" His tongue laved underneath Lucas's ear as Lucas's leg kicked out. Jack squeezed his arsecheek as he purred, "Lucas," and slotted their lips together. Another gentle moan vibrated into Lucas's mouth, their kisses slow and wet.

"You're lush." Lucas's words tumbled into Jack's panting mouth. "So fucking lush. Worth every penny, I'm sure."

Jack sighed high in his voice and hugged Lucas closer with his thighs. Their heads tilted in opposite directions as they kissed, saliva building on the bottom ridge of Jack's chin. Lucas swiped his tongue over his bottom lip, sucking and nibbling until Jack trembled beneath him. Jack squeezed Lucas's arse and ground upward.

Jack murmured, "Put your hands on me."

His voice melted into the thick layer of soft noises that had built around them, and the room filled with tiny sound waves. Lucas followed the motion of Jack's slender fingers as he popped each button. His shirt fluttered open. The light material framed his tanned, muscled torso. Jack's heavy, half-lidded gaze landed on Lucas's face before he kissed him, their lips softly melding together.

"Touch me. See how your hands fit on me." Jack held Lucas's hand and flattened it on his hip. Lucas's face was motionless, unreadable. "See where it feels right to touch me. Feel the heat of my skin. Get used to it."

He guided Lucas's hand over his rippled abs. Jack had the barest layer of fat stretched over his carefully crafted muscles and long frame. He was blessed with the magic combination of built and muscular with lean and curvy, deep hip dents leading beneath his tight black jeans. He looked like he chopped wood every day and built log cabins. His lean body was devoid of the overstuffed gym bulk so many men strove for.

Lucas's thumbnail scratched beside his navel and Jack's abs clenched. Jack shrugged his shoulders back.

"I've got sensitive spots too, but I don't mind. I'm pretty sensitive everywhere, but you can touch me wherever you want."

When Lucas had seen slivers of Jack's skin in the taxi, unwashed and marred with grime from an overnight, he imagined that Jack was made up of the same cells and particles that every other human was made of. He assumed that Jack showered a passable amount, that his skin got oily and sweaty as needed, and that he had rough patches pop up without reason or a hair or two that sprouted out of a mole only noticeable when the shower light was just so.

His skin did not look or feel real under Lucas's touch. It felt like the literary description of rose petals and the underside of leather, like every fantasy figure wrapped into one thrumming creature. He felt like a human, like a man, but his smooth skin was so evenly warm, so tender and soft, that it felt like Lucas was touching fine fabric, not flesh sweating and stretched over shifting muscles and bones.

"What are you made of?"

True confusion wrinkled Jack's brow as he continued holding the top of his hand. "What?"

Lucas licked his lips. His mouth itched for more of Jack's taste, and his heart pounded rapidly. He gritted his teeth, his gaze scanning over Jack's body.

Jack's torso was hairless, save for a downy line of brown hair just visible above his boxer briefs, and the hint of soft hair beneath his arms. His nipples were darker pink than his lips and slightly puffy, standing out from his chiseled pecs.

Lucas counted four tattoos on his endless upper body. The first was a bird outline on the front of his right shoulder. The bird was flying off of him, its beak pointing toward Jack's arm.

"A swallow?" Lucas asked, brushing his fingers over the bird. Some of his marbles returned to the inside of his head. "Really? In your field?"

Jack smirked. "It's a nightingale, smartarse."

Lucas held on to his bicep and lifted his arm away from his side. Jack's eyes widened slightly. The motion brought the barest tinge of crisp deodorant to Lucas's nostrils. Jack's hips shifted under him.

Lucas used light fingertips to trace his second tattoo, a delicate wire birdcage inked high enough on his upper ribs that it was nearly under his arm. He glanced at Jack and noticed his tight expression, his mouth twitching as he watched Lucas's fingers. Lucas deliberately ran his fingers over the spot again and Jack breathed out a shaky laugh.

"All right, Mr. Tickles. Relax." He lowered his arm. "It's just a tattoo."

Lucas tapped the nightingale. "Does she go in the cage?"

"It's a he."

"Is it?"

"Contrary to popular belief, male nightingales sing the loudest, not the female, and are usually the ones humans hear singing. Males use their song at night to find a mate or to warn other birds of danger."

Lucas nodded along with his explanation. "That actually works with your profession." He touched the filled-in black heart tattooed on Jack's outer shoulder and dragged his fingers to the simple script *R* beside the heart. "Gentleman of the night and all that."

Jack gripped his chin, gently but firmly, and directed his face up. He held his stare, his mouth a straight line.

"The cage is empty and the nightingale is free. I'm no one's caged bird." Jack fluttered his lashes before looking back to Lucas. "That's far too cliché, and I'm far too happy, and well paid, to compare myself to a caged animal."

"Fair enough. Who or what is *R*?"

Jack's warm hands held Lucas's face as they started kissing again. The itchy feeling on Lucas's tongue disappeared, and he puffed a short gasp into Jack's mouth. Jack guided Lucas to lie on the bed, then crawled on top of him, framing Lucas's head with his forearms. He leaned down, but Lucas placed a hand on the center of his chest and sniffed his neck.

"Are you wearing my cologne?"

Jack's smile was slow, forming lopsided before it straightened to a full grin. "Yeah."

"Why?"

"I like it. Smells good on you."

"I thought you wear the vanilla one?"

Jack's long lashes blinked once. There was a small break in talking before he replied. "Not regularly, though that's my favorite. I don't own any cologne. I like to try different types out."

Lucas squinted. "Like, on the job?"

"Yeah."

Lucas prodded his birdcage. "Cologne thief."

Jack giggled and curled his arms around himself. "I think we've had enough practice for tonight," he said, still letting out soft laughs and rolling off Lucas. "Wouldn't want to overwhelm your wee brain."

"Oi!"

Jack pinned Lucas's wrists to the bed and smacked a loud kiss to his lips, nipping his bottom lip and kissing it quickly.

"We can tackle Hand-Holding 101 and Spooning for Lovers at a later class."

"You're such a menace," Lucas grumbled, a small smile slipping out.

Jack got up to his knees on the bed. He cupped his crotch and lifted his leg, gripping himself and pushing his hand to the side. Lucas's smile faded, his eyes glued to the thick line pressing against the upper thigh of Jack's jeans.

"You even got me a little hot." Jack started to chew his mint gum with an open mouth. "Always a rare, rare bonus."

"I didn't mean to." Lucas frowned. "That's inappropriate."

"Getting a semi is inappropriate?" Jack's eyes flickered toward George, who was fast asleep on a mountain of pillows. "No wonder your dog is acting out sexual frustration. It must run rampant in here. Your poor cock and balls."

Lucas sat up and moved to stand, and Jack gently shoved him onto his back. He huffed as he righted himself. Jack grinned and nudged him off balance.

"My cock and balls are just fine, thank you."

Jack's eyes slid to Lucas's middle. His right brow arched. "You've got that right."

Lucas looked down. "Shit," he muttered, pressing his hand to his cock. So that was why the middle of his body had been aching and throbbing for the past few minutes. As his hand pressed harder in an effort to adjust, he winced and jutted his hips backward, and Jack snickered. "Shut up. We shouldn't—" Lucas quickly waved his hand in the air. "This shouldn't happen."

"You're the hottest client I've ever had, and probably will ever have. It makes sense that it happened. Or did they leave out the birds and the bees at Cambridge?"

"I'm not your client in that way."

Jack ruffled Lucas's hair as he got off the bed. "I wouldn't stress about it, babe."

Lucas watched Jack shrug his shirt on, his fingers even faster when buttoning it up.

"I'm not your babe."

Jack glanced at him, mischief lighting his eyes. "You should be happy you can still get hard at your age, fluffy-bum."

Lucas glared at him with the fury of ten thousand blazing suns.

Jack laughed deeply as he bent to grab his laptop bag, then ran out of the bedroom with Lucas hot on his heels.

Chapter EIGHT

Wednesday, April 22

LUCAS BALLED up a sheet of paper and threw it toward his rubbish bin. He sighed and ran his hands through his hair. So much for his carefully crafted quiff that morning. His office phone rang and he snatched it up before the first ring ended.

"Yes?" he asked, cradling the phone on his shoulder.

"You have a visitor, sir," Albert said.

Lucas peered out the open door. Albert was close enough for Lucas to hear him both over the phone and in real life.

Albert asked, "A Mr. Jack McQueen?"

Lucas's mouth went dry. The phone slipped off his shoulder. He threw it on the receiver and stood up, walking into Albert's office with his hands in his pockets. His eyes darted around.

"Is he here?"

"No, he's still downstairs at security. Shall I tell him you're not available?"

"No, no, it's fine. He…." Lucas rolled up on the balls of his feet. "He can come up whenever he wants if he needs to see me."

Albert's eyes widened slightly and his voice dropped to a hushed, secretive tone. "Are you sure, sir? You haven't granted anyone that security clearance."

Lucas nodded. "It's fine. He's my boyfriend." He felt like he was speaking a foreign language that had yet to be invented. "We've been together for six months. We met on Halloween and are very much in love. With each other."

Albert gaped at him, his mouth popping open and closed like a fish. "Oh. I… I'm sorry, I didn't know." Albert clutched his hand over his chest. "I wouldn't have scheduled so many evening and weekend meetings. You always said it was fine, but I am truly, truly sorry, sir. A better assistant would have known—"

"It was fine. Is fine. It's fine. You can send him up, thanks. Why don't you take a coffee break? Charge it to me." He pointed two fingers at Albert. "Lunch! Why don't you get lunch? Whatever you want. On me." He slung an arm around Albert's shoulder and patted the center of his chest. "You're the best assistant. A star of an assistant. Please do not stress about it." He patted his chest again. "All is well."

"Will do. Yes. Thanks. Yes." Albert nodded as he bumbled his words. "Okay. Yes."

Lucas turned away to the sound of Albert placing a call to security. He went back into his office and tried to clear his desk of paperwork while straightening his tie and organizing a pile of rainbow paperclips. He heard a desk chair squeak.

"Hello! I'm Albert, Lucas's assistant," Albert said from outside his office, professional and friendly. "It's a pleasure to finally meet you."

Lucas froze, a bundle of papers clutched to his chest. That was fast.

"Hey, mate. I'm Jack. Lovely to meet you, as well. Luke's said the nicest things."

Lucas frowned down at his desk. Gone was Jack's smoky hustler voice, instead replaced with a deep, honey-sweet drawl.

"You look familiar," Albert said, sounding polite but unsure. "Have we met before?"

Lucas's frown turned to panic. He spun around and tiptoed toward the open door. The gala. Albert must have spotted Jack at the gala, a gala he did not attend as Lucas's date.

"I don't believe so," Jack said. "Did you study at Leeds?"

"No, Warwick."

"Oh, excellent. Beautiful campus." Jack's boots strode across the hardwood. "Hey! Is this the legendary hoop? I hear you're the Michael Jordan of the office."

"Well done," Lucas whispered under his breath.

"Yeah! I mean—" Albert cleared his throat. "—Yes, sir."

Lucas walked into Albert's office in time to hear Jack's easy chuckle.

"I'm not a sir, mate." His eyes twinkled at Lucas as he patted between Albert's shoulder blades. "Luke's the sir around here."

The skin under Lucas's collar heated. "Albert was just getting lunch," Lucas said, glancing at Albert. "Right?"

"Oh! Yes. Right." Albert nodded and picked up his jacket, walking sideways like a crab to get around Jack. "I'll leave you two alone. Would you like for me to bring something back? I'm going to run to the shop down the street for a sandwich, but I should be back shortly."

"No, thanks," Lucas said before Jack could speak. He and Jack exchanged glances. Lucas jerked a thumb toward him. "This one will order the whole menu. Eats like a horse." Jack's cheek dimpled, his eyes crinkling. "Far too much food for one lad to carry."

"I'm only dropping by, as well," Jack said to Albert. "Might not be here when you get back. So glad we were able to meet, finally."

"Me too! I'll have to add you to Lucas's schedule. Do you have a color preference? I believe orange and purple are available, but I could create a custom color to your liking."

"Purple, please," Jack said, looping his thumbs in the pockets of his skinnies. "Love purple."

Albert put on his black jacket. "Excellent choice." He checked his watch. "Are you on lunch too?"

"Sort of. I'm an independent contractor, so I make my own schedule."

"What do you do?"

Jack looked toward Lucas, who continued to smile but widened his eyes ever so slightly. That was one part of their backstory they hadn't talked about.

"Silly, Luke. You didn't tell Albert what I do?" Jack tapped his fingers next to Albert's address book on his desk. "I'm shocked you didn't have him put my business card into your Rolodex." He patted his back pocket. "I believe I have an extra on me, if you need one for record-keeping purposes."

"He's a photographer," Lucas said through a gritted smile. He looked to Albert, blinking once. "He has an amazing artistic eye."

"Aw, babe," Jack drawled. "You're sweet."

"Actually, Albert, would you do me a favor?" Lucas said while still keeping watch of Jack.

"Of course! Whatever you need, sir."

"Would you pick us up a couple of teas on your way back from lunch?"

"Sure!"

"I take it the same way as Lucas," Jack offered. He smiled warmly and glanced at Lucas. "Thanks so much."

Lucas reached into his wallet and handed Albert some cash. "Enjoy your lunch."

Albert accepted the cash and said good-bye seven different times, inching his way away from his desk. He power walked with determined energy toward the bank of lifts.

"C'mon in." Lucas held his arm out. Jack walked in front of him, and Lucas pulled the door nearly shut. "Funny you said you take your tea like me. Albert is a saint but must have some sort of block in his brain about tea. Every time he gets me tea, it's a different type prepared a different way."

"Maybe he's trying to keep you on your toes." Jack tucked his hands in his pockets as he strolled around Lucas's desk. He reached the wall of windows. "Office is nice. Looks exactly how I imagined it." He squinted out the window. "Oh, wow. Albert is literally running to lunch. Look. You can see him from up here."

"He's a fitness guy."

"And a very punctual employee."

"Only the best at Covington Associates."

"The guards here are certainly a lot more pleasant than the doorman at your building."

Lucas leaned his bum against the desk. His gaze followed Jack as he wandered the office. "What makes you say that?"

Jack touched the bottom right corner of a modern art painting and tilted it down an inch. "Your doorman is a bit of a dick, is what I meant."

"What? Who? Clarence? Marty?"

"The bald one."

"Nathan. What about him?"

"He was generally unpleasant. Gave me the old stink eye. Made a comment about how I'm not your usual type." Lucas's eyes widened. Jack sat down on the leather sofa against the wall and crossed his long legs, his boot bobbing in the air. He smirked. "Did you neglect to tell me I'm not your first professional? You shouldn't keep secrets from your boyfriend. Honesty is key in any relationship."

Lucas sighed and threw a balled-up piece of paper at Jack. "You're my first professional, but that doesn't mean I've never brought men back with me. I'm not a monk."

Jack batted another tossed ball of paper from the air. "What's your type?"

"I don't have one."

"Someone like that stud of an assistant?"

"No. He's straight, tomcat. Sorry to burst that bubble."

"Tomcat? What happened to kitten?"

"Next on the news at eleven: Kittens grow up into cats."

Jack chuckled and stood up, stretching his arms over his head. "Oh, how I missed your attempts at humor. Manchester treat you well?"

"Manchester was Manchester." Lucas's eyes followed Jack's path as he came closer, until Jack stood in front of him. His long limbs and wind-ruffled hair were close enough to touch. "I was going to call you later, actually. I'm glad you came by."

Jack's froze midstretch. "Oh, yeah?" He arched his hips side to side; the bottom of his shirt rode up. "Even being swamped with the big-tech merger tomorrow?"

Lucas narrowed his eyes, not in an unfriendly way, but in a look of discernment. “You have a good memory. You’re very perceptive.”

“Thank you,” Jack said, pleased, relaxing his arms at his sides. “So? Why are you happy to see me?” He framed his face with his hand. “Other than the obvious, of course.”

Lucas chuckled softly and leaned his arse against his desk. “I was thinking about our flight. It’s so early on Saturday morning, maybe you should sleep at mine on Friday? Guest room, of course. I’m getting us a car to the airport the next morning, and I assume you don’t want to tell me where you live to pick you up?”

“Correct.”

“If you stay at mine, you can sleep later, since you won’t have to come over at three in the morning. Unless you have plans or a client that night or something.”

“That’s… a good idea. A really good idea.” Jack nodded as he spoke, dragging his fingers through his hair. “I, uh… I do have work that night, but it’s an early dinner thing. I could be over by around eightish? Does that work for you?”

Lucas nodded as if Jack said he was working the night shift at the office. “Sure. That’s fine.”

“Excellent,” Jack said. Surprise softened his voice. “Sounds good.”

“So? What’s the real reason you dropped by? Trying to hustle a lunch? I don’t have time for a marathon quiche-and-sandwich session, but I think I’ve got some crisps kicking around somewhere.”

“Nope.” Jack popped the *p*, standing with his hands on his hips. “I’ve already eaten, but thank you for the generous offer. I came by because I started to pack last night and realized I don’t really have any family-friendly swim attire.”

“What does that mean?”

“It means that I don’t think Lane will appreciate Maggie asking questions about why Uncle Lucas’s boyfriend is wearing a sheer white thong on the water slide.”

“I see. Nude pool parties and all.” Lucas pulled his wallet out, thumbing the leather open. “Do you want money for clothes?”

“No, no money needed, thanks. I came by to see if you needed me to pick anything up for you while I was at the shops. I know you have a busy week.”

Lucas pocketed his wallet. “I think I have enough swim trunks.”

Jack sighed, but was smiling. “You have two pairs. One pair is basic black, which is passable. The other pair is so ugly and unflattering that I think I’d rather see you in a sheer thong.”

"I think you'd want to see me in a sheer thong anyway, regardless of what I already had in my closet."

"You might be right." Lucas rolled his eyes, his mouth twitching in an effort to remain neutral. Jack raised his eyebrows. "You sure you don't want anything? Two bathing suits won't be fun when we're going to be in and out of water every day. You'll have to keep rinsing and hang drying them."

"I suppose if you see swim trunks that merit your seal of approval"—he pointed one finger at Jack—"and offer full coverage, I could use another couple. You're right. We'll be in and out of water the whole trip."

Jack's face lit up. His long fingers steepled together and fluttered. "Oh, goody. I was hoping you'd say that."

Lucas snorted, his stomach shaking beneath his gray suit jacket. "You sure you don't want money? I can at least pay you back for mine."

"Don't worry about it. I've had a lovely day so far and am feeling generous."

"Yeah? What'd you do?"

"Gym. Excellent green smoothie. Long shower. Amazing facial. Lovely salad with seared tuna. I love a good piece of fish."

Lucas nodded along with his list. "I'd have thought the shower would come after the facial, but that all sounds pleasant enough."

"What? Why…." Jack's mouth dropped open and he barked out a shocked guffaw. "Not that kind of facial, you horny minx. I got a facial at a spa. For skin care purposes."

"Ah," Lucas said, holding out the sound. "My mistake." He tugged on the bottom of Jack's blue flannel shirt. "Looking less like Captain Jack today. Well." He jutted his chin up at the red and blue patterned scarf wrapped around his hair. "A bit less."

"I'm off. Felt like being casual."

"I see." Lucas smoothly moved his face to Jack's neck, taking a slow sniff. Jack's body froze in place, the tip of Lucas's nose brushing the buttery skin. "No cologne either. You smell of lavender."

"Spa."

Lucas pulled his face back and found Jack's eyes. The right side of Lucas's mouth rose. "Lovely."

Without breaking eye contact, Jack said, "We should kiss again."

"What?" Lucas snorted, his brows furrowing. "Why?"

"We need the practice, and Albert will be back soon. We should be kissing when he gets back."

Lucas's lips pursed for three silent seconds. "You're still not making sense, love."

Jack stepped closer, his body heat moving into Lucas's space. He ran his fingertips over the tops of Lucas's hands, tracing his middle knuckles. "Albert is going to the wedding, yes?"

"Yes, but I don't see how that's important."

"If he comes back and catches us kissing, he'll remember it. Even if it's just light kissing. It might come in handy if questions pop up during the trip about how valid we are."

"Who would question that?"

Jack smirked at him, innocent and closemouthed, and leaned down, brushing his lips beneath Lucas's jawline. Lucas stiffened, his hands shooting out to hold Jack's hips.

"Nosy family members." Jack kissed his pulse point. "Confused friends." He mouthed beside his Adam's apple. "That sort of thing."

"What…." Lucas's voice cracked. He roughly cleared his throat. "What are you doing?"

Jack dragged his nose to Lucas's ear. "You wear your cologne so well." He sniffed. He looped his right arm around Lucas's lower back. "Smells so good on you."

"Trying to get a contact high?"

"Trying to figure you out. What's your deal?" Jack murmured. Hot air teased the inward arch of Lucas's neck and he felt goose bumps rising on the sensitive skin. "One minute you're doing this to me, the next minute you're shocked someone would want to do it to you." He nosed along the soft skin. Lucas's Adam's apple bobbed beneath his kisses. "What makes you tick? You can tell me. I'm very good at keeping secrets."

"Why do you care?"

Jack's mouth pursed to place small, light, barely there kisses along the side of Lucas's neck. Lucas's hands fell from his hips to grip the edge of his desk.

"Pleasure is my business, and I'm usually quite good at identifying what people want."

Lucas swallowed again, his pulse flickering faster beneath his jaw.

"People want their necks mauled during business hours? They want to be interrupted at work?"

Jack lifted his head, his eyes heavy and full of mirth. "Sometimes. Most clients would pay hundreds for me to do what I'm doing right now out of the goodness of my heart." He looked at Lucas's lips and leaned closer. Lucas tilted his head away, his mouth twitching. "Aw," Jack drawled deeply, holding out the word. He pecked his cheek, running his fingers through Lucas's well-coiffed hair. "You're shy, is that it?"

"I'm not shy."

Jack started to kiss along the other side of his neck. "No?"

"I think you're used to having clients who want you. I don't want you, which ruins your little game."

"Is that so?"

"Yes."

"Just like how you didn't need a date for the wedding?"

"That—" Lucas's even, steady voice cracked, and he blinked rapidly. He could feel Jack chuckling against his skin, as if he could smell blood in the water. Jack suckled beneath his ear with deep, tender swirls of his tongue, humming low in his throat as he sucked. Lucas clenched his toes in his leather shoes, directing his gaze at the ceiling. "Jack, I…" He stretched his head to the side. "I'm at work."

Jack hummed even lower, kissing up to Lucas's chin. "Do you like being pursued? Is that it? That must be it. You're always in control at work. You have a stressful job. So, in your private life, you want someone else to tell you what to do. 'S why you were so hesitant at your place when we were practicing, and it took you a bit to warm up. You—"

Lucas cackled, the sound startling Jack midkiss. "What's so funny?"

Lucas's cackles softened to giggles, and his eyes glistened. He leveled his stare on Jack and curved his hands around Jack's hips. He narrowed his eyes, his fingers toying in the billowing bottom of Jack's flannel button-down.

"You're not as good at your job as you think you are."

Jack's eyes lit. "How would you know?"

Lucas spun them and fit himself between Jack's thick thighs, pressing Jack's arse against the edge of the desk. Jack made a soft, high sound of surprise as papers shifted beneath his bum. Lucas's thumbs rubbed over the front of Jack's hipbones. "If you think telling me what to do and using your hustler voice on me is going to push my buttons, you are angling for the wrong buttons, darling."

Jack smirked. "Tell me which buttons to push, if you even know where they are."

"Ah, but aren't you in the pleasure business? I wouldn't want to disrespect your art."

"Fuck, you're such a wanker sometimes," Jack said tightly. A genuine smile crinkled Lucas's eyes and Jack's brows furrowed further. "What, you want me to call you a wanker? Is that your kink? You want to be humiliated and talked down to?"

Lucas grinned. "Not quite."

Albert's footsteps in the distance filtered into Lucas's office. Jack glanced at the small space between the open door and the doorframe.

"It's now or never, love. Either we kiss or we…." Jack trailed off and looked down. Lucas let his lips brush over Jack's mouth. Warm fingertips slid up the bottom of Jack's shirt, drawing small circles over the fronts of his bare hips. "Or… we…." Lucas brushed their lips so softly, so gently, that Jack's body tilted forward, finding nothing but air and the blaze of Lucas's teeth. "We…."

Lucas squeezed his hips and tilted his head an inch to the right, pressing their lips together. Jack's hips flexed beneath his thumbs, his hands flattening on the small of Lucas's back.

"Can I kiss you?" Lucas asked.

Jack breathed, "You already have."

"You're right. I suppose I have."

"You like to be in control all the time. You like to tease," Jack whispered, following the tilt of Lucas's head to kiss him more firmly. "That's it?"

"You'll never know now, will you?"

"No, I suppose not."

"Feel the weight of my body," Lucas drawled, mimicking Jack's deep voice. He slid his hands around to the backs of Jack's hips and pressed their groins flush. "Feel how my hands feel on your skin."

"Using my own words against me." Jack gave his arse a playful spank. Lucas's lips curved amusedly. "Bad wolf."

Lucas's teeth closed on Jack's full bottom lip, gently sucking once before Jack pulled him closer, their mouths pressing together. Lucas exhaled through his nostrils and thrust his tongue against Jack's, unable to stand the light tease of his tongue along the seam of his lips.

"You happy now?" he rasped, kissing Jack with more firmness.

Both of Jack's hands cupped Lucas's thick arse, grinding against him. "You certainly are."

Lucas smiled into a kiss, softening the motions of their lips. "I think that's you, darling."

Jack hummed with their lips connected, and swiveled his hips. Lucas's breath stuttered into his mouth, his fingers clutching in the back of Jack's hair.

"Mmm." Jack tilted his head and approached from another angle. "Pull my hair again."

For whatever reason, Lucas's hand followed Jack's murmured order and tightened to pull. Jack whimpered ever so softly, and Lucas pressed harder against him. Their lips opened together and their tongues slid between them.

"I have your tea, sir—*rrrroh*! Oh!" Albert rapidly moonwalked out of the office with a takeaway tray of tea in hand. "Oh," Albert whispered, out of breath. "Oh my."

Lucas rolled his eyes at Jack's smug grin and broke away from him. He licked his lips, dabbing the back of his hand to his mouth. "Sorry, mate." He stepped up to the door and gestured for Albert to come inside. "Didn't mean to startle you."

Albert poked his head back into the office, his eyes tightly shut. "I didn't mean to intrude, sir. Sirs. Erm. I. Well. I apologize."

"It's okay," Lucas chuckled, taking the tray from him. "It's fine. Honest. We shouldn't be fraternizing at work, anyway."

"Yeah, sorry, mate," Jack said, stepping up next to Lucas. "Didn't mean to make you uncomfortable."

"It's no problem! None at all."

Lucas handed Jack a paper cup, then took his own cup out of the carryout tray. They sipped at the same time. Jack tilted his head just so, smirking over the edge of the cup.

"How is it?" Albert clasped his hands tightly in front of his chest, looking from Lucas to Jack. "Did I make it to your liking?"

Jack said, "It's delicious." He licked his lips and nodded. "Thank you so much."

"Yeah, thanks for picking them up," Lucas said. Jack snuffled as he sipped again. "The tea is… great."

Albert snapped his fingers and pointed at Jack. "I know where I've seen you!"

Lucas sputtered into his tea and hot liquid stung inside his nostrils. He coughed, and Jack patted between his shoulder blades.

"Y'all right, love?"

"Fine," Lucas said, sounding strained. Albert rushed toward him with outstretched hands and Lucas held one palm out. Albert had applied CPR to people before at various office events. Lucas knew his safety patrol stance when he saw it. "I'm fine. Just fine."

Jack kept his touch gentle to continue rubbing between Lucas's shoulder blades.

"I think we go to the same gym," Jack said. "Is that where we've seen each other?"

"Oh, erm, no." Albert scratched the back of his head. "I don't believe so?"

"Ah, sorry, man. You look just like one of the trainers at my gym. You must work out, what?" He scanned Albert's body. "Five or six times a week to look like you do?"

As Lucas sipped his tea, Albert's face flushed. Albert fumbled as he touched his own chest.

"Well, I—" Albert exhaled a light laugh. "—I do try to be healthy. I usually go at least four times a week, five if my schedule allows."

"I've been doing a lot more body-weight training lately," Jack said, rubbing the front of his left shoulder and rolling it forward. "Press-ups are killing me. I think I'm doing them wrong."

Albert's eyes lit up. "I could show you how I do them, if you'd like?"

"Could you?"

"Sure! I mean," Albert stopped unbuttoning a shirt cuff and stood up straighter, looking to Lucas. "If that's all right, sir. I can get back to work immediately, if you'd like."

"Please." Lucas swirled his cup in a circle. "By all means. Press-up to your heart's desire."

Albert ran out of the office, saying, "One moment!" over his shoulder.

Jack and Lucas glanced at each other. Jack brought his lips to Lucas's ear. "Who puts milk in blueberry tea?" he whispered.

"We do, apparently," Lucas whispered back. He scoffed, "Blueberry tea. As if we'd have such poor taste."

Jack smiled with his bottom lip pinched between his teeth. Albert returned and dropped to the floor like a soldier. Jack reached into his pocket and pulled his iPhone out.

"Now, when I do press-ups," Albert said, doing them with the same enthusiasm he possessed as Lucas's assistant, "I usually alternate taking one limb out of the equation." He lifted his right hand, never missing a beat. "I've found it helps confuse my muscles."

"You're like an Avenger," Jack said. "You're a total badass."

Albert chuckled breathily, now lifting his left foot while doing press-ups. Jack held up his phone and tapped the screen. The marimba ringtone sang from the phone.

"Ah, shoot, I've got to take this." He leaned down and pecked Lucas's lips, sliding his teacup into Lucas's free hand. "Work call." He kissed Lucas one more time, plush and slow. Lucas's mouth was motionless and his gaze followed Jack as he stepped back. Jack floated around Albert with light feet. "Sorry to have to run." He bent over and grinned at Albert's sweating face. "Was amazing to meet you. Excellent form."

"You too," Albert panted out, starting to stand. "And, uh, thanks!"

Jack patted his shoulder as he walked to the door. "Can't wait to see you at the wedding, mate." He stepped backward and threw a flirty wink at Lucas. "I'll talk to you later, babe."

Lucas watched the entire scene play out in silence. He was aware of Jack's ability to read situations and manipulate as needed, but even he was impressed with how Jack was able to dispense with Albert to get himself out of a potentially uncomfortable revelation about being Mr. Carson's gala date. Jack didn't exaggerate about having an uncanny ability to make himself disappear. Something heavy sank in Lucas's stomach. The uncomfortable feeling made him frown.

"Oh," Albert panted, looking sideways as he held a plank position, "he's gone. That was quick." He smiled up at Lucas. "He's nice!"

"I'll walk him to the lifts. He forgot his tea."

Lucas walked briskly through the office, searching for a tall figure looming above the secretaries busy at their desks. He checked over his shoulder and, when there was no sight of Albert, tossed both of their teas into a garbage can. He caught up with Jack just as he reached the main reception desk.

"Jack," he whispered.

Jack's eyes were wide when they landed on Lucas's face. He looked around for nearby employees.

"What are you doing?"

"Walking you out," Lucas said, flattening his hand on Jack's lower back. "*Babe*."

Jack smirked softly, leaning into his touch.

"Good to see you finally getting it."

"Getting what?"

Jack turned toward Lucas and lifted his hands. He tugged on the knot of Lucas's tie, smoothing his hands over his stiff shirt collar. "In business, you've been successful because you think ahead." The lift pinged open and people hurried around them. "Not one step ahead, or even two steps ahead, but multiple, long-term steps ahead."

"Yes? And?"

Jack entered the lift and pressed the ground floor button. His lips curved in amusement. "Do you not think that I do the same in my business?"

"What are you talking about?"

"You were so reluctant to kiss me in front of Albert. To kiss me at all." Jack adjusted his headscarf. "All it took was me putting the ball in your court, letting you think that you were in control, for you to give in to me. Which you did. Within seconds. And I'm telling you, this will come in handy on the island. Same with you getting more comfortable with me."

The doors started to close, but Lucas's arm shot out to halt them in place. "A few babes and fake kisses do not a mastermind make. I don't think you're that bright, love."

Jack chuckled, a light, bubbled sound. "You don't?" He fixed his eyes on Lucas, brushing his fingers over his bottom lip. "My goal was to get you to kiss me. You kissed me. I got you to want to kiss me. Sounds like I met my goal, doesn't it? Even if I had to take a few twists and turns to get there." He pressed the Door Close button and Lucas's arm stopped it again. "You still don't think I'm bright? You're the one who has not yet grasped who you're dealing with. Call me a hustler, call me a whore, call me a rent boy. I may be all of those things, but I'd imagine a businessman like you would recognize I'm a businessman at heart, and a very good one."

"If I'm the wolf, who are you, then? The snake? The spider? Weaving webs with neck kisses and bad jokes? And I've never called you a whore. Never will."

Jack grinned and ran his right hand through his hair; its shiny waves tumbled over his shoulders. He pressed the Door Close button. "If I'm the spider or the snake, does that make you my prey? I quite like that image."

"Well? What are you? For a man who babbles constantly, you rarely say anything of use."

"I'm a whole other animal." The doors started to close. Lucas stood with his arms at his sides. Jack winked and blew him an air kiss. "See you Friday, love."

The doors pinged shut. Lucas stared at the brushed metal.

Chapter NINE

Friday, April 24

"YOU'VE OUTDONE yourself yet again, little bear," Mr. Carson said. "Bravo, my boy, bravo."

Jack scraped his fork on a plate. "I was hoping you'd like those chicken tacos." He glanced over his shoulder from the sink and saw Mr. Carson hobbling into the kitchen with an empty plate in hand. "The recipe seemed too good to be true, but it's totally heart-healthy. We'll have to add it to our usual repertoire."

"You should become a personal chef," Mr. Carson continued in a creaky but still bright voice. He held his plate out to Jack. "Your healthy food tastes nothing like the rubbish my chef makes me. Sawdust. He makes me sawdust, I swear it."

Jack laughed quietly and took the plate. "Why don't you get ready for bed? I'll be in shortly."

Mr. Carson weakly squeezed Jack's shoulder, before patting his back. "You're too good to me, sweet boy."

Jack smiled down at the sink of suds, running warm water over their dinner dishes. He opened the dishwasher and started to load it, even though Mr. Carson would scoff and tell him to leave the mess for his housekeeper.

Once the kitchen was cleaned up, he went to the enormous master-bedroom en-suite. The room was covered in light marble with gold fixtures, and was twice the size of a regular person's entire apartment.

He searched through the medicine cabinet and pulled out three bottles. He opened one bottle and frowned. He set that bottle to the side and divided the other medications into a white paper cup. He walked into the bedroom with the cup and the extra pill bottle.

Mr. Carson was already under the covers, wearing scarlet silk pajamas, his eyes closed and his mouth slackened.

"Did you want me to split these?" Jack asked, wiggling the bottle. "Dr. Hilary said to take half a dose at night from now on, remember?"

"Did she?" Mr. Carson said, sounding exhausted. He took his glasses off, his age-spot-covered hands rubbing his eyes. "My brain is a bit fried. I apologize, love."

"That's all right," Jack said, gentle and quiet. "We only saw her yesterday. It's still new. I'll bring your meds in a moment, just relax."

After preparing the split pills and double-checking the medication within the white cup, Jack went back into the lavish red and gold bedroom. Mr. Carson was snoring with his head dropped back and a thin line of drool glistening between his cracked lips. Jack went to the left side of the bed and placed his hand on Mr. Carson's shoulder, squeezing once.

"Meds then beds, just like always," he whispered. Mr. Carson struggled to sit up. Jack slid his arm beneath his lower back. He eased him into an upright position and offered him a glass of water. He dropped a collection of pills into Mr. Carson's other hand. "Here we are."

Mr. Carson threw the pills into his mouth and lifted his glass of water with a shaking hand. He gulped the pills down, taking small sips of the remaining water as Jack tucked the blankets around his chest. "Are you going away with Lucas Thompson next week?"

Jack's hands paused on the blankets, and he blinked twice. He smiled tightly at Mr. Carson, smoothing his hand over the duvet. He took the empty water glass and placed it on his bedside table.

"I'll—" He held out the word before slowly continuing. "—be out of town next week."

"He's a very nice boy, like you are. Smart. Very smart, just as you are. And lonely." Mr. Carson wrapped his thin, bony fingers around Jack's forearm. Jack looked at him. "He could use someone like you."

Jack's brows shot up, but his smile softened. "Me? He could use someone like me? I don't know if I believe that. He seems just fine on his own."

"He could use someone kind. Someone big-hearted and patient. Someone to make him laugh." Mr. Carson's eyes started to flicker shut and he weakly squeezed Jack's wrist. "You'll be very happy together, I'm sure."

His nasal, clucked snores took over the conversation. Jack stared warmly at his slackened face. His pale skin was so thin it resembled tissue paper, with veins and capillaries standing out from the wrinkled surface. He eased Mr. Carson's hand off his arm and shut the lamp off on his bedside table. Jack bent over to press a kiss to Mr. Carson's forehead, stroking his palm over his thinning white hair.

He left Mr. Carson's penthouse with his luggage in hand. He had been on enough holidays to know how to pack, needing only one rectangular suitcase and a black leather overnight bag as his carry-on. Lucas lived a mere two-minute walk from Mr. Carson's luxury building.

Jack stood in front of the sky-high structure and gritted his teeth, huffing a slow breath out of his nostrils.

The main doorman, someone who looked older than Mr. Carson, opened the door for him and offered him a nod. "Good evening, sir."

He nodded at the doorman, murmuring, "Thank you," and continued into the modern lobby. He approached the security desk. His muscles felt tighter as he walked and his spine stuck up straighter. He took one more breath as he reached the security guard, but his steely gaze softened.

"Good evening, sir," a sparkly-eyed ginger said to him, smiling wide behind the tiny lenses of his round, gold glasses. "How may I help you?"

"Oh, um." Jack ran his hand over the back of his neck. "I'm here to see Lucas Thompson? In 30A?"

"You must be Jack," the man said. He held his hand out. "Come on in, then. He told me to expect you. Shall I help you with your bags?"

"Thank you, but there's no need." He tightened his grip on the rolling bag's handle. "I've got it."

"All right, sir. Please don't hesitate to ask if you do need anything during your time here. Welcome."

"Thanks so much." Jack walked past his desk then paused, taking a step backward. He turned to face the guard. "Excuse me, sir?"

The ginger guard popped up from his chair, standing at attention in front of Jack. "Yes, Mr. McQueen?"

"Jack. Please, call me Jack."

"Okay, Jack. What can I do for you?"

Jack shuffled his boots and squeezed the handle of his bag. "What happened to the other night guard? Nathan, I think?"

"Oh," the man said. His happy expression faded fast. "Top secret, of course, but—" His voice dropped, his hand flat next to his mouth. "—rumor has it he was fired. He made inappropriate comments to guests and divulged private information about residents. Terrible. Just shameful." Jack's eyes widened, and the guard checked around the empty lobby. "To be honest, everyone seems relieved he's gone, myself included. He was a right dick." He adjusted his uniform, gruffly clearing his throat. "Pardon the language, sir."

"That's quite all right." A small tingle started to form in Jack's lower belly. "Thank you for telling me."

"Happy to help! I'm Marty, by the way. Whatever you need during your time here, please let me know."

Jack clasped Marty's hand. "Thank you. That's very kind of you to offer." A mix of shyness and flattery warmed Jack's cheeks. "Have a lovely evening, sir."

"You as well!" Marty patted the top of his hand and winked. "Best not keep Luke waiting or else he'll send Sir George out as a search party."

Jack chuckled and stepped away. He went to the lifts and got inside. He leaned back on the smooth wall for his journey to the thirtieth floor, and started to smile. His stomach fluttered and he grazed his fingertips over his lips.

The doors pinged open as his smile fully bloomed. The wheels of his suitcase had barely made their first rotation on the tile when Lucas's front door swung open. Lucas walked barefoot into the foyer. His face was relaxed and friendly but with sleepiness softening his eyes. He took the handle of Jack's suitcase.

"Hey, mate," Lucas said. He slid his free hand under the strap of Jack's leather overnight bag and shouldered it himself. Jack sputtered a soft sound and went for his suitcase, but Lucas rotated his grip before Jack's hand could clasp the handle. "Good dinner?"

"Yeah, was fine, thanks. Made tacos. But you—you don't have to do that." Jack gripped the strap of his overnight bag in an attempt to take it back. Lucas's forward steps dragged them both into the flat together. Their feet clopped awkwardly in a sideways shuffle. "I could have done that."

Lucas pushed the door shut. "It's no problem. Uh-oh." Tiny nails clicked on the hardwood, louder and louder until frantic panting could be heard. Jack grinned and looked toward the sounds. "Here comes trouble with a capital G."

Jack's grin spread even wider. "It's my Georgie!"

He dropped to his knees in time for George to barrel into him. He lifted George into his arms and cuddled their faces together, mumbling dog nonsense sounds.

Lucas hummed. "He certainly has taken a shine to you."

Jack stood up, holding George to his chest. That shy, bashful feeling fluttered in his stomach again. "He's sweet."

"Want to know a secret?"

Jack's brows rose. He lowered his face closer to Lucas. "Sure," he whispered, matching Lucas's hushed tone.

"When Zamir first came over to meet George," Lucas said as he rubbed George's belly, "this little beast pissed in his boots. Not just on his boots, but *inside* both of his boots."

Jack guffawed and gasped at the puppy, and tangled his fingers with Lucas's. "Naughty Georgie!"

Lucas scratched the top of George's head. "He's a cuddle monster, but he doesn't always warm up to new people right away. At least, not as fast as he warmed to you."

Jack dropped a soft kiss to George's head. "I'm honored, mate," he said into his fur. George wiggled and licked Jack's nose. "Aw, such a little lover."

Lucas tucked his hands in the pockets of his gray sweats. "So, you're all packed and ready? The car is picking us up at half three, sharp."

"I am," Jack said, nodding and placing George on the floor. He smoothed his mauve floral button-down and smiled at Lucas. "I can't wait for you to see your new swim trunks."

Lucas rolled his eyes and turned away, but not before Jack caught his small smile. He walked into the kitchen and grabbed a black kettle. "I shudder to think of the patterns you chose."

Jack laughed and perched on top of the kitchen island. He crossed his ankles, gently tapping his heels into the cabinet below. Lucas glanced at the front door. Jack's brown suede ankle boots rested beside his blue Adidas trainers.

"You'll love them," Jack insisted. "I'm sure of it."

Lucas stuck the kettle under the faucet. "Tea?"

"Yes, please." Jack lifted the unbuttoned vee of his shirt to his nose, letting the material fall back on his chest a second later. "Though I'd love a quick shower first, if that's all right?"

"Sure, yeah, of course. Whatever you want." Lucas turned off the sink and plopped the kettle on the stovetop. He turned on the heat. "I'll show you to your guest room."

Lucas took hold of Jack's luggage handle. Jack shouldered his bag. They, including George, walked to the first guest room.

The room was decorated in warm purples and grays, the floor in the same dark hardwood that ran through the flat. The large bed was outfitted with all-white linens; a flat-screen was mounted to the wall in front of the bed.

"Lovely," Jack said, then dropped his bag at the foot of the bed. "I love the colors."

"Thanks." Lucas lifted his hand and pointed at an open door. "There's a full en-suite, plus fresh towels and shower things if you need them."

Jack started unbuttoning his shirt. "Great, thanks." He walked to the en-suite and turned on the lights. A long white soaking tub beside a glass-walled shower awaited him. "Oh, wow. Nice tub."

Lucas crossed his arms over his chest and leaned his bum against the bedroom doorway. "Feel free to have a soak. The last person who stayed in here was Maggie, and she avoided having a bath like the plague. The only way I could get her to bathe was filling the Jacuzzi tub in my en-suite with mostly bubbles so we could have a"—he made air quotes—"'Princess Pool Party' in our swimsuits. I actually don't know if this tub's ever been used."

Jack's shirt melted off his long torso. The material dangled from his fingers and brushed the floor. Lucas averted his eyes.

"Nah, I'm too lazy for a bath." Jack tossed his shirt on the bed. "A shower will be lovely."

George climbed on a decorative padded leather bench at the end of the bed and launched himself onto the mattress, burrowing into Jack's colorful shirt. Lucas pushed himself off the wall.

"George, no." Lucas pointed from George to the floor. "Down, George. No bed. Down."

Jack inserted himself between Lucas and the bed. "I don't mind." His arms spread at his sides; he was shirtless and had his jeans unbuttoned. "I don't mind at all." He sat on the end of the bed, the motion causing his abs to ripple and his pecs to swell slightly. George toddled over to him. His small paws sank into the rich linens. "Unless it's a household rule?"

"He'll never leave you alone if you let him up, just a warning."

"That's all right. I don't mind."

Lucas shrugged. "As you wish."

Jack squeezed the back of George's neck, smiling down at the pup. "He'll forget me after tonight. I can manage one pug cuddle night."

"What do you mean?"

Jack looked up at him. "Well, because I won't be back here after the trip."

"Ah. Right." Lucas looked to George. The dog's chin was propped on Jack's thigh and his tail was whirling. "Right. Of course."

Jack looked down and scratched behind George's ears. His bicep flickered while he scratched, and every muscle in his torso lazily stretched as he stood up from the bed. He picked up George and walked to Lucas.

"Be good for Daddy," Jack whispered, placing George in Lucas's arms. He smirked and slowly batted his lashes. Their toes touched. "Right, Daddy?"

"That's not my thing," Lucas said. Jack clicked his back teeth and snapped his fingers in the air, making Lucas laugh. "Are you—" He held George against his shoulder like a burping infant, and sniffed the air in front of Jack's bare chest. "—wearing women's perfume?"

"Chanel No. 5."

Lucas stepped back. "A male client asks you to wear it? Wait, is that…." He blinked twice, the memory of too much pale ale still bitter on the back of his tongue. "You wore it at the gala. Is that… is that Mr. Carson's thing? Women's perfume?"

Jack turned away from him and picked up his shirt from the bed. The muscles framing his lower spine fluttered. "I normally wouldn't divulge any information about a client, but you know him, and he knows you know about our arrangement." He held his shirt out, fingers pinching the shoulders. "His wife used to wear it. She passed away a few years ago."

"I remember. I sent a fruit basket."

Jack glanced over his shoulder. "How generous of you."

"He has you wear his dead wife's perfume while you do, erm,"—Lucas shifted George to his other shoulder—"whatever you do with him?"

Jack's smirk softened as he carefully folded his shirt against his chest. "He said it reminds him of her. He likes it. Likes to smell it around the house."

"Does he call you her name?"

"No," Jack chuckled, laying his folded shirt on the bed bench. He faced Lucas with his hands on his bare hips; his jeans rode low enough to reveal a hint of brown hair. "It's not like that. I think it's a comfort thing. She was a really lovely woman."

"You knew her?" Lucas asked, shocked.

"I did. I met her before I met him. She actually set me up with him when she knew she was dying."

"What?"

Jack unzipped his jeans, lowering them in one easy motion. He stood up straight. Lucas stared at the ceiling. "She knew she'd be leaving him, so she wanted to make sure someone would be there for him. Someone whom she liked. Their kids are not very involved. They've got families of their own."

"So, she picked a prostitute? A gay prostitute?"

Jack kicked his jeans aside. "She liked me and so did he. It worked out for everyone." He placed his hands on the waistband of his black briefs, his hip dents flexing. "I think the kettle's on."

"Huh?"

Jack quirked his hip. "Kettle." He started to roll the waistband down, swaying his right hip up, then his left. "Unless"—he pushed the material below his arse—"you want to see the goods?"

"Kettle, right," Lucas said, tearing his eyes away from Jack's thighs. He blinked rapidly; the kettle howled in the kitchen. "Yes. Right."

Lucas turned away to the sound of Jack's sniggers.

"Hey," Lucas said, pulling a sock off his ear.

Jack threw the other sock at him. Lucas swatted at it and glared over his shoulder.

"Only one more thing to throw." The thick base of Jack's cock was revealed. "You sure you don't want a peek?"

Lucas fixed him with a bored stare. "Please refrain from flashing anyone on holiday."

"Even you?"

Lucas stepped into the hallway and sucked in a gulp of fresh air. "Especially me," he said, leaving Jack to snicker in the guest room.

When Jack returned to the kitchen after his shower, Lucas was peering into a white ceramic teapot, two bags of Yorkshire tea floating inside. "Good shower?"

Jack said, "Yup," and sat at the island, swaying his bare feet underneath the padded leather stool. "Excellent pressure."

Lucas looked up and stared at him. He placed the lid on the teapot. "Are you naked right now?"

"Nope." Jack propped his chin on his palm. "I promise I've got pants on. I sleep naked, though. Just a warning."

"Congratulations. We have separate beds in our hotel. I couldn't care less how you sleep."

"You mean you don't want to wake up to my sausage up against your arse every morning? A full English wake-up call?"

"Oh my God," Lucas laughed, holding his hand to his upper stomach. "Already with the sausage jokes? We're not even there yet."

"I've been practicing."

Lucas laughed again, the sound bubbling uncontrollably out of him, and then placed a mug in front of Jack. A bowl with tiny sugar cubes and a small glass pitcher of milk rested on the island. Lucas picked up the pitcher. "I don't know how you take it. This is whole milk, but I've got semi in the fridge, if you prefer."

Jack watched Lucas pour a splash of milk into his empty white mug before placing the pitcher in front of him on the countertop. "Whole is fine. Thanks."

Lucas stirred his tea. "This is decaf, which almost eliminates the purpose of tea, but I figured being wired would not be good for either of us."

Jack nodded. "Good thinking. We have an early morning."

They sipped in silence. Football highlights quietly played on the telly in the living room, and toenails clicked closer on the hardwood. George bounded into the kitchen and went to his water bowl; his tiny tongue licked ripples into the smooth surface. Lucas smiled around his mug. George's little bum and tail wiggled with excitement, and his flat nose snorted as he drank.

"I should take him out one more time before bed," Lucas said, licking tea off the corner of his mouth. He looked to Jack and Jack immediately dropped his eyes to his mug. Lucas frowned. "What?"

"Nothing."

"You're smiling. What?"

Jack sipped his tea. "Nothing. Just…. Your eyes crinkle sometimes when you smile." He spun his mug once on the island. "It's cute."

"Oh," Lucas said, the single word pure and high.

Jack broke their stare to look down. "Wow, Georgie. You're a leg guy? Me too, mate, me too."

LUCAS RAN around the counter. George was happily humping Jack's ankle. Lucas let out a horrified cry and bent over, bundling the pup into his arms. "Fucking hell." His amusement sneaked into his attempt at a stern voice. Jack's abs scrunched as he laughed softly. "What's the matter with him? He's obsessed with you."

"Most men are. Some women too."

Lucas scoffed, still snorting. "I'll take him out. Maybe the walk will calm him down."

Jack swayed his feet below his stool. "Is that what you do to calm yourself down?"

Lucas tilted his chin. "Ha-ha," he deadpanned, walking to the door. He slipped his bare feet into a pair of black Toms and took George's leash off the wall. Lucas pulled a plastic bag out of a container hanging on the leash hook. The crinkling of plastic seemed to signal something to George, who started to yelp and wiggle in Lucas's arms. "I'll be right back."

"Okay."

Lucas brought his eyes to Jack's face as he clipped the leash to George's collar. "You can practice your sausage jokes."

"Okay." Jack watched Lucas lower George to the floor and pat his sweats, making his keys jingle in his pocket. "Hey, Luke?"

Lucas turned toward him as George jetted out the open door with his leash straight and tight. "Yeah?"

Jack stood from the kitchen stool, revealing that he was not naked, but wearing a small pair of dark gray briefs that hit below his hips. Lucas's throat bobbed as he wondered if anyone could see in through his wall of windows at that very moment. There he was, short and covered in sweats, while Jack strode toward him like some sort of modern god, his long limbs and lean muscles all moving as one to transport his tall form closer and closer.

"Did you get that guard fired?" Jack's bare feet padded, near silent, on the hardwood; he held his hands relaxed at his sides. "Nathan?"

Lucas's tongue flickered over his bottom lip, their eyes never breaking contact. "I did."

Jack's features pinched slightly inward. "Why?"

"Because he was rude to you," Lucas said simply, as if it were the most obvious answer in the world. "Unacceptable."

"Me? You mean your fake boyfriend slash escort?" Jack chuckled, widening his eyes and scratching the back of his hair. "Quite a fuss for someone like me."

"Don't speak of yourself that way," Lucas said softly, his brows furrowed. "Your job does not measure your worth. Being an escort is not who you are. You're a human, and a seemingly decent one, at that. You deserve to be treated with respect and kindness."

Jack's gaze dropped to the floor. His long toes curled against the hardwood.

Lucas could feel George tugging at the leash and hear his frantic breaths panting into the silent air. "Besides," Lucas said, his voice regaining its normal tone, "in addition to being rude to you, he divulged something private about me to a stranger. I pay far too much to live in this overpriced glass box to deal with that. I won't stand for that sort of unprofessionalism. People should be allowed privacy in their own home, no matter how their doorman feels about their chosen activities or bedmates."

Jack nodded once, his fingertips brushing the outside of his thighs. "I agree."

Lucas's arm was tugged straight by George's leash. "Good."

"But—" Jack ran his fingers through his damp hair; its ends hung wet against his shoulders. "—But what if he had a family?" Lucas's head tilted at his question. Jack stepped closer and dropped his arm. "He was unprofessional, yeah, but what if he has a family to support? And now he's unemployed?"

"Aw, kitten. Your heart must be on the same level as your sausage."

A pout wrinkled Jack's forehead. "Was that a riddle?"

"Research, love."

The pout dissolved, Jack's eyes going round. "What do you mean?"

"He's divorced. No children. He cheats regularly on his girlfriend of two months. He posts horrific sexist, homophobic, transphobic, and racist messages on public online forums for guns, sometimes while logged into the computer at the security desk, all of which I was able to find out in three minutes at his computer." Lucas curled his lips as if he sipped sour milk. "The elderly truly don't understand how to lock down their online presence."

Jack inhaled and tucked his thumbs against his palms. He watched Lucas pull a treat from his pocket, a tiny brown biscuit in the shape of a chicken leg, and bend over to hand it to George.

"Did you interrogate him in the bonsai garden downstairs or something?" Jack crossed his hands in front of his groin. He placed his clasped fingers flush to his cock. The motion drew Lucas's attention to the tight, slightly tented material. "Is that how you found all this out?"

Lucas stood up straight and brushed his hand over his sweats. "I'd never sully the bonsai garden with such filth. He told me all of this himself. Happily. All it took was a simple conversation and a few well-placed comments for him to start blabbering."

"Sometimes that's all it takes," Jack said, his voice quiet. "A sense of security and an open ear."

Lucas nodded slowly. "You were right."

"About?"

"We're very similar, you and I."

Jack grinned, the motion of his lips slow. He ran his fingers through the back of his hair as one knee bent in to touch the other. Goose bumps prickled over his entire body. "Oh," he said, his voice shivering with unsung laughter.

"Oh?"

"Thank you." They locked gazes; a wave of hair fell over Jack's eyes. Softer, he said, "I meant to say thank you, but an *oh* came out, so…." He swallowed and pushed his hair back. "Thank you."

"For?"

"For saying that. For doing that. And…." He bit his bottom lip and laid his hand flat on his abs. He rubbed up to his chest. "For thinking the way you do. About… about how humans should be treated."

They stared at each other. Jack's chest heaved visibly beneath his flat palm as Lucas's eyes traced the flushed skin beneath his long, spread fingers. The hollow of his throat was damp with sweat and his other hand was clenched in front of his groin.

"You're welcome," Lucas said, his tone as simple as his regular delivery. His eyes snapped back to Jack's face. "You're very welcome."

"I wish there were more people like you in the world."

Lucas's lips twitched. "We'll see how you feel in ten days."

"I don't think ten days of seeing you half-naked and oiled up is going to change my opinion for the worse."

True shock emerged on Lucas's face. Jack's cheeks burned bright red and he pressed his hand tighter to his groin. Lucas let his gaze float down Jack's body and back up within half a second; his eyes were blazing but still gentle.

"Is that so?" Lucas's voice was half there.

"Right. I, um." Jack chuckled breathily and started to walk backward. The fronts of his thighs flexed as he lifted himself up on the balls of his bare feet. He thumbed over his shoulder and his nightingale stretched. "I'm gonna go get ready for bed."

Lucas nodded. "All right."

"Have a nice—Ouch," Jack said at the same volume as his speaking voice, bumping into the island and his body rolling sideways. Lucas's lips curled into a smirk. "Have a fun walk with Georgie."

Lucas's arm jutted out due to George pulling on the leash. "We will."

Jack let out another breathless sound and turned away. He glanced over his shoulder to find Lucas still staring at him, his expression unreadable. Jack half laughed and padded away, rubbing the back of his neck. The guest room door nicked shut behind him.

JACK FINISHED up his nighttime routine, then wandered from room to room. He was not usually a snooper, but he couldn't sit still, even after washing and moisturizing his face, brushing his teeth, and stretching out on his cloud of a bed.

He checked out the other guest room. It was decorated almost exactly like his own, but the color scheme was based around the colors turquoise and sandy taupe. He had seen Lucas's bedroom before; that room didn't require a stop on his tour.

He returned to the open-plan living room and kitchen. He opened the fridge and saw a shorter stack of labeled meals, plus three different containers of milk, two eggs in one carton and four eggs in another carton, and a half-eaten block of sharp cheddar hastily wrapped in foil.

"Nice balanced diet," he said, closing the fridge. He opened the pantry and smirked. He pushed a mountain of crisp packets aside to reveal multiple jars of peanut butter and Nutella. "Very balanced."

Lucas's living room was fairly boring, save for the amazing view of the city. The white apple of a MacBook Air glowed on the glass coffee table; the television remote lay wedged between the cushions of his buttery leather sofa.

Jack took the remote out and switched channels until he found *Marvel's Agents of S.H.I.E.L.D.* He tossed the remote on the sofa. The sofa was dented in on the right side cushion near the arm. The dent was diagonal, as if Lucas liked to sit sideways with his feet on the middle of the coffee table. There was a smaller dent on the left side of the couch, large enough to accommodate George's pudgy body.

He looked away from the sofa dents and went back into the kitchen. He grabbed their empty cups from the counter and went to the sink. He was placing the clean teapot in a stainless steel drying rack when he heard the lift ping.

LUCAS WALKED out of the lift with George proudly leading the way. He bent over and picked the puppy up, and George lavished his neck with licks. Lucas hugged him to his chest. "Mate, I know he's scorching hot, but you've got to tone it down," he whispered in George's ear. "Consent is key in our house. You can't just go around humping everyone you find attractive."

He looked at George's scrunched little pug face. The dog snorted as if to ask "Why not?"

Lucas sighed, "Good question."

George resumed his licks. Lucas opened the door to his flat and lowered George to the floor, kneeling in front of him. "Glad to see the walk calmed you down," Lucas said, struggling to unclip the leash from George's collar. "All right, all right, mate."

Jack happily cried, "Is that my Georgie?"

George took off the second he was free.

Lucas stood up but swayed on his feet. His stomach lurched upward and intruded on the space meant for his lungs. "Is everything…."

Jack smiled at Lucas from the kitchen while drying his hands on a towel. George ran in circles around his bare feet. Their mugs were lined up next to each other in the drying rack.

"Is everything what?" Jack asked, shifting his weight and quirking his hip. George slid on his stomach and bumped into his ankle. Jack chuckled and bent over. He took him in his arms, cradling him against his chest and scratching behind his ears. "Welcome back."

"Is… is everything with your room all right?" Lucas placed his hand on the wall, toeing his Toms off. He swallowed down a dry patch in the lowest part of his throat. "Are you ready for bed? I mean"—he scrunched his eyes—"is everything all right? Do you need anything?"

"No, I'm good, thanks."

Lucas dropped his keys on a narrow black table beside the door. "All right, then."

Jack lowered George to the floor, but the puppy whined and sat on top of his foot, panting up at him.

"Go to Papa," Jack said quietly, swaying his hands toward Lucas. He stepped backward and George followed, plopping on his feet again. "It's bedtime."

Lucas went into the living room and picked up the remote. "Shit, I forgot to watch that tonight," he whispered to himself, turning *S.H.I.E.L.D.* off. He went into the kitchen and saw Jack hopping from foot to foot, with George attempting to keep up but mostly sliding on his belly from spot to spot. "I'm going to head to bed, but you can stay up and watch telly or whatever."

"Nah. I need to sleep too." Jack huffed and made his longest jump yet. George scampered after him. He giggled, with his face toward the panting dog. "I'm tired."

Lucas watched Jack's long legs jump side to side, his muscled torso following each graceful sway. "Yeah, looks like it."

Jack grinned at him, with his hair tumbled over in his eyes. He pushed his hair off his forehead and scrunched his face in a serious expression. He waved one stiff finger at George. "All right, Georgie. Time for bed. Get serious."

George stared up at him, motionless. A tiny, high-pitched fart came from beneath the dog's bum.

"Oh my God," Lucas groaned, moving toward George. "You've rendered him completely stupid." That sent Jack into heartier laughs, his arm shooting out to grip the island as Lucas chuckled and lifted George. "I swear, he was a very bright, normal dog before he met you."

Jack's laughter calmed and his eyes sparkled with tears. He petted George's head. "He's still a very bright, normal dog—farts and raging libido and all." Lucas chuckled, thumbing over George's ribs. "Hey," Jack said, brushing his fingers against Lucas's as they petted the dog. "Where is he going when we're gone?" His eyes sagged. "Does he stay here alone the whole time?"

"Nah. He goes to this doggie spa place."

"Lucky Georgie."

"He loves it there. If I was only going to be gone a day or two, I'd have David, his dog walker, come over to care for him. But since we're going for over a week, he gets to stay at the spa. He even has friends that'll be there from this dog park we go to. We're all on a mailing list for dog hangouts."

"Is his e-mail georgieboy@mostadorablepuppyofalltime.com?"

"Dot org, actually."

Jack snuffled.

Lucas asked, "If you sleep with him in your room, do you mind keeping the door open a crack? He's usually fine through the night, and he just went out, but on the off chance he needs to go out again, I'd rather him be able to get out of the room and find me."

"Yeah, of course. Sure." Jack nodded. "I can take him out too, if you want."

"That's all right. He usually sleeps like a rock, but I'll leave my door ajar, just in case."

"All right."

Jack broke their stare to look down at the pup cradled in his arms. George had his tongue hanging out the corner of his mouth as he stared, besotted, from his owner to his new best friend, and his stubby legs bobbed with each rub to his belly. Jack's voice was softer, gentler, as he asked, "Does that sound good, Georgie boy? A sleepover with me?"

"His name is George," Lucas said, smiling only a tiny, tiny bit.

Jack pulled George into his arms, cradling him against his chest. George started to lick the bottom of his neck. "I think he's a Georgie."

Lucas sighed and touched a panel on the kitchen wall that dimmed the lights of the entire main space. "I know a lost battle when I see one." They started to walk toward the bedrooms. "All right. Well…." Lucas swallowed. "Good night."

Jack opened his mouth to say good night but froze as Lucas's lips tenderly pressed to his cheekbone. "Oh," he said, the sound popping out of his mouth. "Um."

"Sorry. Shit, I'm—" Lucas stepped back and held his hands out in front of him. "That—that was so weird. That was weird, right?" He shook his head, grimacing. "I shouldn't have done that." He rubbed his hand over his nose, muttering, "I'm as bad as Georgie."

"No, it's—it was fine," Jack said with wide eyes, stepping closer. "It wasn't weird. It was good. It—we're probably going to do that in front of people, like, that kind of kiss. It's good practice."

Before Lucas could reply, Jack swooped down and kissed his right cheek, kissing closer to his temple with gentle pressure. Lucas's hair smelled of a sporty, basic shampoo that a uni student would buy because it was the cheapest in the store, but his skin felt like velvet, as if he bathed in the luxury skincare products a uni student could never dream of purchasing. Jack kissed his left cheekbone. Lucas kissed Jack's jawline once, his slight stubble rough on Jack's skin.

"Right," Lucas sounded strained, "it's…." His half-lidded eyes landed on Jack's mouth. "It's good—"

Jack bent down as Lucas lifted himself on the balls of his feet. Their lips met in the middle. A fizzle of bright light nipped at the base of Lucas's neck, and tendrils of heat teased up to the top of his brain.

Their lips pressed together, closed but firm. Their eyes met and Jack started to laugh silently. Lucas smiled and ducked his face down. Jack chased after him, offering his puffy lips to Lucas's mouth.

"—practice," Jack finished for him. "Like… we…."

Lucas's hand molded around Jack's hip and he lifted his other hand to Jack's hair. Jack wilted down again and their mouths softly sucked together. Georgie squirmed, squished between their chests. Jack's back bumped into the wall, Lucas's toes nudged his own, and they took turns kissing each other's cheeks.

"Practice," Lucas murmured, his voice barely audible.

Jack held the dog with one arm but looped his other arm around Lucas's lower back. Lucas kissed the corner of his lips. Jack's head tilted to bring their lips together, and Lucas exhaled a hot breath.

With their lips tenderly pressed together, Jack let out a soft whimper and linked his foot behind Lucas's ankle. Lucas slid his palm down the damp skin of Jack's lower back. When Lucas reached his arse, his hand curled around the plump mound of his right arsecheek. Jack made a needier, throatier whimper, air running through his moans, and he arched his hips forward.

Then Lucas stepped back and Jack's warmth was gone.

"All right, then. Good night," Lucas said, conversational in tempo but frantic in pitch. He flattened his back to the wall on the opposite side of the hallway. Jack blinked at him. "See you in the morning, bright and early."

Lucas kept his gaze on Jack's doe-eyed, round-lipped face, though his peripheral vision could not ignore the tightened gray fabric stretched over Jack's bulge. He swirled his hand in the air and babbled, "Good practice. I mean, good night. Yeah. Thanks." Lucas nodded and started to slide along the wall, with wide side steps. "All well? Good. Yes. Good night."

"Night," Jack said, licking his shining lips. The highest points of his cheekbones were pink. A flush was visible on the center of his chest and the skin just above his waistband. "Yeah, we'll, um…" He swallowed and shifted George in his arms. "We'll see you tomorrow."

Lucas nodded and pushed off the wall, walking quickly to his bedroom. He didn't turn around to watch Jack go into the guest room. He could feel Jack's stare as he closed the door, leaving it open a tiny crack. He went to his bed, stood on the end, spread his arms, and belly flopped into his pillows, letting out a weak scream. He curled into the tightest ball he could manage, clutching a pillow to his chest.

He contemplated smothering himself but decided against it, instead going into his en-suite and following his bedtime routine. He rid himself of his clothes, crawled into bed, then took a deep breath and stared up at the ceiling, exhaling a smooth line through his lips.

"All right. Sleep."

He shut his eyes and wiggled lower under the heavy covers. His nose twitched and he slid his feet against the cool sheets. There was a quiet sound from the hallway and Lucas's eyes opened. It could be the building settling, or the ventilation blowing air through his flat, or Jack turning over in bed. He would never know.

From then on, every small sound he thought he heard caused his eyes to pop open, and he tossed and turned in bed. He fumbled to open his bedside table drawer and pulled out his emergency flask, a small silver bottle. He brought it to his lips and chugged. Liquor stung the back of his throat.

He placed the flask in the drawer and lay back. Staring up at the ceiling, he ran his tongue over his teeth.

"Vodka's sterile," he reasoned aloud, slapping his lips together. "Don't need to clean my teeth again. Nope."

He sighed and turned onto his stomach, falling into a weak sleep.

After mere moments, the sound of music pinged his ears. He opened his eyes, despite the grogginess that had finally started to pull at him, and swung his legs over the edge of the bed. He padded out of his bedroom and down the hall. The music became clearer the closer he got to Jack's room.

Lucas stood outside the door for a moment and listened to the sound of a flute and a brash voice singing, the volume low but audible from outside the cracked door. He knocked gently. There was no answer. He pushed the door open enough to peek inside as strings started to tremble, and a sweeter voice sang into the room.

In the center of the bed, Jack had curled on his right side with the white duvet at around shoulder height. His hair formed a wavy halo on the white pillows. The remote control had fallen to the floor beside the bed. George was a tight ball against his chest, wheezing snuffly dog snores into the front of Jack's long neck. George's leg twitched in his sleep.

The television was on and playing *Cinderella*, the last DVD Lucas had put in the flat-screen when Maggie had slept over. Light and colors flickered over Jack's motionless body and sleep-slackened face as the music swelled to female voices singing in perfect harmony. Something warm surged in Lucas's belly as their voices grew.

Lucas stepped into the room to turn off the television but stopped with his hand on the button. The colorful bubble part was always his favorite.

He looked at Jack for one more long beat, taking in the shadows cast over his high cheekbones. Jack's lashes shivered involuntarily. His full lips were puffed forward and a sleepy flush darkened his skin like a fever. Lucas thought back to the first time he'd seen Jack, then the second, then the third, trying to catalog all his expressions and looks, just as he'd catalog facts about a client to help keep his blood pressure low, to give him an edge when negotiating.

As the song came to its abrupt end, due to a mean cat making a mess of Cinderella's clean floor, Lucas watched Jack's bare back swell and sink. Jack might have a goofy laughing face, but he looked like Disney royalty when he slept, fair and lovely and gentle.

A combination of jealousy—Lucas was a mouth breather who drooled while he slept—and endearment flooded his body. Jack shrugged his shoulder and moved his feet under the covers. The small motion fully pushed endearment past jealousy in the race for how he felt at that moment.

Lucas turned off the television and backed out of the dark room. The simple melody of the nightingale's song, and Jack's soft, even breaths, floated in his ears.

Chapter TEN

Saturday, April 25

JACK LET his head drop back on the plush cushion of his chair. His silky white shirt fell open to reveal his left nipple, the top of his abs, and his long neck stretched backward. He pulled black aviators over his eyes, his shiny hair tumbling down the sides of his face.

"Why did we have to fly so early?" Jack asked around a yawn. Another yawn overtook him and his tongue extended sideways out of his mouth. "So early. Single digits are far too severe for a wake-up call."

Lucas chuckled and kept his eyes on his iPad. His foot swayed his brown leather flip-flop in the air. If he was going someplace warm, he planned on wearing as little footwear as possible, though he still wore dark jeans and a gray long-sleeved tee for the journey. A burgundy hoodie, zipped up halfway, completed his ensemble, with a gray beanie pulled over his hair.

"Too early for you, Mr. McQueen?"

"There's a reason I'm a gentleman of the night, emphasis on night."

"Poor kitten. I'm up this early every day with my trainer."

"I weep for your future spouse," Jack said dryly. "Morning sex all but eliminated for the sake of physical fitness."

Lucas glanced Jack's way, still scrolling over his iPad. Jack's limbs were artfully draped over his chair, one arm covered his eyes, and his legs were spread wide. Lucas stared at his exposed nipple for a moment. "Why did you dress like a B-list celebrity from the early nineties?" He looked back at his iPad. "We're going to the Bahamas, not the land before time."

Jack grinned and arched his back. "It's called style, love."

Lucas's shoulders bobbed with a quiet laugh. He refocused on his reading as more people settled around them in the British Airways VIP lounge. Jack wondered if London Heathrow ever had a quiet moment.

"Besides," Jack said as he propped his hands behind his head and his sleeves slunk down his biceps, "I thought the first thing isn't until the barbecue dinner on the beach? Why the rush?"

Lucas quirked a brow. "Memorized the itinerary, did we?"

"I'm nothing if not a prepared professional."

Lucas looked at him. The soft brown hair under Jack's arms contrasted with the white silkiness of his shirt; the roundness of his biceps contrasted with the delicate, pale skin on the undersides of his wrists. Lucas locked his iPad and crossed his legs. "I want to have time to get settled. I want you to be able to get settled before we have to meet everyone. We have our own unofficial itinerary before the official one begins."

Jack slid his sunglasses into his hair, leaning an arm on his chair and turning toward Lucas. "What do you mean?"

"I thought you, erm, *we* could use some relaxation before what will surely be a week from karaoke craft hell." Lucas ruffled the back of his hair, still damp from his shower. "This last merger about killed me, and I've been sleeping pretty poorly this whole week. I need to unwind before facing my family, or it won't be pretty."

"Why didn't you say anything last night?"

Lucas rolled his head on the back of his seat. "About what?"

Jack sat up straighter and leaned closer. "About not feeling well after work. I wouldn't have kept you up so late."

Lucas used his pointer finger to scratch the side of his neck. "It's all right. We went to bed early enough. I'm glad we talked and played with Georgie." He looked straight ahead, his fingers whirling over the front of his throat. "That helped me unwind, actually. Was good."

"Oooh," Jack drawled, fluctuating his pitch.

Lucas's fingers paused. "What?"

"You called him Georgie," Jack said, grinning slowly. He widened his eyes. "My master plan has come to fruition."

Lucas sighed in exasperation as Jack nudged his boot against his ankle. They stared at each other for a moment, and flashes of their morning raced through Lucas's head.

He remembered Jack walking around for the majority of their morning with only a towel around his waist, a smaller towel looped around his hair. George happily chased after Jack as he went from room to room with ease, filling the kettle and using Lucas's cologne and refilling George's water bowl and suggesting that Lucas not bother with his hair because it looked sweet messy and it was so bloody early.

That montage was replaced by watching Jack get down on his knees to hug George tightly in his arms, both Jack and George making soft, sad sounds to each other before they left the flat.

"So." Jack nudged his ankle again. "What's the plan?"

Lucas's eyes snapped to attention. "We should get to the resort by around noon their time, well before most of the other guests have arrived. I, uh…." He licked his lips, glancing away. "I booked us massages in the spa." Jack made a tiny, happy noise beside him. "Plus lunch in a private beachfront cabana." The happy noise was louder; Lucas was able to hear Jack's clothes shifting. "I wasn't sure what to order for us, but thanks to your quite thorough client welcome e-mail, I know you like healthy stuff, so there should be plenty of fresh fruit and vegetables for you. Maybe we can even have a swim before facing the masses."

Lucas looked back at Jack as Jack's mouth opened, his eyes scrunched, and his chin tilted.

"That…." Jack's mouth closed. "That was really nice of you to do."

Lucas rubbed his hand over the back of his neck. "Um, I could only manage to get us in the couple's room. For the massages, I mean. Is that okay? Are you comfortable with that? They were fully booked, otherwise."

Jack thought for a moment, his stare leaving paths of heat over Lucas's face. "You mean I might get a glimpse of that arse during this trip after all?"

Lucas's cheeks pinked but he smirked, facing forward. "Don't you see enough arses in your daily life?"

"Quality, not quantity, love." Jack bumped their shoulders together, prompting a snuffled sound from Lucas.

Lucas checked his watch. "Wanna walk around a bit?" He rolled his ankles. "I need to stretch my legs. Might get a tea, as well. We've got some time before boarding."

"Sure," Jack said, uncrossing his legs. "I could use a latte. Maybe a scone too."

Lucas's brows arched. "A latte? And carbs? Not a green juice or some sort of grassy substance?"

"Normally, you'd be right, but seeing as this is a no-sex, no-nude-pool-party sort of holiday, I plan on eating my way through the Bahamas." Jack rubbed his flat stomach. "The airport is included in our holiday."

Lucas hummed as they shouldered their carry-on bags—his was a brown leather duffel, while Jack's was a black Tom Ford bag shaped almost like a doctor's tote. They wandered toward the duty-free shops, blaring lights bouncing off the white tile and walls. They started in a shop with walls of high-end liquor.

"I don't understand why you're on a diet to begin with." Lucas replaced a bottle of scotch on a shelf. He peered at Jack through a row of clear vodka bottles. "You get plenty of physical activity."

Jack's face was warped by the glass. "It's not so much a diet as I feel better when I watch my carbs and sugar. I eat whatever I want, but usually I want salads and stuff. I listen to what my body tells me."

"How Zen."

"Someone wise, or who *thinks* he's wise, once said I was the Buddha of hookers. I'm merely living up to my reputation."

They laughed from either side of the row of bottles.

"You're such a liar." Lucas dragged his fingertips on the front of the shelf as he walked. "Who actually wants a salad? Next thing you'll tell me is that you love working out."

Jack appeared at the end of the row, chirping, "I do!"

Lucas snorted and joined him. They moved on to a shop full of scarves.

"Dunno how you do it," Lucas said, poking at a leopard scarf. "Carbs and sugar are my favorite."

"Yeah, I noticed." Jack moved toward a clothing rack at the front of the shop. He pulled a paisley scarf out, running his fingers over the fabric. "You've got enough crisps and Nutella in your flat to last through the apocalypse."

Lucas appeared at the rack of scarves. "Excuse me, but were you snooping? How unprofessional."

"Maybe. Maybe you're too trusting."

Lucas moved to Jack's side of the rack and halfheartedly started to pick through the scarves. "How so?"

"You left me alone in your flat. What if I stole something? What if I was a spy?"

"A sp-spy?" Lucas sputtered. His eyes crinkled from across the scarf display. "Please. You'd make a sexy spy, I'm sure, but I'm far too boring for anyone to want information about me."

"Is that what you're into? Role play?"

"Not quite, Captain Jack."

They moved on to a display of men's shirts, each print more flowery than the last.

"Still"—Jack's long fingers danced over the padded hangers—"I'm a stranger, and you left me alone in your flat. You don't know what I'm capable of."

Lucas pinched the bottom of one shirt; its pattern was a rainbow of floral print. "Did you steal anything?"

"No, of course not."

Lucas let the shirt flutter down from his fingers. "Good. That's what I thought you'd say."

Jack followed Lucas as they walked into a shop full of expensive watches. “It is?”

Lucas glanced over his shoulder without actually looking at Jack.

“You haven’t given me any reason not to trust you. I tend to have a pretty good instinct about bad eggs.” He did a slow scan over Jack’s bare chest before landing on his face. “Unique fashion choices aside, I don’t believe you’re a bad egg.” He gave Jack a small smile. “I trust you.”

Lucas strolled down the line of watches.

Jack stood motionless in front of the row of glittering boxes. Light reflected off the glass case, brightening the green of his eyes. He glanced outside the shop.

“Uh, there’s a cafe.” he said, his voice deeper than usual. He flattened his hand on the front of his throat, tilting his head out the door once Lucas looked his way. “I’m gonna get a drink. Do you want anything? Tea?”

“I think I’ll actually wait until we’re on the plane, but thanks for asking.” Lucas reached into his pocket. “How much do you—”

Jack’s hand wrapped around Lucas’s wrist. “No,” he said softly, shaking his head. Lucas stared at his hand on his wrist, bringing his eyes up to Jack’s face. “No money needed. I’ve got it.”

“You sure?”

“Yeah, it’s fine.” Jack let go of his wrist. The hot pads of his fingers left near-invisible white fingerprints on Lucas’s wrist. “Thanks, though.”

Lucas relaxed his arm at his side, nodding once. “All right.”

Jack looked at Lucas’s mouth, at his tongue smoothing over the inside of his bottom lip. He leaned down with a slow, growing smile, and Lucas’s eyes widened. Jack’s head swayed left at the last minute, his lips pressing against Lucas’s cheek. Lucas’s head tilted involuntarily toward him. Their cheeks were warm pressed together, and Jack kissed the strong line of his jaw.

“I’ll meet you in the lounge, okay?” he whispered, fingering the tender inside of Lucas’s wrist. “Text me if you change your mind.”

Lucas nodded, breathing in at the same time as he attempted to say, “Okay, cool.” It came out as a hollow, raspy sound, and Jack grinned slightly. Lucas’s chest rose and fell. “Okay,” Lucas repeated, clearing his throat, “cool.”

Jack pecked his cheek, faster and more playful. “I’ll be back. Don’t have too much fun without me.”

Lucas watched him walk away. Jack slid his sunglasses over his eyes before throwing a look over his shoulder. His teeth sparkled as he grinned at Lucas. He wiggled his fingers; Lucas exhaled and, ducking his head down, focused on the ticking watches in front of him.

When Lucas returned to the lounge ten minutes later, Jack was nowhere to be found. The lounge was filling up. Passengers were drinking flutes of fizzy champagne, even at the early hour, and glasses of colorful juices. There were also a number of flight attendants behind the boarding desk, chatting with each other in their neat uniforms.

He checked his watch. They still had some time before boarding, but Jack's absence lit a hint of worry in his gut. His feet itched to run laps around the airport.

He watched a small boy push a toy car across the floor, weaving the car around his parents' shoes. His parents watched him as they spoke with another couple beside them. After ten round-trip car rides, Lucas pulled his phone out of his pocket and typed a text to Jack.

On your way back to the lounge? I know the scarves were very pretty, but they're not nearly pirate-y enough to cause you to miss the flight.

Jack replied within seconds.

I can't believe you typed out the word pirate-y. St Andrews has burst into flames. Cambridge is a pile of smoldering ashes.

A proud grin lifted Lucas's lips, his fingers tapping on his screen.

Very descriptive. Did you get lost in a library? The squares with scribbles inside are called books.

Jack's next message did not come through, nor did the small bubble appear to indicate he was typing. Lucas looked up from his phone, scanning the lounge. His mouth scrunched to the side. Still no sign of Jack.

"Ladies and gentlemen," a female flight attendant said into a microphone. "Good morning and welcome to Flight BA0253 to Nassau, Bahamas…."

Lucas tuned her announcement out as his thumbs tapped against the sides of his phone. He crossed his left leg over his right, then switched legs, then flattened both feet on the floor. He sent another text to Jack.

Not to rush whatever you're doing, but I think they're going to begin boarding soon.

When no response came through, Lucas stood up and shouldered his carry-on. He left the lounge and did a quick check of the stores they had wandered through, but there was still no sign of Jack. Lucas glanced up at a flat-screen displaying boarding gates, and frowned. Their flight was very close to the top of the list.

On a last-ditch effort, he went into the men's room just outside the lounge. He walked from stall to stall. A quiet moan sounded in the echoey space. Lucas's brows rose. His feet remained frozen in place.

"Um, Jack?"

Boots shuffled on the floor, followed by a loud sigh.

"What are you doing in here?" Jack asked.

"Oh, thank God," Lucas said, leaning his bum on the counter. He crossed his arms over his chest. "I was worried you got lost or something. What are you doing?"

There was a pause. A humorless laugh was exhaled behind the stall door.

"I'm… in a restroom. Sitting on a toilet. What do you think I'm doing, painting my toenails?"

"No need to get touchy." Lucas smiled, tilting his head. "You should be honored I came looking for you." With a quiet huff that carried through the door, he watched Jack's boots shuffle again. "I could have left you here to…."

The automatic flush went off in the empty stall in front of him. Realization dawned on Lucas; it pulled a sudden, loud gasp from the deepest point of his gut. His hand flew to his mouth. "Oh my God," he laughed through his fingers.

Jack whined, "Please, just get out. I'll be there in a minute."

"Why didn't you say so?"

"I know we have an unconventional relationship, but I don't inform my friends of my toilet habits," Jack said, sounding more frustrated. "Could I please get some privacy?"

Lucas held his fingers in front of himself, using his thumbnail to push down a cuticle. "What if I wanted to leisurely wash my hands?"

"Lucas."

"All right, all right," Lucas said, backing toward the door. "I'll leave you be. A man needs his dignity."

"Thank you," Jack sighed deeply. Relief was evident in his voice. His boots shuffled. "I'll be there in a minute, I promise."

Lucas left the restroom and went back to the lounge, stopping in a few shops on the way. He placed his carry-on on the seat beside him and pulled out his phone, scanning through some e-mails. He sensed a tall figure standing in front of his carry-on and removed it from the chair without looking up. Muscled thighs swayed in his peripheral vision as Jack sat down. Jack rested his black bag against Lucas's ankle.

"Welcome back," Lucas said without looking up. His foot bobbed at the end of his crossed leg. "Good latte?"

"Fine."

"And your scone?"

"Also fine."

Lucas pocketed his phone. He rubbed his hand in a circle over his own stomach. "And your wee little tum-tum?"

"We're not talking about that," Jack said, adjusting his sunglasses on the bridge of his nose. He snapped his gum in the back of his teeth, staring straight ahead. "Ever."

"Ah. All right." Lucas nodded, studying his serious profile. "I suppose you were right, though."

"Wh—" Jack pursed his lips to speak, then paused. He steeled his face and ground out, "Don't."

Lucas continued, "You should have—"

"Don't," Jack repeated.

"You should have brought your enemas after all."

"I absolutely hate you." Jack's voice trembled, a smile plumping his rosy cheeks. "I hate you."

"Oh, pishposh, love." Lucas placed a bottle of ginger ale on the small table between their seats. "Everybody has a stomach and the issues that come with it." He dropped a packet of Pepto-Bismol tabs on Jack's lap. "I hope you're not getting sick, though. Kind of fast for a scone to upset your stomach."

Jack's voice dropped, mortification deepening his tone. "I also had a hash brown from McDonald's. Maybe two. Or three."

Lucas started to giggle, and it quickly grew to a head-thrown-back, stomach-clutching sort of belly laugh.

"Oh, fuck off," Jack mumbled good-naturedly, chewing his Pepto tabs. "I was hungry."

"Three at once? I'm impressed."

"They were buy one, get one free. Plus, the lady behind the counter said I had a beautiful smile, so she gave me an extra."

"Awww," Lucas drawled, grinning at Jack, his voice jumping. "That's actually sweet. And now it makes sense. Those are so good. I don't blame you."

Jack tucked his hair behind his ears with both hands as a bright flush spread over his neck and cheeks.

"Yeah, well, I couldn't take the grease, I guess." He rubbed his stomach, running his tongue over teeth. "I usually don't even like that stuff, but they smelled amazing. Next thing you know, I felt like I was having a gallbladder attack or something. I felt actual pain in my stomach. It was awful."

Lucas patted Jack's leg and rolled the back of his head on his chair. "Oh, Baby Mick. Your body led you in the wrong direction." Lucas's eyes narrowed. "Blasted, traitorous body."

Jack chuckled. He spread his leg closer to Lucas. He asked, "Been reading lots of those scribble squares?" Lucas pinched right above Jack's knee and Jack guffawed. "Oi," he said with a frantic look in his eyes. He started to giggle and pushed Lucas's hand away; Lucas grinned.

Their heads snapped forward at the sound of the female flight attendant's voice. Boarding would begin shortly.

Jack pushed his sunglasses up into his hair, and Lucas uncrossed his legs. Both checked their carry-ons for their passports and phones, pulling their boarding passes out of their wallets.

"Oh, yeah," Lucas said. "I got you this, in addition to the Pepto."

Jack looked up from his carry-on. "What did you get me?"

Lucas placed a small black gift bag on the table between them and stood up.

Jack tilted his head back to ask, "What is it?"

"I saw it and it made me think of you." Lucas shouldered his carry-on. He nudged the gift bag with his knuckles, pushing it closer to Jack. "Think of it as a thank-you for agreeing to this trip."

Jack stood and said, "You didn't have to get me anything," with confusion clouding his face.

"I didn't have to, no, but I wanted to. Now, hurry those giraffe legs up. We're about to board."

Jack picked up the bag. The heaviness of it made him frown. He carefully stuck his hand inside the black tissue paper and pulled out a box. Tom Ford Private Blend Tobacco Vanille Eau de Parfum. His mouth popped open as Lucas started to walk.

"Luke," Jack said, walking faster to catch up. He reached Lucas's side. "Lucas, this size bottle costs, like, two hundred pounds!"

Lucas smoothed wrinkles out of his boarding pass, holding the paper against his stomach. "And? Were you expecting a magnet? It was duty-free. I couldn't resist."

They got in line to board. Jack ran his fingers through his hair with his gaze on the box of cologne.

"No, I wasn't expecting anything," Jack said slowly. "But… you didn't have to do this."

They stepped up as the line moved. Lucas kept his face forward.

"I wanted to. I don't have anyone to spend my money on besides Georgie and a few family members and friends. A dog can only eat so many bones, and I don't want to spoil him. If I had a boyfriend, I'd want to buy him things if I saw something that reminded me of him."

Jack stared at Lucas, silent, as Lucas felt a slow flush creep up his neck. Lucas's pulse visibly hammered beneath his jawline as he stared straight ahead.

"That's really… sweet of you." The shock in Jack's tone softened, his voice quieter as he said, "Thank you."

"I'm not sweet." Lucas scratched the back of his hair, looking away from Jack's stare. "Spend enough time with me and you'll find sweet is not in my descriptive vocabulary."

Jack's fingertips curled against Lucas's palm. Lucas's hand twitched once before he laced his fingers through Jack's and they faced forward at the boarding gate.

"We'll see," Jack cooed.

Lucas broke into a smile.

THEIR WIDE seats were spread out in such a way that they could turn their seats into beds, if they wished. Jack sat at the window, Lucas across from him but far enough to the left to give their legs room to stretch.

Lucas tried his best to remain awake for the flight, but dozed off upon sitting in the plush seat and buckling his seatbelt, holding his belt while he slept. A split second before he fell asleep, he watched Jack untangle his headphones. He wondered if it was rude to pass out before the flight even took off, but then his entire week of work, travel, and stress about the trip caught up to him. The choice to stay awake faded into fuzzy darkness before he could even tell Jack he was going to nap.

He had no idea how long he'd been out for when he started to register sounds and his eyes moved beneath his lids. He flexed his feet and felt soft fabric on his toes. He peered down his body. His legs had been elevated and his seat pulled out into a bed. His flip-flops were on the floor at the end of his bed and a white duvet spread over his body from neck to feet.

"I can do it, love, no worries," Jack's voice filtered into his brain. Lucas rubbed his fingers over his eyes and started to sit up. He watched Jack pour milk into a white porcelain teacup. "He takes it milk first, the diva."

The flight attendant chuckled and her gaze landed on Lucas's face. "Welcome back, sir," she said soothingly. "Would you care for anything to eat? A hot towel?"

"No, thank you," Lucas said gruffly. He sat up in bed and pushed his beanie off his hair, running his fingers over his scalp. Jack placed his cup of tea on the table beside his chair. Lucas blinked from the cup to Jack's face. "Thanks."

Jack reached out and thumbed the corner of Lucas's mouth. "You're welcome."

Lucas wiped the back of his hand over his mouth. Jack returned to the flight attendant to fix his own tea. Lucas saw that Jack had placed his boots beneath his seat but had not reclined his seat into a bed, a glossy home-and-gardening magazine wilted open on his table. Jack's socked right foot was tucked under his bum, his left leg straight ahead.

"Thank you so much," Jack said, cradling his tea in his lap.

Lucas offered the flight attendant a nod, pulling his beanie back on his hair. A packet of truffle-dusted almonds landed on top of his blanket.

Jack asked, "Why aren't you eating anything? You didn't even eat one of your weird robot food containers at home. And you're not drinking enough water. Flying is dehydrating."

"I'm listening to my body," Lucas said, his pinky poised to sip his tea. "And that robot food is personally prepared for me by a chef and nutritionist, thank you very much. I'm a well-fed robot."

Jack snorted, stretching his legs in front of himself. He exhaled a small groan as he stretched, clutched his arms behind his head, and arched his back.

Lucas licked his lips, replacing his teacup on its saucer. He pulled at the almond packaging, dragging his eyes up from the shiny wrapper to Jack. "You know," he said as he got the wrapper to open. Almonds spilled onto his lap. "Albert's worked for me for well over a year, and he has yet to make me an accurate cup of tea. You know me a few days and, somehow, you make me a perfect cup."

Jack grinned, releasing his stretch. He crossed both legs under himself on his seat. He picked up his teacup. "Sounds to me like it's your responsibility, as the employer, to provide your staff with proper training, not assume Albert can read your mind."

"I've definitely mentioned I like my tea with just milk. Yorkshire tea. Milk. That's it. I don't know when this blueberry nonsense started."

"But did you tell him milk first?"

"No," Lucas said slowly, eyeing Jack. "You figured that out all on your own." Jack dropped his gaze, sipping his tea. "Perceptive as usual."

"Maybe I should be your assistant." Jack's eyes shimmered. Lucas started to smile as Jack painted the scene. "You could boss me around. I could prance about your office in a mini skirt and thigh highs." Jack pinched a bit of his bottom lip between his teeth. "I could pretend to drop things in front of your office desk. All the time. Rulers could be involved. Desktops, as well."

Lucas took a sip of tea. "We'd never get any work done. I need someone productive."

"I can be very productive when necessary."

"You've got the legs for a skirt, though."

Jack's eyebrows arched and he sat up straighter. "Is that it, then? You like your men to dress up for you? Or is it the bossing around part? Both?"

Lucas tilted his head and blinked at him, his smirk kind. "Sorry, love. You've yet to hit the mark. But it's very amusing to watch you try, so, by all means, please continue."

Jack stuck his tongue sideways and popped his earbuds back in; the white and pink cables stood out from his dark hair. Lucas chuckled and sipped his tea, rubbing his feet together under the blanket.

Jack took a black elastic off his wrist and lifted his hands to his hair, running his fingers up his scalp to gather it in a bun. Lucas focused on munching almonds and not looking at Jack, who somehow made the act of putting his hair up into a bun an erotic act. His abs visibly crunched beneath his draped shirt. His arms strained and a small, thoughtful wrinkle formed between his brows.

"You're staring," Jack said, not meeting Lucas's gaze but smiling. He rolled his head toward Lucas, his bun bobbing. "What?"

"You have nice cheekbones."

"Oh. I wasn't expecting that, but thank you."

"You know, with all your hair and stuff out of the way."

"Hey, I like my hair."

Lucas flattened his palm toward Jack. "You have lovely hair, don't get me wrong. I've just never seen you with your hair like that."

"Ah."

Lucas chewed on a mouthful of almonds, and Jack reclined in his seat. Once he was down, Jack pulled a sleep mask out from his carry-on, tucking his sunglasses into the bag. He put the sleep mask elastic over his head, tangling his headphones with the mask.

"Hey," Lucas said.

Jack looked at him, still trying to untangle his headphones. "What's up?"

"Can I ask you a question?"

"Depends on the question, but you can certainly try."

Lucas turned on his side with his blanket pulled up to shoulder height. He put the empty almond bag on his seat-side table. A bottle of sparkling water he couldn't remember requesting waited for him on the table as well. He opened the bottle. "How did you get into what you do?"

Jack smiled slowly, dropping his gaze down to the mess of wires in his hands. A small curl sprung from his bun, wispy and fluttering on the very center of his hairline. "Why do you ask?"

"Because you're not an idiot. You seem employable."

"You're making me blush, babe."

"I'm serious." Lucas propped himself up on his elbow. Jack finally freed his headphones from their tangle. He released a small cry of victory. "How did you even get into your field? It's not like there's an office for Escorts Inc. posting ads online. Unless, is there?" He frowned. "I should have researched more thoroughly."

Jack chuckled. "No, not that I know of." He narrowed his eyes, running his tongue over the left corner of his mouth. "Why should I tell you my secrets? Maybe you should try to be as perceptive as me if you want to learn more."

Lucas smirked, holding his stare for two heartbeats. "Do you really want to play this game with me?"

"What game?" Jack shrugged his shoulders forward. His shirt wilted down his collarbone as his eyes urged Lucas on. "C'mon, love," he whispered. "Show me what you're made of. I'm starting to think you're all talk, no brain."

Lucas chuckled quietly, fluffing his pillow beneath his head. He relaxed on his side; his gaze landed on Jack's face.

"You take your tea light with one sugar. Two if they're sugar cubes, which I'm guessing is because you think the cubes are cute," Lucas said, emphasizing the *t*. "Even on your special diet, you choose white sugar as opposed to one of those"—he flicked his hand at the air—"chemically enhanced sugar alternatives, likely because you prefer to have natural, whole foods in your body, which you take pride in, but not so much pride as to appear vain. You're very, very fit, but you're still growing into the idea of being physically attractive, even though that's the main area of your success. A late bloomer, possibly. You're still growing into your height, as you have a habit of slouching when you're not parading around like a peacock. That contrasts with your comfort to take your clothes off or walk about naked, which I'm sure is irresistible to your clients. The perfect mix of boyish and cocksure. A true sex kitten if I've ever seen one."

"You've never seen me naked."

"I've seen enough to know you're uncut and pretty heavily groomed, leaving just enough hair to distinguish yourself as a sexually virile male but not so much hair as to be a bother with fussy clients."

"Size?"

Lucas weighed his head side to side. "Well, I've felt your cock more often than I've seen it, so I'd approximate…" He thought for a moment. "Probably around seven and a half hard? Above average. Eight, maybe. Large enough to do the job, but not so large as to appear cartoonish."

Jack said nothing as amusement teased the corners of his mouth. "Continue."

"You're educated. Whether that means you went to uni or not, I can't be one hundred percent sure, but I'd guess you did study somewhere for some period of time, based on how clearly you can communicate in writing."

Jack did not have a reply for that. His face was motionless.

"You wear almost exclusively designer clothes," Lucas continued. "Lots of pricey Yves Saint Laurent and Tom Ford. I'm guessing that's due to a client you have who is connected in the fashion world, seeing as you were hesitant to purchase a bottle of cologne that costs a mere twenty minutes of your time. Chump change."

"Maybe I like to try different colognes, and lack commitment."

"Maybe," Lucas said, airy and casual. "I was pinning that decision more on you being smart with your money, which is a good thing and yet another trait that sets you apart from others in your field."

Jack gasped and flattened his hand on his chest. "Was that a compliment?"

"Take it as you will. Any decent numbers man can calculate that, even if you see clients for a mere five hours per week and give yourself four weeks off per year for illness or holidays, you are well over the average income for a family of four, let alone one single mouth to feed. You do well for yourself."

"All those natural, whole foods are pricey with an appetite like mine."

Lucas grinned. Jack's attempt at dry sarcasm was ruined by his growing smile. "My hope for you," Lucas said, licking his lips and exhaling a quick breath, "is that you're socking away as much money as you can and investing wisely, so you don't have to do this for the rest of your life. Or until your looks fade. Whichever comes first."

"How do you know my looks will fade?"

"I have no doubt you'll age into a handsome old fart, but your clients are men. Rich men. I know that most rich men want young, which I've never quite gotten, but that's the way the world turns. You'll be lucky to last in your field until you're thirty. Thirty-one, maybe, since you have a baby face."

"Drat." Jack snapped his fingers. "There go my hopes of hustling you when I'm ninety. I was so looking forward to sucking your wrinkled balls."

"And, please," Lucas chuckled. "You could never lack commitment. You're organized, methodical, and smart. You like to be in control of your affairs far too much to ever lack commitment, and that's not even taking into account how much you respect your clients and keep their secrets. Lack of commitment is not on the docket, love."

"All right, then. That's it? That's your read on me?"

Lucas let his head fall to the side. "Come now, darling. You and I both know that neither of us is going to reveal his hand quite yet."

"What are you waiting for?"

Lucas's eyes flickered up to meet Jack's gaze. "A reason."

Jack grinned, his head mirroring Lucas's angled position. "Good answer."

"And your good answer to my good question would be?"

Jack stared at him for a moment. A flight attendant walked past with a tray of drinks, their cubes clinking in the fizzy tumblers. Lucas held his stare easily.

"I can keep secrets too," Lucas said, softer. He crossed his heart. "Promise."

Jack held his gaze for one more moment before he started to speak. His tone matched Lucas's soft promise. "I was studying during the day. Classics. I was a waiter at night. Every night, seven days a week, since I was trying to pay for everything myself. It was a tiny Italian restaurant where the kitchen stank of rotting fish all the time, even though we sold mostly cheap pasta and pizza." His face crumpled. "Ugh. I absolutely hated it. Hated the smell of the place." Jack adjusted his shirt, righting it on his chest. "Plus, I'm terrible at carrying things."

"Ah ha."

Jack rolled his eyes. "Yes, yes. Congratulations. You were right about the uni thing."

Lucas sipped his tea. "Please, continue. This is like learning about when Spider-Man was bit by the radioactive spider."

That pulled a dimpled grin from Jack. He ran his hand through his hair. He bumped his fingers into his bun and his eyes darted up. "I was on the brink of not making rent every single month despite working what felt like twenty-four hours a day." He smoothed his hair. "For weeks, I hadn't eaten anything but whatever I could convince the cooks to slip me when I was at work. The customers were wretched and, after one particularly nasty night, I was in desperate need of a drink. I didn't even care that I shouldn't have spent the money, I just wanted to sit somewhere quiet, drink something cold, and then go home to bed."

"Age?"

Jack licked the front of his bottom teeth with his lips closed. "Twenty."

"All right."

"I went to the bar of this posh hotel I walked by every day." His words slowed, and he shifted his gaze over Lucas's shoulder. "I liked the bar because it had a fish tank around the whole bar with all these pretty fish swimming around. Lots of different colors and types."

"The Kingston," Lucas said. Jack nodded. "I've been there for drinks. It's nice."

"It is. I went straight from work in my"—Jack chuckled—"dorky black trousers and white shirt. I think I even had sauce on my collar. I was a mess. I sat down at the bar and, before I could even order, this guy started chatting with me. I was lo—" Jack paused for a moment and pressed his lips together. His throat bobbed and his gaze returned to Lucas's face a split second later. "I had transferred to a new uni and moved into a new place on my own," he said, choosing his words carefully. "I was so busy with work and study that I hadn't really met anyone. I didn't mind the conversation, which he apparently liked. I don't even really remember what we talked about, to be honest. I was so tired and he was nice. So we just… chatted a bit. In the course of one drink, which he insisted on paying for, he liked me enough to ask if I wanted to go back to his room with him. I was confused, because he was, like, significantly older than me, and I'd never done anything like that before. I'd never even fucked someone in a hotel, at that point, let alone a stranger."

"How old was he?"

"Let's say sixty-five."

Lucas nodded. "All right."

"I'd never been with anyone that old and I didn't understand he was trying to pick me up until he asked my rate." Jack laughed quietly and looked down, fingering the edge of his duvet. "I thought it was a joke, that the bartender had put him up to it or something, so I asked what he wanted me to do in his room." He tilted his head left. "He said he wanted to suck me off." His head went right. "I said it would be a thousand, thinking there's no bloody way anyone would pay that much to give a blowjob." He brought his eyes to Lucas. "The man said, 'Lovely. I'd have paid you two.'" Jack gracefully flared his fingers in the air near his face. "The rest is history."

Lucas asked, "You just let this old guy suck you off? Without your whole background check process? What if he murdered you?"

"He didn't murder me, obviously. What he did do is pay me fifteen hundred cash, let me order whatever I wanted off room service, and asked if he could be added to my regular client list for a standing appointment twice a month, which I didn't even know was a thing."

"How did you get hard if you weren't into him?"

"I lay back and thought of my bank account, to be honest." They laughed, and Lucas's brows shot up. Newspapers ruffled in a nearby seat, so Jack lowered his voice. "The thought of more than one zero brought me to the Big *O* with no issue."

Lucas groaned. "God, you're so cheesy."

"I was able to quit that shitty restaurant job and figure out how to build my business, all because that guy felt like a fling with a younger guy. He traveled a lot for work. Was divorced. I get a lot of those."

"And uni? What made you pick Classics if you wanted to be a photographer?"

Jack's smile faded. "I couldn't make up my mind what I wanted to be and thought Classics would be… I dunno. Malleable for whatever career I ended up in. But poor Classics never stood a chance once I started to make enough money to support myself. I'd always wanted to travel. I wanted to go everywhere and anywhere. My new career made that possible, where being a teacher or copywriter wouldn't give me that sort of flexibility." He snorted. "Or paycheck."

"But you're having sex with people on these holidays."

"So? I like sex."

"I'd hope so."

"Like I said, doing what I do does not always involve sex. Sometimes it's sex with someone I'm not attracted to, and I have my ways of dealing with that, but in general I'm very lucky." He ticked a list off on his fingers. "I've never had a violent client. I've never had trouble getting paid. I've never been forced to do something I'm uncomfortable with. I've met a lot of really interesting people and traveled to a lot of beautiful places. I have friends in the industry who have dealt with a lot of issues that, for whatever reason, I have been lucky enough to avoid. I have no complaints."

"You keep talking and giving great answers, and yet my brain is exploding with all sorts of inappropriate questions," Lucas admitted, laughing only after Jack did. "I don't know why, but it's true."

"What do you want to know?"

"No, it's all silly nonsense. I won't burden you with my curiosity. You already gave me a very detailed blow-by-blow of your origin as Spider-Hustle."

Jack snorted, "Captain Cock or Iron Arse," and Lucas started to chuckle with him.

"I quite like Captain Cock. Does your shield have a cock on it instead of a star?"

"It has cocks arranged in the shape of a star."

They laughed and the newspaper rustled in the seat behind them.

Lucas sat up straighter in his seat and said over his shoulder, "Give it a rest. Like you've never heard the word *cock* before. We're not even talking that loud." He slouched back down, tugging his blanket up his stomach. He muttered, "First class snobs," and looked to Jack, who was staring at him. Lucas quietly asked, "What?"

Jack's smile grew before he dropped his face, shaking his head. Another small curl popped from his bun, this curl at his temple. "Nothing."

"All right." Lucas settled back on his pillows. He crossed his ankles. The blanket ballooned on top of his feet. "I guess we have nine nights of pillow talks to look forward to."

"True. Except, for those talks, I'll be naked." Jack curled on his side, pulling his blanket up to his chin. He shut his eyes, yawning. "Will be much more comfortable."

Lucas chuckled, "Yeah," and swallowed, looking out the window. He saw powder-white beaches and pure turquoise water, dots of vibrant green scattered over the serene island. He whispered to himself, "Real comfortable," and shut his eyes.

Chapter ELEVEN

UPON LANDING, they were escorted to a shuttle van, which took them to a ferry port. Their luggage had already been transported and packed on the tiny boat by the time they got there. Jack took his bun out, ruffling his hair as a warm, humid breeze blew his shirt up his stomach.

"Lovely," he murmured, dropping his head back on his seat. He let the blazing beams heat his face, fluttering his eyes shut beneath his aviators. "Hello, sun. I've missed you."

"You listen to your body and talk to the sun. Are there any hippie clichés you don't participate in?"

"Um…." Jack sucked his bottom lip as Lucas put his beanie in his carry-on. "Oh! I like making money. Does that count?"

Lucas grinned, making the skin beside his eyes crinkle. He popped his sunglasses on. "Fair enough."

One ferry ride later, and they were in The Exumas, an island south of Nassau. The Exumas Cays, pronounced *keys*, was their specific destination, along with being their exotic, exclusive, and luxurious home for the next ten days. Another shuttle van took them to the resort itself.

After a short drive, the van stopped in front of a tall, wide gate made of dark wood. The driver buzzed the intercom and introduced them. The gate swung open. The way was smooth for the drive up the long road to the resort. Both Jack and Lucas turned away from each other to watch out the windows.

Rich, tropical trees and plants lined the path, the green so thick it was impossible to see more than a foot into the brush. The landscaping opened up once the sprawling resort came into view, giving them a look at the impressive beachfront real estate the resort was built upon: powdery sand without a single jagged shell marring the pure surface, cerulean water dotted with early morning swimmers, and a sun burning white heat over the entire scenic paradise.

Jack whistled between his teeth. "I've been to some posh resorts in my time, and even private island homes, but this place might take the cake."

"The wedding cake?"

"Yes," Jack chuckled. "The wedding cake."

They pulled up to an enormous hotel. The building was all white, contrasting with the colorful nature surrounding it. The carved wooden sign on the doorway read "Welcome to Flamingo Cove!"

The driver came around and opened the door for them, helping them out while a crew hurried to the van and removed their luggage. Air conditioning brought goose bumps to any exposed skin once they walked into the pristine lobby. Before they could even approach the desk, two tanned men in crisp white polo shirts came up to them. There was a tiny magenta flamingo embroidered on the left side of each of their chests.

"Welcome!" one said, holding his hand out toward the concierge desk. "We're so happy you have arrived!"

Jack and Lucas smiled at him. Everything about the resort screamed fresh, clean, and rich.

"Thank you," Jack said quietly. They all shook hands. "We're very happy to be here."

They made it to the concierge, who rose from her white leather chair with a welcoming smile. She held her arms out, her uniform all white with a soft magenta blazer on top. A tasteful pearl necklace and earrings complemented her dark skin and shiny black hair. "Welcome!"

"Thank you," they both said.

"My name is Marie, and I'm one of the concierges at Flamingo Cove," she said, resting her fingers on the marble desk. Her fingernails were short and filed round, manicured in a pale pink. "I'd be happy to help you with whatever you need during your stay."

Lucas pulled out his passport and wallet. "We're here to check in. The reservation is under Thompson."

"Excellent! I'll check you in right away."

She typed eight letters into her computer and hit Enter, her eyes scanning over the screen. "Hm. I'm not seeing your room, though I see your spa and lunch reservation."

Jack's brows rose while Lucas's furrowed. Lucas reached into his carry-on front pocket. "I got the confirmation e-mail last night." He unfolded a white sheet of paper and placed it on the desk. "We're here with a group. Does that change things?"

She tilted her head to read the paper and gasped. "Oh! Are you with the Matin/Moran wedding?"

Lucas nodded. "Yes, that's us."

"That's why I'm not finding you in the regular reservations." Her eyes remained on Lucas's face as her mouse clicked over the screen. Lucas respected a good multitasker. "You're in a special group of rooms, Mr. Thompson."

"Ah, okay."

Her expression went sheepish, her cheeks pinking. "I truly apologize for the delay."

"No delay. No worries. Take your time."

"Lucky you," she said slowly, a grin spreading across her face. "You're in one of our private, beachfront bungalows. Bungalow D." She looked between them. "Very romantic. Wait until you see the bed. It's massive with the most luxurious linens we offer. It was recently featured in a travel magazine. Very chic."

Lucas asked, "Private bungalow?"

"Romantic?" Jack asked. Amusement made his voice shake. "And bed, as in"—he glanced at Lucas—"one bed?"

"Oh, um, yes," she said, confused. She looked between them again, and her hand froze on her mouse. "Is that… a problem?"

Jack thumbed over his bottom lip as his gaze rested on Lucas. Lucas rose up on tiptoe to lean across the marble countertop, lowering his voice in both pitch and volume.

"I believe I booked us a regular room in the main resort." He circled his hand in the air. "This building, I think. One with two beds?"

"Ah. All right, let's see where the mix-up is. I do apologize, sir." She clicked her mouse twice as she scanned the screen. Lucas pointedly avoided Jack's face. "It seems the grooms-to-be made a change to your lodging reservation, noting that I should tell you…." She cleared her throat and spoke in a loud Irish accent, "Don't be silly, Lukeybear! You're staying with all of our families this week! You can't escape us this time! VIP, baby! VIP!"

Jack whispered, "Lukeybear," behind him and broke into airy giggles. Lucas tapped his credit card once on the counter.

"Well then. I suppose that's that. You do an excellent Cillian impression, by the way."

She grinned and signaled to an attendant waiting behind them. "Jacques, please bring their luggage to Bungalow D." She whispered conspiratorially to Lucas and Jack. "Mr. Moran was very involved with the planning process. We've become 'booking buddies.' His term, not mine."

A man in a white polo and khakis offered them a friendly nod as he pushed their luggage cart toward the exit; two other muscled men followed him.

Marie offered Lucas another smile, fingers tapping away on her keyboard. "It really is a lovely suite. Very, very spacious. You have access to room service and a private concierge twenty-four hours a day for whatever you may need during your stay. There's a private hot tub and outdoor shower on your property, along with a darling front deck. You can walk to the beach from your room." She slid a form across the counter that explained his room deposit and the rules of the resort. "The decor is absolutely divine."

"We're thrilled to see the decor." Lucas scribbled his signature on the bottom line and handed his credit card over. "Here you are."

"Oh, that's not necessary, sir," she chirped, sliding it back toward him. "Mr. Moran has his card on file for all rooms. However, it's our policy to get a signature of consent from the actual room guest."

"I see." He took out his wallet, sliding his card into it. "Very well, then."

"Give me one moment and I'll have your key cards ready for you."

Jack nudged Lucas's ribs with his elbow. "Hey, did you see my headphones?" He searched through his leather bag, then unzipped the front pocket. "I can't find them." He patted his back pockets. "I hope I didn't leave them on the ferry."

"Oh, yeah, they're in mine. Sorry." Lucas bent over. "I grabbed them when we were getting off and forgot to mention it."

Jack flattened his hand on Lucas's lower back. "I can get them." He smiled crookedly, a thick wave of hair falling from the sunglasses propped on his head. "Thanks for remembering. They cost all of a tenner, but I'm quite fond of the Hello Kitty graphics."

Lucas hummed. Jack squatted down as Lucas started to stand up straight.

A high-pitched, ecstatic voice echoed through the mellow lobby. "Lucas! Luke! Oh, Luke! You're here! Finally!"

Lucas was swept into his mother's oil-covered arms before he could say anything or even look toward the sound of her voice. His flip-flops slapped on the tile and he grasped the counter.

"Yes, hi, Mum," he said, squeezing her once. Oil from her shoulder slid under his squirming cheek until he reached the strap of her gauzy Creamsicle-colored beach cover-up; her warm skin smelled like fruit punch. He searched for Jack, who rose to his full height next to Lucas's carry-on. "So happy to"—Jo planted a loud, smacked kiss on his cheek—"see you."

Jo pulled back to cup Lucas's cheeks with both hands. Lucas could already feel pimples popping up on his skin from her sun oil addiction. "I'm so excited for this week!" She shook his head side to side and her short, curvy body jiggled as she jostled him. "We haven't had a family holiday in years! Probably over ten years!"

"Yes"—his mouth was pushed forward by her hands—"very excited."

While making a long, squealed sound of joy, she planted another kiss on each of his cheeks before staring at him. Their noses nearly touched.

Jo said, "You look wonderful, love. I like your hair longer." She ran her fingers through it. "Takes attention away from your forehead and crow's-feet." She tapped her thumbs beside his eyes, whispering, "Bloody genetic curse." Lucas flushed. Jack's boots shuffled behind him as he chuckled softly. Jo patted his shoulders. "That gorgeous trainer you've got has been doing good work!"

Lucas eased her grip from his face. He stepped backward, sucking in a breath of fresh air. His reflection stared back at him in his mother's wide black sunglasses. In the reflection, Jack stood beside him.

Jo pushed her sunglasses up into her hair, looking from Lucas's face up to Jack. "Hello," she said. She gestured between Lucas and Jack. "Do you two know each other?"

Lucas placed his hand on the small of Jack's back. Jack's heat radiated against his side. "Actually, Mum, I'm sorry you two didn't get a chance to meet before this trip, but this is my boyfriend—"

"Teddy," Jack said, extending his hand. A dimpled grin lit his face. Their hands joined, and Jo's brows shot sky-high. "Teddy Bennet. It's so great to meet you, Mrs. Mackey."

Lucas blinked at Jack. Questions swirled wildly in his head. Who was Teddy Bennet, and what had happened to Jack McQueen? Jack's tone while speaking to his mum was so kind and warm that Lucas almost forgot what his hustler voice sounded like—almost forgot that he *was* a hustler. Was Teddy another character that Jack pulled out on the job? Who else would appear during their vacation together?

They were all silent for a moment. Even Marie was quiet behind the desk, pretending to type without touching the keyboard.

Jo finally laughed a bubbly, airy sound. "Oh! You're—" She searched for her next word, as her mouth moved silently and she shook her head. "Real! You're real! Luke actually has a boyfriend!"

Jack glanced at Lucas, who stared blankly at his mother. "Yes, I'm all real," he said, causing Jo to giggle even louder. Her fingers fluttered against her collarbone.

"I meant—" She clenched her eyes shut and laughed, waving her hands in the air. "Of course you're real! I apologize, Teddy. Teddy," she repeated firmer, as if she were familiarizing herself with the name. "I'm just thrilled to meet one of Lucas's boyfriends!"

"I only have one boyfriend, Mum." Lucas looked to Jack with narrowed eyes. "Only one… Teddy."

Jack pulled Jo into an easy hug. "I'm very happy to meet you all, as well," he murmured into her hair. "You have a wonderful son. I can only imagine how wonderful his family is."

Jo stared, shocked, at Lucas. The bottom half of her face was blocked by Jack's shoulder.

They broke apart, and Jo patted Jack's face, pressing a quick kiss to his cheek. "Please, love. Call me Jo."

Jack nodded. A slight flush dappled the back of his neck. "All right. Jo it is."

Jo stared at Lucas for a long moment; her mouth hung agape as she looked between them. "Sorry, loves, that was—" Giving a throaty laugh, she knocked on her own forehead. Her seashell bracelets jingled around her wrists. "I don't think I've ever been so caught off guard! I'm out of breath." She patted Jack's shoulder. "Of course you're real. We all just thought"—she directed her attention to Lucas—"that you were joking when you said you had a boyfriend."

Lucas's jawline twitched as his lips tightened in a closemouthed smile.

Jack grinned and pulled Lucas into his body by the bottom of his tee, slinging his right arm around his narrow shoulders. He flattened his left hand on the center of Lucas's chest. "He does have a very interesting sense of humor, doesn't he?"

Jo's blue eyes crinkled at the corners, reminiscent of some of the rare, full-faced grins Lucas had graced him with. Her nose even scrunched in the same way. "He does. My little comedian."

Marie slid two key cards across the counter, whispering, "Sorry to interrupt, Mr. Thompson, but your room is ready for you."

Lucas snatched them up and beamed at her. "No interruption at all! Thank you for your excellent service." He wrapped his arm around Jack's waist. "Well, we'd best be getting to our room to settle—"

"Luke!"

Before he could finish his sentence, he was tackled by two skinny bodies, one with blazing blond hair and the other sporting a shaggy mess of shiny black hair. Neither wore shirts or shoes with their matching neon green floral swim trunks.

"You're here!" Zamir cried. His normally soft voice blared in Lucas's ear. "We didn't think you'd be here until tonight, mate! This is magical! Fate!"

"I'm so happy to smell you," Cillian said, sounding choked up. He hugged Lucas tighter, clenching his eyes shut. "I've missed your aura, mate." He rubbed his palm over Lucas's face, still hugging him. "You have no idea!"

Lucas met Jack's eyes. Jack held a hand over his mouth, but his eyes curved with a smirk.

"I've missed you guys too." Lucas patted Zamir's back. "This whole thing is going to be great. I'm so thrilled for you two."

Zamir and Cillian hugged him tighter for one long beat before stepping back. They pressed their palms together in front of their chests and bowed. Cillian's eyes floated over Lucas's shoulder to gaze at Jack.

"You're stunning," Cillian said, almost starstruck.

"You really are," Zamir added.

Cillian waved his hands in the air in small circles. "And your aura is just—" He fluttered his fingers and breathed in deeply. His nostrils flared. "—incredible. Chakras galore, mate."

"Thank you." Jack stepped forward and held his hand out. "I'm Teddy, Lucas's boyfriend. So great to meet both of you."

Cillian and Zamir's chatter quieted. Their lips remained open in smile shapes, but their brows shot up. Their chins tilted left as they stared at Jack.

Zamir looked at Lucas, quietly asking, "Oh, that… that wasn't a joke?"

Lucas shut his eyes and dropped his head backward, and Jack's deep laugh echoed around the lobby. A crowd of people with heavy Irish accents came into the lobby and swarmed around Cillian and Zamir.

"Sorry, mate." Zamir waved at Lucas as he was carried away. "We'll catch up with you and, um, Teddy later, yeah? So, so happy you're here."

Lucas opened his mouth to reply but was interrupted by something clingy and wet latching onto his shin and a mushy bum sitting on top of his foot.

"Uncle Luke!"

The tightness in his chest evaporated and a wide grin crinkled his eyes. "Miss Maggie," he said, getting down to the floor. Maggie peered up at him. Her face was smudged with sun cream and her wet curls dripped on her shoulders. She still had on her bright orange water wings and her pink one-piece bathing suit featuring a pattern of cartoon grapes, orange slices, and strawberries. "How is my favorite niece?"

"I'm your only niece, silly man," she giggled, hugging his leg tighter. Lucas chuckled and kissed her forehead, smoothing his hand over the top of her head. She scrambled to sit on his bent leg, and Lucas wrapped his arm around her back. Her flip-flops swayed in the space below his thigh. She blinked her big brown eyes at him; her lashes were wet and her skin smelled of chlorine. "Where is Georgie?"

Jack gasped. "You call him Georgie too?"

Maggie looked up at him. Her eyes widened, and a loud, high-pitched shriek of joy radiated from her tiny vocal cords and her feet kicked in the air. Lucas looked at her, alarmed, and squeezed her closer to his body.

"Are you all right?" Jack kneeled down next to Lucas, and Maggie peered at him. "I know I'm new, but I'm very excited to meet you," he said, his voice pitched low and gentle. He held his hand out and smiled softly. "I've heard so much about you from your Uncle Lucas."

She grew very quiet; the lack of sound and movement alarmed Lucas further.

Maggie reached out and touched Jack's hair, her tiny fingers stroking through his waves. "Are you Snow White?" she whispered.

Jack grinned, delighted. "No, but your uncle could be one of the Seven Dwarves, couldn't he?"

Maggie cackled and Lucas stared at him. "Very funny, love." He jutted his chin toward Jack. "Maggie, this is my boyfriend, Teddy." He cleared his throat before repeating, "Teddy. Do you know what a boyfriend—"

"Tazzy!" she cried.

Jack chuckled and jerked his head sideways at a tug of her hand.

Maggie hopped off Lucas's leg, leaving wet marks on his jeans. She marched over to Jack and latched onto his shin.

Jack pulled her up to sit on his knee. "Are you having a fun holiday? The weather is lovely, isn't it?"

"Oh, yes," she said excitedly. "Wanna swim with me?"

"Um, yeah, maybe in a bit." He glanced at Lucas. "We've got to, uh, check into our room."

"Where's your mum?" Lucas asked, standing up. Jack went to stand, but Maggie held on around his middle. Wet marks appeared on his silky white shirt. "Or did you fly here all by yourself, young lady?"

"I'm right here," Lane sang.

Her flip-flops slapped the marble floor. She walked up to Lucas. Her black sundress hung loose off her athletic, petite figure. The siblings shared a long hug; Lane was two inches shorter than Lucas. She kissed his cheek, hugging him again.

"Little monster took off like a shot when Mum texted that you arrived." Lane pulled back, sliding her large, round sunglasses to the top of her head. Her dark brown hair was piled in a high topknot. "She also mentioned that your boyfriend was here," she said, putting her hands on her narrow hips. "Way to shock the shit out of Mum on day one." She smirked down at Jack, who hurried to stand, placing Maggie gently on the floor. "Hi, I'm Lane."

"Teddy," he said, holding his hand out. "Ah." He wiped his wet hand on his jeans embarrassedly. "Sorry about that."

"That's quite all right. Pool water is no big thing." She hugged him. Jack's long arms wrapped around her back and his head set on her shoulder. "Once you have children, you lose your fear of any and all liquids." He chuckled and glanced toward the sound of Lucas's laugh. Lucas was back on his knees, with Maggie on tiptoe to whisper in his ear. "Don't mind those two." Lane patted his shoulder. She pulled back. "Thick as thieves."

"Thick as thieves," Maggie repeated, scrunching her face up at her mother in an evil grin.

Lucas stood, moving to Jack's side. "We actually do have to get to our room and drop our stuff."

"Come swim after," Lane said, scooping Maggie into her arms. Maggie whined and reached toward Jack. Jack stuck his tongue out the side of his mouth. Maggie giggled. "Love, he'll come swim soon too. Leave him alone."

"It's all right," Jack said. "I don't mind."

Lucas shouldered his carry-on. "Did I miss the memo that everyone was getting here early?"

"Why waste the whole day of sunshine?" Lane asked, bouncing Maggie on her hip.

"True. We can swim in a bit." Lucas picked up Jack's bag and Jack took it from him. "We've got to settle in and then eat. We haven't had lunch yet."

"Ah, all right," Lane said, turning her face toward Maggie. "Glasses, please, little miss." Maggie pinched the sides of her sunglasses and carefully placed them on her; Lane kissed the tip of Maggie's nose. Maggie giggled, squirming on Lane's hip. "Thank you, love. You're very helpful."

"We'll see you later," Lucas said, waving at Lane and Maggie.

"It was great to meet you both," Jack said. "Everyone. It was great to meet everyone."

"You as well," Lane said, her gaze sliding to Lucas. She arched an eyebrow above the line of her sunglasses. "Was a lovely surprise."

Lucas blinked at her, his lips twitching.

Maggie reached toward Jack's hair. "Come swim with me, Tazzy!"

Jack placed the strap of his bag over his shoulder. "Soon, I promise."

Maggie giggled, "Okay!" and waved.

Lucas and Jack turned away from the group. Cillian and Zamir took a quick break from their throng of family members to snag Lucas and Jack for hugs.

"Still blown away by your amazing aura," Cillian whispered, cradling Jack's face in his hands. "Just amazing."

"Thanks, mate," Jack said.

Beside them, Zamir whispered, “Why didn’t you say anything?” as he hugged Lucas. “You never mentioned you were seeing anyone seriously.”

Lucas swiped his tongue over his dry lips. He stepped out of the hug. “We… I didn’t want to say anything until it was certain, and then we both were busy at work and, you know, time sort of got away from us.”

“Ah.” Zamir nodded, but his eyes were squinting. “I see.”

“We’d better get to our room,” Jack said, brushing his knuckles over the back of Lucas’s hand. Lucas’s fingers laced with his.

“Yeah, of course.” Zamir’s eyes gained some warmth. “Get comfortable. Settle in. Relax. We’re all sticking by the infinity pool today, I think. There’s a whole area roped off for our group. We kind of took over the resort this week. You’ll read about it when you get to your room. There’s a welcome booklet.”

Lucas nodded. Jack’s thumb soothed over his knuckles. “Thank you for, erm….” Lucas looked from Cillian to Zamir. “Upgrading us. That was really generous.”

Cillian slung his arm around Lucas’s shoulders. “Of course! I told Albert to book you in the bungalow to begin with. I’ll have to give him a spanking when he gets here Thursday.”

“And why wouldn’t you be in one of the bungalows?” Zamir asked. He squeezed Lucas’s chin, smirking. “Your family is there, our families are there, and our house is there. It’ll be amazing.”

“House?” Lucas asked.

“It’s like we’re on MTV Cribs!” Happiness radiated from Cillian’s voice. “We’re big pimping! You guys should come over to use our shower. It’s like an orgas-ma-tron.”

Zamir smiled. “Yeah, it’s lovely. Right on the beach. All the bungalows are in a row leading up to it. The house is kind of large, but when in paradise, you know?”

“Right,” Lucas drawled. Jack squeezed Lucas’s hand and received a squeeze in reply. “Well, we’d better be going.”

“No disappearing, you hear?” Zamir prodded Lucas’s stomach. “Though now it makes sense why you wanted your privacy in the main house.” He winked at Jack. “I promise you’ll both love the bungalow.”

“If you need lube, we’re four doors down,” Cillian said, conversational and cheery. “We brought a lot.” Jack pursed his lips while nodding. Lucas and Zamir both rubbed their hands over their faces.

“Very generous, thanks.” Jack’s smirk grew to a grin. “I think we’re set, but we will keep that in mind.”

"Yeah," Lucas said, quicker. He squeezed Jack's hand. "We'll see you at the pool later." He gave them a rushed smile and pulled, and Jack followed behind him.

Jack called, "Nice to meet you!" over his shoulder.

"Maybe the talk of lube turned them on," Cillian whispered behind them.

Lucas sped up his steps.

Jack chuckled and caught up to Lucas as he pushed the lobby door open. "What's up? What's the rush? Do you have to pee?"

"We have massages to get to," Lucas said.

Jack frowned. "That's not why you're running."

"I'm not running."

"We are literally running together on the beach right now." Jack's arm swayed while Lucas bent over to pull off his flip-flops. "Are we a couple of retirees from Boca?"

Lucas sighed and went to release his hand, but Jack held firm, still scrunching his face in a frown. They stepped up on a boardwalk, following signs toward the row of pastel-painted bungalows. Each bungalow was larger than an average person's house.

Lucas whispered, "Oh, I dunno, maybe I'm mortified that my family and best friends all assumed it was a joke that I could have a boyfriend." He dropped his sunglasses onto his nose. "Or the fact that I actually don't have a boyfriend—I convinced someone to come play pretend with me, which only validates their view of me."

They stopped in front of the steps to Bungalow D. The house was painted pale yellow with light pink shutters and a crisp white deck with high bamboo growing on either side of it. There was plenty of room between bungalows to ensure privacy.

Lucas recognized one of his mother's beach bags on the deck of the baby blue Bungalow C to the right of their house. Some of Maggie's pool toys were on the deck of the mint green Bungalow E to the left.

"Lovely," he muttered.

"Hey," Jack murmured, pulling Lucas into his body. He pushed Lucas's sunglasses up to his hair, and Lucas lifted his head to look him in the eye. Jack shook his head. "Don't say it like that—like there's something wrong with you. You could have a boyfriend if you wanted to. You could go out on the street right now and say, 'I want a boyfriend,' and you'd have blokes flocking to you like seagulls to a sausage."

"Fuck, you're so weird." Lucas's voice trembled with muffled laughter. "And you don't know that. How can you say that?"

"I'm perceptive, yeah? If you wanted a boyfriend, you'd have a boyfriend. You don't want a boyfriend right now, and that's fine. There's nothing to be ashamed about. Yeah, it can be awkward going to group events alone, but that doesn't make you a bad person."

Lucas released his hand and reached into his pocket, walking up the steps of their bungalow. "I'm not ashamed."

"What was with everyone telling you not to disappear?"

Lucas huffed as he stuck the key card into the door. "What is this, an interrogation?"

"Nah, I left my sexy spy costume at home. We'll have to postpone the interrogation."

Lucas exhaled a laugh and his head fell forward. Jack's warm hand flattened on his lower back, sliding beneath his shirt to scratch between his shoulder blades. Jack pressed his mouth against the back of Lucas's neck. The kiss and soft scratches somehow signaled Lucas's heart to stop pounding out of his chest, despite the rush of blood to his groin.

"You don't have to be like this, you know," Lucas said. Jack kissed along the arch of his neck. Lucas's head dropped to the side, his eyes falling half shut. "You're not here to be my counselor or therapist."

"No, I'm not, but I want to help you feel good. I like listening." Jack nudged his nose on top of Lucas's shoulder. He squeezed Lucas with both arms and pressed his front to Lucas's back. "We're in this together."

Lucas said nothing, but he nodded, pushing the door open.

The sunlight-filled room that greeted them looked almost exactly like one featured in the home and garden magazine Jack had browsed on the plane. Sprawling hardwood floors were warm and welcoming beneath the luxurious white fabric draped over the wood furniture, its design a mix of modern and beach chic. The walls and high ceiling were white with dark wood beams running across the top; a bamboo fan whirled lazily above the bed. The dark, hardwood bed was so wide that they would have no problem staying apart in the night; the mattress sported equally luxurious white linens.

A set of glass french doors led out to their hot tub and outdoor shower. Floor-length tan curtains blew in the gentle breeze of the air conditioning. Their luggage waited for them on a long bench at the end of the bed, along with a glass-front fridge filled with fizzy beverages and fresh fruit. A flat-screen was mounted in front of the bed, and a seating area consisting of a white sofa and overstuffed armchair lay to the left of the bed beneath a large window. Jack ground his hips against Lucas's arse and whispered, "Fuck yes."

Lucas grinned and gently shoved his shoulder, and they both stepped into the room. The heavy wood door clicked shut.

"I'm not sure how sausage can be so lucrative, but this place is incredible," Jack said, placing his bag beside the bed. He lifted a handful of red rose petals from the bed and let them slip through his fingers, grinning over his shoulder. "How romantic. They must have known we were coming."

Lucas snorted and dropped his bag. He stretched his arms over his head. "So."

"So, what?"

"So, Teddy?"

He faced Lucas. "Yes?"

"I would have appreciated if you told me ahead of time that you were going to use a fake name with my family," Lucas said, lowering his arms. "I don't care what name you use, but it would have been nice not to be blindsided like that. I thought you were Mr. Preparation and Practice? No more surprise secrets, please. My blood pressure can't handle it. What if I already told them your name was Jack?"

"Teddy's my real name. Jack is my fake name for work."

Lucas's brows pinched. "What?"

Teddy reached into his carry-on and tossed his passport on the bed; the tightly tucked duvet caused it to bounce in the air.

Lucas picked it up and studied the photo for one *Theodore Bennet*. In his photo, Teddy looked significantly younger, and soft in the face. His hair was a wild mess of chocolate curls. A check of the expiration date told Lucas that Teddy was probably around twenty in the photo. "Is that… is that why you make your own travel bookings? So clients don't know your name?"

"It is. I don't need clients knowing who I am. Safety first, right?" Teddy reached out to grab his passport. "Plus, I like to keep the frequent flyer miles for myself."

Lucas looked at Teddy's bare wrists, no security bracelet in sight. "But why did you tell my mum? Why did you tell me?"

Teddy's motions slowed. He shrugged a casual shoulder, redirecting his attention to his luggage. "This is a different situation. You're not even really a client."

"You had me sign all your normal paperwork and jump through all your security hoops. My background check told you I'm not a psycho?"

"It feels different, all right? It's too many people to lie to at once. It's one thing if one person thinks I'm called Jack, but a huge group? That can cause confusion if I run into one of them on the street. Your mum seems like a nice lady. Your whole family seems nice."

"They're overbearing."

"They love you. You should be thankful."

Lucas pushed his tongue against the inside of his cheek. "You were… good. With my family. With Maggie, especially. I can barely handle them and you fit right in, despite your family fears."

"I didn't say I was bad with kids or families. I said that I don't usually deal with families while working."

"Fair enough." Lucas sniffed the center of his tee. "Ugh. I need to take my nasty travel clothes off and get rubbed."

"All right, then." Teddy sat on the bed and patted his thighs. "C'mere."

Lucas snorted as he walked toward the en-suite.

TEDDY FELL onto his back on the bed, sending his hair fluffing around his head. He heard Lucas unzip, followed by the hissed sound of peeing. Teddy shifted his hips and pressed his hand to his groin.

"Hurry up or I'll wet myself, babe," he said.

"Golden showers are not my kink, Theodore."

"Damn it, and I was so close," Teddy whispered, smiling wider. He got up off the bed and went to his luggage. He stepped on the back of his boots to toe them off. "Should we wear our swim stuff to the spa?"

The sink stopped running in the en-suite. "Yeah, makes sense. We're taking our clothes off anyway," Lucas said, passing by as Teddy unzipped his luggage. "We can go straight to lunch."

"Cool."

Teddy tossed a pair of swim trunks at Lucas's head. Lucas squawked but caught the trunks as they slid off his ear. "Um, these are small." He held the geometric-patterned blue shorts in front of himself. "They'll hit above my knee."

"Which is a good thing. You've got great legs. Try them."

Lucas sighed and placed the shorts on the bed. He unzipped his hoodie and shrugged it off, shucking his tee over his shoulders. Lucas's head popped out of his tee and Teddy gasped.

Lucas glanced in Teddy's direction. "What?"

"You're, like, hairy."

Lucas followed Teddy's gaze, blinking down at the dusting of reddish brown hair spread over his chest. A matching line of hair led from his navel to below his waistband. He looked up at Teddy. "Not really. What, you figured I'd be dolphin smooth like you?"

"I'm not dolphin smooth," Teddy scoffed, moving toward Lucas with slow steps. He reached out, and the pads of his fingers lightly stroked the center of Lucas's chest. "This is nice." His fingertips traced a series of circles over Lucas's heart. "A nice surprise."

Lucas's jawline tensed, his body otherwise motionless. "It's chest hair, Theodore. Not really a revelation."

The right side of Teddy's mouth rose. "Still nice, though. You have adorable nipples."

Lucas swallowed and stepped back, gesturing toward the en-suite. "You should pee and change." He put his hands on his hips. "We've got to get going."

"Yeah, yeah. I don't see your shorts on, bossy."

Teddy brushed his fingers beneath Lucas's navel and Lucas crumpled in on himself. Teddy grinned.

"Go change," Lucas said, unbuttoning his jeans. "I'll change too."

"I'll be quick, lover." Teddy batted his eyelashes and started unbuttoning his shirt as he backed away. "Wouldn't want to keep you waiting."

Lucas flicked both of his hands toward the en-suite. He changed into his swim trunks and started to dig through his luggage. The toilet flushed and Lucas heard water running behind the half-closed door.

Teddy came out of the bathroom wearing nothing but short black boxer briefs; his waistband drooped well below his hip dents. Lucas kept his eyes on his mess of clothing as Teddy pushed his suitcase open beside him.

Where Lucas's clothing was thrown into his luggage at random, Teddy's was rolled and arranged in a perfect mural of fabric. Teddy pulled out a white tank top, a black baseball hat, and a pair of short, bright yellow swim trunks.

Lucas pulled his eyes away from Teddy's long legs as he stepped into his shorts. "Who is Jack McQueen? Where did he come from?"

Teddy looped the white tank over his head and turned toward him. "Is this my interrogation?"

"Shall I dress like a spy?"

"I have a black turtleneck you could borrow," Teddy said, sounding far too excited about a turtleneck. He put his hat on backward. "I love a good interrogation."

"I'll pass, thanks. We need to get massages and eat. And nap."

"'Jumpin' Jack Flash' is one of my favorite Rolling Stones songs," Teddy said, pocketing his keycard. He tapped the screen of his phone, then turned it off and tossed it in his bag. "I thought Jack was a good name in my line of work. It's short, easy to remember, works well during sex, yet still sounds like a guy who can fix a car or talk football."

"Jack. Jack. Jack." Lucas's voice grew deeper as he repeated the name. "I suppose I can see that. And McQueen?"

Teddy slipped his feet into black flip-flops. "I was admiring an Alexander McQueen scarf at the time, plus I thought the name sounded kind of… dunno. Dramatic or something. Jack was simple. McQueen was for the more selective clients."

"Did you ever get that scarf?"

Teddy delicately placed black aviators on his nose. "I bought it for myself one month in."

THEY WERE greeted at the spa by two women, named Pam and Melody. The massage therapists wore the telltale flamingo white polos; they had dark ponytails fastened in identical pink hair clips and their tan skin glowed.

"Welcome," Pam said. Her voice was a soft, calm coo. Perfect spa tone. She held out a tray with two frosty glasses, mint-colored cubes clinking amid the foamy, white beverage inside. "Would either of you care for a drink? Fresh coconut with lime-infused ice."

"Yes, please." Lucas reached for a glass. He handed the glass to Teddy, taking the second glass for himself. He sipped once and felt his stress level drop on the spot. He exhaled, "Thank you."

"Please come with us." Melody indicated toward a skylit hallway. "We'll be in the Love Suite for your treatments."

Teddy smiled around the rim of his glass, wiggling his eyebrows at Lucas. Lucas muffled a laugh with a longer sip, and they followed their therapists. Pam opened a frosted glass door and stepped aside, bowing her head as they passed.

"This is your private locker room," she said. "Please disrobe, shower, and dress in the robes provided. If you are more comfortable being clothed during your massages, there are soft clothes provided for you in each locker."

"Great, thank you," Teddy said.

"Allow me to show you to your shower." Melody walked farther into the locker room. She opened a glass door; a large sea-blue-tiled shower was lit by yet another skylight. "There is an optional sea-salt scrub provided for you to apply during your shower, but please do not feel pressured to use it."

"Excellent," Teddy said, sliding his arm around Lucas's lower back. "He's got a few rough spots that need polishing."

Had anyone else said that to him, Lucas would have spat fire as fast as his brain could manage. When Teddy said it, Lucas's tongue flopped out of his mouth, like when Georgie rolled over to beg for belly rubs.

Pam and Melody smiled at them. Kindness radiated from their brown eyes.

"We will see you when you are finished," Pam said.

They left the locker room and shut the door behind them. Lucas pulled his tee off; Teddy neatly folded his tank and placed it in a locker.

"Do you go nude?" Teddy asked.

"I do." Lucas pushed his swim trunks down. He turned toward Teddy, who diverted his eyes upward as he fumbled with the strings of his swim trunks. "I like getting my glutes rubbed. My lower back acts up from sitting at my desk all the time."

"That why you're always taking walks?"

"Yep."

They faced each other in their black boxer briefs.

Teddy slowly drawled, "So, I'm fine with sharing the shower, but do you want to take turns or what?"

Lucas stared at the shower for a moment, exhaling a long breath. "I suppose turns will do."

"Do you want me to come in to scrub your back?"

"No," Lucas said pointedly. "I'll be fine, thanks."

Teddy held his hand out. "Age before beauty."

Lucas grabbed a fluffy white towel out of his locker. "Ha. Very funny."

He walked into the shower and pulled the fogged glass door shut. After sliding his black boxer briefs down his legs, he started the water, then soaped up.

MINUTES LATER, Lucas pushed the shower door open and Teddy fell sideways, grappling to hold on to the lockers.

"You all right?" Lucas laughed, taking another towel from his locker. He dabbed his hair. "You can shower now. The scrub stuff is nice, though I wouldn't use it on your moneymaker."

"My moneymaker," Teddy said and arched his eyebrows.

"Yeah. You seem like the type not to realize that salt scrub isn't needed on your cock and balls and such."

"You really think I'd salt scrub my cock?"

"You mean you don't season your sausage with salt?"

Teddy's mouth fell open, his cackle echoing around the locker room. "That wasn't really that funny, and was borderline gross, but I love that you said it!"

Lucas chuckled and bumped his hip to Teddy's. "Shower. You stink of pirate."

Teddy brought his mouth to Lucas's neck, growling "*Arrrggg*" and biting beneath his ear. Lucas smiled and pushed his face away. Teddy grinned and pecked his cheek. "I'll be back."

Teddy's shower was even shorter than Lucas's. His torso glistened when he came out, only a tiny white towel low around his hips. Lucas was sprawled on a white couch, with his mouth agape and his bare feet propped up on the arm. Teddy poked the bottom of his right foot.

"I'm up," Lucas snorted, sitting up straight. He held his towel in place, blinking extra wide. "Fuck, what's wrong with me? I keep passing out."

"You work too much."

Lucas breathed in deeply, swinging his feet to the tile floor. He slipped on his flip-flops. "That's… sort of true."

"Come on, darling," Teddy said, holding his arm out. "Time to get rubbed and forget all about those mean, mean men at work. Get those glutes nice and loose."

Lucas linked his arm with Teddy's as they walked into the treatment room. It wasn't so much a room as a private patio. Sheer white curtains billowed in between the wooden pillars that framed the space; birds chirped outside the screened-in walls. They could see and hear the ocean from the patio. The spa was built high enough to ensure privacy during their massage.

"Welcome back," Pam said, standing next to a white padded table. Melody stood next to an identical table. "Please relax facedown, underneath the sheets. We will step out while you make yourselves comfortable."

They nodded and waited for the therapists to step into the hallway. Teddy dropped his towel before the door even shut. Lucas looked away, which was useless when Teddy strode naked to the farther table. His plump arse swayed on top of his endless legs. Teddy placed his towel on a counter that ran along the wall.

"I'm not looking," Teddy said and turned his head away as he slid under the sheets. "Sadly." Lucas got on the table and dropped his towel onto the floor. Teddy murmured, "You've got a nice little body. Great arse, obviously, but everything else is lovely too."

Lucas turned his head toward Teddy's table. Teddy was already smirking at him. "Cheers. I'll send your positive feedback to my trainer."

There was a soft knock on the door before Pam and Melody came inside. Quiet, relaxing music piped into the room.

"Are there any areas you would like special attention on?" one asked, their voices starting to blend.

"Glutes, please," Lucas said, turning his head to place his face in the cloth-covered cradle. "Legs in general. Lower back is always nice."

Teddy's voice was muffled by fabric. "Shoulders and upper back for me, please."

Lucas hummed, adding, "Yeah, those for me too."

"Are you two on your honeymoon?" Melody asked.

Both burst out laughing, then stopped for a split second and resumed laughing upon hearing each other's reaction. Their bodies relaxed on the padded tables and their hysterical laughter calmed.

"Not quite," Lucas said.

"Maybe one day, fluffy-bum," Teddy said, still chuckling in his face cradle. "I'll make an honest man out of you."

"Yeah, maybe, honey bunch. You'd be a dashing groom, I'm sure."

"YOU REALLY didn't have to set all this up."

Lucas chewed his final bite of salad while cutting into a slice of juicy cantaloupe. "I didn't set anything up." He dabbed his mouth with a white cloth napkin. "I legitimately just sent an e-mail saying that my boyfriend likes healthy food, and we'd like a light lunch on the beach." Lucas swirled his fork in the air with a piece of bright orange melon speared juicily on its prongs. "I hate to break it to you, but I didn't run over here to cut and arrange our fruit platter. This was all Flamingo."

Teddy bit into a slice of watermelon. "I like flamingos."

Lucas chuckled lightly, popping grapes into his mouth. He pressed the back of his head into his white chaise lounge. The ocean calmly lapped mere feet away from their cabana.

"That was such a good massage," Teddy said. His voice sounded sleepy and low. "Such deceptively strong hands."

"It really was."

"You were asleep most of it."

"For some reason, whenever I get my legs worked on, I pass out. It's like an off button or something."

"Good to know."

Lucas reached toward the fruit plate between them, taking two more slices of cantaloupe. "You keep your grabby hands away from my legs."

"I'd never want to threaten your chastity, love."

They munched on their fruit, and Teddy sipped the last of his piña colada. A waitress came over with a tray of fresh drinks. Teddy accepted his frozen cocktail. He handed Lucas a new glass of rum punch, and Lucas stretched across and took it from him.

"Thank you."

"Are you feeling relaxed?"

Lucas's lips popped off his straw. He licked a drop of red punch from the corner of his mouth. "Getting there."

"Your family seems so nice. Why don't you like spending time with them?"

Lucas shut his eyes and lay back down, propping his straw in his mouth. "What were you saying about relaxation?"

"C'mon, I'm not trying to stress you out," Teddy said gently, turning on his side, his muscles flexing with the motion. He had taken off everything but his yellow shorts. He sipped his drink, crossing his ankles. "I'm trying to learn so I can better understand the situation."

"It's weird. And silly." Lucas glanced at Teddy, looking wry. "Though family stuff always is, right?"

Teddy said nothing, sipping his drink and studying the sea.

Lucas stared at him for a beat as the breeze ruffled their cabana curtains. "I don't always like to do everything with everyone all the time, which makes me an outcast to my mother, who doesn't seem to understand boundaries." He took a long suck of rum punch and relaxed on his back, sighing slowly. "That's what they meant with the whole 'disappear' thing. They tease me because I tend to disappear on long group trips like this. Not the whole trip, but sometimes I need to be alone for a few hours. I don't know why, but I do."

"You're an introvert, maybe?"

"I don't think I'm an introvert, but I think I do have a few characteristics that are common in introverts. My family—which includes Zamir's entire family as well—has never understood why I don't always want to be involved with everything all the time, but they also.... They've never understood other things about me."

"Like what?"

"Like... it's hard to explain, but when you're around a big family all the time, for your whole life, and everything is shared, sometimes you like to keep some things for yourself. It sounds selfish, but that's who I am, I guess."

Teddy licked frozen coconut off his lips, pushing himself up on his forearm. "I don't think you're selfish. Far from it. I've met a lot of selfish men. You're not selfish."

"Selfish isn't the right word. Um. Withholding? I don't know how to describe it. It's like, ever since I was born, it was assumed that I'd share everything I ever did, every quid I ever earned, every secret thought I ever had, with my entire extended family. I like spending my money, and I like being generous. If anyone in my family told me they needed something, *anything*, I'd do everything in my power to give it to them. But I don't like assumptions. I've never liked how my mum presumes, not even when I was a kid. I'm not describing myself clearly, I'm sorry."

"No, you are."

Lucas stirred his drink, snorting down at the bright red punch. "You didn't lie about being a good listener."

"I don't believe I've lied to you about anything in our time together besides my name, though you now know the truth about that."

"I haven't lied to you about anything."

"Feels good, right?"

"Good," Lucas said, his voice quiet. "Weird, but good."

Teddy placed his half-full cup on the table between them. "Ask me a question."

Lucas chewed a chunk of extra sharp cheddar. He furrowed his brows. "About what?"

"Whatever you want. We'll even it out."

"Hmm," Lucas hummed deeply, still chewing. He swallowed and pointed at the fruit plate. "Can I have the last piece of cantaloupe?"

Teddy laughed. "Yes, by all means. That's my least favorite melon."

Lucas gasped. "How is cantaloupe your least favorite melon? I thought everyone's least favorite was that green watery one?"

"Honeydew!" Teddy's voice dropped, and he cradled his hand over the remaining slices of green melon. "How very dare you? That's the second-best melon behind watermelon!"

"No way."

"Was that really your question?"

"I don't want to pry."

"You? You don't want to pry?"

"I don't pry. It's not my fault most people are easier to read than the Sunday comics."

"Very well."

"Let's see, let's see," Lucas said, scratching the top of his head. He arched his back as he yawned, propping his hands behind his head. "Do you have female clients?"

"Not really. I'll straight-up escort for women sometimes, but no sex. That's how I met Mr. Carson's wife, actually. At a charity luncheon I went to with a friend of hers. Once in a blue moon, I'll get a male-female couple who wants a three-way, but that hasn't happened in well over a year. Maybe even longer. It's usually me and two other men if I'm doing that."

"Do they get a discount? Like buy one, get one free?"

"No way. I charge the same per hour per person, unless one just wants to watch, then I charge a flat fee to the second person."

"Do you like three-ways?"

"Eh," Teddy said, shrugging. "It's usually all right for me, because I'm the outsider. The guest. Whether it's men or women, they're pretty revved up to be with me. It can be a technical nightmare, though, trying to keep everyone satisfied. I much prefer one-on-one."

"Hm. Interesting."

"Would you do a three-way?"

"In theory, I guess? In reality, probably not."

"Why?"

"I'm so rarely into one person for more than just a fuck, let alone two people at once."

"Even if they're both physically attractive?"

"That has very little to do with it for me."

"Are you maybe demisexual? You need an emotional bond for sexual attraction?"

Lucas whistled quietly. "Boy, oh boy. Introvert. Demisexual. Did you actually study Psychology, not Classics, at uni?"

"Ha. No. I just like to read."

"Fair enough." Lucas arched his lower back and propped an arm behind his head. "I don't believe I'm demisexual, based on what I've read about it, but sexuality is such a fluid, changing… thing. Who knows. I have plenty of… attraction, I guess. I'm sexually attracted to strangers and such without an emotional bond. I just so rarely find people I can tolerate for extended periods, who I also want to fuck. I don't think it has to do with sex, it's more like their personality meshing with mine. It doesn't often happen."

"I see. What do you find attractive?"

"You little sneak," Lucas chuckled, stirring his drink. "You're still trying to find out what turns me on."

"I am not," Teddy insisted, grinning. He flipped his sunglasses up to hold his hair off his forehead. "We're having a conversation. I didn't ask what turns you on. You're the one who brought up group sex." He scanned down to Lucas's bare feet, delicate in size with high, pale arches. "Why would I care what turns you on?"

"Aw, you want to be surprised? Are we going to have a true wedding night tonight? A proper virginal honeymoon?"

Teddy bit his straw. "I'm very traditional, you know."

"Hello, lovely boys!"

They looked toward the cheerful voice, and then heard other voices chattering around their cabana. Lucas sat up straighter and put his plate on the table between them; Teddy slid his sunglasses over his eyes and sat up with his feet on either side of his lounge. Jo popped into their cabana. Lane, Maggie, Zamir, Cillian, and a number of other family members came in from every side of the open space. They spotted the fruit platter and pounced.

"Oh, um, hi," Teddy said, shocked. Jo sat at the end of his lounge chair, fanning herself with her hand. He looked to Lucas, who was hugging some family member he had yet to meet; a line of tension ran up Lucas's bare back. "What happened to the pool?"

"We felt like visiting!" Jo reached out and took the last piece of cantaloupe on Lucas's plate, then popped it into her mouth. She smiled at Teddy as she chewed with her mouth shut. "The pool is lovely, but a little birdy told us you two were having lunch over here, so we all took a field trip."

"Nice," Teddy said, swallowing thickly. He reached for his piña colada and sipped through his straw, widening his eyes at Jo's rapt stare. "So… um…." He saw Lucas standing to hug who he thought was Lane's husband. Teddy's lips twitched to whistle a bird noise, then stopped, instead sipping his drink for longer. "Where is John?"

Jo's eyes lit up. "Oh, Luke didn't tell you? He's flying in tomorrow. Business calls."

"Ah," Teddy nodded. "I don't think he knew that, actually. He didn't say anything to me."

"Typical," she chuckled, taking Lucas's glass from the tabletop. She sipped, wrinkling her nose. "Yuck, too rummy."

"He's been really swamped at work," Teddy said, keeping his tone friendly. "He's exhausted. It probably just slipped his mind."

She waved her hand in a dismissive flutter, chuckling. "Always so serious with work. Work, work, work. I don't know where he gets it."

Teddy continued to smile, but his eyes narrowed behind his sunglasses. "Uh-huh."

"Not that I'm not proud of his accomplishments," she said quickly, waving her palms at him. "Far from it! I know he's the best at what he does. The hardest worker."

A beautiful woman with short black hair popped her head into their conversation. "She tells everyone all about her golden boy," the woman said. Teddy remembered her to be Zamir's mother, named Tracy. "Lucas is her little star."

"I just wish he'd relax more," Jo said, shrugging. Her body bounced on the lounge. "Oh! Maybe being with you will relax him! You can keep him regular, if you know what I'm saying."

Teddy laughed, and shock flushed his body.

"Tazzy!"

Teddy had never been happier to be tackled by a small, chlorine-scented child. He fell back on his chair, letting out a dramatic grunt. "Holy moly, Miss Maggie, did you swallow all the water in the pool?"

"No, car-ay-zy," Maggie giggled, perching on top of his chest. Teddy chuckled and lifted her to sit next to him on his chair. Maggie sat with her small legs crossed and her knees bumping Teddy's side. "Will you swim with me?"

"Sure. Where's Mummy?"

Maggie flung her tiny hand toward the front corner of the cabana, where Lane and Lucas were standing together and chatting. She poked the nightingale on Teddy's shoulder. Teddy looked back at her and smiled.

"Is this a bird?" she asked, shy.

"It is." He sat up straighter. "It's called a nightingale."

Maggie's eyes lit up; she wiggled closer. In a pure, high-pitched singing voice, she softly sang a line from Cinderella's song to the nightingale. She opened her mouth as wide as she could, leaning back to sing the word "High."

Teddy chuckled and nodded his head side to side to the beat. He sang two octaves lower to repeat the line as a duet with Maggie. "I just watched a little bit of *Cinderella* at Uncle Luke's flat, but I fell asleep before that part. It's my favorite part of the movie."

"Me too!"

IN THE corner of the cabana, Lane adjusted Lucas's sunglasses. Lucas tore his eyes away from Teddy's lounge.

"I like those trunks," Lane said, stepping back and staring at his shorts. "They're amazing on you. The blue's the same color as your eyes. I love the pattern."

Lucas looked down at his swim trunks, then remembered that he had on tiny geometric-patterned shorts instead of his usual black board shorts. "Oh. Thanks. Teddy bought them for me."

"Good. Your other ones are ugly."

"Hey, they're bloody swim trunks. Who cares what they look like?"

"Your hot-as-fuck boyfriend, apparently."

Lucas's mouth fell open. "Such language. You kiss your daughter with that mouth?"

Lane grabbed a fruity cocktail off the tray of a passing waitress. "I'm on holiday. I can't be mummy all the time. Sometimes, I need to curse and ogle hot men."

"I'm right here, babe," Dean, Lane's husband, said from next to her.

Dean flexed his arms and spun, wiggling his bum against Lane's thigh. Lane and Lucas applauded his display.

Lane downed half her drink, crunching ice between her back teeth. "So, should I be concerned that my daughter is taken with your hot-as-fuck boyfriend? And is he…. Is he actually getting her to eat vegetables?"

Lucas looked toward Teddy's lounge. Teddy and Maggie were taking turns throwing crinkled slices of carrots in each other's mouth. Maggie, the child, was more accurate than Teddy, the adult. Each throw caused Maggie to squeal.

"I wouldn't be concerned," Lucas said. "Georgie liked Teddy more than me within seconds of meeting him. He humped Teddy's leg multiple times. It wasn't his finest moment. Teddy's very…."

Teddy looked up toward him as a carrot bounced off his cheek. His hair was wild behind his pushed-up sunglasses. Teddy winked.

Lucas dropped his eyes and grinned at his bare feet. "Captivating," Lucas finally said. "Harmless, but captivating."

Lane looked between them, humming. "I'm sure."

MORE FAMILY members came up to Teddy to introduce themselves. He met Lucas's maternal grandparents, two aunts, three uncles, five cousins, and a few people whose place in the family tree he wasn't able to pinpoint. He'd have to quiz Lucas later.

Lane came by to relieve him of Maggie duty. "You're a saint to play with her, and I'm so thankful for the break, but you're here on holiday," Lane whispered to him. She had Maggie propped on her hip and dozing on her shoulder. "Don't let this little stinker wiggle her way into your schedule. Luke has already done enough babysitting to last a lifetime."

"Well, she did manage to convince me to accompany her to shell painting, but I already highlighted that in my itinerary. I love seashells and sparkle paint."

Lane laughed loudly and Teddy stood from his chair, stretching his arms over his head. She stared at him as he stretched. He glanced down his body and winced, holding his hand over his nightingale.

Teddy whispered, "I already told Maggie she can't get any tattoos until she's at least fifty years old, and she will need your parental permission."

Lane laughed again, softer, bouncing Maggie on her hip. "No, not that. I'm just really happy Luke picked you."

"You've only known me a couple of hours."

"Doesn't matter," she said simply. "I'm still happy he picked you."

Teddy nodded, brushing his right toes over the sand-dusted floor. "Yeah," he exhaled, joy breaking over his face. "Me too."

"Now, go rescue him. My mum's got her lecture look on." Lane tilted her chin across the cabana. "Go get your man."

Teddy chuckled, running his fingers through his hair. He walked toward Lucas, who was in the middle of a conversation with his mother. He watched Lucas nod; his posture wound tight.

"I wanted us to have lunch together, just the two of us," Lucas said quietly. "It's a lot for him to have to meet everyone at once. We didn't mean to insult you, we just wanted to eat together. I made the plans, not him. Teddy had nothing to do with it. I didn't know the entire group would be here already."

"I don't understand your behavior. How could you be so cold?"

Lucas sighed. "Mum, please. Not everything is such a big deal. I haven't had a serious boyfriend for nearly a decade. Are you really already annoyed with me for spending time with him?"

Teddy's feet slowed. His body tilted right as he sought out more of Lucas's words.

"Oh, Luke, of course I'm not annoyed with you or him. I'm thrilled for you! He's lovely!"

A warm flush raced through Teddy's body. He held on to one of the billowing curtains at his side.

Lucas replied, "Yet you're already giving me a hard time for not participating in an unscheduled event."

Jo frowned, her hands holding Lucas's outer biceps. "Stop talking like that. You're not at work. Lighten up."

Teddy watched Lucas's jawline tighten even more, flexing his hands against his thighs.

"I've already apologized to you for not including you in our plans." Lucas's voice was almost inaudible within the large, chattering group. "What more do you want?"

Teddy stepped up next to Lucas, offering Jo a warm smile. He placed his hand on the small of Lucas's back. Lucas's skin was hot beneath his palm and his muscles twitched. "I'm not interrupting, am I? Oh, I'm sorry! So sorry," Teddy said, taking a step back. He lowered his head, running his fingers through his hair. "I'll leave you two to your mum-son chat. So sorry to—"

"No, no, love," Jo said, reaching out and grasping his shoulder. She smiled kindly at him. "No interruption. Not at all. I'm so happy you're here." She squeezed his arm and looked to Lucas, nodding. "Truly."

"As am I," Teddy said, leaning into her touch. "Oh, before I forget to ask, do you use Jo Malone candles? Luke told me you like candles, and I've been meaning to try a new scent. I think of you every time I see the name in stores. I like their fig one. Fig and cassis."

"Oh! Yes!" Jo clucked in surprise. Lucas swallowed and kept his expression natural. "I like Jo Malone's selection. I love Dyptique, as well. Have you ever tried those?"

"I've seen them in stores, but I couldn't get into any of their scents." Teddy's fingers tiptoed around Lucas's hip; his palm warmed the curved dip between his hip and ribs. "Have you ever heard of Volcania?"

Her face lit up, her hands gesturing wildly in the air. "Yes! From Bali!"

Teddy took a small step backward with his hand still on Lucas's hip. Lucas said nothing, but his feet mirrored Teddy's tiny steps.

Teddy said, "Yeah, I like those a lot. All natural. Made from the earth. Hey." He pointed from Lucas to Jo, then back to Lucas. "Would you mind if I borrow him a moment? I saw these gorgeous birds flying around down by the water. I wanna check them out."

"Oh." Her hands reached toward Lucas. "Well, I—"

"Thank you so much," Teddy said before she could finish, squeezing her outstretched hand. "We'll be back in just a minute." His fingertips moved to the hem of her cover-up, the fabric billowing away from her body. "I love that caftan on you, by the way. The colors are perfect for your complexion."

"Oh, thank you," she said and laid her palm flat on the center of her chest. "I heard you bought Lucas's trunks." She snorted. "Thank God."

Lucas huffed out a breath, but Teddy pulled him backward by the hip. He brought his lips to Lucas's ear and whispered, "Come with me," while lightly running his knuckles up the bottom of his spine. Lucas kept his head facing toward his mother as he nodded, glancing sideways at Teddy.

They slipped around the mass of people and walked down the wooden steps of the cabana. Teddy held his hand out and Lucas laced their fingers together as they walked barefoot in the sand.

"Where are we going?" Lucas asked. He dropped his sunglasses onto the bridge of his nose and squinted. "I don't see any birds."

Teddy looked around as he walked them to the left of the cabana; his mouth pursed side to side. He pointed toward a large bank of smooth, gray boulders on the shoreline.

"There."

Teddy walked them around the side of the rocks closest to the sea. They were hidden from Lucas's family in the cabana. Warm water lapped at their ankles.

"You're a candle expert, or was that research?" Lucas asked.

Teddy's smile went shy, and he tucked a wave behind his ear. "I like candles."

"Candles, flamingos, sparkly seashells. What else? Potpourri?"

Teddy chuckled and stood with his back against the boulders. He held Lucas's hips with both hands and guided him to stand between his slightly spread legs. Lucas blinked at him, bracing himself by gripping Teddy's lower ribs.

"Kiss me," Teddy said softly.

IF IT were a week ago in his bedroom during their kissing practice session, Lucas might have put up a fight or said something sarcastic in reply to Teddy's request. After their early wake-up, hours of travel, the stress of his family, and enduring seeing Teddy nearly naked multiple times in twenty-four hours, Lucas could not begin to formulate a response.

He shrugged and stood on the balls of his feet, gripping the back of Teddy's hair. He angled his head and nudged his face forward, tenderly sucking on Teddy's lips. Teddy's mouth responded immediately. His answering sucks were just as gentle and slow, and their faces tilted in opposite directions.

Teddy's brows arched, and he hummed into the kiss, smoothing his hands to the small of Lucas's back. Sweat and sun cream slid under his palms as Lucas's toes dug into the sand in front of his feet. Teddy let his tongue tease into Lucas's mouth; Lucas's chin lifted as his tongue chased Teddy's. Sticky, sweet saliva slurped between them. Lucas felt like he was trying to find a cherry in a bowl of melting coconut ice cream, his hands tightening in Teddy's hair.

"Lucas," Teddy breathed.

Lucas flattened his hand on Teddy's chest, then kissed him again.

Lucas's brows furrowed, his eyes closed. Teddy's strong jaw opened wider to guide their kisses, their sweaty chests pressing flush together. Lucas tugged on the back of Teddy's hair. Teddy groaned and palmed his arse, squeezing his plump right cheek. Lucas's hips pressed against him. Teddy's hand squeezed tighter and pulled Lucas in. Lucas's feet skidded over the wet sand.

"O-oh!"

Lucas's eyes popped open. He sucked a shaky breath in and pulled his face back. Teddy pressed his face to Lucas's damp collarbone, the pads of his fingers drawing small circles just above Lucas's waistband.

"Sorry, loves!" Jo winced, holding her palms toward them, with her face bright red. "Didn't mean to interrupt!" She pulled down one lens of her sunglasses and winked at them, backing away. "Have fun!" She retreated quickly, waving Lane back to the cabana. Farther away, she said, "They're busy, love, leave them be!"

Teddy started to kiss Lucas's neck, sweat and coconut tanning oil mingling sweetly on his tongue. Lucas let his head tilt to the side.

"They won't bother us anymore when we walk off if they think we're fooling around," Teddy whispered, teasing breath over Lucas's hot skin. Lucas's eyes closed without his control. His smile widened, and a tingly, hot feeling buzzed in his lower belly. Teddy chuckled as he dragged his lips to his sharp collarbone. "At least not for the next two hours or so. Then we might have to do a repeat performance."

Lucas looped his arms over Teddy's shoulders; his head fell backward. Teddy's lips mouthed around his Adam's apple, kisses trickling over the lowest point of his stretched neck.

"You're, like, smart," Lucas said on a groan. He opened his eyes and peered at Teddy. "How is that fair? You look the way you do, and yet you also got some brains in the deal."

Teddy pressed their foreheads together. He tilted his head to peck Lucas's lips and squeezed his arse gently. Lucas lifted himself to peck Teddy again. Teddy watched Lucas's eyes flutter shut, even for the short press of their lips.

"Just some." Teddy lifted one hand to pinch the air. "Just a little bit of brains."

"I mean, honestly. How do you walk around like this"—Lucas gestured from Teddy's sandy feet up to his face with one quick flick of his hand—"and not get distracted by your own reflection?"

Teddy slid his right hand down the front of Lucas's arm, stroking over his wrist before he laced their fingers together. He pulled their joined hands up to rest on his muscled, sun-warmed stomach as they strolled around the boulder.

"Well, it *is* a daily struggle," Teddy said seriously. "But, somehow, I've managed to avoid falling into any reflective bodies of water or mirrors, hypnotized by my own beauty. I was a Classics major, after all. I've read my fair share of Greek mythology."

Lucas saw a pair of birds land on top of one of the boulders. They were small with smooth yellow bellies and a bit of slate blue on the undersides of their necks. There was a dab of red on their beaks, almost as if they were wearing lipstick, and a white stripe on the sides of their faces.

"Oh, look, they're back." Teddy pulled Lucas closer to the rocks. He kept his voice quiet, their steps careful and slow. "Aren't they cute? I love their little outfits."

Lucas stared up at the birds and pursed his open lips.

"Oh, so… there were actually birds you wanted to show me?"

"Yeah!" Teddy beamed at him. He looked back to the birds, squeezing Lucas's hand and swaying their arms between them. "Our room has Wi-Fi, right? Maybe I can download a bird-watching book onto my iPad."

"Yeah, we… we've got Wi-Fi."

"Cool."

As Teddy watched the birds hop around, his eyes widened as soft lips pressed to the outside of his bicep. He placed his hand on the small of Lucas's back and turned his upper body, dipping down and gently kissing Lucas's bottom lip. Lucas's hand ghosted over Teddy's cheek, holding his face for a split second, then fell to his chest, thumbing between Teddy's pecs.

"Christ. I think we need to go in the water," Lucas murmured, pressing the bridge of his nose to Teddy's bicep. "I'm losing it."

Teddy stepped into Lucas's space, guiding his back against a boulder. His lips dropped open in a goofy grin, a drawn-out breath hissing into his throat. "Are you… drunk?" Teddy asked slowly, his dimple deepening. He thumbed the dip of Lucas's waist. Lucas brayed a laugh and covered his face with his hands. "Drunk off one and a half cups of rum punch? Wow, Lukeybear. I didn't take you for that cheap a date."

"I'm not drunk. I'm just…." Lucas pushed his sunglasses up to his hair, rubbing the heels of his hands over his eyes. "I don't know. I think I'm…."

Teddy prompted, “Having fun?”

“Yeah, kind of,” Lucas said, dropping his hands from his face and squinting. “Is that weird?”

“Um, no,” Teddy giggled. He gripped both of Lucas’s hands and swayed their arms in and out. “That’s great. That’s the goal, love.” Teddy gently kicked warm water at Lucas’s ankle. “Do you want to go swim? The water’s perfect.” He gave his hips a little swivel. “If you can manage seeing me wet, of course. Wouldn’t want you to scandalize the family with an untimely stiffy.”

Lucas pinched the sides of his sunglasses. “I can manage.”

Chapter TWELVE

THE WELCOME barbecue dinner wrapped up at around nine, right as a karaoke company started blasting music and laser lights from a large stage set up on the beach. Their enormous group was spread out over picnic tables placed on the sand, with Tiki torches lit around the perimeter of their space. At most backyard grill outs, people ate burgers and hot dogs, and maybe drank a few beers. At the welcome barbecue, guests were served Kobe beef hot dogs, lobster tails, and mugs of Cristal champagne.

"These guys do the lights and stage design for U2," Cillian shouted over the music. Red barbecue sauce dotted his bottom lip. He bit into a hot dog. Mustard smeared on his top lip to complete his duo of face sauces. "Fucking incredible," he said out of the side of his mouth. He swallowed. "Magicians of light."

Zamir wiped Cillian's mouth with his thumb, then sucked the pad of his thumb. Cillian leaned in with his tongue already out, both starting to kiss as if there wasn't a children's tea party going on at the table behind them, and their elderly relatives weren't seated at the table in front of them.

Lucas and Teddy glanced at each other. Lucas smirked against the rim of his beer bottle. Teddy grinned with his straw crunched between his back teeth, then discreetly rolled his tongue at Lucas. Lucas muffled a throaty laugh with a sip of beer.

"And the crew who organized the Zill-ympics work for *Survivor* and *MTV Real World/Road Rules Challenges*," Zamir said, saliva and mustard shining on his mouth. Now Cillian reached out, dabbing the spots away with a napkin. "We wanted it to be fair for us to compete, so we actually have no idea what kind of events and stuff they're planning."

Lane and Dean sat down at their table, and Maggie crawled onto the bench beside Teddy.

Teddy whispered, "Up past your bedtime?"

"Yup," Maggie sighed, her eyes falling shut. Her small head plunked against his shoulder. "Tired."

Teddy could sympathize. It had been a long day.

They had showered after spending the entire day on the beach, and then changed into actual clothes. Lucas's cheeks already showed the beginnings of a caramel tan, contrasting with his loose powder blue V-neck. Comfortable khaki shorts clung to his thighs, and his bare feet were crossed beneath his bench in the fine sand.

Teddy had chosen a billowy, short-sleeved chambray shirt, unbuttoned to midchest, along with a pair of darker jeans with the cuffs rolled up past his ankles. He had also kicked his shoes off.

Lucas spun his beer bottle on the table and asked, "So, we could show up thinking it's all fun and games, but then these guys could be setting up legitimate athletic events? Like, hard ones that require skill?"

"No worries, bro," Lane said cheerfully. "Dean and I are going to own those games. We've been training. You don't have to worry about difficulty, because we're going to own it. Own. It. Bro."

"Us too," Cillian offered. Zamir nodded at his side.

Lucas and Teddy glanced at each other.

"I guess we should have practiced more," Lucas said, his eyes twinkling. Teddy's brows arched and his full lips popped open in shock. "Silly us."

"Yeah," Teddy laughed out. Lucas grinned, looking away with flushed cheeks. Teddy dipped his head lower, brushing his lips against Lucas's ear. "We could always practice tomorrow," he murmured. "Tonight too, if you'd like."

The warmth of Lucas's cheeks surged hotter.

"All right, all right, all right!" the DJ's voice boomed. "We're ready to take requests up at the stage!"

"Yes!" Zamir and Cillian exhaled in the same, excited voice, jumping up from the table. Mobs of people ran toward the stage. Cillian pulled a thick packet of paper from his back pocket and shouted, "I've got our rep list, babe!"

Lane lifted Maggie's limp body from the bench and sat down in her spot. Dean took Maggie into his arms. Lane propped her hands on her cheeks, her gaze scanning around the table.

"Well?" she drawled, fluctuating her voice. "Who wants to karaoke with me?"

"Not me, thank you," Lucas said.

Lane wrinkled her nose. "Aw, c'mon, Loo Loo. You always say that!"

"I hate karaoke."

Lane's eyes rolled to Teddy. She shrugged and nodded. "He really does."

"I know." Teddy slipped his hand onto Lucas's thigh. He squeezed once; Lucas's leg shifted closer. "He made that very clear."

"Will you sing a duet with me?" Lane asked, her voice sugary sweet. She clasped her hands under her chin. "Please? Please, Tazzy?" Teddy's smile broke into a bashful laugh and he rubbed the back of his neck. "Maggie said you have a beautiful voice."

Lucas's brows furrowed. "What? You sing?"

Teddy shook his head. "It was nothing. But…."

Lane drawled, "But?" and widened her eyes.

Teddy lifted his hands. "I guess I could try to sing with you?" he said with a shy grin, his voice slow. "I haven't sung karaoke in, like, forever. I might be terrible."

"Yes!" Lane cheered, fist-pumping. She gripped Teddy's hand and stood from the table. "C'mon, we need to put our song in the queue."

"I don't even know what song to sing," Teddy said as he was forcibly pulled out of his seat. He looked at Lucas over his shoulder. "I told you they'd be our biggest competition. She's got a stronger grip than I do."

Lane pulled him along. "Damn straight I do."

LUCAS STOOD from their table and walked to where his mother was sitting in front of the stage.

"Lukeybear!" she cried, scooting over on her bench. She petted the wood beside her. She held a fishbowl-sized glass of red sangria sloshing in her hand. Lucas leaned down to kiss her warm cheek. "Sit, sit! Look at that tan after one day! You lucky little ducky!"

He sat down at the table full of his mother's friends, including Zamir's and Cillian's mothers. They all had similarly large glasses of wine-based mixed drinks, some drinking red sangria and some drinking white.

Cillian and Zamir concluded their performance of Bon Jovi's masterpiece "Livin' on a Prayer" and bowed deeply at the front of the stage.

"Nice one, Zill, nice one!" the DJ shouted over the cheers. Cillian and Zamir jumped off the stage with their hands joined. "Next up, we've got the lovely Lane and terrific Teddy!"

Lane and Teddy walked up the stage steps, each holding a mic. The crowd was already cheering and whistling. They had been drinking in the sun for hours. The crowd would cheer for a conch shell propped near a microphone.

Lucas clapped while staring at the strutting duo. Teddy met his gaze and smiled from the stage. A peppy drumbeat kicked off the up-tempo Madonna song "Open Your Heart."

Lane and Teddy grinned at each other and strutted right for four beats, then left for four beats. They planted their spread feet in the center of the stage and extended their hands toward the crowd, right hand then left hand, their straight arms doing a "Greased Lightning"-type motion with each set of four beats.

"Oh, choreography!" Jo shouted, clapping louder. "Lovely!"

They repeated the choreography for the next set of sixteen beats, and the crowd only grew more enthusiastic. Lane crooned the first verse in her best throaty Madonna impression; she dragged her flat hand down her cheek to the front of her neck. Teddy read the words on the monitor, bobbing his chin forward to the beat. Then he opened his mouth.

Teddy started to sing in a soulful, raspy voice that spread over the crowd in a hypnotic layer of honey. Lucas could see Teddy's lips moving in time with the words, but Lucas's mouth remained agape, his eyes unblinking.

"Oh my God, he can sing!" Jo exclaimed, pulling Lucas to his feet.

Teddy gripped his belt buckle and gave a small roll of his hips toward where Lucas sat. The women at Lucas's table got to their feet, hooting and hollering and outright shrieking. Teddy's dimple popped. His grin was sly and he directed it toward Lucas before he turned and walked across the stage.

Lane and Teddy strutted up the middle of the stage, Lane singing the bridge to the chorus. The chorus included both Lane and Teddy jumping to the beat with their right arms fist-pumping into the air. They alternated that move with forming a heart with their arms over their head. The audience mirrored their dance motions and sang along while rainbows of laser light spilled from the stage.

They split the second verse, each singing two lines, and then jumped off the stage into the audience, continuing their heart choreography. Lane went to Dean, rubbing her back against Dean's front and giggling while singing. Dean's bellowed laughter picked up on the mic.

Teddy prowled up to Lucas during Lane's solo. His long legs flexed and snapped as his hips swayed like a trained supermodel. He got close enough for Lucas to feel his hot breath over his lips. Their gazes locked as he sang the bridge alone, his words more like a growled statement than singing random lyrics. He rubbed his groin against Lucas's crotch, and his top lip snarled upward. The crowd roared. Lucas stood still, but he smirked and held his stare.

Teddy turned toward Lane and pumped his fist in the air. Both sang the final chorus as they ran back up to the stage, completing the song with even more strutting, spins, and heart shapes. The audience clapped and screamed when they finished. Lucas found himself screaming along with the crowd. Teddy caught his eye and winked, pursing his lips in an air kiss.

"Oooooh, I like him," Jo said in Lucas's ear, squeezing him to her side. "What a cutie!"

Lucas clapped, and his lips twitched upward. "Yeah, he's real cute."

Teddy and Lane walked back to their original table, where Lucas, Zamir, Cillian, Dean, and a few of the younger cousins were sitting. Their quick chatter got louder the closer they got to the table.

"Oh shit, yes! That's the one!" Lane cried, hugging Teddy to her side. "'Love Is A Battlefield'! Let's do that one tomorrow!"

They stepped apart and did the classic Pat Benatar shoulder shimmy. Teddy's eyes lit up a split second before he threw his head back to laugh.

"You were beautiful, love," Dean said, jumping up and hugging Lane. He kissed her temple as they swayed together. "I almost threw my bra at you, it was so amazing."

Lane beamed up at her husband. She thumbed toward Teddy. "I owe it all to this gentleman." She held her hand out for a high five. "Who knew you'd be such a bloody dynamo? I felt like I was on stage with Mick Jagger!"

Teddy chuckled breathily and sat down next to Lucas, returning her high five.

"Yeah, man, those moves," Cillian said, swaying his hips. "How do you do that wormy thing?"

"Erm, I dunno," Teddy said, chuckling again. "It comes naturally, I…." His breath hitched and Lucas squeezed his thigh. "I guess."

"It was amazing," Lucas said, offering Lane a thumbs-up. He brought his eyes to Teddy and squeezed his thigh tighter. His gaze fell to Teddy's plush mouth. Teddy leaned in and tilted his head, and Lucas met him halfway to peck his lips. "You were amazing."

Teddy grinned. His nose scrunched and faint pink dappled his cheekbones. "Thank you."

As Lane and Teddy got settled with the group, Zamir waved down a waiter carrying a tray of tropical drinks.

Lucas took one piña colada and one rum punch off the tray, and brought his lips to Teddy's ear, placing his rum punch on the table. "Yeah, so, you and Lane choreographed, and mastered, a dance to match your perfect Madonna duet in the span of, what, five minutes?" Teddy accepted the piña colada, sucking the straw into his mouth. "Surely that's some sort of record."

"You're not the only one who can move fast."

Lucas propped his elbow on the table and rested the side of his head on his palm. "First, you seduce my dog. Now, my entire family. What's next?"

Teddy's smile was slow, his foot brushing Lucas's ankle. "Oh, love," he whispered, borderline patronizing. His tongue darted out to lick the left corner of his lips. "Weren't you listening to the song?"

Lucas leaned in, but Teddy pulled back and nibbled his bottom lip. Lucas stared at him for a beat. The hair on the back of Teddy's neck stood up, his pupils dilated, and his cheeks went rosy.

Lucas rubbed along his inner thigh. "To be honest, Theodore, you looked so good that I had trouble focusing on anything else."

"Good answer."

When they could take no more karaoke (one can only take so many groups of teenagers screaming into mics so many times before even the strongest cocktails can no longer dull the pain), they excused themselves and headed toward their bungalow, joining the steady stream of family members stumbling back to their rooms.

"Don't these children know about the Spice Girls?" Teddy asked, slurring slightly. He leaned into Lucas. Lucas's arm was warm around his lower back. "What sort of rubbish are they learning in school? Whatever happened to music education?"

Lucas threw his head back and laughed, and Teddy rested his cheek on his shoulder as he laughed. They reached their bungalow and let themselves in, dropping their flip-flops outside the door.

Teddy broke away from Lucas's side and unbuttoned his shirt, letting the fabric fall down his arms. He unzipped his jeans and pushed them down, stepping out of the fabric. Lucas was already inside the en-suite with his mouth full of foam when Teddy got to his sink. Teddy caught eyes in the mirror with Lucas as he set up his toothbrush.

"I'll keep my pants on," Teddy said, sticking his brush under the water. "Promise."

Lucas said, "How generous," and spit into his sink.

"Sharing is caring, mate."

Lucas watched Teddy line up a long row of products on the countertop: more and more bottles of serum, moisturizer, toner, and other potions appeared out of his shaving kit.

"Do you use all those?"

"I have a routine," Teddy said, dunking his face into the sink.

"Here's my routine." Lucas slapped cold water onto his face and scrubbed his skin with a towel. Teddy blinked at him, bored, while applying a serum that smelled of oranges. Lucas dropped the towel on the counter. "Done."

Teddy let the serum sink into his skin and fanned himself. He picked up Lucas's towel and folded it on the rack to the side of the sink. Lucas turned away from him to pull down his khaki shorts, letting a sliver of his arse become visible as he peed.

"No wonder you put up such a fuss about putting on sunscreen," Teddy muttered as he dabbed on eye cream.

The toilet flushed. Lucas knocked his sink on and stuck his hands under the water. "My skin tans." He turned the water off. "It doesn't burn."

Teddy snorted, smoothing moisturizer on the apples of his cheeks. "Be sure to tell your doctor that when you drop dead from skin cancer. How are you so smart about some things but so ignorant about others?"

Lucas blew air through his lips, staring at Teddy and dropping his towel on the counter.

Teddy picked up the towel, pointedly glaring as he put it on the rack. "I'm not here to be your maid this week."

"But what if maid costumes turn me on?"

Teddy batted his eyelashes. "I'm no one's maid, darling. And you're a liar," he said, his top lip snarling upward. "I've already mentioned every fancy dress option, and you've given me a negative for each one." He walked out of the en-suite, leaving a hint of sweet oranges behind him. He called over his shoulder. "Clean up after yourself."

Lucas went back into the room, holding his balled shirt in his hand. His belt flared out from his hips. He dropped the shirt into his luggage, watching Teddy carefully hang his shirt and jeans in the walk-in closet. Lucas took off his khakis and laid them on top of his luggage, forgoing pajama bottoms to sleep in only his black boxer briefs. Maybe he'd have to ask the concierge if they could send someone to unpack for him tomorrow.

"You ready to sleep?" Teddy asked, his hand on the light switch.

"Yeah," Lucas said. He stretched his arms above his head, walking to bed. He tapped the screen of the air conditioner and checked the temperature. "I'm good. Temperature okay for you?"

"Yep. I like it cold."

The lights went out, moonlight blaring into their room from the glass patio door. Lucas pulled the curtains shut. "I like it dark when I sleep, is that all right?"

"Fine with me." Teddy pulled the duvet down on the left side of the bed, closest to the sofa and door. He fluffed his hair. "That way you won't be distracted by my beauty. Wouldn't want to keep you up at night."

Lucas snorted and got into the right side of the bed, closest to the patio. He lay down and pulled the duvet to his chin. They both exhaled slow breaths at the same time, staring up at the ceiling. An ocean of mattress stretched between them.

"We should go in the hot tub tomorrow," Teddy said, his voice beginning to fade. "And the outdoor shower."

"Sleep now." Lucas took a deep breath. "Shower tomorrow."

"Mmm." Teddy's eyes were too heavy to keep open, his arms bent at the elbows and rested flat above his head on the mattress. "This day felt endless," he said on a soft rasp. "Like I've known everyone for years. So many people."

"Mmm, travel will do that to you," Lucas murmured. His eyes moved beneath his closed eyelids. His mouth continued to move to speak, but the motions of his lips were small, his voice low. "That happens when you spend so much time together in one day. Some internships I did were in foreign countries over the summer, and after a week with the same people, you feel like you've known everyone forever, just because you're together for twenty-four hours a day. It's like… sped-up friendship, or something."

"Makes sense." Teddy turned onto his stomach, cradling his pillow to his face. "What time do we have to wake up?"

"Breakfast is at half eight in the main house."

Teddy whimpered through his nose, rubbing his feet over the cool sheets. "Gross."

"I know. Who plans a holiday with actual breakfasts? If it was up to me, we'd spend all day in bed."

There was a pause. Lucas tensed.

"Oh yeah?" Teddy asked coyly. "In bed together all day? Whatever would we—"

"Sleeping. I meant sleeping."

"Mmm, sure you did."

Lucas turned onto his stomach too, angling his face away from Teddy. "Enough chitchat." He pulled the duvet up to his chin and the sheets hissed around him. He curled into a ball, with his ankles crossed and his knees nearly touching his chest. "I'm tired."

"All right, Grumpy Gus, all right. No need to get your unfortunate swim trunks in a bunch."

"And I'll just get this out of the way now," Lucas said, tilting his face to the ceiling but keeping his eyes shut. "I sleep with my mouth open and I drool, no matter how much I try not to. I don't want to hear any cracks about it tomorrow."

"Okay." Teddy chuckled, low and lazy. He mock saluted. "Noted."

Lucas relaxed his neck and curled tighter. Teddy's easy breaths puffed into the silence.

"Hey, Luke?"

Lucas opened his eyes. "Yes?"

"You sure you don't want to, you know." There was a pause, long enough for Teddy to lick his lips and smirk. "Practice? Before bed?"

His voice was teasing beneath the layers of raspy depth. Goose bumps sprung up over Lucas's entire body.

Lucas swallowed, his throat clicking. "We don't need to practice. Just sleep."

"All right, whatever you say," Teddy said, practically singing his words. He took a deep breath in through his nose, exhaling and stretching his long legs to the end of the bed. "Kinda nice to have a sex-free holiday." He snuffled, rubbing his cheek against his pillow. "Can actually relax."

Chapter THIRTEEN

Sunday, April 26

LUCAS STRETCHED his head, digging his cheekbone into his pillow. The bed shifted beneath him. Something heavy and hot ran diagonally between his shoulder blades, and his right inner thigh sweated on something equally warm. He curled his shoulder forward and licked his lips. His tongue bumped into something salty, something that shuddered under his lips. The line of heat over his back lifted and thudded on the pillow.

His eyes fluttered open and he saw hair. Soft brown hair, specifically. The sight of Teddy's underarm matched up with the scent of faded Tom Ford cologne and sweet, metallic sweat flooding his nose. Teddy's head was turned away from him on the pillow with his arms stretched upward.

Lucas glanced down and winced; half of his body lay on top of Teddy. He tensed, and his right leg slid off Teddy's thigh. He tried to pull away and he gritted his teeth, keeping watch on Teddy's calm, sleeping face. He looked down their bodies and tried to lift his leg.

"Good morning, lover."

Lucas relaxed at the sound of Teddy's deep, syrupy voice. Low laughs rasped into his hair and Teddy's chest bumped under his face.

"I'm sorry, it was an accident," Lucas said, scooting sideways. "I usually sleep alone."

"It's all right." Teddy slid his hands behind his head. Lucas glanced at him. Sleepy amusement warmed his face, and his long hair tumbled down his shoulders. "I don't mind."

"Well, I do." Lucas turned away from him and put his feet on the floor, holding his hand against the fly of his boxer briefs; his cock throbbed beneath the fabric. "It was an accident."

Lucas could hear Teddy stretching behind him, yawning and making a squeaking sound.

"That why you have all those guest rooms in your flat?"

When Lucas said nothing, his spine stick straight, Teddy chuckled low in his throat.

They both took quick showers and dressed in swim trunks and T-shirts. Teddy wore tiny black shorts and a loose white V-neck tee. Lucas wore one of Teddy's gift bathing suits, featuring a yellow fabric with vintage roses on it, and a matching white V-neck. Flip-flops and sunglasses completed their beach look. Lucas shouldered a black backpack while Teddy carried a simple canvas tote bag.

"We don't have to bring anything with us to pay to eat?" Teddy leaned his bum on the bannister of their deck. "No ID?"

"Nope." Lucas pulled their door shut and checked the handle. "We can tell them our room number and that we're with the wedding. You can do that all week whenever you want a drink or snack or whatever."

"Is there karaoke at breakfast?" Teddy peeked inside his tote. "I think I left my itinerary inside."

"I pray to the gods of the Bahamas that there is not."

Teddy chuckled, and both men walked down the steps of their deck.

Breakfast in the main house was the first of many group meals that would take place in the airy, large meeting space. Round tables covered in white tablecloths were arranged around the space and magnificent bouquets of exotic flowers dotted the center of each table. Buffet tables bursting with fresh fruit and pastries were set up along both sides of the room and would be refreshed all day, in case guests wanted something to nibble on between meals.

In addition to the breakfast buffets, the hotel waitstaff glided between tables to take orders for drinks and special items off the chef's menu, which had an elaborate selection of gourmet breakfast foods. Lucas quietly ordered himself a bowl of cornflakes, crispy bacon, and tea while scratching his throat. His eyes were still heavy with sleep and his sunglasses propped crooked on top of his head.

The waitress looked to Teddy. "And for you, sir?"

"I'd like the special artichoke and spinach omelet, please, and, uh." Teddy glanced at the buffet and spotted an overflowing fruit bowl. "I'll get a banana myself." He handed the waitress the menu and smiled. "Thank you."

"Tea?"

"Yes, please. And orange juice."

"I'll bring a carafe for the table," she said with a friendly nod, moving on to take Jo's order.

Teddy stood up, rubbing his hands down his T-shirt. "You want any fruit?"

"No, thanks," Lucas said through a yawn, placing his hand over his mouth. His eyes crinkled up at Teddy. "Sorry." He cleared his throat. His voice was raspier than usual. "I'm still in work detox."

Teddy stared down at him and stroked his messy fringe, letting his fingertips play through the feathery strands. "S'all right."

Lucas could feel his cheeks heat. He started to nibble his bottom lip, and Teddy grinned down at him. Teddy stroked his hair once more before stepping away, walking with Dean toward the breakfast bar.

Lucas cracked open a bottle of water and swallowed half of it down, making a point to ignore the sway of Teddy's arse in his short swim trunks as he held a few ripe bananas in his hands. Lane dropped into the empty seat beside him.

"Am I the only one hungover as fuck?" she rasped. Her voice was even deeper than Lucas's.

"No," Lucas said with water in his mouth. He gulped another mouthful. "I didn't even know I was drunk, but apparently I was."

"Um, yeah, you were officially drunk." Lane opened her own bottle of water. "For hours. We all were."

"Why do you say—" Lucas pushed his chair back far enough for Maggie to crawl up on his lap; he cradled her to his body. "Good morning, love," he said, softer, running his fingers through her curls. He redirected his attention to Lane. "Why do you say that?"

"Because you were all cuddly with Teddy. Duh."

"I like Teddy," Maggie whispered, curling her hands in Lucas's tee.

"So does Uncle Lucas." Lane handed Maggie a cup of water. "Now—drink, please."

Teddy returned to the table with two bananas in hand. He placed a small white plate in front of Lucas, then sat down and pulled his chair in to the table. Lucas blinked at the smiley face crafted out of cantaloupe chunks and slices. He rolled his eyes toward Teddy as Teddy innocently ate a banana. Lucas leaned over and tugged the neckline of Teddy's tee, pressing a kiss to his bare shoulder.

"Thank you."

Once everyone had been served their breakfast, a screen lowered from the ceiling in the front of the room. The lights dimmed. Cillian and Zamir appeared in front of the screen.

"Good morning, beautiful spirits!" Cillian shouted into the mic.

Hungover groans harmonized around the room.

"Babe, you're amplified." Zamir chuckled and pushed the mic a few inches from Cillian's mouth. "You don't have to shout."

"Ah! Right!" Cillian whispered, grinning. "Sorry, all. We're here to kick the day off with one of our favorite things: Home movies!"

Zamir explained. "We felt it was a good way for everyone to get to know us and our families, for anyone who is new to this big, crazy group."

"And we love everyone!"

Lucas clenched his eyes shut, sipping his tea. Teddy murmured, "And you prayed for no karaoke," in his ear. Lucas smirked around the rim of his cup.

Zamir and Cillian finished their intro and stepped off the stage. Home movies started to play on the screen. It was an even mix of baby Zamir and baby Cillian in chronological order. They had put graphics on the films, comic book action bubbles popping up once in a while to point out various family members. With most of Zamir's movie moments came Lucas and his family, Lane and Marcy eventually mixing in with Zamir's sisters.

"Oh my God, it's you," Teddy whispered, light reflected from the screen flickering over his face. He squeezed Lucas's knee. "You're so cute! And chubby!"

Lucas watched himself on the screen, at around six months old. He and Zamir sat like little overdressed blobs in their prams; Jo and Tracy waved at the camera in formal wear. It must have been a family event or birthday party, though Lucas couldn't place the moment.

A particularly mortifying moment popped up where Lucas and Zamir were running around his mum's house in their matching Superman underwear with sheets tied around their necks. Lucas glanced at Teddy as Jo came onto the screen and waved. There was a bowl of brownie mix in her arms and a big, warm smile on her face as Lucas and Zamir ran around her. Teddy's throat bobbed and he shut his mouth in a straight line as he blinked faster.

They reached their teenage years, flying through films of school concerts and footie matches, Cillian's set of movies surprisingly similar despite his family's wealth. The scene changed from Cillian doing cannonballs off a diving board to an icy, snow-covered forest. Lucas shifted in his seat, with Teddy staring rapt at the screen.

Lucas could sense someone come up behind him. Zamir's chin cuddled down on top of his shoulder; his familiar spicy scent tingled in Lucas's nostrils. Teddy looked at Zamir's profile, appearing confused, but he looked back to the screen. Cillian's chin dug into Teddy's shoulder and he settled a lanky arm around his back.

"Oh, uh, hi," Teddy whispered.

Both of Cillian's arms wrapped around his upper body. "This is an emotional moment," Cillian whispered, pressing his cheek to Teddy's cheek. "Prepare your chakras."

The film showed Zamir, Lucas, and some other teenage boys playing footie on top of a frozen pond. Their distant voices had been picked up on the old video camera. There was a loud crack and the chatter stopped abruptly. The boys all ran away from the pond amid a chorus of shouts.

The camera jumped as whoever was holding it ran closer, an out-of-breath male voice saying, "Oh my God, Z-Zamir! Zamir!" There were more cracking noises and muffled screams barely picked up on the microphone. "Lucas, no, don't—you'll fall in! Luke!"

On-screen, Lucas sprinted to the other side of the pond and flopped on his stomach. His back heaved as he punched down through the frozen pond; shards of ice and splatters of water flew up from each punch. He shoved his upper body into a hole in the ice. The shouts of too many male voices crackled on the jumping film, the camera moving closer.

After a few seconds, Lucas pulled back from the hole. His hair was matted down with ice and water, and his frantic breaths created clouds of steam in the gray air. He moved backward with his arms wrapped around Zamir's chest, and pulled him out.

"Oh, darling," Jo said at the breakfast table, dabbing her eyes with a napkin. The other guests let out a collection of nervous breaths, followed by quiet applause, people turning in their seats to look at Lucas.

The film transitioned to the boys all joking around in the backseat of a beat-up SUV. Zamir shuddered but smiled, wrapped in blankets with his lips tinged blue.

"The best," Zamir said in the film, with chattering teeth, laying his head on Lucas's shoulder. Teenage Lucas giggled. The sound was bubbly, and he put his beanie on top of the two knitted hats Zamir already had on his head. "The absolute best. My brother from another mother."

The montage switched to a new scene, Cillian performing an impressive gymnastics routine on the rings in a neon green unitard. The air in the room returned, and the breakfast crowd hooted.

Teddy swallowed. He had a lump in his throat with tears wet on his neck. He blinked, but didn't feel any tears on his lashes. He looked to the side and saw Cillian was silently crying, staring at the screen with a huge grin on his face.

"He saved my love's life," Cillian said, hugging Teddy tightly. Teddy rubbed Cillian's forearm, patting the top of his hand and squeezing his wrist. "He's our hero."

"Still my best." Zamir planted a loud kiss on Lucas's cheek. Lucas exhaled a breath that sounded almost like the bubbly giggle in the video. Zamir ruffled his hair. "Always."

They left breakfast to head to the beach. Lucas was silent for the beginning of the walk, and sunglasses shielded his eyes. Teddy walked beside Lucas while chatting easily with Cillian and Zamir, until Zamir's mother came up to them. Zamir and Cillian waved at Teddy and Lucas before they were guided to Zamir's grandparents.

Teddy moved closer to Lucas. The backs of their fingers brushed together. He wordlessly linked their pinky fingers. When Lucas said nothing and didn't pull away, Teddy curled his hand to lace their fingers together.

Lucas looked at him. "What's up?"

"Nothing." Teddy squeezed his hand. "Just…." He tilted his head toward the fading main house. "That was pretty incredible."

"I know. Who knew Cillian was such a gifted gymnast?"

"I meant the ice thing, silly," Teddy chuckled quietly with their arms pressed together. "That was incredible."

"Anyone would do that for a friend."

"I don't understand where you got the idea…. Why you always think of yourself as the bad guy. I've met bad guys. You're not a bad guy."

Lucas swallowed dryly, then faced forward and kicked off his flip-flops. "Yeah? Ask the many mom-and-pop companies I've swindled into selling out for a paycheck. Or found loopholes for partners to stage a surprise takeover. Or mergers that completely fucked one party because the other party had enough money to secure my firm." He bent and picked up his flip-flops. Their joined hands stayed together. "Ask those people—the people I've lied to and manipulated—if I'm a good guy or a bad guy."

"That can't be all you do at work, and even if it were, what you do at work does not dictate the person you are."

"No, it's not all I do at work, but I do it. Isn't that just as bad as if it was all I did? Doesn't matter what percent of the time I do it. I do it."

They walked on the sand together. Teddy's steps slowed. He bent over to take off his shoes, and Lucas waited patiently at his side.

Teddy peered up at Lucas from behind his aviators. "So what does that say about me?"

"You're not a bad person."

Teddy stood to his full height, now looking down at Lucas. "I lie to people on a daily basis and for extended periods of time."

"You lie to protect yourself. Like an actor with a stage name. You're not hurting anyone. On the contrary. You actually give pleasure to people, whether that's sex or company or whatever your clients ask for. There's a difference."

"Do you lie in your personal life?"

"No."

"Are you lying to me?"

"No. Are you?"

"No. Not at all."

"I've been—" Lucas scratched the top of his head. "—shockingly candid with you, actually. You could have been a priest, you're so easy to talk to."

Teddy turned to face him, holding Lucas's hand with both of his. "So, stop playing the role of bad guy. A bad guy wouldn't even remember any of the scenarios you just mentioned. He'd just move on with his life and cash his check. A bad guy wouldn't treat his niece like gold or humor his nosy family or donate thousands of pounds to animal adoption charities." Lucas's mouth opened and Teddy squeezed his hand. "I'm sorry and didn't mean to snoop, but I saw a letter on your kitchen counter. So, you see? You're *not* a bad guy." Lucas looked away and Teddy arched to maintain eye contact. "You're not. You're not a bad guy. Say it. Say that you're not a bad guy."

The corners of Lucas's lips twitched down. His head shook ever so slightly. "No."

Teddy's jawline tensed. "Lucas."

"I'm not a bad guy," Lucas said over him. "Happy?"

"You're not a bad guy."

"You've made your point, Baby Mick, all right?"

"All right. Now." Teddy's serious expression evaporated to a breezier one. "Let's go take our clothes off. I wanna rub something shiny all over you."

Lucas barked out a laugh and arched his brows. "You're nuts."

Teddy started to walk. Their hands were still joined and swaying between them. "I even have an oil with a little SPF in it, I think. Smells amazing. Your glutes will love it, I promise."

LUCAS ALLOWING Teddy to rub oil on him started as an act of convenience, as he couldn't reach his entire back without assistance. It was cautious, and logical, to accept Teddy's offer to keep him protected from the blazing sun. He was doing it for medical purposes.

If he felt the floor, or sand, drop whenever Teddy's large hands squeezed over his muscles, it was only because he liked getting massages. It had nothing to do with the fact that Teddy's touch was comforting, thorough, strong, and gentle all at the same time.

It made sense for him to do the same to Teddy, who let out the softest moan Lucas had ever heard when he ran his hands up the backs of his ribs.

Lucas dropped the bottle of oil on their blue-and-white striped blanket and turned onto his stomach, burying his face in his folded towel.

Four hours, one nap, five dips in the water, and one massive sand castle with Maggie later, Lucas had grown used to Teddy massaging coconut-scented oil on him each time they dried off. He, in turn, would do Teddy the same courtesy until both were so used to touching each other that it seemed like clockwork.

And if Lucas couldn't look Teddy in the eye when Teddy smoothed his oiled palms over Lucas's chest and the heels of his hands dragged over Lucas's nipples, it was simply because the sun was shining so brightly.

Teddy dozed on his back, with a book open on his stomach and his arms bent over his head. His left arm was stretched almost completely straight while his right hand rested on his bun. The breeze gently ruffled the pages of his book and the tiny, loose curls along the front of his hairline.

Lucas lay on his stomach to read his own book; sweat beaded on the back of his neck. He glanced at Teddy and saw sweat shining in the center of his chest. Sweat dripped down his neck to pool at his collarbones, the brown hair around his navel darkened. Lucas swiped his hand over his face and refocused on his book. They'd have to take a dip soon before the heat became unbearable.

"Wanna swim?" Teddy asked. His voice was heavy and rough. Lucas lifted off the blanket and caught the eye of a waiter, who rushed over with two frosty glasses of the coconut-lime concoction they first drank at the spa. "I'm hot."

"Yeah, me too. Thanks so much, mate." Lucas took two glasses from the waiter with a grateful nod and rolled onto his side, holding one glass out. "Here. Drink first."

Teddy pursed his lips and Lucas snorted, balancing the cup on Teddy's towel and angling the straw into his mouth. "Here you go, honey bunch."

"Thank you." Teddy grinned.

They went into the water and splashed around for a bit. Teddy took his bun out, dunking himself and scratching his fingers through his hair.

"Do you still want to go to pottery?" Lucas asked.

Teddy flipped his hair back, rubbing his hands over his eyes. "Yeah, if you want to."

"Is that even a question? Of course I want to sit in a pavilion that isn't even air conditioned and watch you pretend to be Patrick Swayze."

Teddy laughed with his whole body and replaced his sunglasses. "Please. You look more like Patrick Swayze than I do."

"I do not." Lucas smirked and rubbed over his outer arms. "The heat's getting to you."

They finished their swim and went back to their blanket. Jo and John, her husband, lay on a blanket two groups to their right with the other parents. Lane and Maggie were asleep on a lounge chair to their left, and Dean was snoring loudly under an umbrella at their feet.

Lucas lay on his stomach and searched through his backpack, retrieving his waterproof watch. He put it on. “We have time to relax for another half hour before pottery. I set my watch.”

“All right.” Teddy sprawled on his back, stretching his toes toward the sea. “Sounds good. Can you hand me the oil?” Lucas passed it over and relaxed, hugging his balled T-shirt to his face. “Want me to do you?”

“No. I don’t want to be sticky if we have to put clothes on.”

Teddy hummed and placed the oil bottle in his tote.

“Hello, boys!”

Lucas squinted up at the sound of his mother’s voice. Teddy tilted his head back to look at her upside down.

“Hi,” Lucas said, shielding his eyes. “What’s up?”

“You two look so cute over here.” She held her iPhone forward and chirped, “Say cheese!”

“No, Mum, no.” Lucas held up his hand up. “Don’t—” He glanced at Teddy, who was looking confusedly at him. “We don’t like photos.”

“Okay,” Jo said slowly, lowering her phone.

“Nah, it’s all right.” Teddy turned onto his stomach and held his arm out toward Lucas. “C’mere, love.”

Lucas stared at him for a moment, confusion wrinkling his brow. Teddy’s fingers crawled over Lucas’s side. Lucas chuckled, bumping Teddy’s hand with his hip, and scooted sideways. Teddy laid his arm over Lucas’s upper back. They both looked up.

She cooed, “Smile!” and lifted her phone. They smiled, Teddy’s cheek dimpling as they twisted to rest their heads together. “Lovely! Adorable!”

She leaned closer while still snapping photos. Teddy chuckled and dropped his gaze

“All right, paparazzi, that’s enough,” Lucas said with a good-natured grumble in his voice. He flicked his hand toward Jo’s blanket. “You got your photos.”

“So”—she took a photo. Teddy’s face was hidden by Lucas leaning over him—“cute!”

She went to take another photo, and Lucas held his hand out. “Mum, please. You took, like, fifty. Isn’t that enough?”

“All right, all right,” she said, smirking. “I’ll leave you be.”

"Thank you."

She went back to her blanket. Lucas exhaled and rested his cheek on the blanket. Teddy rubbed his toes over Lucas's ankle.

"What a gentleman," Teddy drawled quietly. "Shielding me from the mum-arazzi."

"Hey, I'm just trying to follow the rules."

"What rules?"

"No photos, of course. That's one of your rules, is it not?"

Teddy rolled onto his back, propping his hands behind his head.

"Well, yeah, for normal work gigs," he whispered, mindful of nearby ears. "This is different. You know that." He bent his legs and dug the tops of his toes into the blanket. "I didn't even include the photo clause in our agreement."

"So, you don't care if people take photos of you here this week? With me?"

"No, I don't care. I've already gotten Facebook friend requests from a few people here. It was bound to happen."

"Wh-what?" Lucas guffawed, rolling on his side and propping his head up. He whispered, "You have a Facebook? Under your Teddy name?"

"Yeah. Haven't you checked your phone? I friended you. You should probably accept, genius."

"No, I turned my phone off when we got here and don't plan on turning it on again until I'm dragged back into my office."

"I respect that," Teddy said with an impressed nod. He straightened his legs. "Good for you."

"The firm has Albert's contact information, and he knows where I am. If there's an issue that requires my attention, I'd find out sooner or later. I'm not a brain surgeon."

Teddy rolled toward Lucas with his T-shirt in hand. He laid his T-shirt over both of their heads, white fabric softening the light on their faces.

Lucas pushed his sunglasses up to the top of his head to squint at him. "What's this?"

"C'mere," Teddy whispered.

"Why?" Lucas whispered back.

"Mum-arazzi is nearby." Teddy rested one hand on Lucas's cheek, his other hand on the front of Lucas's sweating neck. "If she thinks we're—"

Lucas tilted his head and pressed their lips together. Teddy's eyebrows shot up and became visible over the line of his sunglasses. Lucas's hand flattened on the small of Teddy's arched back, pulling him closer as they sucked hot kisses. Water lapped along the shore, birds cawed in the distance, and grains of sand dug into their skin as they moved together. Teddy's hand cradled Lucas's face while Lucas rubbed both hands up his spine. Their toes bumped at the end of the blanket.

"Oh, whoops!" Jo whispered. "Sorry, loves!"

Sand crunched under her fast steps away from the kissing duo. A few teasing hoots and whistles came from nearby blankets. Lucas let out a quiet hum, and Teddy leaned into their kisses. The gentle, nudging motions of Teddy's head were hypnotizing. Lucas mirrored the rhythm.

"I think she's gone," Lucas whispered, puffing warm, coconut breaths over Teddy's open mouth. He put his sunglasses back on and grinned. "Good call. Masterful."

"Oh, uh, yeah," Teddy said, sounding lost. He licked his own lips while staring at Lucas's mouth, and leaned in. "I mean, um." His eyes snapped up as he pulled back. "Thanks."

Lucas took the T-shirt off their heads, tossing it on Teddy's face. "Get your smelly pirate clothes away from me."

"Yeah, cause your feet smelled like roses after yesterday."

"Hey," Lucas warned, poking Teddy's stomach. Teddy gasped as he pushed Lucas's hand off. "I'm sorry we're not all owners of feet worth six hundred pounds an hour." Teddy laughed lightly at that, rolling onto his back and replacing his hands behind his head. They were close enough to feel each other's body heat. "Tell me, do you offer Mr. Tickles a buy-one-get-one-free deal?"

"What?"

Lucas flattened on his stomach, stretching his hands forward. "Yeah, like your hash browns. Buy one armpit, get one free?"

"No," Teddy said, still laughing, his dimples on display. "Silly. It doesn't work that way."

"No work emergencies? No Jack McQueen penis signal up in the skies of London?"

"Nope. I wouldn't know." Teddy dimpled up at the sun. "I left my work phone off in my suitcase before we even flew out, and I think my personal phone died this morning. Need to charge it. You have a fascination with my clients." Teddy poked his index finger into Lucas's ribs. "Mr. Tickles, especially."

Lucas scoffed, "I do not," and pushed his hand away.

"You do. So many questions."

"I just think it's… interesting."

"Sex?"

"Well, yeah. Sex is interesting. It should be, right?"

Teddy nodded. "I agree."

"I guess because… I always imagined people in your field as, like…." Lucas scrunched his nose, pulling his elbows to his sides. "I dunno." He placed his fists under his chin, letting his toes dig into the blanket. "Not like you."

"I know the feeling."

"And, like, sex is so… weird. And embarrassing, at times. Doesn't it make it even weirder to be with a stranger like that?"

"Sex is weird, yeah, and embarrassing at times, yeah, but it's like that whether you know the person or not."

Lucas swayed his head side to side. "I suppose that's true."

Teddy directed his face toward Lucas. "Sex, even the most planned, scheduled of hookups, is always going to have some element of spontaneity to it. Hopefully. The things you say and do before, during, and after sex are the spontaneous part, not the mechanics of something in, something out. Someone sucks, someone licks. If you had a script of everything you said to the person you're having sex with, and then showed it to someone else, it wouldn't read as hot or sexy because it's not happening in the moment. Whether money is exchanged or not, I strive to achieve that."

"And the kinky ones? The ones who might even manage to embarrass the unflappable Jack McQueen?"

Teddy grinned and bulged his biceps. He tilted his face toward the sky. "I quite like the kinky ones."

"Yeah?"

"Every kinky one I've come in contact with was very nice and much more polite than your average closeted businessman. They're happy to be there and explore. Not so stuffy or angsty."

"Excuse me, but I'm not a closeted businessman."

"Did I say you were?" Teddy smirked and gently kicked Lucas's shin. "I meant it as a generalization. People with more imagination can usually verbalize exactly what they want, instead of hemming and hawing and expecting me to read their mind. If they're new to their kink, or they've never had a chance to explore in real life, like Mr. Tickles, it's kind of nice to be a safe space for them. To let them try things out without worrying about feeling embarrassed. To guide them along in such a way that when they find an actual partner, they know how to treat their partner well."

"That's… almost nice. That *is* nice. That's kind of you to think that way."

Teddy shrugged. "In truth, I don't get too many kinky ones. That's not my thing. Kinky or not, the key is usually just knowing what the other person wants to hear, when they want to hear it, and saying it the right way."

"Like, dirty talk?"

"No. You're cute."

"No, I'm not."

"You were a cute chubby baby and you're a cute full-grown adult."

Lucas sighed and relaxed on his stomach, pillowing his face on his folded arms.

Teddy continued, "Whether a person is kinky or not, sex is very much a mind game. The mental is what takes it to the edge, rather than the physical."

"Oh really? And what, sexual Buddha, do people like to hear?"

"It's all a personal thing. Buddha isn't sexual, I don't think. Isn't that the point of being Buddha?"

"I don't know. I thought Buddha was cool with sex, but you're the sexpert."

"Ugh, I hate that term. It sounds like I host a morning talk show or something."

Lucas swayed his feet in the air. "That would be a ratings star, I'm sure. Welcome to *Your Morning Cup of Fuck* with sexpert Jack McQueen."

Teddy threw his head back into the blanket to howl, his stomach jumping, his arms spasming. "Oh my God. Insane," he laughed, tilting his head toward Lucas. "I'm no sexpert, I promise you that. And Jesus, the things that come out of your mouth."

"The things that go into your mouth."

Teddy's mouth fell open. "Filthy. You're filthy."

"I thought you like the kinky ones best?"

"Filthy does not equal kinky. And like I said, not every client puts something in my mouth. I'm not having sex with every single one of them."

"Yet you somehow manage to get them to pay you thousands to chitchat."

"One time I got a client to pay me plus a mate of mine to supervise, because he wanted to tie me up and watch me struggle. That's it. No touching. No sex. Just me, naked, struggling to get out."

Lucas blew a breath through his pursed mouth, a confused chuckle following. "What?"

"Yeah, sounds crazy, right? The client was into that, but I never agree to be bound in a way I can't get out. I said that if he wanted to do that, he had to pay my mate, Nick, a supervision fee. I think Nick was writing a paper on his laptop in the other room of the hotel suite, actually."

Lucas framed his face with his hands. "Again: What? I feel like I'm in this bizarro world where people are paying prostitutes enormous amounts of money for everything but sex. What's the point of hiring someone for sex if you don't have sex?"

"Like I said, for some it's the mental above the physical. Some people get off on…." Teddy reached high above his head, arching his back and quietly chanting, "Harder. More. Please. *More*." His voice returned to normal. "While others are more into…." He crossed his wrists and pretended to pull at invisible restraints. He arched his back again; breathiness and the hint of laughter lightened his voice as he pleaded, "Oh please, no more, *please*, no more, please." He relaxed his posture, turning his face in time to see Lucas look away with his jaw clenched. "You know what I mean?"

Lucas stared at the blanket. His legs and feet were perfectly straight, his arms held tight at his sides. "Um, yeah. I get it. We, uh"—he checked his watch, rolling his back to Teddy—"should pack up and get to pottery."

"Oh," Teddy said, looking surprised. Lucas stood up, his back still to Teddy as he packed up his backpack. "All right."

TEDDY SCRUBBED his fingernails with a brush, squirting more soap into his hands.

"And Patrick made clay look so hot," Lucas whispered from beside him. Teddy grinned down at the suds-filled sink.

Cillian came up between them and shoved his hands under the water. "That was a seriously spiritual session, mates. I haven't felt so connected during group pottery since Zamir and I were in Portugal for the winter solstice."

Lucas dried his hands. Teddy was still rinsing.

"How'd you get all these pottery wheels in here?" Lucas asked. "And that oven thing? It's huge."

"Money," Cillian said cheerfully. He had a dollop of soapsuds on the end of his nose. His eyes lit up. "Oh, good, the seashells have arrived."

He ran off with wet hands, and Teddy and Lucas exchanged an amused look. Both stepped aside to let more clay-covered people wash up.

"I told Maggie I'd do seashells with her," Teddy said, taking the towel out of Lucas's hands. "Do you want to stay and do them?"

"Erm." Lucas scratched the back of his neck and looked over his shoulder toward the beach. "I kind of want a nap."

"Oh, okay, that sounds good. Are you all right with me being with your family alone?"

"Yeah, of course." Lucas dropped his arm and arched his eyebrows. "Are *you* okay with being with my family alone? They can be a lot."

"Yeah, sure. I'll be fine."

"All right." Lucas glanced at his watch. "How long is shells supposed to take?"

"Erm, I believe—hi, love." Teddy ruffled Maggie's wild curls. Maggie latched on to his left shin and beamed toothily up at him. "Is it seashell time?"

"It is," she said, drawing out the words.

Teddy grinned and looked to Lucas. "I think it's only, like, forty-five minutes? How long could we possibly paint seashells for?"

"Forever!" Maggie cried.

Lucas and Teddy chuckled.

"There you have it," Teddy said as he stroked Maggie's hair. "I'll be here in this pavilion forever."

"At least you'll have lots of glitter for eternity."

"Very true."

Lucas bent down and kissed Maggie's forehead. "Have fun, little love. Take care of Teddy." He brought himself to his full height, and softly kissed Teddy's cheek. "You have fun too."

"Ew," Maggie droned, burying her face in Teddy's kneecap.

Teddy stared at him with twinkling eyes and curled his hand on Lucas's hip. His thumb snuck up under his tee, drawing soft circles on his hipbone. "I always do."

Lucas ducked his head down as heat raced over the back of his neck. "Right."

He went back to their craft table and got his backpack. By the time he said good-bye to his sister, Maggie had already dumped a mountain of seashells on the table in front of Teddy, who exclaimed, "I love your ambition!"

"Damn sexy Buddha," Lucas whispered to himself, legging it back to their bungalow.

He threw his bag on the floor and made a beeline for their bed. He shoved two towel swans off the center of the mattress, mentally sent an apology to their maid, Cynthia, for her careful folding skills, and ripped his tee off. He dropped his shorts and got into bed on his side. He licked his palm twice and shoved his hand under the blankets. He lowered his head back on his pillow with a relieved, extended sigh.

"Fuck," he whispered and started to pump himself.

It wouldn't be his finest wank, or his longest, but speed was of the utmost importance. After so many hours of seeing Teddy oiled and nearly naked, his brain was bordering on useless. He had to fit in at least two wanks before Teddy got back, or he would end up accidentally drowning during water polo that afternoon.

He moaned softly and opened his mouth, biting on his bottom lip as his toes curled against the tucked-too-tight duvet.

Fucking Teddy, he thought, speeding up his hand.

Small shorts and long legs and perfect abs that only a select few genetically gifted people could achieve. His mind flashed to their time on the beach earlier that day: Teddy relaxing on his back with his arms stretched above his head, his voice fluctuating from his natural rasp to a kittenish purr, his fake begging hotter than any begging Lucas had heard in any porn he'd ever watched.

All the kissing and touching was starting to become so second nature to Lucas that he felt strange not touching Teddy. He felt strange when they weren't kissing… when he couldn't smell Teddy's shampoo or sweat or silly coconut oil.

Lucas's eyes clenched tighter, his balls ached, and his hand flew fast over his throbbing cock. Sweat prickled his temples. He arched his lower back and moaned a bit louder, his chest heaving to pant, "Fuck," and suck in a breath.

The tightness in his belly coiled and unfurled, coiled and unfurled, and his arm started to tremble as he stroked and stroked and—

The door clicked.

Lucas's eyes flew open, but his hand still worked over his cock.

"O-oh," Teddy blurted out. His mouth was a perfect circle. He froze in the doorway. "I… I…."

Lucas regained his wits. "Get out!" He flailed his arm toward the door. "Get out of here!"

Teddy stepped into the room and shut the door as he started to cackle, which rapidly grew to a full-blown, hysterical belly laugh. Tears shone in his eyes and he braced himself with his hand on the door, his body bent in half. Lucas gritted his teeth, and Teddy leaned back against the door, crossing his ankles. His laughter lightened to bubbly, breathy giggles. He dabbed under his eyes with the back of his hand.

"Well, well, well. Would you look at that," Teddy drawled, low and teasing. "You're human after all. I was beginning to wonder."

Lucas tightened his grip on the duvet, dropping his head back with a sigh. "I'm human and getting very annoyed that you interrupted my nap."

"Your nap? You're annoyed I interrupted your"—Teddy made the universal jerk-off motion near his groin with practiced ease—"nap? Aw, I'm sorry, baby. So sorry you're annoyed. But don't you mean frustrated?" He pushed himself off the door, running his hands over his chest and putting extra breathy moans between his words. "Backed—*unghhh*—up?" His head dropped back as he rolled his neck, clutching at his shirt and panting out, "*Ohhh*, maybe?"

“You were supposed to be at seashells,” Lucas said through clenched teeth, “for at *least* another half hour.”

Teddy kicked his flip-flops off, flicking one hand in the air. “Maggie fell asleep on me, so we brought her back for a nap.”

“Cockblocked by my own goddaughter.” Lucas huffed, sending an annoyed look Teddy’s way without actually looking at him. “Lovely.”

“Ooh,” Teddy cooed as he widened his eyes. He crawled on his knees up from the end of the bed. Lucas pulled the duvet higher and it untucked itself from beneath the bed. His legs stuck out from under the puff of white fabric. Teddy batted his doe eyes and walked his fingers toward Lucas’s bare feet. “Am I going to get detention for skipping out on arts and crafts? You gonna spank me for being naughty?”

Lucas wrapped the duvet around his middle and stood up. He must look like a swan wearing a large, fluffy diaper. “I’m taking a shower. Alone. Please don’t come into the en-suite until I come out.”

Teddy nodded and held his palms out. “Of course.”

Lucas turned away from him and started to walk. He took three steps before the duvet got caught on something. He pulled it once and slingshotted two steps backward. He turned and looked at the stretched duvet. A long foot stood on the corner of the fabric. He rolled his eyes and glared at Teddy, who had his hand over his mouth. His eyes sparkled.

“Excuse me.” Lucas stepped away from him. The duvet pulled taut. “Are we children?”

Teddy lifted his foot and sent Lucas tumbling backward, arse over elbows, in a whirling mess of duvet. Teddy’s loud laughter rang in the room. “Ooh, I think I saw a peachy cheek!” He fanned himself, blowing out a harried breath. “I might need to turn the AC higher.” He peeled his shirt up his stomach. “It’s getting hot in here, babe.”

Lucas huffed and waddled into the en-suite. He tried to slam the door, but the luxury resort had outfitted all doors, drawers, and windows to glide shut quietly.

He opened the door a crack and said, “I’d slam this if it were possible,” prompting another chuckle from Teddy.

Lucas turned the stone-tiled shower on and cranked each of the jets to their highest, most pounding setting. He folded the duvet as best he could, placed it in the bathtub, then got into the shower and leaned his forehead against the wall.

“Fucking hell,” he whispered.

He wrapped his right hand around his cock and started pumping, hard and fast, hot water racing down his stomach to slick his strokes. He clenched his eyes shut. Water dripped over his bottom lip. He felt the familiar tension at the root of his belly, and bit on his left hand, muffling a high-pitched whimper as he shot against the stone tiles. His hips jutted unevenly. His grip bordered on pain and he squeezed his eyes tighter as he jerked himself through his climax.

Lucas reached to the wall and exhaled. Drops of water sprayed from his mouth and he hung his head. The muscles between his shoulder blades ached, and his bicep was slightly sore. He opened his eyes and stared at his shampoo, listening to the water drip and slap against the steam-filled shower.

After loosening his grip from his cock and stepping back, he let the shower spray his stomach and groin. Come slid off him and was sucked down the drain. He picked up his bodywash and uncapped it, squirting gel into his hands.

He started to wash himself, but each time his hands came even close to his cock, he felt a jump in his stomach. He checked his watch and sighed, then unbuckled it and placed it on one of the built-in shelves.

Stroking himself tightly with his soapy hand prompted him to hiss through his teeth. The original plan had been to wank twice in bed. Might as well follow through in the shower.

Lucas emerged from the en-suite fifteen minutes later in a cloud of steam, a thick white towel tied around his waist. His eyes landed on the bed.

Teddy was sprawled in the center wearing nothing but a small pair of black briefs with his long limbs stretched toward each corner. His briefs were shucked low and bunched up at the legs, and the thick outline of his cock was visible through the thin material. Any bit of hair dusting his body, such as the hair under his arms or at the very highest crease of his inner thighs, was darkened. His chest puffed up and down rapidly, sweat shone in the dips of his body, and his long toes curled and relaxed with each panted breath.

Lucas raised his eyebrows.

"I couldn't help but join you," Teddy said. His voice was deeper than usual, his words even slower. He grinned, no doubt noticing a matching flush of heat dusting Lucas's cheeks. He pushed himself up on one elbow, his abs flexing. "But let the record show that you"—he pointed at Lucas, then sucked his thumb into his mouth—"cracked first."

Lucas's mouth ached to smile, and he ground his teeth to halt the motion. "Whatever. Had nothing to do with you."

He went to the dresser and pulled open the top drawer. Teddy came up next to him and fished out a pair of black boxer briefs from within the same drawer. Lucas's nostrils flared. The heady, slightly too-sharp scent of Teddy's sweat walloped his brain. Sex. That was what Teddy would smell like after sex.

Their forearms brushed just before Teddy walked away, and Lucas's hand faltered, his fingernails clacking against the bottom of the drawer.

Teddy stepped out of the en-suite. "Oh, yeah, sorry about the sheets." He dimpled brightly. "Since the maid did our room already, I guess we'll just have to sleep on them, even though I got them a bit… sweaty." Lucas watched Teddy start to push his briefs off, his lower abs lengthening, but he looked away and turned his back to Teddy. He heard the soft whoosh of briefs hitting the floor.

"Whoops," Teddy whispered, air licking beneath Lucas's ear, body heat teasing Lucas's bare back. Teddy's long fingers pinched a pair of boxer briefs. "Forgot these."

Lucas swallowed tightly, keeping his eyes toward the front door. Then Teddy's body heat was gone, his bare feet padding into the en-suite. The shower started up.

INSIDE THE shower, Teddy soaped up his groin. He rubbed his hands under his arms and over the back of his neck, then held his arms out and let the shower jets pound over his skin.

The glass door opened.

Teddy covered his soapy nipples and froze. His tension melted immediately into a wide grin. Lucas stepped into the shower, naked, his expression bored, and pulled the door shut behind himself.

Lucas's cock was soft but hung heavy from the thatch of dark brown hair spreading from his groin to the creases of his thighs. The small slit of his cock was just barely visible at the end of the smooth, dark pink foreskin bulging around the head.

Teddy gripped Lucas's arse with one big hand on each thick cheek, then leaned back slightly. His gaze ran down Lucas's wet abs to the base of his uncut cock. He groaned softly and dug his fingers into the meaty flesh, sucking a kiss to the front of Lucas's throat.

"Wanted to join me? Fucking finally, Luke. Been dying here." He pressed back against the wall and pulled Lucas in to his body, mouthing up to his jawline. "Look at that cock. You're so fucking thick, love."

Lucas reached up and plucked his waterproof watch from the shampoo ledge.

"Forgot this." He started to buckle his watch while maintaining eye contact. Teddy stared at him, stunned. He pushed Teddy's hands off his arse with a small, teasing smirk. "But let the record show that you wanted me first."

"Lucas—"

Lucas opened the shower door and stepped out, but reached back in to turn the left faucet off. Teddy shouted nonsense and hurried to turn the hot water back on. Lucas cackled as he walked into the bedroom. Teddy, frazzled and cold, only caught a glimpse of Lucas's wet arse and bowlegged walk before the en-suite door glided shut.

"Jesus Christ." He dropped his head back on the tile and shut his eyes. Warm water sprayed over his body. He pressed his palms together and peered up at the sunny skylight. "Buddha, if you're up there, please give me strength. Please strengthen my chakras, whatever or wherever they are. Please give me the strength to resist that big arse and pretty face and…."

Teddy looked down at his cock. Being hard wasn't the divine intervention he was looking for, but he sighed and wrapped his hand around himself, biting his left hand and starting to stroke.

THEY FILED into the main-house dining room for dinner with the other wedding guests. They went toward the table they'd been sitting at with Lucas's family since arriving. Teddy pulled Lucas's chair out for him. Lucas murmured, "Thanks," and slipped into his seat.

"Dunno, guys," Lane said, sitting in her seat beside Lucas. "You didn't fare well in water polo. What if there's a swimming race in the Zill-ympics tomorrow?"

Lucas snapped his cloth napkin in the air. "We would have fared well if some people hadn't decided to have a chicken fight midmatch. I didn't see that on the itinerary."

Teddy grinned across the table at Cillian. They stood up to slap hands, both giggling.

"Aw, Loo Loo, don't be sore that we lost." Teddy settled in his seat. "Not my fault you couldn't balance on my shoulders properly." He sipped water out of a crystal goblet, with his pinky poised. "Too bottom heavy, I guess."

The table burst out laughing. Lucas smirked at Teddy, and batted his lashes. "You're just so funny, aren't you, Theodore? Full of laughs."

"Laughter is good. It relaxes us." He wrapped his arm around Lucas's shoulders, stroking the side of his neck. "You seem much more relaxed yourself, love." Heat radiated between them as both shared a smirk. "That nap must have done you good."

Lucas's smirk softened. "I'm very relaxed, darling."

"Excellent."

A waiter appeared and placed a plate of artfully arranged food in front of each guest. Among the colorful sauces and vegetables was an enormous bratwurst, resting across the fine china plate.

"Aw, yeah! It's sausage night!" Cillian cried, pumping both fists in the air. "Look at these big boys. Moran's finest, everyone! Moran's finest. I think I stuffed these myself."

Lucas prodded at his sausage and murmured, "Speaking of my nap." Teddy guffawed while sipping his water, sputtering into his goblet. Lucas primly cut his bratwurst. He kept his voice low enough for Teddy's ears only. "I'm not often wrong in my hunches about people, but"—he swayed his fork toward Teddy's bratwurst—"I don't mind so much this time around. An extra inch or so can be a pleasant surprise."

"Don't know why that's any concern of yours." Teddy stabbed his fork in the very center of his bratwurst, smiling sweetly at Lucas. "Not like you have any use for it."

Lucas hummed as he chewed. He swallowed. "Very true, though I still appreciate a nice-sized sausage. I am human, love."

Teddy sighed and started to eat, focusing his energy on the sausage on his plate rather than the sausage in his pants.

THAT NIGHT, Lucas forgot to close the drapes on the patio door and the large front window. Teddy blinked at the slivers of starry sky he could see through the bamboo blinds, rubbing his feet together under the covers.

It had been another busy day with lots of sun and people and activities. He knew he should be asleep, but his racing mind had other plans. He shifted from his left to his right side and the duvet loosened over the dip of his waist. He propped his head on his hand.

Teddy studied Lucas's wrinkle-free, slackened face. His skin was starting to brown with an even caramel warmth. His narrow chest swelled up with each breath exhaled from his open mouth. He pushed Lucas's fringe off his forehead with light fingers, revealing his long eyelashes and shimmering eyelids. Lucas didn't miss a beat with his breathing, but his body remained motionless. Teddy stroked his hair again, playing in the soft strands.

What would it have been like if they had met in any other way than they did? Teddy had spent a fair amount of his daily life asking himself that question since their meeting in the taxi. Even at his snippiest, Lucas had burrowed his way into the center of his chest, sending shocks of electricity to his heart or groin, or both at the same time, depending on what he said or did at each moment of the day.

Maybe they would have met on a blind date. They would fumble through the meal at an overpriced French place or a round of burgers at the pub. Maybe one would spill something on the other, both drinking too much wine to calm their nerves. The night would end in a giggly shag in one of their flats, or a jumpy duo of hand jobs in the car outside the restaurant, or maybe just kissing on the walk home. Teddy liked just kissing.

Maybe Teddy had a dog of his own and would take him to a dog park every morning before work. He'd always wanted a puppy: a schnauzer or a golden lab, maybe. One day, Lucas would start taking Georgie to the same park at the same time. Their dogs would become friends and then, eventually, one of them would work up the guts to ask for the other's number. For strictly doggie hangout purposes, of course.

Maybe they would have met in Tesco when they went for the same bunch of grapes at the same time. Their hands would brush, fireworks would go off in the produce aisle, and everything would be happily ever after from there, including a wedding where the color scheme revolved around purple to honor the start of their relationship.

Or maybe Teddy worked a more normal kind of job. He would work in an office in a tall building with big windows and breakrooms with espresso machines. A publishing office, maybe. Or a magazine focused on photography, where he could look at pictures all day. His biggest concern would be remembering to iron his clothes the night before work. The thought of wearing a safety bracelet or waxing himself raw or using a fake name would never even enter his mind.

Maybe he would go to lunch in the building's cafeteria every day at the same time. Some days he would bring his own lunch. Sandwiches made with whatever leftovers he had in the fridge or thermoses of soup and chili he made each Sunday to last him the whole week. Other days he'd splurge on one of the cafeteria's fancy salads with dried berries and pecans. Goat cheese, maybe.

One day, he would see Lucas come into the cafeteria with his quiffed hair and tailored navy suit and leather briefcase. He'd think to himself, "Wow, he's gorgeous," with his soupspoon paused inches from his mouth. Bright orange butternut squash bisque would drip onto his white Oxford shirt. A bit of soup lingered on the corner of his mouth.

His work friends would notice him staring at Lucas and gently tease him about his crush, but he wouldn't care. Lucas would be that unattainable businessman he could gaze at on lunch breaks before he went back to work, providing him with a daily sixty-minute mental holiday into a life that he'd never have.

And then, on a day like any other, Teddy would be running late for lunch, only remembering he had to eat when his boss popped her head into his cubicle and said, "Boy, you really are a hustler! Go to lunch, Bennet. Take an hour."

He would go to the cafeteria and sit at a table alone, all of his work friends already back upstairs. He'd shove his sandwich in his mouth and gulp down a cup of tea, only then remembering that he wanted to use his lunch hour to pick up his allergy pills at the pharmacy.

Lucas would walk by Teddy's table. His scrunched face would be buried in a book, an apple would be balanced on the edge of his tray. Maybe his apple would roll off, or his book would slip from his fingers, but Teddy would be there to catch it, whatever it was that dropped, and they would meet like normal people do, given the chance to get to know each other the way normal people do.

Normal, he thought. He pulled his hand back from Lucas's hair, curling his fingers on the mattress. He swallowed, repeating the word in his head. For all his hard work to be legal and legit and professional, his job was not normal to someone in Lucas's world.

Teddy dragged his wet, stinging gaze from Lucas's face. He stared at the sheets stretched over the mattress and tapped his fingertips on the bed. The inches between them might as well have been leagues.

He pulled the duvet up to his neck and rolled over with his back to Lucas. He wrapped his arms around himself and curled into a ball, shutting his eyes tight. He'd had enough of his fictional mind montages for one night.

Chapter FOURTEEN

Monday, April 27

THEIR ROOM lit up the minute the sun rose. Sunlight warmed the wooden floors and caused Teddy's organized jewelry collection to glimmer on top of their shared chest of drawers. The air conditioner kicked on and blew at the open curtains. Cool air teased over any bare skin not covered by the duvet.

Teddy breathed in through his nose and cuddled his bum backward. Something warm and firm pressed against his back. He woke enough to realize that the arms wrapped around him were not his own. His hands rested in front of him, loosely curled on the mattress. Lucas's palm lay flat on top of his stomach.

He shifted his head back against his pillow. Lucas's nose brushed the curve of his neck and shifted with him. Teddy hummed, receiving an answering hum from Lucas. Teddy's pout eased away.

Teddy started to drift back asleep. The air conditioning was a perfect cool contrast with the beams of sunlight heating his bare shoulder. Lucas made another sleepy hum, and the sound grew louder and higher as his bare feet started to shuffle.

"Bloody hell," Lucas grumbled under his breath. "Again?" He went to move, but Teddy's hand shot out, gripping his forearm. Lucas licked his lips and croaked, "What?"

"Stay. Please?" Teddy rubbed his feet together, cuddling his face against his pillow. "I'm comfortable like this."

Lucas sighed. "I suppose." He settled down and blinked a few times, his gaze scanning their sunlit room.

Their pottery creations sat on the windowsill in front of the bed. Teddy's creation was a perfectly symmetrical candle holder, painted purple with even, smooth strokes. His own creation was a lumpy green blob with a hole dug into it, a last-ditch effort to make his ball of clay look sort of like Teddy's candle holder. Teddy declared it was the perfect vessel to hold keys and made no mention of its hideous appearance.

Lucas pressed his face against Teddy's sweet skin. "Are you ready for the Zill-ympics?"

Teddy hummed deep in his throat and shifted back against him. "Ready as I'll ever be." He stroked the bony top of Lucas's hand, tracing around his knuckles, his touch light and teasing. "Are you?"

"Whenever there was a group activity that required partners, I usually paired up with one of my aunts, who are all certified senior citizens. We didn't care about winning. Just wanted to do it for fun. I don't care about winning today, either. I just want you—I mean, us. I just want us to have fun doing it."

Teddy nodded, pulling Lucas's arm up to his chest. He rested Lucas's hand in the crook of his neck, snuggling against his forearm.

"We'll have fun. Let's sleep. Zill-ympians need their rest."

THE ITINERARY for the Zill-ympics said to meet on the beach directly after breakfast. Each pair who wished to compete was recommended to wear their swimsuit beneath whatever athletic clothes they preferred, plus trainers and plenty of sun cream. They would be in the sun all morning, with a celebratory barbecue lunch immediately following the competition.

The official Zill-ympics competition was for guests over the age of eighteen, but Cillian and Zamir had also asked their crew to arrange a mini Zill-ympics, which would be held for the little ones the following day, so as not to leave anyone out.

They arrived on the beach as one big herd of people. Lane and Dean raced Teddy and Lucas onto the sand.

"We're reserving our strength," Lucas said. Their joined hands swayed between them.

"Wimps!" Lane shouted over her shoulder, sprinting to pass Dean.

Teddy squeezed his hand. "Your sister's athleticism is slightly terrifying."

Lucas chuckled. "Wait until you see who Cillian's with."

"He's not with Zamir?"

Cillian and a man with close-cropped brown hair came up to them. "Teddy, meet my lovely mate, Chessie." Cillian hugged Teddy to his side. "Chessie, this is Luke's boyfriend, Teddy."

Chessie nodded warmly at him and held his hand out. "Nigel Chester."

"Teddy Bennet." They shook hands. "Nice to meet you."

"Chessie's from my hometown," Cillian said, stroking Teddy's hair as if he were hugging an oversized cat. "He's also a former professional footballer and did two triathlons last month, so, you know—" Cillian bowed, his palms pressed in a gesture of prayer. "—Best of luck competing with us, happy spirits."

Zamir ran around them, grinning and patting Cillian's bum. "Yeah, right." He kicked sand back at Cillian. "Me and Asa are going to own this."

Zamir's younger sister, Asa, sped up and launched into an impressive gymnastics combination of roundoffs, back handsprings, and backflips. Teddy's mouth fell open.

"We'll be fine, love." Lucas squeezed Teddy's hand. "Those giraffe legs of yours have to be good for something."

Teddy let go of Lucas to jog forward and attempt a cartwheel. His baggy white tank flopped up on his abs. Nearby guests cheered and clapped, while Lucas wheezed, with his hand clutching his stomach. Teddy's bent legs stuck out of his black Nike swim trunks, which—combined with his not-so-perfect landing—only made Lucas laugh harder. Teddy pumped his hands in the air as if he were Kerri Strug at the 1996 Olympics, complete with lifting one neon yellow trainer off the sand.

Lucas jogged up to him and hugged him around his middle, and Teddy's arm curved easily over his shoulders. Lucas had also worn black swim trunks and a white tank, though his trainers were blue Adidas. They had not talked about wearing matching attire, but given that some teams wore homemade uniforms, they were in good company.

Teddy came close to Lucas's ear. Softly, he said, "You being cuddly is another pleasant surprise. Mmm, you smell so tropical."

Lucas squeezed his waist. "I'm not cuddly or tropical," he scoffed. A laugh was hidden in his voice. He looked at Teddy and found his dimples on display. Long waves of hair whipped around his tanned face. "I'm simply trying to instill team spirit."

They all gathered at the starting point of the competition. A section of the beach right off the path from the main house was decorated in flags from different countries and a large "2015 ZILL-YMPICS!" banner.

"I can't believe Flamingo Cove okayed all this," Lucas murmured to Teddy. Teddy bent his head lower to hear him over the chatter and wind. "This is… kind of a lot. This isn't the usual type of activity for this level of resort. This is more of a private place for, like, celebrities and stuff. Not this." He gestured forward. "This."

Multiple athletic stations were set up across the sand, plus some events set up in the water. There was a section of the beach blocked off and hidden at the end of the athletic stations, a banner proclaiming that area to be "THE FINAL COUNTDOWN!"

"Yeah," Teddy said, nodding. "Must have cost a fortune to reserve the entire beach all morning. What'd they tell the other guests? Stay inside?"

Lucas peered around the beach. No one but their group was present, not even on the path to the beach or the sections outside their reserved area. "Maybe they said to use one of the pools until after lunch."

"Maybe."

Guests not competing were provided with comfortable seating on the edge of the beach, close enough to see the action but far enough to accommodate the waitstaff bringing them cool drinks and snacks.

"Ladies and gentlemen," a male voice suited to announcing boxing matches boomed from a lifeguard stand. "All teams to the start, please! All teams to the start!"

Lucas snagged the bottom of Zamir's shirt. "Is he going to announce everything the whole time?"

"Of course!" Zamir said, happy as a clam. "He's going to do commentary and everything! Like the real Olympics!"

There was a table holding a rainbow of bandanas at the starting line. Each duo was given a choice of team colors.

"Purple?" Lucas asked, already reaching for two purple bandanas. He held one out to Teddy. "It's your favorite, yeah?"

"Oh, uh, yeah." Teddy accepted his bandana. Lucas smirked at him as he tied his own, and Teddy bent over, tightening his to keep his hair off his flushed face. "Purple's my favorite."

Once all competitors were set with their bandanas, two bearded, muscular men in white polos and khaki cargo shorts came out with clipboards. Their name tags proclaimed them to be Phil and Bill. Phil was a brunet while Bill was blond. They both wore black aviators with black whistles hanging around their necks. A crowd of eight similarly dressed people stood behind them.

"Greetings!" Phil raised one meaty hand to wave.

Bill proclaimed, "Welcome to the Zill-ympics!"

The competitors and crowd clapped. A small crew walked around with video cameras on their shoulders.

"Before we start, let's talk rules and safety," Phil said, gripping his clipboard. "We are your judges." He held his arms out to the athletic-looking group standing behind him. "We also want everyone to have fun and be safe."

There were six qualifying events, centered on specific sports or skills, though none of the events were so dangerous that anyone need worry. There was also a medic crew at each station, just in case.

Station 1: Football

Competitors have thirty seconds to score as many goals as possible. They then must defend the net for thirty seconds and block as many goals as possible. The kicker during the defense portion of this station will be one of the neutral judges. The highest total number of goals scored combined with goals defended receives the highest points.

Station 2: American Football

Competitors must throw an American football through a hanging tire. There are ten potential tires to throw through. The highest number of accurate throws receives the highest points.

Station 3: Puzzle I—Checkers

Competitors must complete all moves on an oversized checkerboard. The fastest team to finish the board receives the highest points.

Station 4: Track & Field

Competitors will sprint, jump, and leap through a small obstacle course. The fastest team to make it through receives the highest points.

Station 5: Puzzle II—Trivia

Competitors will be asked ten trivia questions. The most accurate team receives the highest points. In the event of a tie, the fastest team to accurately answer all questions correctly receives the highest points.

Station 6: Swimming

Competitors must swim out into the sea, retrieve a flag, and bring it back to shore. The fastest team back receives the highest points.

Each pair was to compete as a team, working their way through the qualifying events in order. The team to place first in each event received the most points, with point values decreasing the lower you placed. The three colors with the highest cumulative score would move on to the Final Countdown, which was a massive obstacle course combining sports and puzzles.

Since there were more teams than stations, some teams would start their rotation sooner than others. In an effort for fairness, teams not competing would be kept away from the competition so as not to give away any strategy or secrets.

"Be aware that each station might include a surprise puzzle or athletic event," Bill said in his thick Southern accent, peering at the competitors over his aviators. "If you choose not to complete any event, you will DQ—be disqualified—and will be awarded zero points for that event."

Bill was not joking about the surprises. For every athletic event, there was some sort of puzzle or trivia attached. For the events that seemed strictly athletic, competitors were confused to find silly additions. Instead of difficult hurdles and sprints, competitors faced an egg race or parts where they needed to cartwheel or skip or leap together. Even the puzzles had athletic twists, such as the oversized checkerboard being so large that both competitors needed to run from piece to piece in order to finish the game.

IT SEEMED the Olympic gods were smiling upon Lucas and Teddy as they went from station to station. There was no rule that said both competitors had to participate in every aspect of each event, only that they had to be present, which made certain sports very cut-and-dry.

"Are you good at football?" Lucas asked as they approached Station 1.

"Erm…." Teddy tightened his bandana. "No. Sadly."

"All right." Lucas patted Teddy's shoulder. "I'll do both. Kick and defend."

Teddy opened his mouth to offer his goalie services, but Lucas had already gotten into place to start kicking. Teddy watched Lucas's thighs and arse flex beneath his black shorts as he kicked goal after goal. The ref blew the whistle after what seemed like fifty.

Lucas jogged back to Teddy. A pink flush brightened Lucas's cheeks. Teddy pulled him into a hug and squeezed him tight. "That was amazing, Luke!"

Lucas rubbed Teddy's lower back. "Thanks, love."

"Want me to defend the goal?"

"Do you want to? I can do it, if you're not comfortable. I play a lot in a work league."

"You're sure you don't mind?"

Lucas's gaze flickered over Teddy's body and he crooked a smile. "We all have our gifts. It's fine if football isn't yours."

Lucas managed to defend all but one of the goals kicked toward him by the judge, earning an impressed nod from the man when they moved on. Their high score for the first station lit a fire under their arses, both growing more excited to keep competing.

American football was one of Teddy's gifts. He nailed all ten throws in a row. Lucas stood slack-jawed on the sidelines.

"Jesus Christ, Bennet!" John, Jo's husband, exclaimed, with his hands cupped around his mouth. "You've got a cannon on there!"

"Yeah, where the hell did that come from?" Lucas asked softly, squeezing both of Teddy's shoulders. He massaged his biceps. "Who knew? That was incredible."

"Thanks, Fluff." Teddy lifted two thumbs up and raised his chin toward John. "Go, Pack, go."

"The Packers?" John exclaimed, horrified. "Ugh! They suck!"

Teddy said, "The Cowboys suck!" with Lucas pulling him to the next event.

They went to the life-sized checkerboard, which was set up as if the game was half-finished. Lucas ran straight at the board, but Teddy held his arm out, catching him around the stomach.

"Let's look at it a second," Teddy whispered. Lucas stepped back. "See what pieces are left."

"We're already being timed."

"So? Let's just look. Just for a second to plot our moves."

Lucas nodded and looped his thumbs in the waistband of his black trunks. He and Teddy stood in silence for a few seconds, then gasped in unison. They took off toward the board, both flying silently from piece to piece to make their moves.

"Done!" Lucas said as he and Teddy jumped off the board.

The judge gave them a thumbs-up while noting their time.

Their weakest section, by far, was Track & Field. No one was perfect.

"Teddy," Lucas chuckled, nearly stumbling and flopping on his stomach. He dragged Teddy along, his right leg bound to Teddy's left. "You're doing so good, move those legs! Left, right! Left, ri—*Ai-yi-yi*, what are you *doing*?"

Teddy's laughter grew louder as he teetered. His long legs did not match up with Lucas's compact strides. Teddy tried, truly he did, but he couldn't keep them up, and Lucas followed him as he fell sideways on the sand. By the time they were untied and made it to the egg race portion, they were a sandy mess.

They grabbed their eggs and spoons and took off, though Teddy lagged behind. Lucas turned and looked over his shoulder.

"Teddy, it's an egg! You can't—" Lucas ran back and put Teddy's egg on his spoon, urging him along. "C'mon, love! Deliver that little egg like the flamingo you were born to be!"

Teddy made it to the finish and fell on his stomach as he was overcome by belly laughs. His fall sent his egg flying. Lucas tried to pick him up, but Teddy pulled him down to the sand.

"Oi!" Lucas burst into high-pitched, babbled giggles, pushing Teddy's fingers away from his sides. "I guess those legs are truly for cosmetic purposes only! Theodore!"

The next team reached the start of Track & Field. Zamir and Asa waited patiently with their hands on their hips and identical knowing smirks. Teddy and Lucas both blushed and stopped their beach wrestling match. They got up and moved on to trivia.

Each question came with a physical challenge. For some, both team members had to do jumping jacks while being quizzed. They had to answer some questions with one teammate performing a handstand, or chug a beer each before getting interrogated.

"Your knowledge of useless rubbish has finally paid off," Lucas said, both jogging to the final swimming station.

"Perfect ten, baby," Teddy said, slightly out of breath.

They high-fived.

"Well done, love," Lucas said.

Both toed off their shoes and socks at the final station, leaving their tanks beside their trainers. Instead of a simple swimming race to get a flag, they had to answer a long math problem before they could even get in the water. Lucas's hand flew over the chalkboard. He dispensed with the math problem with as much ease as Teddy confidently answered that the capital of Belgium was Brussels.

"I didn't know maths could be hot," Teddy said as they ran into the water at full speed.

He heard Lucas scoff playfully as he dove under. They both swam as fast as they could to a dinghy about twenty-five meters out. They picked up their purple flags and swam back to the shore, running to the judge waiting for them on the sand.

"Done," Lucas gasped out. He fell to his knees on the sand with his hands on his thighs. The judge blew her whistle, and Teddy fell down beside him, rolling onto his back. "Ugh." Lucas tugged at his damp, sandy swim trunks. He looked up at the judge. "Can we swim to rinse off?"

She nodded and pointed toward an area of the sea not being used for their competition. The solo events were wrapping up by the time they rinsed and dried off. They waited at the starting line with the other competitors, sipping bottled water and reapplying sun cream.

Bill and Phil came over with their clipboards, and Bill said, "What an impressive display of athleticism! Here are the results."

They started calling pairs out, everyone clapping politely for each group. Most of the older competitors had done the competition for fun. The atmosphere was friendly and laughter-filled as they revealed who had opted out of what event. Jo and Tracy even competed with frozen drinks in hand, opting out of more events than they competed in.

Eventually, there were only four pairs left: Zamir and Asa (Team Blue), Lucas and Teddy (Team Purple), Cillian and Chessie (Team Green), Lane and Dean (Team Red).

"In fourth place, a mere two points away from the top three," Phil said, dragging out the announcement. He did work for reality television, after all. "We have… Team Blue: Zamir and Asa."

The other three pairs all burst into loud, excited cheers, their shouts varying from Lane exclaiming, "*Yessssss*!" while fist-pumping with both arms, to Teddy and Lucas giggling, "Oh my God!" at the same time. Phil cut a line in the air with his flattened palm. "Your scores from the qualifying round have no say in your place for the Final Countdown. It's all a fresh start. However, the rankings after the qualifying round are: Green in third, Purple in second, and Red in first."

"HELLS YES, baby," Lane said. She and Dean slapped their hands high over their heads. Dean picked her up and twirled her. She pointed at Lucas, with a silly grin on her face. "Told you we'd own it!"

Lucas and Teddy swayed in a tight hug.

"Hey, babe, second place! That's awesome," Lucas said, oblivious to his sister. "Proud of you."

Teddy pecked the lowest curve of his neck, then kissed the front of his shoulder and murmured, "So proud of you."

Lucas inhaled a deep breath of Teddy's sweaty, yet still soapy, skin. "Thank you for being my partner. You're…." Lucas's voice softened. "You're amazing. Kept us both calm and killed the puzzles."

Teddy squeezed him and stepped back. He cradled Lucas's face with the heel of his hand. "Thank you for being such an amazing teammate. And enduring my legs."

"I rather enjoy your legs, so it was my pleasure."

Teddy's brows arched, and Lucas smirked, running his hands through his own hair. They went to Zamir and hugged him. Lucas reached out to Asa to rub her back.

"S'all right," Asa said, squeezing Lucas. "We sucked at the puzzles."

"We really did." Zamir pulled Lucas into another hug and whispered, "I'm so proud of you, Lukeybear," and ruffled the back of his wet hair.

Lucas snorted and wiggled in his arms. "Aw, thanks. Sorry, mate. 'M all sweaty."

"We all are." Zamir stepped back and patted Lucas's cheeks as he grinned. His hazel eyes sparkled. He lowered his voice to whisper, "Don't tell Cillian, but I hope you and Teddy win."

"I heard that!" Cillian shouted from across the beach. He waved a warning finger at Zamir. "You'd better watch it, bud, or we're only having sex once tonight."

Asa dry heaved, then held her hands over her mother's ears.

The announcer corralled all the competitors at the front of the Final Countdown. The crowd was moved along the strip of closed-off beach marked by the long curtain that blocked the competitors from seeing what the Final Countdown actually consisted of.

Bill and Phil appeared, and both nodded at one of the judges. The judge pulled the curtain aside. The crowd cheered.

The course was full of colorful foam blocks, nets, and climbing walls erected between puzzle setups. Even parts of the sea had colorful floating objects scattered throughout.

Bill stepped forward with his clipboard held to his chest. "The Final Countdown is a massive obstacle course, combining sport, smarts, and quick thinking. As you can see, it is quite long, with lots of running in between each event. You must collect a flag after completing each event." One of the judges came forward with three gold foam sticks. "You then must place each flag in your torch. If you lose or forget a flag, you will have sixty seconds added to your finish time."

The crowd gasped as the competitors nodded. Loss of a flag would ensure a team would lose the entire competition with that steep a penalty. Teddy, Lane, and Chessie accepted the stumpy foam torches.

"I repeat," Bill said, slowly. "You must finish with all event flags in your torch to be considered done. Any lost flag will result in a sixty-second penalty. Judges will be at each station and will give you the flag only once they have deemed you are successfully finished with that particular course."

Phil stepped forward. "I believe it goes without saying that opting out of one of the events will result in a DQ, which will add two minutes to your time and would likely end your shot at winning. There is no points system for the

Final Countdown. The team that successfully makes it to the finish with the fastest course time wins gold, second silver, and third bronze."

Bill said, "Though you may prefer to have shoes and your gear on, you will be in and out of the water the entire time, so keep that in mind. Please be aware that none of the events should cause injury if you choose to run the race barefoot. There are numbered signs at each event explaining what task must be done, and judges can explain the rules to you, but they will not offer you any help or suggestions. Any questions?"

The competitors shook their heads. They took off their trainers and socks, leaving them beside the starting line. The men took off their tanks and tees. Lane was already down to her athletic black bikini and a pair of neon orange running shorts.

"God, I'm loving all this beefcake," she said, grinning at the men, with her hands on her narrow hips.

Dean pointed two fingers at Lane and flicked them toward his face. "Hey, eyes up here, babe. I know my physique is stunning"—he flexed one arm and turned sideways, showing his slight beer gut sticking out—"but no need to be rude."

The finalists all laughed. Lucas adjusted Teddy's bandana, tightening it around his hair. Teddy straightened Lucas's sunglasses.

"This is going to be so fun," Lucas whispered, as he and Teddy shared a warm look of bemusement. Teddy pecked him and squeezed Lucas's arse with both hands. Lucas laughed quietly, wiggling his bum beneath his hands.

"Is this an athletic competition or prom?" Cillian stepped between them. He grinned and bumped his shoulders into Teddy and Lucas. "I'm sensing Team Purple for the big L." He held his hand up to his forehead with his thumb and pointer finger forming the letter *L*.

Teddy crossed his arms over his bare chest. "Aren't you supposed to be all peace-on-earth and Zen?" Lucas chuckled into his water bottle. "Where's this competitive streak coming from?"

"Oh, I'm still Zen, bud. Don't you worry. And I'm going to peacefully"—Cillian pressed his palms together and bowed—"kick some arse."

The finalists got into position at the starting line. They could see that there was a short run to the first station, which appeared to include a swimming portion.

"On your mark," the announcer said in a dramatic, booming voice. "Get set." Team Green and Team Red got down to a sprinting position, Teddy and Lucas glancing confusedly at them. "Go!"

They all ran toward the first station. Lane and Chessie reached it first, Lucas and Teddy coming up next, followed by Dean and Cillian.

Station I

Teammates are to take turns swimming out to their team-color-designated buoy and retrieving their foam puzzle pieces. One teammate must be on the shore at all times. Once all pieces are retrieved, they must complete the puzzle in their raised puzzle box.

"I'll swim first." Teddy patted Lucas's back and took off.

Lucas went to their puzzle station and stood with his hands on his hips, squinting through his sunglasses. He watched Teddy dive in the water and swim toward the floating pieces. His long limbs sliced through the clear blue water. Lane was just a few strokes ahead of Teddy, but Cillian was lagging behind.

Teddy scooped up as many purple foam puzzle pieces as he could and swam toward the sand. He ran up the shore and dumped the pieces. Lucas sprinted toward the shoreline at the same time as Dean, both hitting the water as Cillian finally made it back.

"C'mon, mate!" Chessie cried. Quick bits of chatter from both Cillian and Chessie carried to the other competitors. "Get up here!"

Lucas returned to their station with as many puzzle pieces as he could hold. Teddy had already laid out a possible arrangement on the sand. Lucas dropped his pieces and slicked his hands over his dripping face. Teddy ran toward the water.

TEDDY RETURNED moments later with their remaining pieces and dropped them on the sand, noting that Lucas had started to arrange more of their pieces in possible positions. Lane and Dean were slamming pieces into their puzzle box a few yards away, Lane grumbling while Dean sighed and tried to fit pieces together.

"What do you think?" Lucas whispered.

Teddy hummed and reached down, plucking a small triangle from Lucas's pile. He switched two other pieces, placed the triangle in the arrangement, then added three of Lucas's larger pieces and one smaller piece from his last swim.

"This is it," Teddy whispered. He glanced at Lucas, who nodded. "Yeah?"

They started calmly placing pieces in their puzzle board. Within seconds the board was full, all pieces smoothly sliding together. They both lifted their hands.

"Done," Teddy declared. A judge came over, then looked from their board to her clipboard.

"You're good!" She held out a red flag. "You may move on."

Lucas accepted their flag and stuck it in the top of the torch. Both ran at full speed to the next station. They were met by a rock wall that needed to be climbed on both sides. The walls were angled in such a way that it was too steep to walk straight up, but if they fell off the wall they would not be injured. They quickly scanned the sign.

Station II

Get ready to climb! Competitors must make it through a military-style obstacle course, complete with climbing walls, a rope wall, walls to jump over, and a belly crawl on the sand. Watch out for grenades!

Lucas and Teddy moved to the wall. Lane and Dean ran up to the instructions behind them as both Teddy and Lucas started to climb.

"All right, not too bad," Teddy said, conversationally. His long toes gripped the rubbery holders, and his hands easily found the quickest path to the top. "Rock climbing is actually a really fun fitness activity, don't you think?"

He swung over the top of the wall, Lucas's hands grasping a few rubber markers from the top. Teddy looked back and saw Lane and Dean starting to climb.

"Jesus, what are you, a monkey?" Lucas panted and pushed himself up with his feet.

Teddy held his hands out and pulled Lucas up by the underarms, and they quickly moved down the other side. They reached a row of five walls, each around shoulder height.

Lucas said, "All right, so we just—Ugh!" He lifted his foot and found it to be covered with magenta paint. Teddy saw his pink foot at the same time as something wet slapped him on the back. Teddy turned to reveal his teal back.

The grenades came in the form of children throwing paint-filled water balloons. Maggie cackled—she had thrown the teal one right at Teddy.

"Traitors," Lucas shouted at the sidelines.

TEDDY AND Lucas scaled all five walls in tandem, both finishing in no time, despite the paint pelting them from either side. They dropped to their stomachs and started to crawl beneath the low canopy of rope that stretched across the sand.

"You've got the torch, yeah?" Teddy said, winded. His long limbs were not as helpful on the ground as they were when scaling walls.

Lucas emerged from under the far end, patting the torch shoved in the back of his swim trunks to be sure their first flag was there. "Yeah." He bent over and held his hands out. "C'mere, babe. You've got this."

Teddy gripped Lucas's hands, and Lucas pulled him out from beneath the rope. He helped Teddy to his feet. Paint and sand covered both of them.

"Ugh," Teddy chuckled, rubbing his hands over his chest. "This is gross."

They reached the final part of the section, which was a rope wall that led to a wide, curved water slide. They quickly climbed up the rope, Teddy making it to the top first.

Lucas got to his knees on top of the slide. "Oh no. And you thought the paint was gross."

They sat on the slide and went down, landing in a large inflatable pool filled with whipped cream and sprinkles. The crowd erupted with cheers. Teddy and Lucas's fall caused the whipped cream to fluff up into both of their faces.

Teddy scooped a handful of whipped cream and slapped it on Lucas's head. Lucas squawked and reached for him. His fingers slid over Teddy's back, but he successfully smushed Teddy's face in the thick cream. Teddy wrestled Lucas as best he could, both laughing loudly.

Lane and Dean got to the top of the slide, while Lucas and Teddy pulled each other out of the slippery pool and ran to the station judge.

They got their second flag, orange, and stuck it in the torch. A judge held out two water bottles for them to grab. They both said, "Cheers!" and took a bottle. They attempted to douse their faces and gulp at the same time as running. They found two small purple stationary bicycles facing each other with a bucket resting next to each bike. There were similar setups with red bikes and green bikes. A tall pole stretched high above each bike setup, with hooks hanging from the top and ropes dangling down the poles, and a platform at the top of each pole.

Station III

Time to clean up! Competitors must run to the sea and fill up their buckets with water. Once full, they must affix their buckets on the provided pulley system and lift them to the top of the bike rigs. Check with judges to be sure your bucket is safely secured. Each bicycle's pedals coordinate with the bucket hanging over their partner's head. Competitors then must pedal as fast as they can until the platform tips the bucket forward to spill on their partner. Beware of the bike locks!

They both grabbed their buckets and ran to the water.

"Oh, shit." Lucas saw Cillian was hot on their heels. "Where'd you come from?"

"Dean got stuck in the whipped cream. Was fucking hilarious," Cillian said, giggling and dunking his bucket. "And Chessie hit the pool so hard he went flying out onto the sand. Gave us a leg up!"

They ran back to their bike setups, quickly rigging their buckets and pulling on a rope to lift their water.

A judge appeared. "You may now pedal," she said, smirking and nodding at them.

Teddy and Lucas sat on their bikes and placed their feet on the pedals. They were met with resistance, and they frowned.

"Ah, fuck, the lock. We can't pedal yet." Teddy got off his bike and down to the sand. "It's a puzzle."

Lucas kneeled next to him, and they read a small sign beneath the oversized lock.

Digit One: [(The last year London hosted the Olympics – 2000) / 2] x 6
Digit Two: (Number of Olympic medals diver Tom Daley has won x 7) + 10
Digit Three: (Month of Zamir's birth + Month of Cillian's birth) x 4

"What is this notation? Have they never heard of order of operations?" Lucas muttered to himself and furrowed his brows, squinting at the sign. "Erm, January and September birthdays." He started to write with his finger in the sand, mouthing along as his brain worked. "Fuck, what year was that? The Olympics?"

"Two thousand and twelve," Teddy whispered. "Tom Daley got one medal."

"Right." Lucas underlined three numbers in the sand and reached for the lock. "Thirty-six, seventeen, forty," he whispered as he turned the dials.

Teddy nodded along with him while rubbing between his shoulder blades. "Fucking amazing, Luke."

The lock popped open, and Teddy smeared Lucas's math away on the sand. They jumped on their bikes and pedaled. After a few seconds, the platforms beneath the water buckets started to tilt. The more they pedaled, the steeper the angle of the bucket. Water started to drip out of each bucket and they pedaled faster. Lucas doused Teddy first. Teddy cackled, with his head tilted back. The bucket over his head emptied within seconds.

"C'mon, c'mon! Do me too," Lucas shouted as he laughed. Teddy started to pedal again and, finally, the bucket over Lucas tipped and doused him. He rubbed his hands over his face. "All right." He spit water out of his mouth. "Let's go."

"Flags!" Teddy cried, running backward. He picked up their torch, accepting their new yellow flag from the judge and shoving it in the foam tube.

"Close," Lucas said, running faster. Teddy was a few strides behind him, and Lucas slowed his pace to bring them even. "C'mon, love. It's a long run to the next one and Lane can—"

"Ta, boys!" Lane called, flying ahead of them.

"—run really well," Lucas finished.

Dean ran past them. Cillian and Chessie's loud chatter and heavy steps were audible in the distance.

"I'm fine going faster," Teddy said, speeding up his strides. "I didn't want us to get exhausted."

"I think we're almost done. We can push."

"HOW ARE you so good at talking and running at full speed?" Teddy asked. Perspiration dotted his face. He rubbed his forearm over his brows, finding a mixture of sweat, seawater, and whipped cream on his skin. "Lungs of steel."

They approached the next station and saw a table full of water bottles.

"Good," Lucas panted, slowing his steps. "Go to the directions."

Teddy continued on to the tablet of rules. Lucas ran up seconds later with two bottles of water and a wet towel.

"What have we got?" Lucas handed over a bottle. Teddy cracked the bottle open and sucked on the end before dumping it on his head. Lucas read over the rules. He glanced forward and saw Lane and Dean standing at an enormous red bowl. "Oh, gross."

Station IV

Eat up! Competitors can share a chilly, sweet snack after such a long run (spoons not included). Both competitors must participate in the eating of their team sundae, and their bowl must be licked clean to be considered finished. A bit of cardio to work off your ice cream and you'll be on your way to the next station. Bon appétit!

Lucas and Teddy ran to their large purple bowl. A mountain of colorful scoops of ice cream awaited them—mounds of whipped cream and heaps of toppings and cherries spilled out of the bowl. As the rules proclaimed, there were no spoons.

"We can use our hands?" Teddy asked their judge. The judge nodded. Teddy grinned at Lucas. "You ready?"

Lucas took a deep breath and stuck his hand in the bowl. "Cillian can eat like no one on earth. We need to suck this down." He pulled out a handful of pistachio. "Fuck me, this is cold."

Teddy couldn't see how much ice cream was left in Team Red's bowl, but both Lane and Dean looked a bit green in the face.

Cillian arrived. "Yay!" he chirped. "Ice cream!" He dunked his face in the bowl.

"Right," Teddy said, nodding once. He stuck his hands in and brought them to his mouth, swallowing down gobs of ice cream. He watched, wide-eyed, as Lucas hoovered ice cream, swallowing fistful after fistful with ease.

Lucas looked at him. His mouth was covered in melted strawberry ice cream and hot fudge dripped off his bottom lip. "Wah?"

Teddy leaned in and sucked the hot fudge off. Lucas smiled against his mouth.

"Lick the bowl, not me." Lucas's cheeks heated. "We need to hurry. Cillian's enjoying this too much."

"Fuck yes, I am!" Cillian cried with his face still in his bowl.

They sped up their swallows, now understanding why Dean and Lane looked sick. Ice cream was delicious when you had a bowl or two as a treat. It was not such a treat to use filthy hands to dig into mountains of the stuff and swallow it as fast as possible, and saliva and sweat mixed in the bowl.

"Ugh, I don't know if I can eat any more," Teddy groaned quietly, clutching his stomach. "I keep tasting sand."

"I got it, love." Lucas looked to their judge. "Can I lift the bowl to finish it?"

"Yes."

Lucas picked up their bowl and angled it, gulping the conglomeration of melted ice cream left in the bottom. Teddy ran to the water station and got them both fresh water bottles and towels. When he returned seconds later, Lucas was licking the bowl clean. Chocolate ice cream smeared all over his face and his nose was green with mint chip. He even had sprinkles in his hair.

Lucas dropped the bowl on the table and said, "Done," on an exhale. His stomach puffed out.

Their judge checked the bowl. "All right, boys, go ahead to your cardio."

They followed the line of her arm and groaned. They both held their stomachs and then ran to the row of treadmills she'd indicated.

"You're a sick fuck, Cillian," Lucas called over his shoulder. He accepted a bottle from Teddy and doused his face, thumbing his eyelids. "How do you even get treadmills on a beach?"

Cillian just groaned with his face in his bowl. Lane shouted, "C'mon, babe, eat!" and clapped her hands next to Dean's head, but her gaze was on Lucas and Teddy.

The duo reached their treadmills and got on. A judge set their time for two minutes, and they started to jog.

"Oh my God," Teddy whimpered, gripping the rails of the treadmill. He and Lucas jogged while making quiet, pained noises. "Who knew ice cream could be evil?"

THEY FINISHED their jog and got off. Lane and Dean were halfway through their treadmill time, but Cillian and Chessie were just getting on their treadmills. They went to collect their flag but found another obstacle. A judge stood with a bucket of baseball bats. He handed one to each of them.

"Ten spins, then run through the tires to get your flag."

They shared a nauseated glance but took the bats, bent over, and placed their foreheads on the handles. They started to spin with their bodies hunched forward, their feet running sideways in a circle on the sand.

"One," the judge counted aloud. "Two. Three. Four. Five!"

Lucas saw Team Red running toward the bats as they finished spinning.

"Go to the tires, boys, you're doing great," the judge said, holding his arm out.

Lucas went to run, and immediately fell onto his side. Teddy cackled.

Teddy wrapped his hand around Lucas's forearm. "And you said my legs were useless." Teddy hauled Lucas to his feet. The sky and sand were spinning. "C'mon, babe, you're doing amazing." Teddy held Lucas to his side. They wobbled toward the rainbow of tires. "Just go with the sway."

"That makes no sense. How are you better at walking after spinny bats than in your everyday life?"

"I'm gifted. Ready?"

They broke apart to stumble through the tire course. They reached the end and both whimpered upon receiving their green flag. Lucas pulled out the torch and stuck the flag in. He and Teddy counted their flags before running to the next station.

Station V

This is not your lazy Sunday crossword! Teams must complete the word puzzle before collecting their flag. Need a letter? A quick trip to Alphabet Island should help!

Teddy stared at the list of clues, glancing from the clues to the empty puzzle. There were three identical puzzle boards set up, a bag of letters hanging from each board. A buoy bobbed in the sea with a large sign in the middle that read "ABC ISLAND!" Teddy dumped the letters on the sand. He and Lucas flipped them until they were all letter-side up.

"Right, so, these are all wedding words." Teddy glanced at the board. "We need vowels. That space is—" He lined up the letters G-R-O-M-S. "—'GROOMS,' but we only have one *O*." He pointed at the board. "This space is 'FLOWERS,' but we need the one *E* we've got for the word 'CAKE.'"

"I'll get us some letters."

Lucas ran to the sea and dove in, welcoming the warm water over his sticky skin. He swam to the buoy and grabbed as many letters as he could, including multiple vowels. He was swimming back as Lane dove in and Chessie ran into the water.

He ran at full speed back to Teddy and saw Teddy had arranged the puzzle on the sand, similar to how he had completed the first puzzle. Lucas dropped his letters. Teddy wordlessly grabbed vowels and placed them in empty spots.

"What do you think the fifth clue is?" Teddy asked, keeping his voice low.

Lucas glanced at the nearby teams. Their boards were angled away, but they were close enough to hear each other's voices. He focused on the clue list. "Erm." He scratched the top of his wet hair. "Is it… garter?"

"Garter," Teddy whispered excitedly, snapping his fingers. He grinned at Lucas. "Thank God you received slightly more brains than me."

"Psh. You figured this whole thing out on your own."

Teddy stood up. "We need another *A* and *T*. I'll get them. You wanna start the board?"

"Yeah, definitely."

Teddy turned and ran to the water as Lucas started to place tiles in their boxes.

"Shit," Cillian cursed loudly. Lucas looked from their puzzle and saw Cillian frantically digging in the sand. "Where's the yellow flag, Chess?"

"Must have dropped. Fuck. I'll go," Chessie said, sprinting back toward the last station.

Teddy ran up the beach. Bright sunlight highlighted the dips and curves of his long, slick body.

"Thank fuck," Teddy gasped, handing Lucas two dripping tiles. "I needed to get wet. I stink of dairy."

Lucas placed the final tiles and stepped back, calling, "Done."

A judge came over. She compared the puzzle to her clipboard. She handed them a blue flag, which they tucked into their torch. "Only one station left," she said. "Almost there."

"Can we dump the board?" Lucas asked, holding the side of their puzzle.

A small smile emerged on the judge's face. "Yes. Very wise." Lucas and Teddy pulled the pieces off and dumped them on the sand.

"We see your wandering eyes, Team Red," Teddy said, pointing two fingers from his eyes to their station.

Dean snorted, while Lane stuck her tongue out at them. They started to run. Lucas double-checked their torch for all flags.

They reached the final station.

Station VI

Almost there! After such a long race, you surely need a beverage!

Teams must inflate an inner tube and take turns sliding in it to the bar. There are four drinks for each team (two per teammate). You must slide back and forth for each cup, using the inner tube for each trip except the final one. Their teammate can hold the tube on the finish line side. When you finish each drink, it's time for a little Flip Cup! You must successfully flip the cup on the edge of the table by putting your cup facedown and flicking it until it stands up the right way.

Bottoms up! We'll see you at the finish line!

Three lines of bright blue Slip'N Slides led to a table with three rows of four plastic cups on top. The cups were purple, red, and green to match the competing teams. Fountains sprayed the plastic Slip'N Slides with water and inflatable palm trees surrounded the area. The cheering crowd was at the finish line, which was around thirty meters from the bar.

Lucas and Teddy started unfurling a neon purple inner tube.

"Cillian lost a flag," Lucas said quietly as their hands moved fast.

"Lane's coming." Teddy pulled the rubbery valve out from the tube. "Let's do this."

He sucked in a deep breath and started to blow, Lucas continuing to spread the tube out. He let Teddy blow five times before he tapped his shoulder and took over, and they traded back and forth. Their tube was half-full when Lane started to fill Team Red's tube. The siblings eyed each other. Cillian and Chessie ran up to the rules. Teddy took over blowing again, Lucas sucking breaths in and fanning himself.

"I think we're good," Teddy said.

He and Lucas squeezed the taut tube. They glanced up at the judge, who nodded. They fastened the valve and stood up, then ran to the Slip'N Slide.

"Want me to go first?" Teddy asked. "You'll be faster than me and it'll be better for you to anchor the race."

"Good plan."

TEDDY HELD the tube to his stomach, exhaled a quick breath, and took off toward the Slip'N Slide. He bent over and slid on the tube across the wet plastic. In theory, a Slip'N Slide worked for small children. In practice, large, adult bodies covered in sand were not the easiest to propel across cheap plastic, even with the tube's assistance.

Teddy's running start got him to the halfway point, but upon hitting the middle of the slide, he flopped off the tube and landed in a pile of limbs.

"Oh my God," Lucas gasped out between hysterical giggles. Teddy laughed as he tried to right himself, using his feet to push himself the rest of the way. When Teddy stood up on the sand, Lane went flying across the Slip'N Slide. Lucas cupped his hands around his mouth. "Go, Theodore, go!"

Teddy ran to the table and chugged the first purple cup of beer. The cup was not even filled halfway, and Teddy finished it in two gulps. He placed it upside down with the rim hanging over the edge of the table, then started to tap his fingers underneath the rim to get it to flip. He took only three tries before he got the cup to flip and stand right-side up. "Is that good?" he asked the judge. The judge nodded.

"Ugh, who approved warm beer?" Cillian groaned. He gave a horrified grimace as he tried to flip his cup.

Teddy ran to the Slip'N Slide at the same time as Lane. No matter how much of a lead he and Lucas seemed to get, Lane and Dean came roaring back at them.

"Shit, you Thompsons are"—Teddy threw himself onto the slide—"relentless."

Lane said, "You have no idea," as she whizzed past him.

Teddy stumbled up and handed Lucas the tube. Lucas grabbed it and sprinted away. When Lucas hit the wet plastic, he used his hands and feet to keep momentum going. His trip across was much smoother than Teddy's.

"Yeah, Luke!" Teddy shouted, clapping loudly. "That's it! Good one!"

Lucas ran to the table and downed his beer. He placed the cup upside down and tapped the bottom, flipping it in one. He went flying back across, Dean hot on his heels and Chessie sliding toward the bar.

The crowd's laughter almost overpowered its cheers. The sight of six sweating, frantic adults trying to squeeze into inner tubes and fling themselves across a Slip'N Slide was quite something to see. Combine that with said adults trying to flip plastic cups while drinking warm beer, and the video crew basically became a necessity.

Teddy was neck and neck with Lane for his final trip across. He flipped his second cup on one try and held his hands up. "Come on, Luke!" he hollered, running to the end of the Slip'N Slide. He clapped. "Come on, love!" He clapped louder and watched Lucas fling himself down the line on his belly without the tube, Dean and Cillian coming down at the same time. Teddy helped Lucas up. "You got it, babe."

"We're so close." Lucas coughed before sucking down a gulp. Dean and Cillian were also beginning to chug, and Lucas's eyes widened at the sight. He grunted out, "Shit."

"You're totally fine. We're doing amazing."

Lucas started to flip his cup and Teddy gasped.

"Oh no." He spun Lucas to look at the torch tucked in the back of his swim trunks. "Where's the green one?"

Lucas took the torch out of his swim trunks, halting his flip attempts. He and Teddy looked to the Slip'N Slide and spotted a sliver of green fabric snagged on the middle.

"Flip," Teddy said, already running. "I'll get it." He ran to the Slip'N Slide asking the judge, "Do I have to use the tube?"

The judge nodded and Teddy sighed, launching himself forward. He scrambled to get the fabric, clawing his way back to the sand.

"Teddy!"

Teddy looked toward Lucas, who was jumping up and down at the bar while waving a purple flag.

"I flipped! Come on, love!"

Teddy got himself upright on the sand. The second he reached Lucas, they took off. There was a cheer from Team Red's table. Lane and Dean were inches behind them.

"Fuck, run, run, run," Lucas chanted. He and Teddy ran at full speed to the finish.

Ice cream and warm beer and the lingering dizziness from their time with the spinny baseball bats lurched in their stomachs, but Lucas and Teddy grasped hands and ran harder. They ran over the rainbow line drawn in the sand mere seconds before Dean and Lane. Teddy's long legs spread wider as he ran and Lucas's chest heaved. Lucas handed Phil their torch and sagged backward, and Teddy held him against his body. They looked to the judges with their eyes wide, heaving to breathe.

Bill lifted their torch, a rainbow of soggy fabric hanging from the gold foam tube. He brought a microphone to his mouth. "Winner," he droned, dragging out the word. He grinned. "Team Purple."

Teddy and Lucas screamed and laughed and flung their arms around each other, jumping up and down as if they had won the actual Olympics, the crowd cheering loudly. The Queen song "We Are The Champions" blared on the beach. The other finalists swarmed them. Lane hugged her brother tightly, and Cillian snorted so hard that sprinkles came out of his nose and got stuck in Teddy's hair.

When the finalists backed off, Lucas somehow ended up with his legs wrapped around Teddy's waist. Teddy twirled them as they babbled nonsense to each other, then fell onto the sand and took Lucas, who was still straddling his waist, with him. Lucas cupped his face and leaned down, both exhaling through their noses with their lips hotly joined together. Their chests heaved. Teddy slid his hands up Lucas's sweaty lower back as they sucked firm, smacking kisses.

"You taste like strawberry ice cream," Teddy purred. Lucas's fingers ran through his wet, matted hair as their kisses pressed harder. Lucas moaned into his mouth and Teddy's hands squeezed his arse. "Delicious."

"You taste like victory." Both laughed and Lucas kissed him with tiny, barely there pecks. "So proud of you, puzzle master." Lucas smoothed his hand over Teddy's hair. "Thank you for being my partner."

Teddy cradled Lucas's face, guiding him down for another soft kiss. "Anything for you, love."

Lucas's lower back arched and he hugged Teddy tighter as they sucked kisses, both moaning weakly into each other's mouth.

"Ahem."

They froze. Teddy retracted his lips from his kissy pout, and Lucas looked over his shoulder with his crooked sunglasses half off his nose.

Bill, Phil, the competition judges, the camera crew, and the entire wedding group stood in front of them. Even the announcer up in his lifeguard chair was staring down.

Cillian chuckled and slung his arm around Zamir's shoulder. "And they said they wouldn't need to borrow lube." His attempt at a whisper was loud enough for the crowd to hear. They burst out with whoops, and Zamir covered his face with his tee.

LUCAS SCOOTED backward, flattening his hands on Teddy's stomach. He glanced down and found Teddy to be blushing, his smile shy, his thumbs gently rubbing the tops of Lucas's knees. His purple bandana was crooked, the knot sticking out from the top of his head like a unicorn horn. His sunglasses were a smudged, whipped-cream-smeared mess, and rainbow sprinkles and sand were ground into his hair.

Lucas's breath caught. His heart pounded faster than every high point of the competition combined. A flurry of warm, ticklish energy swirled inside his rib cage.

"We'd like to proceed with the medal ceremony and celebratory barbecue," Bill said, with amusement peeking through his sportsmanlike judge exterior. "If that's all right with our gold medalists, of course."

"Yes, definitely," Lucas said. His bum thudded on the sand. Teddy sat up and brushed some sand off his torso. "We can, erm, proceed. Can we rinse off before the ceremony?"

"I suppose," Phil said. Bill was beside him. "But make it quick." Phil rubbed his stomach. "I'm hungry and the chicken smells amazing."

Teddy stood and dusted off his bum, then peered down at Lucas, with mischief curling his lips. He held one hand out.

"What?" Lucas asked as he stood. They clasped hands. Teddy grinned and looped his arm under Lucas's arse, swinging him up in the air and over his shoulder. Lucas squealed, "Oh my God, what are you doing?"

Lucas's shouts could be heard by the clapping crowd even as Teddy took off toward the water. Teddy ran until the water was at his waist then dumped Lucas into the sea. Lucas popped up like an infuriated Ariel.

"You sneaky shit." Lucas laughed and jumped on Teddy's shoulders. Teddy dunked under the water with Lucas's fingers laced in the back of his hair. Lucas's eyes bulged as rapid giggles rushed out of his mouth and he kicked his legs wildly. "Fuck!" He threw his head back as Teddy blew a raspberry on his navel. "What are you—"

Lucas cackled and squirmed to get away from the fingers squeezing both sides of his hips. Teddy's beaming face popped out of the water. The other finalists waded into the warm water.

"You're so dead," Lucas warned, swimming toward Teddy.

Teddy swam backward, taunting, "Oh, I'm so scared! I'm so—I'm so—" He started to laugh throatily and sputtered water with all four of Lucas's limbs suctioned to him like a starfish. "Luke!"

Chapter FIFTEEN

AFTER A delicious barbecue lunch, everyone planned on going in the pool. They'd had enough sand for the day, plus it was going to take some time for the beach to be cleaned up in the wake of the Zill-ympics extravaganza.

Teddy and Lucas walked back to their bungalow for proper showers. The resort's picturesque pools were kept in pristine condition, and they didn't want to foul the water with whipped cream and sprinkle remnants.

"You wanna go first?" Lucas asked, scratching behind his ear. "Ugh. I think I'll be finding sprinkles for weeks."

Teddy dropped his trainers on the welcome mat. He reached for Lucas's discarded trainers and tossed them on the deck. "Do you wanna try the outdoor shower?" He pinched Lucas's sandy tank top from the floor and put it in his own designated dirty clothes bag. "We've already seen each other's cocks. It'll save time."

Lucas watched Teddy stand to his full height.

"Erm, yeah." He dropped his hand. "Sure. I'll get bodywash."

Teddy peeled his swim trunks off in one smooth motion. The loss of his swimsuit revealed tan lines running around his hips. The skin of his lower back was bronzed warm brown while his plump, damp arse was a contrasting creamy color. Teddy turned toward him, his hands on his hips, his swim trunks in hand.

His cock hung heavily from the tawny, wet skin of his groin. His foreskin was a touch darker than the shade of his slightly puffy nipples. Teddy's abs twitched and his left pec clenched upward as he walked. A groomed triangle of close-cropped, dark hair thinned out as it rose and tapered into the line of hair leading to his navel.

Lucas swallowed dryly. His gaze twitched up from Teddy's groin. Teddy stepped closer, and the head of his cock slapped against his inner thigh.

"Shower stuff?" Teddy arched his brows and took one step toward Lucas. "Or do you need help locating the bodywash?"

"Yes. Right. No." Lucas shook his head and pointed at the glass patio door, turning away. "Shower stuff. Yes."

Lucas went into the en-suite, ignoring the soft, slapping sounds that Teddy's cock made as it bumped against his leg. He walked outside with one bodywash and one bottle of shampoo.

He walked up the path to the wooden outdoor shower. Lush grass pillowed his bare feet and steam already rose from within the wide wooden box. The door was half-open, revealing a sliver of a view. Teddy stood under the gushing stream of the shower, with water racing down the front of his body.

"Lord Jesus," Lucas whispered to himself, blinking rapidly. He inhaled deeply, exhaling as he stepped into the shower. "Hi."

Teddy's eyes opened. Drops clung to his dark lashes. He smiled softly and took the bottles from Lucas, who dropped his swim trunks to the floor, kicking them aside.

"Want me to do your back?" Teddy popped the bodywash open. "Quite a bit of paint still there."

Lucas pushed his shoulders back, stretching his shoulder blades and clasping his hands above his arse. "Sure."

Teddy gripped the tops of his shoulders and turned him around, pulling him under the water. Lucas shut his eyes as Teddy's fingers dug in all over his back. His strokes were soft but firm enough to ease paint from Lucas's skin.

"Feels nice," Lucas said quietly. His head lolled on his neck. He heard another bottle pop. "What are you doing?"

Teddy's long fingers massaged his scalp, making fruity foam puff around his hair. Lucas clenched his eyes shut tighter; he furrowed his brows and rolled his head forward. Teddy squeezed up and down the back of his neck as he washed his hair. Lucas's mouth was agape, water dribbled off his bottom lip, and his arms hung limp at his sides.

"There we are," Teddy's soft voice murmured near his ear. He smoothed Lucas's clean hair back. "Sprinkle free for the time being. Though—" He chuckled quietly. "—you still have pink toes."

Lucas opened his eyes and watched the shower water for a moment. Sunlight filtered in through the open roof to illuminate the lightest grains of the smooth wood walls. "Want me to do you? Help, I mean. Want me to help you?"

Teddy hummed and handed over the bottle of shampoo. He kept the bottle of bodywash. "I'll deal with my body, but you can do my hair, if you'd like."

Lucas turned and wordlessly started to wash Teddy's hair. Teddy scrubbed his hands over his paint patches and sticky bits. In an attempt to mimic Teddy's tingle-inducing touch, Lucas dug his fingernails into his scalp. Teddy moved his head at the same time, Lucas's fingernails scratching over his ears in the shift.

"Ow," Teddy chuckled, tilting his head. He grinned lopsidedly at Lucas with soapsuds sliding down his cheeks. "Watch the ears, please. They're sensitive."

"Sorry."

"S'all right." Teddy ducked his head down to Lucas's level while soaping his own groin. His eyes flicked up through his wet hair. "Well?"

Lucas blinked at him. "You're… done." Lucas released the shampoo bottle and the plastic clattered to the floor. "Your hair's clean."

Teddy tipped his head back. He stroked over his hair, suds flowing down his back to swirl in the drain between their feet. The muscles of his torso stretched, the hollows under his arms deepened, and his hip dents flexed.

Lucas asked, "How does anyone ever resist you?"

Teddy blinked water off his lashes and looked at Lucas. He smiled as he did one final swipe of his hands through his hair before lowering his arms. Their bodies, so different in size and structure, held the same position, and their arms hung straight down at their sides.

"You tell me." Teddy licked his wet lips. "You're the only one."

Lucas swallowed thickly, his jawline tight.

Teddy's eyes softened, and he slowly moved closer. "What do you want, Lucas?"

Lucas opened his mouth, then shut it. He sucked a shaky breath in through his nostrils.

"Do you want me?" Teddy's quiet question hung in the humid air. "If you do, all you have to do is say so."

Lucas shook his head. The motion brought a small smile to Teddy's closed mouth. Teddy lifted a hand and Lucas's gaze followed the motion.

Instead of reaching to Lucas, Teddy wrapped his hand around his own cock. He pumped himself once, slow and tight. He tilted his hips backward and his lower back arched for one stroke, all while nibbling a pinch of his bottom lip. His abs fluttered as his hips relaxed, and his hand continued its smooth, steady motion.

"Needed a wank whether you were in the shower or not." Teddy's voice was already rougher and his eyes had darkened. "Rolling around on the sand with you got me hot and bothered." The reddened, shiny head of his cock popped out of his fist for each deliberate stroke with a slick click. He let his knuckles brush the tip of Lucas's cock on an upstroke. Lucas inhaled sharply. "Looks like you could use one, as well."

Lucas's thumb and middle finger twitched against his thigh. He brought his eyes up from Teddy's pumping fist. "Yeah," he said gruffly, bringing his hand to his cock. "You're right."

They stared at each other as they pleasured themselves, the growing pace of their arms syncing and Lucas's chest heaving a split second faster than

Teddy's. Their heads jerked forward and back, faces tilting as if going in for a kiss, but always pulling away at the last second. Water continued to pound over them as fat drops slapped the stone tiles.

Lucas's toes nudged the outer edge of Teddy's foot. Teddy watched the water sway to mold to Lucas's Adam's apple as he swallowed. Teddy lowered his face, lingering at a breath from Lucas's mouth. No matter how Lucas's head twitched and turned, Teddy's mouth was there, huffing soft, hot breaths against his face, their fists clicking faster over their cocks.

Softly, ever so softly, Teddy whimpered, "Luke," and Lucas turned his head just so, pressing their lips together with searing heat. Teddy whimpered again, lower. One hand shifted to grip Lucas's cock and the other flattened on the small of Lucas's back.

Lucas's fingers slid down Teddy's stomach to wrap around his cock. Their tongues tangled while their hands resumed their quick-paced strokes. Lucas pressed Teddy against the shower wall and spread his right thigh outward to press himself tighter to Teddy's body. Teddy moaned into his mouth. Lucas felt his way up Teddy's body with nimble fingers. Teddy stuttered faster breaths out of his nostrils from a mere ghost of a touch over one of his nipples.

Lucas gripped the back of his hair and pulled gently, and Teddy's hips bucked against him. Lucas opened his mouth wider. Teddy dropped his jaw to accommodate the harder kiss. A sharp tug to his hair drew another long, low moan from him, and they both huffed uneven breaths between kisses.

"Do you want my pretty mouth?" Teddy whispered, his consonants fuzzy.

Lucas's brows pinched. His growling mouth slid from Teddy's to press his face to his neck. Lucas opened his mouth and sank his teeth into the soft skin beneath Teddy's ear.

Teddy groaned, "Fuck," and tilted his head to the side. The weak, kittenish sound was a complete contrast to his strong hand jerking Lucas through his climax. Come shot onto Teddy's lower belly.

Lucas's hips stuttered. He came, inhaling frantic breaths of Teddy's fruity hair. He squeezed his eyes shut tighter as a nasal, deep bark wailed out of his mouth, loud enough to vibrate against Teddy's skin. Teddy whimpered high in his throat as his toes curled on top of Lucas's.

Lucas sucked Teddy's neck as he came down, tiny blood vessels popping beneath Teddy's skin to meet his sucks. Lucas's hand tightened on his head. He tugged his hair one final time and Teddy gasped another one of his soft, weak sounds. He spilled hotly over Lucas's fist and the dark hair of his groin. His clenching right foot dug into Lucas's calf, and he dragged his fingernails down the small of Lucas's back.

They stayed wrapped around each other for a few moments. They panted together while the shower continued to flow. Teddy's head lolled back to thud on the wooden wall. Lucas mouthed over his neck while trying to regulate his breathing.

Teddy lifted his fingers from Lucas's cock. The motion and loss of warmth drew Lucas's eyes up, and they shared a pair of relaxed, afterglow-softened smiles between them. Teddy opened his mouth and stuck his own middle finger straight inside. His lips closed tight around the digit before he slowly pulled it out. Come squelched on the corner of his mouth as Lucas's pulse pounded beneath his jawline. Teddy gave each finger the same slow treatment. Their eyes locked even when Teddy opened his mouth on his palm and licked the final remnants of come from his skin.

Lucas opened his mouth to speak, but no words came out. Teddy lifted Lucas's hand from his cock and sucked his own come off each of Lucas's fingers, thumb to pinky. His teeth dragged over the pads of Lucas's fingers before his hot tongue swirled the end of each digit. He licked Lucas's palm, letting his tongue slither between Lucas's ring and middle finger. His eyes were so dark they were nearly all pupil.

Lucas's mouth snapped shut. Teddy's hand molded to Lucas's jawline; his wet mouth pried Lucas's lips open to slowly swipe his bitter tongue inside. Lucas's eyes fell shut and his head lolled back. A breath puffed between them, and Teddy angled his head left and kissed Lucas again, their jaws opening and closing as their heads nuzzled in opposite directions.

Teddy moved back, brushing the pink tip of his tongue over one corner of his mouth, then the other.

Lucas's voice was nothing more than a rasped whisper. "What the fuck was that for?"

"You gave me a memory." Teddy's long fingers fluttered near the sore spot on his neck. Red already showed between the sunken indents left by Lucas's teeth. He dipped his gaze to Lucas's mouth. Hunger and playfulness quirked Teddy's smile. "And I gave you one in return. It's only fair."

Lucas licked his salty lips. "Do you want another?"

"YOU MISSED a spot, silly." Jo flicked Lucas's toes. Lucas winced and pulled his foot to himself, not looking up from his book. Jo opened a copy of Vogue and settled on her white lounge chair. "Didn't you two shower? How could you miss the bright pink?"

Lucas hummed noncommittally. He sipped his coconut drink, something Teddy had ordered for him, and looked left. Teddy's long feet swayed in the air as he lay flat on his stomach on a white cabana bed. Teddy's Creamsicle-orange swim trunks were nearly identical to his yellow ones.

"Blue, please," Maggie said, holding her hand out.

"Excellent manners," Teddy said as he handed her a chunky blue crayon. He continued to color a sun with his yellow crayon, turning to look over his shoulder. He caught Lucas staring and smirked, touching his toes together. He held Lucas's stare for a beat, then returned to his coloring, his feet swaying again.

"Tazzy?"

"Yes, love?"

Maggie poked Teddy's neck with her crayon. "Are you hurt? You have a spot."

Teddy rubbed his neck. "What?" She poked again, and Teddy stopped rubbing. Her prod sent jolts of dull pain to his brain. "Oh. Uh. I."

Lane glanced at them over her Kindle. "Yeah, Tazzy, do tell us." She pushed her sunglasses up to her hair. "What happened to cause such a bruise?"

Lucas sat up straighter and turned onto his side, smiling sweetly at his sister. He looked at Maggie's confused, rumpled face. "He's fine, love. When Tazzy and I were beating your mum at the Zill-ympics, he must have accidentally bumped his neck. No worries."

Lane chuckled and knocked her fist on her forehead. "I'm sorry, am I forgetting about a shark event that I didn't participate in?"

"Children." Jo's full lips spread into a poorly hidden smile. "Enough."

"When does Marcy get here?" Lane fanned herself. "She's the mediator."

"You're the actual middle child." Lucas propped his hand behind his head and lay back on his chair. He glanced at Teddy's tropical fish drawing. "Lovely shading, babe."

Teddy grinned over his shoulder, and his legs swayed faster. "Thanks, love. Must be my artistic eye."

Lucas smiled and hummed, refocusing on his book.

Jo folded her magazine on her lap, lightening her voice. "Miss Maggie, what are you coloring? Can Gram see?"

Maggie climbed off the cabana bed and went to Jo's chair, clutching a pile of drawings to her chest. She scrambled up to sit next to Jo, with Lucas's chair to her right. She fell forward and her neon pink bathing-suit skirt flopped over her belly. Jo cradled Maggie to her side.

"Oh, sweetheart, these are beautiful," Jo cooed. She touched a beach scene in crayon. "I love the colors."

"Thank you! Taz helped me. That's Taz!" She slapped her hand on a drawing of Snow White they had pulled out of a princess coloring book. Instead of Snow White's normal dress being colored in, Maggie had drawn a shirt with pink flowers on it and put large sunglasses on Snow White's face. A big row of teeth was drawn over the cartoon's tiny mouth, and brown swirls covered the top quarter of the page.

"The resemblance is uncanny." Lucas turned a page. "Truly."

Teddy continued coloring, feet swaying lazily. "Mags, shall we show Uncle Lucas your picture of him?"

"Yeah!" Maggie squealed.

Teddy reached forward and shuffled through a few drawings. He turned on his side and grinned, angling a paper Lucas's way.

Lucas squinted through his sunglasses. "Dopey. From the Seven Dwarves." His voice was flat but his cheeks plumped. He tilted his head sideways as he studied the picture. Teddy held his hand over his mouth and snorted. Even Jo and Lane were muffling laughter; Jo's shoulders were shaking behind her trembling *Vogue* magazine. "Lovely. Did Teddy help you with that one too?"

"Yes!" Maggie climbed onto Lucas's chaise and shouted, "He has blue shoes!" while flinging her hand toward the drawing.

Lucas scooted sideways, curling his arm around Maggie's shoulders. "I love it," he said, squeezing her. "It's the most beautiful art I've ever seen."

"Uncle Lucas?"

"Yes?" Lucas replied, holding out the vowel and making his voice go higher. He broke into a shocked giggle. "Ah! What are you doing, silly?"

"You have a spot too!" She poked the inside of his bicep as fast as her stubby little finger could. "It's here!" She poked the point of his left collarbone. "Here too!"

Jo and Lane burst out laughing. Teddy pulled a towel over the back of his head and lay flat on his stomach.

"Maybe it was a bug," Maggie said, curiosity lighting her face. "Or an animal!"

"Maybe it was a wolf," Teddy said from under his towel.

Lucas said, "More like the beak of a wild flamingo," and looked at his book to hide his grin. Teddy's towel shook with muffled, slightly embarrassed laughter.

"TELLY ON or off?"

"Off, please," Lucas said, slurring. "I drank too many coconuts." He breathed deeply for a moment, his bare chest rising and falling. "M'tired."

Teddy snuffled and lifted the remote from Lucas's chest. He turned off the television, cutting off the weatherman's voice in the middle of the five-day forecast. The room went dark; they had remembered to shut the curtains before getting into bed that night. Teddy placed the remote on his bedside table and lay on his back.

"We got a lot of sun too." He sniffled, thumbing his right eye. "That always makes me tired."

"Mm."

Teddy stretched his arms up, tucking his hands behind his head. His eyes drifted shut. "Jerking off together probably tired us out, as well."

"Won't happen again."

"Oh, no?"

"Moment of weakness," Lucas said, barely moving his mouth.

"Don't you mean two moments of weakness, numbers man?"

The skin beside Lucas's eyes crinkled, even with his eyes shut. "I'm sleeping," he said. His smile widened at the sound of Teddy's quiet giggle. "Go to sleep, flamingo."

"I think this was the most fun day so far, even excluding the hand jobs," Teddy said, sleepy but cheerful. He nearly fell asleep, but his eyes twitched to the right beneath his closed lids, as if he were looking at Lucas. "What do you think?"

Lucas said nothing. He breathed soft puffs of air at the ceiling, resting his bent arms on his pillow. Teddy hummed and wiggled the back of his head into his pillow. Lucas's breaths faded in his ears as he fell fast asleep.

Chapter SIXTEEN

Tuesday, April 28

LUCAS WOKE up to the feeling of warm air rushing over his neck. The left side of his body felt hot, almost too hot under the duvet, and weighed down by something heavy. He cracked his eyes open and saw hair. This time, it was the hair on Teddy's head, bundled into a loose topknot, not the soft hair under his arm.

Teddy lay curled on his side, with his feet sandwiched around Lucas's ankle. His upper body lay half on Lucas's chest, while his face rested on Lucas's left pec.

Lucas squeezed Teddy's messy bun, beaming at the springy bunch of curls. Teddy's nose sniffled, but he did not wake. He rubbed his cheek against Lucas's chest and curled his fingers on top of Lucas's stomach.

Lucas reached one arm backward, blindly slapping his bedside table. He felt the hard plastic of his iPhone case and lifted the phone. He turned it on while listening to the quiet sounds of Teddy's breathing.

Once the phone was on, he opened the camera and angled it toward Teddy's face. From the camera's angle, Teddy's mouth looked enormous.

"Baby Mick," Lucas whispered, grinning and taking a photo. He pulled the camera out wide enough to get Teddy's clinging body in the picture. "Psh. And he called me cuddly." As he chuckled quietly, he heard Teddy's voice echo in his head. The memory brought him back to one of their first conversations. "Oh my God." He looked at his phone screen. "I *am* that type of creepy."

He dropped the phone.

"Oww," Teddy groaned softly. He squinted one eye up at Lucas. "What'd you do that for?"

"No reason. Nothing."

Teddy settled his cheek on Lucas's chest and sighed. "And I was having such sweet dreams."

"Were you?"

"Mmm."

"About what?"

Teddy took a deep breath in. Lucas was able to see his ribs expand beneath his bare back. "I don't remember."

Lucas walked his fingers in a circle around the tip of Teddy's shoulder blade. "You don't remember?" He tapped one finger on Teddy's bun. "Silly flamingo."

"I don't remember details. I remember how I felt. I was happy. Comfortable. It reminded me of being…." Teddy's body curled a touch tighter as his fingers twitched on Lucas's stomach. "I dunno. It felt good, is all."

"Aren't you happy all the time?"

Teddy leveled his gaze on Lucas. The bright pale green of his eyes coated Lucas's body like a waterfall of mint-infused spring water. Teddy blinked slowly.

"Are you?"

Lucas pursed his mouth and tilted his head side to side. "Depends on your definition of happy. And it's not my dreams we're talking about."

Teddy slid off Lucas's chest. He stayed on his stomach, propping his head up with one hand. Their bodies were close enough to feel the heat of each other's skin. Teddy rubbed a foot behind his knee, causing the duvet to slink down his lower back.

"I'm happy most of the time."

"Most?"

"Most," Teddy repeated, shrugging his shoulder. "Is anyone really happy all the time? I think it's normal to have some moments that aren't high-octane joy. I really can't complain. I'm financially secure, live in a nice flat, and get to travel the world. It's what I always wanted."

"Baby Mick indeed."

Teddy smiled confusedly. "What?"

"Nothing." Lucas turned his phone screen over without breaking eye contact. "Nothing."

Teddy stared at him for one more moment, then chuckled quietly, rolling onto his back. He scooted off his side of the bed and walked toward the chest of drawers. "So," he yawned, stretching his arms to the ceiling, "what do we have today?"

"Group bike ride after breakfast," Lucas said on a groan, rubbing his hands over his face. "Then watching the kid Zill-ympics."

"Which Maggie is obviously going to dominate to continue her family's athletic dynasty."

"Obviously. Then pool volleyball after lunch and jewelry making directly after dinner. Please tell me we can skip jewelry?"

Teddy snorted. His back was turned to Lucas. He rifled through the second drawer. "Of course. Whatever you want to do, or not do, I'm totally fine with." He looked over his shoulder and pouted, cradling the air beside his jawline where an earring would hang. "But whatever will Captain Jack do without new jewelry?"

"I'll buy you a lovely pair. Pearls, diamonds, the bones of rival pirates"—Lucas's hand swirled lazily—"whatever you want."

Teddy grinned and turned back to his clothing. "At least they're keeping their guests active."

"Active and singing." Lucas tossed his itinerary on his bedside table. "There is, as always, karaoke tonight. At least we have some pool time after volleyball. I want more chill and less summer camp."

"You finally going to make your debut on the big stage?"

"Hah! Not a chance. If you see me set foot on that stage, it'll be to sing the overture to the apocalypse."

"Aw, too bad you left your crisp and Nutella bunker at home."

"Ha. Ha."

Teddy laid a pair of jean shorts, a black long-sleeved tee, and an American flag bandana on the bed. He tossed black boxer briefs from the chest of drawers. Lucas leaned on his elbows, prodding the bandana with his toes.

"Are you performing as Bruce Springsteen this evening?"

"No, I wasn't planning on it. I think Lane and I are retiring from the circuit."

Lucas pushed himself up in bed, swinging his legs over the edge. "Makes sense. Your performance of "Rhythm Nation" will never be topped."

Teddy cackled from the en-suite as the shower turned on.

Lucas walked in and leaned on the doorframe, watching Teddy brush his teeth, wearing nothing but small black briefs. "I don't quite understand how you can barely keep yourself upright while walking, could not carry an egg on a spoon for five meters without dropping it, yet you and Lane did Janet Jackson's exact choreography. Where did you even get Britney mics?"

"Some mysteries are better left unsolved."

Teddy pushed his briefs down and Lucas looked to the floor. A hot flush raced up the back of his neck. Lucas didn't look up until he heard the shower door close.

"I'm sorry I lay on you," Teddy said, peering over his shoulder through the steamy glass. He ducked down, snagging shampoo. "I know you don't like it. You could have pushed me off."

"I didn't want to push you off."

Teddy stood up straight. "Oh." Even through the steam, Lucas could see him fighting a smile. "Okay."

Lucas crossed his arms over his bare chest. "But—but don't get used to it."

Teddy's dimpled grin emerged, along with a high-pitched, amused giggle. "Whatever you say." He turned his back to Lucas while sudsing up his hair. "Oh, before I forget." He bent his head down under the water, making his words sound bubbly. "You should probably go into your phone's settings and turn off the shutter sound if you want to take photos of people sleeping."

Lucas squawked, his eyes wide.

"And you call me flamingo!" Teddy said with a quick laugh, flipping his hair back. He opened the door with his hip quirked and his arm outstretched. "What are you doing? Take your pants off and get in here. I'm starving. I want breakfast."

Lucas's mouth remained open and pouted, as if he was singing *ooh*. "You knew I did that?"

Teddy snorted and stepped away from the door. "You dropped your phone on my head."

Lucas blushed and pushed his pants off. His whole body was hot. He felt even sweatier when he got into the shower's humidity.

"I'm sorry," Lucas said quietly. "That was a huge invasion of your privacy and weird and"—he shook his head, dunking under the water—"I shouldn't have done it. I'll delete the photos as soon as we're out."

"You don't have to."

Lucas blinked at him, water flicking off his long lashes. "What?"

Teddy shrugged as he rinsed the soap lingering in the hair around his navel. He smoothed his hand down to his groin. "You don't have to delete the photos."

"But…." He watched Teddy squirt shave gel onto his palm. "I…."

"You'll have something to remember me by." Teddy rubbed the gel over his face and neck. "And you deserve a picture of me looking goofy after sharing a bed with me all week."

"I didn't say you looked goofy."

Teddy blinked at him with his razor poised. A foamy white beard clung to his face. "No?"

Lucas shook his head. "No. You looked lovely."

"Oh."

"Yeah." Lucas reached to fiddle with the bottom of his invisible shirt, but found only his hip bone. His eyes darted from Teddy's face to the floor. He repeated, "Yeah," but it came out breathier. Teddy shaved a long strip up the left side of his throat to his cheek. "You're so pretty you even make a sexy Santa."

Teddy smiled through his foam beard as he carefully shaved his chin. "Thanks." His voice came out as breathy as Lucas's had. His shaving strokes were more like zigzags than smooth lines.

Lucas came up to him and reached for his razor. He took it out of Teddy's hand when the blade was away from his skin, and held it under the shower water, rinsing away the creamy foam and whatever tiny whiskers lingered on the blades.

"And you say I'll have to remember you as if you'll turn back into a pumpkin on Monday as soon as we land." Lucas shaved a smooth line up Teddy's right cheek. Teddy's chest heaved and his breath stuttered. "It's not like you'll disappear once we're back in London."

"But I will. I can, I mean. I usually disappear."

Lucas's closed lips twitched to the left side as he finished up the right side of Teddy's neck. "Don't, please."

"Don't what?"

"Don't disappear."

Teddy's throat bobbed beneath Lucas's careful, slow draws of his razor. "Okay."

Lucas lifted the razor and twirled it with a flourish. Their eyes locked. "Done."

Teddy swallowed, his nostrils flaring. "Thank you."

"You're welcome."

"Can I do you now?"

Lucas handed over the razor and ran his fingers over his face. "I was thinking of letting it grow a bit more."

"But I'll get beard burn."

Lucas snorted and his head recoiled on his neck. "No, you won't. None of that will be happening any longer. Today is not yesterday."

Teddy tilted backward under the shower stream and opened his mouth. He blew a mouthful of water in Lucas's face.

"And I'm the Buddha of this relationship."

"GODDAMMIT," TEDDY said against Lucas's lips. The pressure from Lucas's kiss muffled his words. He gripped the back of Lucas's hair and kissed him harder, even with the slight bite of whiskers against his freshly shaved skin. Lucas pinned his wrists above his head. Cool grass prickled the bare skin of Teddy's forearms and his black shirt rode up on his stomach. "I told you that you should have shaved."

Lucas fit his hand over Teddy's fly while tonguing him. Teddy arched his back on the thick, grassy field they had ridden their bicycles to. "What adult male owns jean shorts?" They both hummed and rutted against each other as they kissed. "It's ridiculous."

The heels of Teddy's Nikes dug into the soft earth. "You're the one turned on by jean shorts."

"They're not turning me on."

Teddy wrapped his legs around Lucas's waist and flipped him. Tiny bits of grass fluttered up onto Lucas's white tank. "Oh no?"

Lucas ran his hands over Teddy's outer thighs. The sweating pads of his fingers sent zaps of tingles into Teddy's thick muscles. "It's your legs, fucking hell," he said, sounding in pain. He squeezed Teddy's thighs. "Your legs are turning me on."

"Aw." Teddy lightly stroked his cheek. "That's too bad, love." He hopped up, leaving Lucas sprawled on his back and baffled. Teddy smirked and brushed his hands together, letting his weight lean mostly on his left leg. "We've got a bike ride to finish." Teddy turned on the balls of his feet, swaying just a touch more than usual to walk back to his bicycle.

"Are you kidding me?"

"Nope." Teddy looked breezily over his shoulder, replacing his Ray-Bans with prim fingers. "Maybe you should check the time. We don't want to be late meeting up with the group. They might send a search party."

Lucas glanced at his watch, scrambling to stand. "What are you—" His jaw dropped, and he lifted his arm toward Teddy, showing him his waterproof watch. "You're seriously still hung up on that first shower?"

Teddy laughed and swung one long leg over his bicycle, lowering himself to the black leather seat. Lucas walked up to his bike and got on. They started to pedal. Lucas's knees jerked up while Teddy glided easily.

"Holding a grudge over a watch," Lucas said on a scoff. They both turned right on the path. "Very mature."

Teddy untied his bun and his hair flowed in the breeze. "No grudge. I don't believe in grudges. I'm just teasing you, love. Besides, as you said in the shower, today is not yesterday, so why would you care?"

"Sounds an awful lot like a grudge to me," Lucas muttered, adjusting his balls on top of the narrow bike seat.

"Holding on to anger is like grasping a hot coal with the intent of throwing it at someone else—you are the one who gets burned."

"You most definitely googled Buddha quotes."

Teddy smiled and looked to the right. He found Lucas was grinning at him, his hair whipping in his face even with a black elastic band around his head.

LUCAS PLACED his hand on the center of Teddy's upper back. "Love?" he asked softly, rubbing his hand up and down. "Do you want another drink?"

Teddy took a slow breath in. His back muscles stretched beneath Lucas's hand. He turned his head to the right and rested his cheek on his folded towel. He gave Lucas a sleepy grin, his sunglasses crooked on his nose.

"Just ice water, please."

Lucas nodded. "Two waters and a fruit plate should do it," he said to their waitress. "Extra banana and watermelon on the plate would be great, if you have it available. Thanks so much."

Teddy's snores mixed in with the raucous chorus of children playing in the splash park. Lucas kept his hand resting on Teddy's neck, drawing soothing circles in the baby-soft dip of hair at the base of Teddy's hairline. Teddy's snores grew breathier and a low hum emerged.

"Purring like a kitten," Lucas whispered to himself.

Lane returned to her chair and quickly wrapped herself in a thick white towel. She rubbed her hands together. "They keep the water so bloody cold on those stupid spray things."

Lucas looked away from the tiny birthmark on the back of Teddy's right hip, just about an inch above his yellow swim trunks.

"Maggie is going wild," he said, chuckling. He watched Maggie spray Dean directly in the face with a child-sized fire hose, her hysterical giggles stretching her tiny mouth as wide as it could go. "This waterpark is cute. Not my usual style of relaxation, but it's still nice for the little ones."

"I think she nearly disowned me when she found out this park existed well over an hour after we got here."

"Well, duh," Lucas scoffed, crossing his ankles. "A good mother would have brought her here upon entering the resort and let her run, in her regular clothes, underneath that weird squirting-mushroom water fountain that looks like a penis."

"I'm out of the running for mum of the year."

"Nah." Lucas rolled the back of his head on his chair and pointed at his sister. "You've still got it in the bag."

Lane smiled brightly, toweling her hair. Behind her, a row of wedding guests turned over in unison; their oily backs sucked in the sun's rays. Jo and

Tracy reached out to get their margaritas. Their hands missed once, twice, three times before they made contact with the frosty glasses.

"Teddy's sleeping?" Lane asked.

"Yeah."

She winced and leaned across her chair, whispering, "Was he mad about volleyball?"

"No, don't be silly." Lucas stroked Teddy's warm shoulder. "Not at all. He thought it was hilarious."

"I swear, I didn't mean to spike it in his face! He's just much taller than everyone else!"

Lucas giggled, then quieted, glancing at Teddy. "He knows that. Did you hear him laughing? I think the dead heard him laughing. Unless—" Lucas pushed his sunglasses down his nose and narrowed his eyes. "—this was your attempt at revenge for yesterday's loss?"

"I stand by my opinion that if the baby pool had been filled with any other substance, Dean would not have been distracted and we would have won it."

"So, you're blaming the silver medal on Dean loving whipped cream?"

"He said he was stuck, but I know he was eating fistfuls of the stuff when my back was turned. Then we get to the ice cream challenge and it's suddenly"—she clutched her stomach and whined—"'Oh, babe, can you handle this one?' and he's complaining about the dairy giving him gas. Like I want to hear about that."

They both snorted.

"Oh my God," Lucas said, "you have no filter."

Dean came up to their chairs with Maggie sitting on his broad shoulders. They were both grinning and dripping.

"Hi!" they shouted together.

He lowered Maggie to the ground, and Maggie ran to Lane's chair. Lane held up a towel for Dean.

"What are you two talking about?" he asked, rubbing the towel over his hair. He plopped down on the end of Lane's chair. "What's so funny?"

"Nothing." Lane bundled Maggie into a towel, and sat back on her lounge. Maggie nestled against her chest with only her eyes and wet curls sticking out of the towel. "I think Marcy should be getting here tonight."

"Just after dinner," Jo's voice said in the distance.

"Jeez, Mum, eavesdrop much?"

"Mothers hear everything."

Lane nodded. "That's true."

"That's great," Lucas said happily, bending his knees and pulling his feet up. "I thought she said she'd only be able to come for the long weekend?"

Maggie's high-pitched voice asked, "Aunt Marcy?" from beneath her towel.

Lane rubbed Maggie's back. "Yes, Aunt Marcy. She's very excited to see everyone." She held her hands over Maggie's ears. "I think she's more excited to have a free open bar and access to Zamir's array of attractive cousins, but we were all in uni once."

"I'm not in uni and I still love an open bar." Dean winked at Lane.

Lane cradled his face, ruffling his wet, sandy brown hair. "And that's why we're married."

Maggie got off the chair and climbed onto Lucas, but only stayed long enough to roll over his legs and jump onto Teddy.

"Woah-oh." Teddy laughed gruffly on his stomach, twitching away from her wet, chilly body. He curled his arm around her to keep her on the lounge. "You are cold!"

"Margaret," Lane hissed.

"It's all right, it's all right." Teddy turned onto his side and opened his eyes, adjusting his Ray-Bans. Maggie was curled up next to him, her nose nearly touching his nose. "What's up, little miss?"

"Will you swim with me? And go on the slides with me? And throw me in the water? And then slides again?"

"We just went on every slide, like, three hundred times." Dean reclined on his lounge beside Lane. "Aren't you tired?" He cracked a beer. "I sure am."

"Nope," Maggie said, popping the *p*. She wiggled closer to Teddy, who shared an amused look with Lucas. "Please?"

Teddy glanced at Lane. "Sure, as long as that's all right with you? I promise to keep a careful eye on her."

"Yeah, of course. Fine with me." Lane wiggled her eyebrows. "I'll even give you twenty quid if you can get Luke down one of those slides with you. Not solo. It has to be you two together in one tube."

"I'll make it fifty," Jo called out.

They all laughed. Maggie laughed the loudest a split second after the adults. The waitress returned, placing their drinks and fresh fruit on the small tables between each chaise. Teddy stood up and held his hand out. Maggie grasped it and started swaying their arms.

Lane lifted her fresh frozen margarita in cheers. "Have fun!"

Lucas sipped his water, sat up on his chair, and planted his feet flat on the ground. "I'll come with."

Teddy squeezed his shoulder. "Nah, you relax," Teddy said. Maggie pulled his arm taut. "Join us whenever you want." He smirked and his dimple deepened. "We can go on the slides together. I could always use an extra fifty quid."

"Yeah, right. Good luck with that. Have fun."

He watched Teddy and Maggie walk away hand in hand. Teddy walked with his normal slow stride while Maggie tried to run ahead, Teddy gently reminding her, "No running near the pool, love," each time.

"Do you think you two'll have kids soon?"

Lucas choked on his water and an ice cube shot out of his throat. It landed on the concrete and started to melt as Lucas coughed into his fist. He blinked at his mother, who had sprawled on Teddy's vacant chair.

"Um, no." He punched the center of his chest. "We haven't discussed it."

"That's strange," Lane said, turning on her side. She sucked her straw for a moment. "He's so good with Mags. He seems like he'd love to have kids."

"We haven't discussed it," Lucas repeated. It was the truth, even if their relationship was a lie. "Just because he's good with Maggie doesn't mean he'd be good with all kids. Maggie's the most adorable, well-behaved child. She's easy to get along with."

He looked over in time to see Teddy waiting at the end of a swirly pink slide and catching Maggie as she hit the chest-high water. He could hear Maggie cackling and Teddy's rough chuckles. Teddy was seemingly unbothered that Maggie had kicked him in both shoulders and knocked his sunglasses off.

"That's not true." Lane grinned and watched Teddy run through the splash park with Maggie, Maggie pretending to chase him with grabby hands. "She terrified two babysitters before we found our current one. She just likes him. I have no idea where Tazzy came from, though."

"*Z* is her favorite letter," Lucas said.

Dean cracked another beer. "At bedtime the first night we were here, we asked her why she liked him so much. She said that she was the new person for a long time, but he's the new person now. She wants to make him feel welcome like everyone did for her and, since he's Uncle Lucas's boyfriend, she wants to make him happy the most because he makes Uncle Lucas happy." He took a long draught. "Fuck, I love my baby girl. She's the shit."

Lucas's eyes stung suddenly.

"Don't call our daughter shit," Lane said.

"I said *the* shit. There's a difference."

"Well, I for one think he'd make a darling father," Jo said, patting Lucas's forearm. "What's his family like? Are they all so tall? And such good dancers?"

Lucas placed his water on the small table and sat up straight. "I have no idea where he got his dancing gene." It was another honest statement to hide a lack of information. He didn't know Teddy's home address, let alone details about his family life. He ignored the strange stinging in his eyes to focus his gaze. "Where'd they go? I lost them."

Lane's phone beeped. "Ah, shoot. That's the sun cream alarm." She silenced her phone, drawing her heels to her bum. "Do you see them? I need to reapply. She already got a lot of sun today."

"I'll go look." Lucas stood. "Need to stretch my legs, anyway."

Jo prodded his bum and said, "You need to go down the slide. Even I went down with Maggie!"

ACROSS THE splash park, Teddy waited at the stone building that housed the restrooms. He leaned on the smooth cream-colored bricks of the doorway and tilted his ear toward the girl's room.

"All okay in there?" he asked.

He heard Maggie yell, "Almost done! Doing hands!" and he half smiled, stepping aside for a mum and two little boys to pass. Maggie ran out with her wet hands outstretched.

"I washed my hands!"

"Well done." Teddy kneeled and eased the hanging strap of her one-piece onto her shoulder. He held out one water wing, and Maggie shoved her arm into the puffy plastic. "I love washing my hands."

"Me too!"

He held out her other water wing, pushing it over her small arm. "There we are. What would you like to do next?"

"Can you throw me? In all the pools?"

"Throw you?" He picked her up, propping her on his hip. "You mean like this?" He gave her a gentle toss in the air. Maggie squealed happily and clung to him.

"Yes!"

Teddy grinned and stepped away from the restroom. "Did you enjoy going to the loo?"

"I did."

"Did the toilets have seashells on them?"

"No." She spread her fingers out. "Starfish."

"Starfish? How cool."

"Cool. Drool. Um." Her face scrunched. "Pool?"

"Are you a rhyming fool?"

"Yes!"

Teddy grinned so wide his nose ached. He could use some more sun cream. "You went to the loo," he whispered, bouncing her on his hip. Maggie shrieked and held him tighter, her laughter deafening his ear. "You took a poo!" He bounced her twice as fast, and Maggie giggled, "Tazzy!" over his chanted, "You went to the loo!"

She said, "I didn't poo!" and tugged on the back of his hair, giggling. "You are a rhyming fool!"

"Oh, no?" He held the back of her head and dipped her, her cackles bouncing over his face. He cradled her to his chest. "What'd you do in there? Read the paper? Write a song? Trade some stocks and bonds?"

"I peeped."

Teddy widened his eyes and bounced her while spinning, quietly chanting, "You took a pee. You went—"

"Jack?"

Teddy turned around. His voice curdled behind his tongue. Maggie looked up at him with confusion as his bouncing knee slowly came to a stop. The happy chatter of guests and soothing splashes of water surrounding him were all sucked into the atmosphere. Teddy had a sudden memory of the sandy blond forty-something man standing in front of him, only the man was sweating and pumping and coming on his back.

"Tazzy!" Maggie kicked his sides with her little heels as if he were a pony. "C'mon!"

"Callum," Teddy said, his voice gruff yet higher than usual. He cleared his throat, hitching Maggie against his side. "Hi." He pasted on a smile. Callum's smile was similarly tight. "How… how are you?"

"I'm good, thanks." Callum put his hands in the pockets of his long blue Hawaiian-print board shorts. His abs were visible but covered by a thin layer of pudge and blond fuzz. "So. Are you—" His face twitched and he cleared his throat. "—here for work?"

"No. I don't do…." Teddy shook his head. "No, I'm not here for work."

"Is this… uh…." Callum surveyed the squirming toddler in his arms. "Your daughter?"

"Oh, um—" Teddy swallowed, shaking his head quickly. "—No." His arms tightened to keep Maggie clutched to his chest, even with her limbs flailing. "She's a friend's daughter." He bounced her once and murmured against her ear, "A friend's lovely daughter."

"I see." Callum offered Maggie a friendly wave. Maggie's giggles halted. "Hi there."

Maggie smushed her face into Teddy's collarbone. Teddy held her closer.

A blond boy of around six years old ran up and attached himself to Callum's stocky, muscled leg. "Dad! Dad!"

Teddy's face fell before he could control it. A pretty woman in a tasteful black one-piece came up behind the boy, chuckling and placing one palm on Callum's back, her other hand on the boy's hair. A large square-cut diamond ring glistened on her finger. Her short blonde bob was kept off her head by a black headband.

"No matter how many times I say no running." Her voice was quiet but sweet. Bile in Teddy's stomach churned and his chest deflated. She looked at Teddy. "Hello." Her kind eyes landed on Maggie's half-hidden face. "Aren't you a pretty girl! I love your curls." She let out a soft, happy gasp. "You were playing with my daughter in the flower fountains, right? She's still there with our nanny, if you want to go play again. I'm sure she'd love that."

One of Maggie's strong kicks landed where Teddy thought he had a kidney, snapping his sadness out of him and replacing it with pain. "All right, little miss," he said on a strained chuckle, lowering her to the ground. He held her hand tight. "You've given me enough internal damage for today."

"Come swim with me, Taz." She blinked her chocolate-brown eyes up at him like the most practiced of sweet-talkers. He respected her game. Her tiny mouth pouted. "Pwease?"

He frowned and bopped her nose. "You don't have a speech impediment, you filthy liar. What was that last word?"

Her wide jack-o'-lantern smile washed over him. "Swim, puh-lease?"

Lucas appeared beside Callum's wife. "I'm here to summon Miss Maggie," he said, pointing two fingers at Maggie. "Time to go, Mags."

Maggie ran around and hid behind Teddy's knees. Muffled giggles tickled the patches of thin skin. Teddy's throat felt like it was extending out through his Adam's apple, and the Bile Olympics in his stomach resumed.

Lucas smirked. "Not even those legs can distract me, little miss. Your mum has a bottle of sunscreen with your name on it."

She groaned, "Oh no," and fluttered her eyelashes up to Teddy, mushing her hand to her nose.

"Do you remember where Mum is sitting?" Teddy asked, holding on to her hand.

She nodded and pointed through the path of the splash park. Lane's chair was visible behind a tall waterfall made of stone sunflowers. He let go of her hand, and she took off toward their group.

Lucas and Teddy shouted, "No running!" at the same time.

Her small, stubby legs slowed down, though she peeked over her shoulder at them and broke into a slightly slower run as she neared her mother's lounge chair. Lane bundled her into her arms, hugging her tight.

Lucas stepped next to Teddy. He placed his right hand on the heated small of Teddy's back, rubbing gently. "I think you need another coat too. Can't have Snow White getting sunburned." His eyes were shielded behind his black aviators, but the twitch of his cheek conveyed his wink. "What do you think?"

Teddy said nothing, his mouth turned down at the ends and the tendons of his neck visibly tight.

The little blond boy pulled Callum's arm and wailed, "Come on the slide with me!"

Lucas looked between Teddy and the family, and his touch faded from Teddy's skin. The loss of his fingertips felt like a whip's lash, Teddy's knees wobbling.

"Do you two know each other?" Lucas extended his right hand, then stopped. "Ah, sorry." He held out his non-oily left hand. "I'm Lucas."

"I'm Callum. We—" Callum began, looking at Teddy while shaking Lucas's hand, "—uh…."

"We used to work together," Teddy said easily.

"Yes!" Callum exhaled, his eyes widening in relief. "Yes. We did. This is my wife, Lisa. Jack, erm…." His gaze darted to his wife. "Jack worked in the mailroom at McDonaugh." Teddy's jawline tightened. Lucas's touch returned to his lower back to draw soothing, small circles. "Are you two… on holiday?"

"Mm-hmm," Lucas said, curving his hand around Teddy's hip. "Our friends are getting married."

"Daddy!"

They all looked down to the boy gripping Callum's wrist.

"I'd better get back to slide duty," Callum said with a gruff laugh, holding his son's hand. His eyes flickered to Teddy, scanning him from head to toe. "Nice to see you, Jack. I hope all is well. You certainly look well." His eyes snapped to Teddy's face. "We should get lunch once we're back in the real world."

"Thanks, all is well," Teddy said. Lucas squeezed his hip. "Nice to see you." He looked at Lisa, his sad gaze drifting toward the little blond boy. "And to meet both of you."

Teddy turned away before anyone could say anything. He clutched the bottom of his throat, marching to his lounge chair.

"Hey. Teddy. Taz. Theodore," Lucas's voice whispered over his neck. "Where are you—"

Teddy heard huffing next to him. Lucas was matching his quick strides.

"What's up, babe? What's the matter? You all right? You look ill."

They reached their group of lounge chairs. Teddy bent to gather his things while Lucas stood at the end of his chair with his hands on his hips. Teddy looked up at him, and Lucas's concern walloped him hard enough for him to grip the chair cushion.

Teddy shuddered out, "I'm sorry. My stomach's suddenly bothering me." He stood up and wrapped his arm around his stomach. "I think I need to go back to the room to lie down."

Lucas picked up his backpack. "All right." He threw his towel around his neck. "I'll come with you."

Teddy hurried to bundle his phone and headphones together in his towel. "You don't have to do that."

"What's wrong?" Jo asked, sitting up on her original chair. "What's going on?" She pushed her sunglasses down her nose, peering curiously at them.

Lane and Maggie sat up on their chair. Zamir and Cillian appeared out of the sunflower waterfall. Cillian ran to Teddy with arms outstretched. So many pairs of eyes on him made Teddy's face hotter than the Bahamas sun. His skin was slick with cold sweat.

"You all right?" Lane asked, Maggie wiggling out of her arms. "You look a bit green."

Lucas intercepted Maggie, swinging her back to Lane. When Lucas reached for Teddy's bundle of items, his arms went willingly limp, and Lucas placed Teddy's things in his own backpack.

"His stomach is bothering him," Lucas said as he zipped his bag. "We're gonna go back to the room to lie down."

"Let me feel your energy," Cillian said as he pressed his wet forehead to Teddy's forehead. Cillian's eyes widened and he flattened his hands on the sides of Teddy's neck. "Mate," he said gravely. "You all right?"

Jo bumped Cillian away from Teddy with her round arse. She pressed the back of her hand to Teddy's forehead. Teddy's eyes clenched shut and his frown deepened.

"Oh, love. Did you have an omelet at breakfast?" Jo thumbed his cheekbones. Teddy nodded, biting the inside of his bottom lip. He'd had a spinach and mushroom omelet that morning. Jo sighed. "John's had a stomach ache all day. That's why he's not here. Samantha and Vincent too. They think there was something off about the omelets. I'll have a word with the kitchen staff. This is unacceptable."

"Asa had one too and didn't feel well after the bike tour," Zamir added, squeezing Teddy's shoulder. "We'll definitely talk to the kitchen tonight."

"That might be it," Teddy said. He nodded and stepped away from Jo's touch, his motions jerky. "Omelets. The omelets." He wiped clammy sweat off the back of his neck. "Might be the heat."

"Maybe both. Poor little lamb." Jo stroked his sweaty hair off his forehead. Teddy diverted his gaze to the ground. "You have a good rest in the air conditioning. Drink lots of fluids. Luke, get him some—"

"I'll get him some juice, no worries." Lucas flattened his hand on Teddy's shoulder. "We should go. Standing around in the sun isn't doing him any good."

Teddy glanced at the crowd of concerned faces, faces he had never seen one week ago and would likely never see again in one week's time. He nodded once, grunting out, "Thank you," and spinning on his heel.

He took off toward the path to the bungalows, able to hear Lucas saying good-bye to their group. His bare feet burned on the small rocks that filled the path. His eyes watered to the point of turning the path into wavy lines, and he huffed out short breaths.

"Hey," Lucas said, jogging up to his side. "I got your shoes. Why don't you head to the room and I'll go to the concierge to see about ordering you a juice. Do you have a fruit preference? Gatorade could be good too. I think I saw that on the room service menu. They've got to have it."

"It's okay," Teddy rasped, his stomach trembling. "You don't have to get me juice. I'm fine."

"You might be dehydrated."

"Lucas, I—Let's go inside."

They reached the path to their bungalow. "But, juice—"

"Lucas, please," Teddy pleaded, breaking into a run as he went up the path.

Lucas nodded and ran in front of him. He opened the front door and hurried inside, and Teddy watched him as he ambled a few steps behind. Lucas dumped their belongings on an overstuffed armchair and hopped up to knock on the air conditioning, dropping the temperature until freezing air pumped out of the vents. He opened the door to the en-suite and met Teddy at the front door.

"Go ahead." Lucas held his arm out. "I'll go for a walk or something. Give you your privacy. Get you that juice."

Teddy's head shook involuntarily as he entered the bungalow with his face scrunched and his eyes shut. "What are you talking about?"

Lucas thumbed at the bathroom door. "Go ahead. You can, y'know—" The corners of his mouth twitched up. "—relieve yourself."

Teddy gaped at him. "I don't have to—what—"

A teasing playfulness spread over Lucas's face. "You said your stomach is upset and, based on your little airport issue from the other day—"

"Oh my God," Teddy groaned, falling sideways on their bed. His sunglasses bounced off his nose. "Please, no more." He curled into a ball and wrapped his arms around his face. "Please," he said, his voice muffled. "Please, don't ever talk about that again."

Lucas sat on the bed, with his bum at the opposite corner from Teddy's body. He reached out and brushed his fingers over Teddy's calf. Teddy curled tighter in on himself and pulled his leg away.

"Hey," Lucas said, flattening his palm on the bed. "What's wrong?"

"That guy," Teddy said, his words muffled.

"Who? That blond guy with the kid?"

Teddy nodded.

"Was he bothering you?" Lucas's voice was a touch deeper.

"No." Teddy shook his head. "He…. I mean…."

Lucas pinched the duvet and pulled it up, lifting a few different spots at random. "Teddy, I get it. He's a client of yours. He called you Jack. Kind of a dick move to say you worked in the mailroom to save face in front of his wife, though."

Teddy nodded, the motion reluctant. "Was. Past tense. Was a client."

"And that's what's got you upset? I know what you do. It's fine."

"It doesn't feel fine."

"Do you want to talk about it?"

Teddy blew a long stream of air out and rolled onto his back. His upper body lay on the bed with his legs bent at the knee, and his bare feet were flat on the floor. He kept his arms over his chest.

"He… he never told me he had a son. Or that he had a wife. Or daughter. No mention of any of it."

LUCAS SCOOTED close and knelt by Teddy's head. "Yeah, but…." He stroked Teddy's hair, tentative and light. He wished, at that moment, he had inherited his mother's natural ability to be tactile and soothing, instead of being someone who caused pain even when trying to wash someone else's hair. "You have to know that some of your clients are married. Or that they have families. It's not your problem if they come to you. You aren't pursuing them, and maybe they have an open sort of thing with their spouse. It's gross if they lie, obviously, but you're not the one married with kids."

"I know that some probably do, but I've never—I've never seen it. I've never heard their kid's voice or seen their wife's face."

Lucas nodded along with him. "I understand how that would be upsetting."

"I…." Teddy's face crumpled. "I feel like absolute shit."

Teddy shot up off the bed and Lucas got to his feet. "Teddy—"

"I'm sorry, please just—"

Lucas stood outside the en-suite as the door shut. He stepped back, exhaling slowly. He tapped his fingers against his palms. His ears picked up on small, gasped, wet noises coming from behind the door. The sink faucet started. He flattened his palms on the door, quietly asking, "Teddy?"

"Please. Go back to the pool. Don't worry about me. I'll be fine."

"I'm not going to do that."

"Why not?"

"Because you're upset."

Teddy sniffled. "Just leave me."

"No," Lucas laughed, pushing himself away from the door. "I could use a kip, myself. I'm going to lie down."

Lucas sat on the bed, but did not lie down. He steepled his fingers together, resting his elbows on his knees. He stared at the closed door, willing it to open, begging the gods of the Bahamas to send rays of comfort into the en-suite.

The doorknob clicked. The door slowly opened. Teddy stared at Lucas, his mouth in an exasperated pout but his shining eyes warm with relief.

"Hi." Lucas sat up straight. "Y'all right?"

"You're neither sleeping nor at the pool." Teddy sighed heavily. "And why do you keep asking me that?"

"Because you faked an omelet emergency to come running back here. You're upset, clearly, and I'm worried. I don't want you upset."

Teddy rubbed his hand over his stomach. The air conditioning prickled goose bumps over his skin. His gaze dropped to his bare torso and legs. Even his feet were bare, sand dusting the tops.

"I didn't want to make a scene. Your family and friends are…." He paused, his voice on the brink of cracking. "They're wonderful. And I didn't want to embarrass myself any further."

"Further? You're not embarrassing yourself at all. What are you talking about?"

"I'm mortified, Lucas," Teddy ground out, his shoulders shivering. "I feel like the most idiotic person on the planet."

"Why, though?"

Teddy swept the air with an open palm. "I'm here, playing pretend with you, and I—" His eyebrows twitched inward. "—I like it. I like everything about it. How I feel, what I'm doing, the people I'm with. Then I see an old client and it's like…." His voice grew thinner, higher, and his bottom lip trembled. "I'm back to being Jack. And I feel even more foolish for forgetting, for pretending. I should know better. I've been doing this long enough. Holidays don't last forever."

Lucas's voice took on a slightly lower, driven tone. "You're not Jack McQueen. You're Theodore Bennet. Don't get it twisted. You're sexy and smart and infuriating and bloody irresistible when you're playing the role of Jack, but you're all of those things and then a shit ton more when you're yourself. You might have fucked that bloke seven ways to Sunday, but that does not mean that you, Teddy Bennet, should feel bad about yourself. Ever. Or feel bad about enjoying yourself here. This trip is as much for you to enjoy as it is for me to enjoy. My family. My friends. Everything."

Teddy whimpered and went toward the en-suite. Lucas stepped closer. He reached out but paused an inch from Teddy's shoulder.

Lucas said, "I'll ask you again: Do you want to talk about it? I'm all ears. I want you to feel good, love. To be happy. Not just…." His voice softened. "Not just some of the time. I know how that feels and you deserve better."

Teddy turned toward him. His face was unreadable. "Why do you care?"

"Because we're in this together. And if you want to scream and barf and throw lamps at the wall—" Lucas tapped his own chest with both hands. "—I'm here for you. Just say the word and lamps will fly."

"No." Teddy's tone was bright.

Lucas's brows slowly rose. "No lamps or no talking?"

"I think I'd rather not talk about it." Teddy shook his head. His mouth shut tight. On the third shake of his head, his face started to twitch and he blinked wider. Each word came out of his throat like a half burp, like air was being forced out of his lungs. "I… I…."

Lucas nodded along with his gasped words. "Yeah?"

"I just…."

Tears poured down both of Teddy's cheeks. His upper lip trembled and his nostrils loudly sucked air in and a mucus-heavy sound was released into the quiet room. Lucas's face fell.

"I just think that, if you have a child, why would you spend any of your free time wining and dining"—Teddy's voice broke with a violent, pained gasp—"and fucking someone like me?"

His volume rose and fell at random. Shivers racked his body. He flexed his arm and sliced at the air.

"Go home to your child," he said on a low growl. "Be with your family. If you have so much extra money, put it in a fucking trust fund for your kid. Don't use it to pay me to let you"—his eyes clenched shut, and his tone weakened—"snort coke out of my arse. Because, sometimes—" He directed his teary eyes at Lucas. "Sometimes people who grow up without a dad, with a single mum, are smart, like you. They become high-powered executives with their shit together. But other times—"

Teddy sniffled rapidly on one breath in through his nose. He tilted his face up with more tears pouring down his face.

"Sometimes a dad dies in a freak car accident, even before he meets his son. And sons wonder why they never got to have a dad, even though they had a good, good mum." His voice cracked and tears dripped off his chin. "A wonderful mum. A saint of a mum." He swallowed thickly. "But she got sick and had to leave him too."

Lucas stepped closer as fat tears rolled down Teddy's face to pool beneath his stuffed nose. He swayed and flattened his forearm over his mouth.

"Teddy—"

"And then the son is alone, with no one to answer to, so he figures, why not? Why not—" Teddy sobbed, hiding his face in his hands. He sank to the floor, shielding his cries with his arms. "—Why not have sex with people for money as a career, instead of a temporary last resort? It's fun, it's easy, and it gets you out of your empty flat. Why the fuck not?"

"Teddy," Lucas soothed, kneeling on the floor. "Teddy, please—You're—" Lucas wrapped his arms around him, and Teddy's body shuddered with shallow, uneven breaths. "You need to breathe. Breathe, love, breathe."

Teddy barked out a painful cough and crawled toward his suitcase. His hands shook as he tried to unzip it.

"Babe, what are you—"

Teddy ripped out a small shaving kit and dumped it on the floor. Lucas tried to follow the path of every random object bouncing on the hardwood—a wallet that spilled open, a necklace, his safety bracelet—but his hand involuntarily shot out toward a white inhaler sliding under the bed.

"Is this what you need?"

Teddy nodded and Lucas held it to Teddy's mouth. Teddy pressed his thumb on top of Lucas's thumb as he tried to breathe in. His sobs had not stopped. His attempts to breathe were deeply thwarted by the jumping of his lungs and his clogged nose, and his sweaty hair covered his face.

"Relax," Lucas soothed, rubbing between his shoulder blades as they sat side by side on their knees in only their swim trunks. Teddy's body threw off waves of heat and the biting smell of sharp sweat. "Breathe, love, breathe in."

Lucas's voice hushed, "Shhh, shhh," the long, quiet sounds lined up with firm, open-palmed circles between his shoulder blades. Teddy heaved air into his lungs, rocking forward and back. Lucas wrapped his arms around Teddy and cradled him to his chest. He rocked him and hushed, "Shhh," until his shudders slowed and his breathing evened, and Teddy fell asleep in his arms.

Chapter SEVENTEEN

WHEN TEDDY woke, it was dark out. He was curled up on his side in the center of the bed. The duvet was cool over his bare skin. His eyes felt swollen, and his chest radiated a dull ache. A burning soreness had settled in his lower throat. He blinked as best he could, sniffling a breath in through his nose.

He heard the stiff sound of a page turning. He focused on a book propped in Lucas's lap, one of his government conspiracy books that Lucas insisted were good reads. Lucas's legs were extended in front of him on the sofa, his bare feet propped on the end and crossed at the ankles. He wore soft-looking gray sweatshorts and a white V-neck tee. His hair was dark and damp as if he'd showered recently. Lucas turned another page of his book, then curled his toes.

"Oh, hi," Lucas said. "You're up."

Teddy ran his gaze over Lucas's body. Lucas folded his book facedown on his stomach.

"Hi," Teddy whispered. He palmed his nose and rasped, "Time's it?"

"Eight."

"Eight?" Teddy sighed and curled tighter. "I'm sorry. I ruined your day and night."

"Don't be ridiculous. I texted everyone to let them know you were still unwell and resting. You didn't ruin anything. How are you feeling?" Lucas asked gently. He pulled his feet off the sofa arm and swung his legs sideways. "Did sleeping help?"

Teddy clenched his eyes for a beat, then released them. He pushed himself up on his elbow. "I'm okay," he croaked. He rubbed the front of his throat. He swallowed once, staring at the rumpled white bedding. "I'm… I'm so sorry. That's…. I've never had that happen in front of someone before." He pressed the heel of his hand over his closed eyelid. "I haven't even used my inhaler in years. I'm so sorry you—" He stopped speaking to suck shaky air in through his nose. He exhaled and pushed his hair off his face. "I'm so sorry you had to deal with that."

"You don't have to apologize for anything." Lucas stood up from the sofa and went to the minifridge. He turned toward the bed with a plastic bottle of Gatorade in each hand. "Blue or orange?"

Teddy surveyed the drinks, his voice even quieter as he said, "Blue, please."

Lucas nodded and stepped up to the bed, offering Teddy the chilly bottle of juice. Teddy took it, sitting up straighter, with the blanket pooled in his lap.

"Everyone was so worried. They've all been texting me nonstop to check on you. Oh, and Lane dropped these off." Lucas picked up a pile of papers from the sofa and placed them on the bed. "Maggie made you Get Well Soon cards. Well, her version of Get Well Soon cards. She's like an abstract artist."

Teddy lifted the drawings as a deep wrinkle formed on his forehead. He looked through them, struggling to hold his bottom lip still. He placed the pile on the bed and flattened his hands on the duvet, hanging his head lower.

"Lucas, I…." Teddy's mouth wobbled wordlessly. Teddy quirked his brows as his eyes welled up. "I don't…."

"Just have a bit to drink. Recharge. We can talk after. My mum'll have my head if you don't replace all your electrolytes."

They cracked open their bottles. Lucas watched Teddy take a tiny sip.

"Lucas, I…." Teddy's throat clicked to swallow. A drop of juice dribbled down his chin. He sniffled and wiped his chin with the back of his hand. His voice was uneven and raw. "I don't know if I can stay after what happened."

Lucas spit Gatorade out in an orange mist. Teddy didn't even look up at the outburst.

Lucas took a few steps closer to the bed. "But… why? Because that guy's here? He's leaving tomorrow, and he's staying in a totally different part of the island than we are. I asked the concierge. We only saw him because we were at the splash park. You won't have to see him again, I promise."

"No, it's not him," Teddy said quietly, shaking his head. "It's… I'm embarrassed. That you saw me like that."

"You're embarrassed that I know you have asthma?"

Teddy tilted his head and puffed a sigh. "You know why I'm embarrassed."

"But I don't care if you got upset. I…." He scratched the back of his head. "I probably should have left you alone, like you asked, but I—I couldn't." He shook his head and dropped his arm. "Not when you seemed so upset. And I don't regret staying."

"I don't either."

"So? What's the problem?"

"I can't stop thinking about my mum." Teddy's eyes watered and he tilted his head to the ceiling. "And it's getting really hard for me to…." He tried to smile, but sadness limited how wide it could stretch. "I don't know what to do in this situation. This has never happened to me before, and I swear to you, I'm normally a very happy person, but being around a family all the time is…. It's…."

Lucas stepped closer, but did not sit on the bed. "I know the feeling and they're my family. What does that say about me?"

Teddy looked up at Lucas and shook his head. "You're a good person," he said, soft and low. "Everyone gets overwhelmed sometimes."

"Then why are you being so rough on yourself? Take your own advice."

"I don't know," Teddy said, dropping his head. He inhaled deeply through his nose. "I just don't know."

Lucas stood at the end of the bed, thumbs looped in his pockets.

"If you want or need to leave, that's fine. It's fine. I'll take care of your flight, your transportation from the airport, everything. And I'll pay you out for the entire trip."

Teddy snapped his head up and shook it quickly. "What? No, you don't have to do that. We had an agreement."

"I don't have to, but I will if you want to leave. I don't want to keep you here if you're not comfortable, and I don't want the week to be a total bust for you."

"I'm very comfortable and I don't need the money. It's not—It's not you, it's me."

"Ha." Lucas smiled with closed lips and looked down, rolling up on the balls of his feet. "Have heard that one before."

Teddy's mouth fell open. "Lucas, no." He got to his knees. "No. That's not what I meant."

"I know, I know. It was a stupid joke. Forgive me."

"You are amazing, Lucas. You're amazing," Teddy said more strongly, crawling on his knees to the end of the bed. "And I've had an amazing time, even though my brain's been…." His mouth moved without sound, and his eyelashes were still damp. "I don't know how to verbalize what's going on inside of me right now."

Lucas sat on the arm of the sofa closest to Teddy. He held his Gatorade bottle on top of his thigh and scratched the back of his head.

"Well, if you want to leave, at any time, please just tell me and my offer will still stand. However, I will say that I…." He unscrewed his bottle and sipped. His gaze slowly scanned up the bed until he reached Teddy's tear-streaked face and wild hair. He placed the cap on his bottle, licking tangy orange off the corner of his mouth. "I don't want you to leave," he said softly. His blue eyes were wide and honest. "I don't want to be here without you. I want you to stay here with me, which is selfish and I'm sorry, but I don't think I would have made it through Day One without you, let alone be having the most fun I've ever had on holiday all the way to Day Four."

Teddy sat on back his feet, and a proper smile slowly emerged.

"So, the choice is yours," Lucas said. "The choice is always yours."

Teddy studied Lucas, then nodded. "I want to stay here. With you."

The skin beside Lucas's eyes crinkled as he tapped the cap of his Gatorade three times with his thumb. "I was hoping you'd say that."

Teddy chuckled breathily, tucking his hair behind his ears. It was curly on the left side of his head and matted with sweat on the right side. He went to gather his hair into a bun.

"Ugh." His nose wrinkled. "I smell."

"A little, yeah."

"Hey," Teddy laughed.

Lucas smirked at him and sat on his foot at the very end of the bed. "Do you wanna go for a walk?" Lucas looked out the window. Stars twinkled in the inky blue sky. "It's nice out. Fresh air will do you good."

"Okay."

Teddy moved out from the duvet. Lucas's hand flattened on his shin. The blanket was a barrier between his palm and Teddy's skin. Lucas raised his eyebrows.

"Do you truly want to go for a walk or are you saying yes because you think it's the right answer? I want you to feel comfortable all the time. Don't say yes because you think it's what I want to hear."

Teddy nodded, the motion slow but firm. A smile teased his lips. "I like walks."

Lucas chuckled and removed his hand, pushing himself off the bed. "I like walks," he parroted. "Such eloquence. Such wisdom." Lucas counted off on his fingers. "Walks, flamingos, sparkly seashells. Am I missing anything else? Oh! Earrings. Right. Can't leave those off the list."

Teddy snorted as he rifled around the chest of drawers. He pulled a thin white tee over his head and stared into the drawer with his hands on his hips.

"Should I put actual shorts on or just stay in these?"

"I've grown very fond of your little yellow shorts, so I'd say to keep those on. It's just a walk."

Teddy turned away from his suitcase with a small smirk. Lucas held out his Gatorade and Teddy accepted it, tapping the bottom of the bottle on his palm.

"You're fond of my little yellow shorts," Teddy repeated. He walked to the door with a sway to his hips and Lucas chuckled. Teddy's cheeks heated. "Good to know."

Lucas met him at the door. Teddy glanced down and noticed that Lucas did not slip on his flip-flops. He chose to forgo shoes himself and stepped, barefoot, out the door. Lucas pulled the door shut behind them.

They walked in silence for a few minutes while sipping their drinks. The humidity of the day had broken and left dry heat in its place. The moon was almost as bright as the sun had been hours earlier. The farther they walked from the row of bungalows, the quieter it got. Their walk was accompanied by nothing but the sound of the sea lapping at the powder-white sand.

They passed a lifeguard's chair laid down on the sand, and walked far enough to pass the preset row of white chaise lounges guests had lain on during the day. Nothing but open, endless beach stood in front of them.

Lucas held his arm out. "Wanna sit?"

Teddy nodded and plopped down on the sand, stretching his legs out toward the water. Lucas dropped his drink and lay on his back. He clasped his hands on his stomach. They were close enough to touch, but far enough to not feel body heat.

"So." Lucas turned his head toward Teddy. "Kids are your Achilles' heel, then? Families?"

Teddy swallowed a gulp of Gatorade. "I guess, yeah. I always thought about having kids one day. As I'm getting older, and—" His voice cracked. "—based on my profession, I'm guessing that won't ever happen for me. Besides, who would ever want me as their dad? I've got nothing to offer."

"Why do you say that? I think you'd be a lovely father. You've got *you* to offer."

"Do you really think any adoption agency will ever allow someone who was a sex worker to adopt?"

Lucas shrugged and propped his hands behind his head, looking up at the sky. "You never know. Sex work is legal. It's worth a shot."

"I'm not ready to have kids."

"Maybe not now, no, but someday. Maybe. You know what it feels like to be alone. Why wouldn't you want to take that feeling away from a child somewhere in the world?"

Teddy said nothing and stared out at the sea. He felt Lucas shift next to him, could sense eyes on his profile. He looked at Lucas. "What?" he asked.

Lucas smiled, looking a touch guilty, then bit his lip. He slid his feet on the sand. "When your stuff fell out of your bag, like, during the inhaler part, your wallet fell out and opened and kind of, um, exploded on the floor. I put your things back in the bag, but I saw a photo." Teddy nodded slowly. "And I think it was your mum?"

"It was."

"She was so lovely."

Teddy smirked, continuing to nod. "She was."

"You're like a clone of her. Same eyes. Same smile. Identical dimple placement. She had better hair, though."

Teddy gave a slow grin. The breathless, frantic feeling that had accompanied his earlier memories of his mother was nowhere to be found. A warm fuzziness washed over him, as if his toes were dipped in the sea.

"Yeah. We were very similar, though she was teeny tiny." His gaze flickered toward Lucas. "Only about an inch taller than you."

"Oi," Lucas warned as Teddy chuckled over him. Lucas pulled himself up to sit facing Teddy, with his legs crossed. "Is she the R?"

Teddy's joy faded for a split second. "The…. Oh." He tugged the neckline of his tee over his shoulder, exposing his tattoo. "Yeah." He looked down at the small script *R*. His soft happiness returned. "Rebecca."

"Did she go by Becky?"

Teddy nodded. "She did. My dad was called Stephen, but he went by Stevie. We were a nickname family, I guess."

"No siblings?"

"Nope. My mum would have had more kids, I think, but money was tight, and she had enough to deal with raising me alone. I was sixteen when she died. Pancreatic cancer." Teddy stared at the small *R* tattoo. A different sort of softness smoothed the lines of his face. "She had her hands full until then. Sometimes, I guess there's just not enough time to do everything you want."

"I've never met my dad."

Teddy released his shirt and the fabric crawled back into place. He turned to face Lucas and straddled his legs around Lucas's thighs. He picked up a small stick of beach wood. "No?"

"Nope." Lucas sat back with his palms on the sand. "He was basically a sperm donor and financial benefactor, as my mum tells it. But she has an interesting view on relationships and marriage. Who knows what the truth is."

"You've never wanted to find out?"

"No. Doesn't matter, does it? If he wanted to be a dad, he'd have been a dad. Not everyone is born to be a parent, and being parents is not the be-all and end-all of why we're here on earth."

"Your conspiracy theory books are warping your vocabulary." Teddy prodded Lucas's knee with his stick, and Lucas huffed quietly. Teddy dragged the stick down the front of his shin. He peered at Lucas as moonlight cast a silvery glow over his eyes. "Are Lane and Marcy your half-sisters?"

"Yep. Not only with me, but with each other. They've both got different fathers."

"S'nice that you treat them like regular sisters. That you don't tell people about your different dads."

"Doesn't matter to me who their dads are. We grew up together as siblings. Nothing could change that in my eyes."

Teddy nodded, poking the stick on the tips of each of Lucas's toes. Lucas scrunched his foot.

"I…." Lucas tapped his fingers on his thighs, light and rapid. "I think you need to change your profession."

Teddy snuffled, dropping his stick to the sand. "Here we go."

Lucas's brows furrowed. "What? I'm surely not the first person to tell you this. Even if your clients are mesmerized by you and the mind-blowing sex, there had to have been one or two blokes in that mix who felt the same way."

Teddy glanced up at him. The seriousness and lack of judgment emanating from Lucas's stare drew his body closer on the sand. "You're right about not being the first to say that. And the mind-blowing sex part."

Lucas stole his stick from him. "I'm just saying, your current job is making it impossible for you to do what you love. Photography. Having a family. You say you're financially secure, so stop. Do something else for a while."

"Thank you for the concise reminder of all the things I want but will never have," Teddy's voice warbled ever so slightly despite his smile. "This walk has been lovely. Should I throw myself in the sea next?"

"Stop being such a pain in the arse," Lucas said, sitting up fully. He reached out and placed his palms on Teddy's knees. "I'm not saying you have to immediately quit your job. I know you have bills to pay and commitments to fulfill and so on. I just think you're selling yourself short."

"Is that so?"

"It is so. You're smart. So smart. Smarter than most of the people that work at my office, though I'd prefer if you don't tell Albert I said that. He's anxious enough about his performance."

Teddy grinned. "Are you insane?"

"What? Why?"

"I'm not going to be an executive assistant for a businessman I once fucked. How weird would that be?" He sat up straight, cradling invisible folders in his arms. He chirped, "Good morning, sir! Tea is waiting on your desk. I have those files you were looking for. Shall I suck your cock or would you prefer a slow screw in the breakroom after lunch?"

"We haven't fucked, I wasn't offering you a job, and ugh, you sound way too much like Albert." Lucas shuddered. "I'm never going to be able to look him in the eye again without your creative imagination running rampant in my head."

Teddy grinned, relaxing to a more natural posture.

Lucas continued. "I didn't mean for you to work for me. I meant that you could probably make enough money to live on, comfortably, working in an office or something. Then you could do photography on the side and build your business. You know how to build a successful business. Do it for photography instead of sex."

"I'm not sure I'm the secretary type."

"Why not? You're personable, friendly, handsome. Those are almost more important secretarial qualities than how many words per minute you type."

"I like having my schedule the way it is. I like making my own money and traveling and not going to the same place forty hours per week. That's never appealed to me. I have no desire to go back to scrounging for money and living in a dump. I'm quite happy with my current standard of living."

"Fair enough. That's understandable."

"But?"

"But what?"

"C'mon, Luke. You've got more to say. You've got that constipated look on your face. Best to let it all out."

Lucas stared at him for a breath. "You could always go straight to the business-building part," he blurted out. Teddy chuckled. "Retire the old moneymaker. Then you could be a photographer or a potter or a bloody ballerina. Whatever you wanted. Or you could intern at a company that interests you. Albert's my assistant because he wants to eventually do what I do. He didn't get into the business to make copies and fetch tea."

"Ninety."

"What?"

"I can type at ninety words per minute." Teddy looked at Lucas, then glanced away. "I took a few online quizzes when I was bored one day."

"Ah. So, those fingers are good for more than just—"

"Be quiet," Teddy chuckled, holding his palm over Lucas's mouth. "Here we were, having a civil conversation."

Lucas made huffing noises under his palm and the vibrations sent tingles up Teddy's arm. Teddy removed his hand, revealing Lucas's smile.

"I think," Teddy said, speaking softly, "I think I've never stopped because… I think I've never wanted to quit because it really is a fun job. Please"—he held up one finger—"no hand- blow- foot-job jokes."

Lucas gasped and clutched his chest. "I would never." He narrowed his eyes. "Are foot jobs really that commonly requested? They seem difficult."

"It's a fun job," Teddy continued on a chuckle, knocking their knees together. "It pays so well I almost feel bad taking the money sometimes. And I've had really, really generous clients. I was being dramatic before about the whole have-sex-for-money thing. I get all wound up once in a while."

"No," Lucas gasped out, faux shocked.

Teddy tossed a pinch of sand at his crotch. "A lot of my friends in this industry have not been so lucky. I could see them wanting out. Absolutely. But my experience hasn't been that way. It's hard to walk away from something so easy and fun and lucrative."

"That makes sense. You've never had a reason to."

"Up until now, yeah. That's exactly it."

Lucas's faux shock shifted to actual shock. Teddy blinked rapidly the second the words left his mouth.

Teddy gaped, "I mean—I—"

"So, I was thinking," Lucas said at the same time.

Teddy's mouth froze, and his brows arched.

Lucas licked his lips, walking his fingers in circles over Teddy's knees. "Do you want to maybe skip the group activities tomorrow?"

"Oh." Teddy's voice popped like a bubble in the air. "Like, all day?"

Lucas nodded. "We'd have breakfast with everyone, but then could have an alone day."

"Uh, sure," Teddy said. His voice was breathier than usual. "Whatever you want to do."

"It's whatever we want to do. Us. Together. Meaning something you want to do."

"I get it, I get it," Teddy said, chuckling and holding his palms out. "I appreciate your concern with my consent more than I can express—that's among your more charming features—but I seriously am fine with doing whatever you want. What'd you have in mind?"

Lucas's shoulders tilted as he spoke and wiggled his bum on the sand. "I read about some amazing scuba diving spots just outside the resort that blow this place out of the water." Teddy's eyes lit up and Lucas spoke more rapidly in excitement. "I haven't gone diving in forever, but I talked to the guy who does diving at the resort. He said he has a friend who takes people out on a little boat and arranges dives at some of these outside spots. He even has all the equipment available to rent and can take us to other spots, like to fish or cliff jump or whatever you want. What do you think?"

"That all sounds great! I'd love to."

"Cool! Okay, cool," Lucas said, exhaling a quick breath seemingly in an effort to calm himself down. "Sorry." They both snorted, and Lucas slid his fingers back through his hair. "I was so excited when I talked to the guy, but you were still asleep, so I had no one to talk to about it."

"Isn't that weird?"

"What?"

"I feel that way too. Like, when we're not together, I have no idea what to do with myself."

Lucas's arm dropped to his lap. "You mean you sit lost and confused on the toilet because I'm not there?" He fluttered his eyelashes. "How sweet."

Teddy started to stand. "I don't think of you on the toilet, thank God. And thank God you're not a client."

Lucas hopped up. "Why?"

"I've embarrassed myself in every possible way. Toilet in the airport, crying, spilling my guts about my dead parents, crying more. I'm really swinging for the fences this trip."

Lucas waved his hand in the air. "Don't worry about any of that. Seriously." Lucas squeezed the tops of Teddy's shoulders, thumbing the thick muscles beside his neck. "You're a human and I'm a human. We all shit. We all cry. It happens. And it's not like you shit your pants in the airport—"

"Oh, God." Teddy groaned on a laugh. Lucas squeezed his shoulders again.

"You had to use the toilet. So what? Who cares? I didn't hear or smell anything—"

"Pleeeease," Teddy said, pretending to be in pain. He held Lucas's face in his hands and shook him gently. "Please don't even say the words *smell* and *toilet* in the same sentence."

"I, myself, have been sneaking out of our room to shit in the fancy toilets in the main-house lobby."

Teddy's throat pushed out a hybrid of a cackle and a gasp. "What?"

Lucas looped his arm with Teddy's and they started to walk, retracing the line of their footsteps on the sand.

"Sorry, is that TMI? It's shocking, I know." Lucas patted Teddy's hand. " But I do need to use the toilet for more than a wee from time to time."

"No, not that. That all makes sense, since you're usually so full of shit."

"Hey!"

Teddy squirmed away from Lucas's prodding fingers. "I'm shocked because I have been using those toilets whenever possible."

"So, by using a toilet out of our room—trying to be considerate, to not embarrass ourselves, and to not gross the other out—we've actually been shitting in the same toilet."

"What a pair we are," Teddy said, rolling his eyes. "Our bums have shared the same toilet seat, like some sort of digestive fate." He fluttered his fingers at the sky. "How very star-crossed."

"And you say my vocabulary is warped."

THEY GOT back to their bungalow and went about their bedtime business quietly. Teddy typed a few messages on his phone while Lucas washed his face. Lucas got into bed first and flicked around the television channels while Teddy showered. He was half asleep and searching for the weather when Teddy came out of the en-suite wearing nothing but small white boxer briefs. His tan was even deeper than hours before, his skin tender and damp above the soft, clinging fabric.

Lucas smiled at him, tight-lipped. He turned off the television and placed the remote on his bedside table. "All good?"

"Yes." Teddy got on the bed and placed his iPhone on his bedside table. "All good."

Lucas pulled his shirt off and dropped it to the floor, choosing to keep his sweatshorts on. He turned out the lights and got under the covers. He and Teddy lay side by side for a few minutes, both staring up at the ceiling. Their breathing synced. Lucas glanced at Teddy and saw his hands clutching the duvet, his teeth grinding behind his closed lips.

"Do you want to… um." Lucas pushed himself up on one arm, making a swirling motion between them. Teddy's eyes flitted to him. "Like… um… spoon? Would that help you feel better?"

Teddy nodded. "Okay."

Lucas went to turn around, but Teddy beat him to it, offering his back and pulling the duvet up.

Teddy peeked over his shoulder. "Well?"

"Right." Lucas shuffled closer. Teddy relaxed his head on his pillow. "So. Like." Teddy reached behind himself and touched Lucas's forearm, guiding it around his upper ribs. "Right," Lucas breathed, swallowing dryly. He pressed himself to Teddy's back. His nose brushed the sweet, damp strands of Teddy's loose hair. "This good?"

"Yes."

"All right. Well, good night."

"Night."

Lucas shut his eyes. Mere seconds into spooning, he had to wiggle his nose—Teddy's hair was brushing over his nostrils. He opened his eyes about a minute in. Teddy's body trembled with small, tight vibrations.

"Are you all right, Teddy?"

"Yes."

"Do you want me to back off a bit?"

"No." Teddy gripped Lucas's forearm and tilted his face up without looking over his shoulder. He stroked the sensitive underside of Lucas's wrist with his thumb. "Please. Stay like that."

"Okay."

Teddy settled on his side again, but the shivering started up as soon as he tried to relax. Lucas lifted himself enough to peer down at Teddy's scrunched face and tightly shut eyes.

"Babe, you're shaking."

"I'm aware," Teddy said, sounding strained.

"What's wrong?"

"Everything and nothing."

Lucas exhaled as he lay down and pressed his face into Teddy's hair. Teddy's shoulders heaved with a similarly heavy sigh.

"I know how that feels," Lucas admitted.

"Do you?"

Lucas nodded, murmuring, "Yes," with his hand flat on Teddy's abs. He rubbed up and down once, the motion stiff. Teddy shifted back into him, his feet brushing Lucas's ankles. Lucas looked down the blankets, able to feel Teddy's clenched toes and tense leg muscles without being able to see them. He attempted another rub of Teddy's stomach.

Slowly, Teddy asked, "What are you doing?"

"I'm trying to soothe you," Lucas said, a touch snappier than intended.

Teddy huffed midshiver. "Thanks."

The last person Lucas had spent the night with who couldn't sleep was Maggie. Lane and Dean had wanted an anniversary celebration in London, which meant they dropped Maggie at Uncle Lucas's for the weekend. Not even Georgie's cuddles could soothe her for the first night away from her parents. Maggie only fell asleep when Lucas agreed to sleep on the floor of the guest room to keep watch for monsters, chatting with the girl until she dozed off, hugging Georgie to her face.

The second night, she'd had no trouble falling asleep, but still requested Lucas keep watch, just in case. He obliged.

"Would you like a bedtime story?"

Teddy's shivers did not stop, but he turned his head slightly. "Are you serious?"

Lucas tightened his arm around Teddy's chest. "It helped Maggie fall asleep."

Teddy settled on his side, bouncing his bum backward into Lucas's groin. His response of "Okay" was so quiet that the air conditioner almost swallowed the sound.

"All right, let's see. Um." Lucas kept one arm around Teddy's body as he stroked the back of his hair. "Once upon a time, there was a boy named Teddy. Teddy loved to take pictures. He had a beautiful mum who looked like a princess. Like a queen." Lucas tightened his grip. "Queen Rebecca loved Teddy very, very much."

Teddy shook uncontrollably, teetering on the edge of sobbing. Lucas tucked his chin on top of Teddy's head, rubbing his hand over his chest.

"Teddy grew up into a strapping young lad with beautiful hair like silk, and eyes like, uh, fresh grass. Or emeralds. Yeah, emeralds. His mum was… promoted. From queen to saint." A small, quiet sob was muffed by Teddy's hand. "And then the sweet little lad was left to fight dragons and wolves and monsters all by himself."

Teddy sniffled, breaking into a shaky gasp, hot tears flowing to pool on the bow of his top lip. "This is the w-w-worst bedtime story of a-all—" He huffed unevenly to take a breath. "—t-t-time."

"It's not over yet, numpty."

Teddy smiled through his tears, pressing his face into a pillow.

"Breathe," Lucas whispered, smoothing Teddy's hair off his forehead. He kissed behind his ear, whispering, "Breathe, love."

"Okay," Teddy said, lifting his face. He sucked cool air into his lungs. He blinked a few times, breathing deeply. "You can continue."

"As I was saying, our hero grew up and things were… not the best. But he was brave and smart and worked hard and had a good heart. Even when things were bad. Even when his luck seemed to have run out. And then, one day, he met another boy when they… argued over who got to take an available chariot."

Teddy gurgled a snuffle, and Lucas chuckled at the watery sound. "What time period is this story set in?" Teddy asked.

"Sort of medievalish."

"They had cameras in medieval times?"

"Just go with it."

"Okay," Teddy said, sniffling.

"And, so, our hero met a new boy. The boy was stunning, truly stunning, with eyes more beautiful than the sky itself and hair spun from gold." Teddy let out a small giggle. "And this boy came with a message for young Teddy."

Teddy's legs shuffled under the covers. "What was the message?"

"The message was that our hero's luck was about to change. Not because the other boy, the rightful chariot-seat holder, was an angel or a prince or a knight in shining armor coming to save the day." Lucas whispered in his ear, "Our hero did not need any of those things."

Soft feet slid between Lucas's ankles. Lucas hugged Teddy tighter, their bodies melding together.

"The boy came as a friend," Lucas said simply. "A friend with the message that even though things were bad at times, young Teddy was still just that. Young. With plenty of time for good things to happen to him. And no matter what he had done in the past, he was still the boy who liked to take pictures. The boy with a saint of a mum who loved him very, very much."

The room was silent. Teddy's back shuddered with each labored breath. Lucas lay frozen, replaying every line of his story he could remember and combing through to find offensive details.

"Are you all right?" Lucas eventually whispered. His palm sweated on Teddy's chest. "Should I get your inhaler?"

"I'm f-fine." The tightness of Teddy's voice broke into an airy laugh. He dabbed the back of his hand on his eyes. "I'm fine."

Lucas exhaled and shut his eyes, willing his heart rate to slow. He drew small circles on the center of Teddy's chest with his fingers, as Teddy rubbed up his inner ankle.

"You're good at making up stories."

Lucas's eyes opened, darting over the back of Teddy's head. "I make up stories for a living. It's nice to tell a true story with a happy ending, for once."

"That was the best bedtime story," Teddy whispered, starting to shiver again. Lucas tightened his arm, rubbing his toes over Teddy's soft arches. "The best. Th-thank you. I'm sorry I keep crying." Saying the word aloud drew quick, shallow breaths from him. Fresh tears prickled his eyes. "I'm not usually like this."

"S'all right. Get it all out. Tomorrow's going to be a fun one, so get those tears out of here." He patted the back of Teddy's shoulder. "Want me to burp you like when Maggie has an upset stomach?"

"No," Teddy laughed. "Contrary to popular belief, I am not a toddler. Thanks, though."

"You're welcome. You want to sleep? I could turn the telly on, if you'd like."

"No telly. I'm fine, um, trying to sleep. But can you...." He tucked his cheek against Lucas's arm. "Can you keep talking?"

"About what?"

"Anything. Wanna hear your voice."

"My voice?" Lucas chuckled high in his throat. He quickly cleared the goofy noise from his system as Teddy chuckled softly. "What about my voice?"

"It's soothing." Teddy's comfort was evident in his voice despite his face being hidden from Lucas. He tilted his head, batting his wet eyelashes. "Please? I like the way you talk."

"What do you want me to talk about? The weather?"

"Anything. Nothing. Whatever you want. Tell me... something funny."

"Such pressure, to be put on the spot like this."

"Oh, c'mon. You're funny all the time."

Lucas snorted, the burst of air from his nose ruffling Teddy's hair. Teddy dragged his thumb over Lucas's forearm.

"Well, let's see." Lucas watched the ceiling fan rotate. "Um." His eyes brightened. "Oh! While you were sleeping, I checked in on Georgie."

"What?" Teddy spun in his arms. His expression was overjoyed even with tracks of tears covering his cheeks. He sniffled once, smiling wider. "At the spa? How? Did you call him on the phone?"

Lucas rubbed the heel of his right hand over Teddy's cheek. Teddy's gaze followed the course of his gentle swipes. "They have cameras in the rooms you can log in to and look at online. Usually the dogs are either sleeping or playing in the group room, but...." He used the pads of his fingers to wipe away the remaining tears on the thin skin beneath Teddy's eyes. "He was awake and playing with this little squirrel soft toy I got him."

Teddy's eyes went wide. "Can we look at him tomorrow? Can I please see him?"

"We can look at him now, if you'd like." Lucas picked up his phone from the bedside table. "He's probably asleep."

Teddy dabbed under his eyes. "I'm such a mess."

Lucas's iPhone exploded with beeps and vibrations upon being woken up. He silenced it, bypassing the alerts. "But you're a pretty mess."

Teddy gently kicked Lucas's ankle, then sat up with their shoulders touching. He reached to his bedside table for a tissue.

"Ugh," Teddy groaned nasally, pinching his nose and blowing. "I smell again. I always smell snotty after I cry."

Lucas pressed his nose against Teddy's neck. Teddy let out a sudden squeal and crunched his head sideways.

"Nope. You still smell amazing." Lucas sniffed again, only prompting more squeals from Teddy. "Better than I could ever hope to smell."

"Lucas." Teddy gently pushed his face away. His eyes shone. "Tickles."

Lucas sat up against the headboard, tapping his phone until a video came through. Teddy rested the back of his head on the front of Lucas's shoulder.

"You can change which room you want to look at," Lucas explained, tapping once. "Like, this is the playroom." The screen showed a large, colorful room with buckets of toys on the sides and a few dachshunds running in circles. "Their entertainment room." He tapped and the screen went to a movie theatre with rows of dog beds. Three snoozing beagles and a frantic Yorkshire Terrier were watching the movie *Lady and the Tramp*. "And their spa room."

"Wow. That looks nicer than the spa here."

"I know, right? What a lucky dog. They play outside here." Lucas tapped again and they saw a sprawling garden. "Ha. Raining, of course. Makes you appreciate the weather here, yeah?"

Teddy glanced sideways at Lucas's profile, a small smile lighting his face. He looked back to the phone. "Definitely."

"And then they have a camera in each…." Lucas squinted, his mouth dropping open. "What the fuck?"

"What? What do you see? Is Georgie…." Teddy's hand flew to his open mouth, muffling a bubbly giggle with his fingers. "Oh my God. Is he—"

"What does that German shepherd think he's *doing*?"

"Aw, they're spooning," Teddy cooed, holding the back of Lucas's phone. "How sweet! Georgie made a friend!"

Lucas's nose wrinkled. "Why is Georgie the big spoon? He's the smaller dog."

"Maybe the German shepherd likes it like that. They're such lovely dogs, German shepherds. Very intelligent. Such a handsome dog face."

"How do you know it's a male?"

"Well, I suppose we don't know for sure if it…."

The dogs turned over. The strength of the German shepherd caused Georgie to roll a foot away from him. The larger dog stretched on his back.

Teddy's mouth fell open as Lucas's eyes bulged.

"It's a boy," they both said.

"Damn." Teddy chuckled. "Get it, Georgie."

"Jesus Christ, what have you done to him?"

"Me?" Teddy held his hand to his chest. He watched the dogs snooze beside each other, his belly going soft. "What do I have to do with it?"

"Georgie meets you and suddenly he's having this, like, gay revolution."

"Gay revolution?" Teddy asked, laughing. He curled on his side, clutching his stomach. "Can we crochet him a rainbow collar during crafts?"

Lucas turned his phone off and tossed it on his bedside table. "Let's give them their privacy."

Teddy giggled quietly and propped his head on his hand, scanning Lucas's bare torso. Lucas lay on his back and stretched his arms to the headboard, resting his hands behind his head. He smiled at Teddy, sleepy and slow. "What?"

Teddy shook his head. "Nothing," Teddy whispered, grinning crookedly. He leaned closer, then paused, their eyes locked. He leaned even closer, pressing a kiss to Lucas's mouth. "G'nite." Teddy's breath rushed over Lucas's face, their lips connecting for another plush kiss. "Sleep well."

Lucas cradled Teddy's cheek, holding him in place. Their lips met, soft and innocent. Teddy's palm was warm on Lucas's upper ribs.

"You, mmm, too," Lucas said. His words were cut off by Teddy sucking on his mouth. Both breathed in through their noses. The sheets hissed around their shifting bodies. "Good night."

"Good night." Teddy linked his foot behind Lucas's ankle. "Sleep…." They kissed again, their gentle hands beginning to wander over skin. "Sleep well."

Lucas rolled onto his side and rested his hand on Teddy's lower back. "Yeah. Good…." Teddy smoothed his palm up Lucas's chest as they kissed tenderly. Lucas panted "Good night" into their kiss.

"We're doing a bad job of going to sleep."

"Are we?" Lucas asked, confused.

Teddy chuckled and studied Lucas's flushed face. "Does it bother you that I like kissing you?"

Lucas blinked with heavy eyes. Teddy drew small circles in the center of Lucas's chest with his fingertips. "No, not at all. As long as…." His words trailed off as Teddy kissed him while gently tugging a pinch of his chest hair. Their lips clicked as they broke apart. "As long as you're fine with it, I'm fine with it. I like it. Kissing you. I like it."

"Yeah?" Teddy pursed his mouth to give Lucas a tiny kiss. "You do?"

Lucas dragged his fingertips up Teddy's spine. Teddy shivered and pressed himself closer to Lucas's body.

"I do. I don't…." Lucas looked away, Teddy shifting to maintain eye contact. "I don't do this sort of thing often."

"I know what you mean. Most of the people I kiss, it's with the implication that sex will happen." Teddy stroked Lucas's hair, then cradled his sharp jawline with the heel of his hand. "It's nice to just do what we've been doing. It's comfortable. Relaxing, almost."

"What a vote of confidence. I'm a total snooze."

Teddy gently slapped Lucas's arm, chuckling, "No, not like that." He soothed his bicep. "You know what I mean."

"No pressure."

Teddy nodded. "Right. No pressure. It's me getting to be me and kissing you." He looked away, Lucas chasing him with his eyes. "It's nice. It's been really nice."

"Yeah, it is. Nice, I mean."

Teddy nodded again, the motion slower. "You mean to tell me you don't cuddle Georgie at night?"

"I sometimes share a bed with George." Lucas spoke pointedly but kept his voice quiet. Teddy smiled and pinched his chest hair again. "That said, I draw the line at snogging my dog."

Teddy whispered, "I'm honored to be one step up from making out with a dog," then sealed their lips together.

"I didn't say that." Lucas smirked into their kisses. "You're at least two steps up."

"Hey." Teddy giggled and pinched Lucas's nipple. Lucas huffed against Teddy's chin. Teddy softened his fingers to stroke over the small, raised circle of skin, then wetly kissed the center of Lucas's chest. "I love your chest hair."

Lucas pulled back, and Teddy moved toward him with his mouth pursed and his eyes hazy. "What? My chest hair? The other day you said I was hairy."

"In a good way." Teddy walked his fingertips just below Lucas's navel. His other hand, at chest level, barely touched the fine dusting of hair around Lucas's nipple. "A really, really good way."

They moved closer. Lucas's arms draped around Teddy's waist, and Teddy cradled Lucas's cheek to kiss him again.

Lucas breathed, "You're…."

"Hm?" Teddy's eyes, so frustrated and pained and sad hours earlier, twinkled at Lucas. Lucas's fingers were gentle as they traveled over the sensitive arch of Teddy's neck. "I'm what?"

Lucas tilted his head as Teddy dropped light, playful kisses beneath his ear. "You're like… that food you end up trying by accident, but are immediately addicted to." Teddy rested his cheek on his pillow, peering up at him with wide, round eyes. Lucas propped his head up on one hand. "And you can't get enough of it, so you run to the shop at three in the morning every night because you feel like you'll die if you don't get more of that flavor or texture or whatever. That's what being with you is like, only you don't have to run to the shop. The food is right here and you can eat as much as you want without getting sick or full."

"Favorite food, hm?" Teddy said quietly, moonlight illuminating his face. "You mean like a big bowl of spaghetti and sausage?"

"My favorite food isn't spaghetti and sausage. What are you.... Oh my God," Lucas started to laugh. Teddy was already nearly hysterical with giggles. "You will do anything to involve sausage in conversation, won't you?"

"Sausage is our official sponsor this week."

Their arms wrapped around each other as they traded soft, openmouthed kisses. Lucas pulled back an inch to whisper, "Like a big bowl of sausage gumbo."

"Ew, gross." Teddy grinned and wrinkled his nose. Lucas interrupted his protest with kisses. "I do not… taste like… sausage gumbo."

"Sausage and peppers on a roll," Lucas said with a quiet moan in his voice. Teddy beamed and cupped Lucas's face. "A full English wake-up."

Lucas cradled Teddy's lower back. They brought their lips together. Lucas's fingers twitched on Teddy's tender skin.

There was a soft knock at the door at the same time as someone half whispered, "Yoo-hoo, anyone up?"

The door swung open.

Lucas's eyes widened. "Mum, what the fuck?" he blurted out, pulling the duvet up to their necks. Teddy blinked, shocked, with the blanket flopped over his mouth. Lucas sat up on his elbows, glaring at her outline. He whispered, "What are you doing in here?"

JO PLACED a tray on the sofa and came up to the bed on Teddy's side.

"How are you, my darling?" She put one knee on the bed and cradled his face. Teddy's eyes widened further. "We were all so worried! I brought soup and sandwiches for both of you, seeing as you skipped dinner."

Teddy looked to Lucas. "You didn't eat?" He squeezed Lucas's thigh under the blanket and warmly drawled, "Luke."

Lucas flushed, and ran his hand through his hair.

Lane entered through the open door. "I have more Gatorade," she said. "I hope you like blue. We didn't know if you'd be up."

"Oh, they're up," Jo said, attempting a wink. She had never mastered the art of winking, instead closing both eyes at the same time while looking at Lane.

She dropped her voice to a husky whisper. "Looked like a whole lot of heavy petting and snogging, and not a whole lot of stomach bug, when I came in."

"Mum." Lucas sighed and rolled his eyes to the ceiling. The back of his head thudded against the headboard. Teddy sat up in bed, using his feet to push himself upright. As soon as he sat up, the wind was knocked out of him.

"Tazzy!"

"Maggie, get off of him!" Lane chided, running to the bed. She dropped four bottles of Gatorade on the mattress. "He's not feeling—"

"It's okay," Teddy said to Lane. "I'm feeling better now." He lifted Maggie to sit on his duvet-covered legs. "I got your beautiful cards," he whispered to Maggie, who preened under the attention. "Thank you so much! I love them. They made me feel much better."

"Can we play tomorrow?"

"Yes, of course," Teddy said, solemn and serious. "Maybe not in the beginning of the day." He glanced at Lucas, who was watching him with a soft smirk. "But maybe tomorrow night."

"Why not tomorrow during the day?" Jo asked.

"We're going to go on an adventure outside the resort," Lucas said.

Lane asked, "Did you get your trip approved by Zill?"

Teddy's mouth dropped open a bit, and he looked at Lucas, concerned. "Did you do that?"

"We don't need approval to leave the resort," Lucas said on a laugh. "Are you both actually joining a cult this week?"

"Well, we did have to pack all white."

Lucas looked toward the raspy, throaty voice and grinned brightly. "Hey!" He sat up straighter and held his arms out. "You got here!"

Marcy came into the room and went to the bed, hugging Lucas. Her deep voice was a total mismatch for her delicate bone structure and cape of shimmering brown hair. A flowing white peasant dress hung off her slender shoulders.

"That's Aunt Marcy," Maggie said, nodding at Teddy.

"Hi, Teddy!" Marcy offered him a smile as she put one knee on the bed and held her hand out. "So nice to meet you."

"You too." Teddy shook her hand. He hitched the duvet up his stomach. "Sorry I'm so, uh, underdressed."

"That's quite all right." Marcy's natural rasp gave that sentence, and any other words she said, an especially heavy adult connotation, even with her innocent face and sunny demeanor. Teddy liked her immediately. "I've heard so much about you," Marcy said, sitting on the bed beside Lucas.

Teddy touched the center of his chest. “Me?”

“Yeah, of course. I watched the Zill-ympics, like, twice already. You’re really good at climbing stuff! Puzzles too.”

“There’s a video?” Lucas asked.

“Of course. They filmed and edited the entire thing.” Jo sat on the bed beside Teddy. “Now, you both should eat.” She held up a spoonful of chicken soup to Teddy’s mouth. “Aren’t you hungry?”

Lucas’s face went from shock to horror in half a second. “Mum, please stop spoon-feeding my boyfriend. I’ll only ask once.”

Teddy snorted and opened his mouth. Jo shoved soup inside. “Mmm, yum,” he said, with his mouth tight around the spoon, rubbing his belly. He swallowed, slowly backing his head away from her. He held his hands under the bowl. “I think I can handle the rest. Thank you, though.”

She beamed kindly at him and let him take the bowl. She pushed his hair back, cradling his face with her small palm.

Teddy heard Lucas say, “Get that away from me, Lane, I swear to God,” and felt the bed shift. Lane giggled, “Aw, let me spoon-feed the wittle Loo Loo.” Teddy saw Marcy’s hand in his peripheral vision, stroking Maggie’s curls. Maggie was asleep and drooling on his bare chest.

“I like this,” Teddy said to Jo.

Jo tapped the tip of his nose with her thumb. “Good. We do too.” She glanced at Lucas for a moment, then back to Teddy. “We all do.”

Teddy smiled shyly and dropped his gaze to his soup. He sipped a spoonful as Jo’s fingers ran through his hair.

Chapter EIGHTEEN

Wednesday, April 29

A SMALL white boat bobbed on pure turquoise water. Lucas and Teddy stared intently at their instructor as he quizzed them on diving terms.

"Okay above?" Ezra, their guide, asked.

Lucas and Teddy lifted their arms and steepled their fingers above their heads.

"Okay below?"

Both held up their right hand with their thumb and pointer fingers touching, their other three fingers sticking outward to make an *okay* shape.

"Help?"

They straightened their right arms and waved them up and down.

"Buddy up?"

They held out their right hands and scissored their middle finger away from their pointer finger.

"Ascend?"

Both jutted their thumbs up.

"Four times two?"

Teddy blinked and scrunched his brows. Lucas held up eight fingers. Teddy glanced at Lucas's hands and quickly mirrored his pose.

"All right, very good." Ezra tilted his head sideways over the edge of his small boat. The dark, leathery skin around his mouth wrinkled as he smirked. He tapped his watch. "Thirty minutes, boys."

BOTH TEDDY and Lucas had many hours of diving experience under their belts from various holidays through the years. They offered their dive cards to Ezra before they even got on board and successfully demonstrated they were knowledgeable about all of their gear and safety rules. Ezra stayed a few meters behind them underwater, giving them the illusion that they were exploring alone. They wouldn't be diving terribly deep for terribly long. Their dive was more focused on beautiful plant life and creatures, not on exploring the depths of the sea.

The rhythmic click of air coming in and out of Lucas's mouthpiece synced with Teddy's flippers swaying in front of him. Whenever Lucas went diving, he was struck by how similar it seemed to what he imagined space was like, even though it was in the opposite direction. They were weightless. Floating. The pressure of clear blue water cushioning them felt unreal, as did the rainbow of creatures and plants they came in contact with.

Lucas's eyes followed a school of large, shimmering fish with yellow scales and iridescent purple fins. He kicked a touch faster and swam up Teddy's body. Teddy turned toward him and held up the waterproof camera Ezra let them borrow. A red rubber cord fastened it to his wrist. He snapped a photo of Lucas holding up a peace sign beside a school of tiny, shimmering pink fish. The school swam so fast it looked like underwater sparkles.

Lucas swam next to him and attempted to get their faces together in the photo. Vibrations bubbled from Teddy's mouthpiece as their cheeks bumped. Both had on matching black shorty wetsuits, the clingy material hitting just above their elbows and knees.

They swam to a colorful patch of coral and posed in front of it, taking turns photographing each other. An enormous turtle swam below their flippers mid-photoshoot. Lucas could hear Teddy exclaim something in excitement and see his fins flipping faster.

After taking a few more photos and trying to race a school of plump magenta fish, Lucas tapped his watch. Teddy nodded and jutted his thumb toward the surface, both starting a slow, careful ascent with Ezra swimming above them.

A BAND made up of steel drummers, guitarists, men on homemade hand percussion, and a lone accordionist played tropical music at the front of an outdoor restaurant. Their straw hats swayed in the gentle breeze. Sandals and bare feet tapped on the sand, and two older women danced off to the side of the band.

Ezra had driven Teddy and Lucas up to the sandy spot by boat. All three men helped secure the boat off the shoreline, where other small boats floated near Ezra's. Luckily, Ezra had a waterproof bag they could borrow to hold their cash for the swim to shore. Ezra preferred to stay on his boat for a snooze.

The restaurant was not a proper restaurant. It consisted of a long wooden shack, or booth, perched in the middle of the beach and an array of wooden picnic tables surrounding the food booth. Some tables were painted with bright patterns, others worn down by the elements.

There were no waiters in crisp white polos, nor a concierge to help patrons choose what they wanted. Guests ordered at the booth and waited for their number to be called. The air was full of the smell of buttery hot oil frying conch fritters and johnnycakes. The chefs made friendly conversation while preparing food.

Guests could not even choose their meal. The restaurant made what they made each day and served it fresh until they ran out. Despite the mysterious, remote location, hordes of people found the restaurant and filled the picnic tables to gorge on fresh seafood.

The picnic tables were pushed into long lines. Guests ate with other guests from all walks of life. Teddy and Lucas chatted with a pair of expert divers, who shared a few secret spots in the area, before they even started eating. They also met a couple on their honeymoon, a family celebrating their parents' twenty-fifth wedding anniversary, and a few American high schoolers on spring break.

Both had left their wetsuits on the boat, wearing nothing but their swim trunks and sunglasses. Teddy's trunks were a soft robin's-egg blue and hit midthigh. Lucas's shorts, another one of Teddy's purchases, were white with black waves sketched along the bottom seams, hitting just above his knees. Three people came up to him while they waited on line for food to compliment his swim trunks. Teddy beamed beside him.

"I've never had conch so fresh," Lucas said, licking the tips of his fingers. "And so spicy." He sucked down a draught of freezing Kalik, the official beer of the Bahamas. The icy liquid felt amazing going down his throat after such spiciness, especially with the sun beating down on his bare back. "I thought the fritters were amazing, but I might love this spicy stuff more."

Teddy smiled and nodded as he chewed a bite of conch with his mouth closed. His dimple deepened. He sipped and swallowed his beer.

"Me too." He picked up the last conch fritter, still hot from the fryer, and popped it into his mouth. "I'm so glad he brought us here," he said out of the corner of his mouth, then smiled. "And that you let me have dessert first."

"As if I could deny you homemade banana ice cream."

Lucas dipped his spoon into the ceramic bowl between them. He lifted a heaping spoonful of fresh conch, chopped peppers and onions, and spicy sauce, prepared in a ceviche style. The heat of the mixture came from the ingredients and some well-placed, but subtle, spices. The crisp bite of lime juice and the lightness of their beers cooled off the mix.

He dropped the spoonful of conch on a flat, tortilla-like bread and rolled it up. He watched Teddy's throat bob while drinking his Kalik. Water dripped off the ends of his hair to trickle over his tanned chest. Teddy put his beer down and loaded up another tortilla for himself, adding a few slices of fresh papaya.

"Strange," Lucas said while chewing.

Teddy licked his thumb. "I'm telling you the spicy sweet is where it's at." He gently kicked Lucas's bare feet under the table. "Try it." He lifted a piece of papaya and placed one piece of conch on top, then reached across the table. "You'll like it," he sang, arching his brows over his Ray-Bans. "I promise."

Lucas lifted his arse off the bench and leaned forward. Teddy's fingers nudged his mouth while he sucked the small, juicy bite. He chewed.

"You like it?"

Lucas swayed his head side to side. "Well…." He held back for as long as he could before his smile became uncontrollable. "Yeah, yeah, you're right." He stole a piece of Teddy's papaya. "It's delicious."

Teddy grinned and thumbed the side of Lucas's mouth, then pulled back and sucked on the sweet juice, lifting a taco with his other hand. Lucas held Teddy's stare and extended his tongue all the way out, placing his taco on top and biting down.

"I do not look like that!" Tiny pepper cubes tumbled out of the corner of Teddy's mouth as he laughed. He caught two cubes and tossed them back in his mouth. His hair flew back with the motion. "You exaggerate."

Lucas picked up a slice and placed it on his extended tongue. "Mmm, papaya," he said, wiggling his tongue at Teddy.

Teddy laughed again, softer, and nudged his foot against Lucas's ankle. Lucas chewed on the juicy fruit, holding still, looking down at his plate as Teddy's foot rubbed against his ankle. The exciting music surrounding them changed to a more mellow cover of "And I Love Her" by The Beatles.

Teddy slowly walked two fingers across the worn wood. When he reached Lucas's fingers, he tapped the pads of his fingertips on Lucas's nails, walking his fingers higher over his knuckles until he reached the top of his hand. He dragged his fingertips back to his knuckles and Lucas turned his hand over, Teddy's fingertips tracing his pale lifeline.

Powdery white sand was slightly rough on their skin as Lucas brushed his toes over the arch of Teddy's foot. He linked their fingers, rubbing his thumb over Teddy's hand. He looked up and found Teddy was grinning at him. The burning of Lucas's cheeks told him he shared Teddy's expression. Both stared at each other for a long beat.

"Would you look at that," Teddy murmured, their feet resting together on the warm sand. "We finally got it right."

EZRA GLANCED over his shoulder, and droplets of water whipped over his cheek and his hand gripping the clutch. Teddy and Lucas were wrapped in one large white towel on a cushion along the right side of the boat. Teddy sat sideways with his legs resting on Lucas's thighs. They stared out the open back of the boat as the restaurant got smaller and smaller.

Ezra raised his voice to carry over the thrumming boat motor. "Where to, boys?" They looked at him curiously, their hair flying in the wind. Ezra lifted one hand and pointed right. "Fishing, or"—he pointed left—"cliffs?" He faced forward again to guide the boat, shouting, "You've already done two dives, and I wouldn't recommend another one."

Teddy and Lucas looked at each other.

"Fishing or cliffs on three," Lucas said. Teddy nodded. They sat up straighter, and the towel wilted off their tanned shoulders. Lucas held up his fingers for each number, counting off, "One, two, three—"

TURQUOISE WATER enveloped Teddy faster than he thought it would. His long body plummeted below the surface in a straight line until his feet hit slightly cooler water. He kicked his legs as hard as he could, rising back to the surface, the water growing lighter as he rose. He stuck his head out of the water and flicked his hair off his face, gasping as he kicked and kept himself afloat.

"Nice one!" Lucas called on a laugh, slapping the water with both hands. "You only looked mildly terrified."

"I wasn't mildly terrified," Teddy said, grinning and swimming over to their spot a few meters from the center. "It was fun!"

Lucas dunked Teddy's head underwater in passing. Teddy reached for him but grabbed nothing but his big toe. Teddy watched Lucas get out of the water and start walking up the path along the side of the cliff. The path led to small platforms carved into the rock. The platforms were not carved by any particular person, but worn into the stone by visitors walking over it.

"Should I try the next one?" Lucas called, pointing to a spot a bit higher. "Or is that too high?"

Teddy gave him a thumbs-up. "Go for it."

Lucas started to climb again, and the compact muscles of his back and thighs flexed.

Teddy called out, "Look at that arse!"

"Shut up," Lucas laughed, attempting to hold his hand over his bum as he climbed.

When Ezra had dropped them outside the secluded cove, he assured them that the water was deep enough below the cliffs for them to jump from as high as they'd like. It was a bit scary not to know how deep the water actually was, but Ezra was waiting on his boat on the other side of the cliffs if any safety issues arose.

The water was a perfect neon blue-green. It grew darker the closer one swam to the center of the water, but looked crystal clear gushing out of the waterfall to the right of their jumping area. The lush plants, exotic flowers, and high cliffs were more colorful and beautiful than any all-inclusive resort could ever recreate.

"All right," Lucas said, holding his arms out to balance. He took a tiny step forward. "Here I come."

Teddy watched Lucas take a running start before throwing himself off the cliff. Lucas straightened his body like an arrow. He stretched his arms over his head and sliced through the water. Lucas's head popped up a few meters away, causing a burst of foam. Both men laughed while treading water.

"That was sick!" Teddy swam closer to Lucas. "Totally sick. Was it scary?"

They faced each other with just about a foot between them.

"Nah. You should definitely try it from that high. It's not scary at all."

Teddy peered up at the rocks. Sunlight beamed into his eyes. They had left their sunglasses on the rocks to avoid having them flying off midjump. "All right, maybe I will."

"I wish we had known about this place sooner," Lucas said, treading water. "This beats smelling like chlorine all day."

Teddy reached out and pushed Lucas's hair out of his eyes. "Definitely." He dropped his hand into the water with a small splash, looking up at the rocks again. He narrowed his gaze. "You're sure it wasn't scary?"

"Nope. You won't even know the difference. Use those giraffe legs to fly."

Teddy tutted his tongue. "Didn't they teach you anything at Cambridge?" He flicked his hair back with a quick jut of his chin. "Giraffes don't fly."

Lucas prodded Teddy's stomach. "This giraffe will."

They took turns jumping and climbing. Other groups of people filtered into the cove to give the cliffs a try. Eventually, everyone else left, leaving nothing but the two of them and their borrowed underwater camera.

"I can dive," Lucas insisted, huffing to catch his breath. "I never took lessons, but I've always been good at it."

Teddy swam closer to the shore; his breath was equally labored. "You're serious?"

"I am."

Teddy peered up at the cliffs and squeezed his nose, wiping water off his face. "Your mum seems to like me, but I think she'd like me less if I informed her you were splattered on the bottom of a cliff."

"I won't splatter," Lucas said, shaking his head. He gently splashed Teddy's face. "What, you don't believe me?"

"Show me," Teddy said, spitting water out and grinning. "Let's see it, big man."

Lucas swam to the front of the cove and pulled himself up onto the ground, swinging up to get his foot on the rocks. He started to climb the cliffs. He went to a jumping point about three-quarters of the way up the cliff, not the highest point but high enough to get air for his jump.

Teddy picked up the waterproof camera from the rocks. He waded back into the cove until the water reached his chest. He looped the red band around his wrist, squinting at the screen as he searched for the best setting.

"You ready?" Lucas called.

"Yup," Teddy said, lifting the camera. "All right, stud." He peered up through the viewfinder. "Let's see what…."

A pair of white swim trunks slapped the water next to him. Teddy's mouth fell open and his finger pressed down on the shutter without his control. His hands went limp around the camera, his arms lowering into the water as his eyes widened.

Lucas threw his body backward to dive off the platform, fearless and graceful, with his arms lifted over his head. His body was straight but relaxed, his arms and legs slightly bent at the elbows and knees. He completed two rotations on the way down before he steepled his fingers to dive into the deep blue water. There was a small flurry of white bubbles around the spot his body dove through. Teddy stared at the spot as the camera floated next to his hip.

Lucas's head popped up amid even more foamy bubbles. He swam toward Teddy, his dark hair matted to his head and his teeth gleaming.

"Well? Do you believe me now?"

"I…." Teddy's mouth gaped open while his feet shuffled on the sandy floor. "You… yeah, you…. That was…." He grabbed Lucas's swim trunks before they could sink too deep. "That was amazing. Um." Teddy held his trunks out. "Here. Ezra might be shocked when he sees some of these photos."

Lucas hummed, appearing intrigued, with about two feet between them. He took the offered trunks, balled them in his hands, and threw them to the shore. Teddy watched the line of their journey, all the way from the flexing of Lucas's throwing arm until the trunks plopped on the sand.

"It feels nice without them." Lucas offered Teddy a crooked grin. "And there are no prying eyes around like at the resort."

Teddy went to pull his trunks off immediately, but the camera got in the way. "Oops," he chuckled sheepishly. He untangled the rubber wristband and tried to get the camera out of the front of his trunks. "Don't tell Ezra his camera was down my pants."

"I'm sure we wouldn't be his first clients with an underwater dick pic or two."

Teddy grinned and wiggled his wrist above the water. "You're right. He's got at least one of you in there."

Lucas's mouth dropped open. "What? *Me*?"

"It was an accident!" Teddy started to giggle as he moved backward. Lucas charged toward him. "I didn't know you were going to jump naked! I took a picture without realizing it."

Lucas stuck the camera underwater and swam closer.

"Oh no, I might have an accident," Lucas teased and Teddy splashed water in his face. "Well, I believe it's only fair for you to jump naked off the cliff and let me have a look."

"But what if my cock hits the water too hard?"

"You mean you don't have your moneymaker insured, like J.Lo's arse?"

"Good idea. I'll have to phone my lawyer immediately."

"You don't have to jump if you don't want to. Skinny dipping is a fine alternative to cliff jumping."

Teddy peered up the cliff, clucking his tongue against the roof of his mouth. "Nah," he grinned, looking back to Lucas. "I'm game."

Lucas smiled so wide his eyes crinkled. Teddy swayed forward to peck his cheek, then swam around him. He walked up the sandy shoreline, taking the long way to get up the cliffs instead of climbing up the flat stone base. He dropped his trunks beside Lucas's on the sand.

"Talk about an arse," Lucas said. Teddy slowed his strides and swayed his hips, prompting Lucas to laugh. "No wonder Georgie humped your legs."

"Projecting much?" Teddy asked. Mischief twinkled in his eyes as his cock slapped wetly against his upper thigh.

Lucas swam backward a few strokes. "Oi, I have never humped your legs."

Teddy looked over his shoulder, his arms raised to grip the side of the cliff, his shoulders bulging. "Not yet."

LUCAS FLOATED for a few seconds, watching Teddy carefully find footing for each section of his climb. He approached the climb much like he approached puzzles, surveying his options before making any big moves.

"This is going to be the least graceful jump ever," Teddy said, standing on a platform. His voice was distant. He held his hands over his groin, taking two wobbly steps closer to the edge. He peered over into the water. "How did it not hurt your junk? I have a very sensitive cock, you know."

Lucas snorted. "It happens so fast, you won't even feel anything."

Teddy looked down at him and quirked one finger. "Will you come up and do it with me?" He pressed his palms together, drawling, "Please?"

Lucas started to swim to the shoreline before Teddy finished his question. He pushed himself up with his hands flat on the rocks. "You want me to hold your cock for the trip down?"

"No," Teddy chuckled. "I just want company. Maybe some of your courage will seep out into me."

Lucas climbed up the side of the cliff much faster than Teddy, reaching him in no time. Teddy shuffled over on the platform and held his hand out. Lucas gripped it for the final steps up. Teddy looked over the edge.

"You ready?" Lucas asked, squeezing his hand.

"Yeah. Yes. Yup."

Lucas brought himself flush with Teddy's side. They swayed their joined hands once, twice, three times before they took off from the edge. Air rushed around their bodies. Teddy's loud shout and Lucas's laughter rang around the cove. Just before they hit the water, Lucas gripped Teddy's cock in his hand.

Teddy shouted, "But your penis!" as their feet slapped the water.

They plummeted underwater with their hands still joined, Lucas releasing his grip on Teddy's groin. Lucas saw Teddy was cackling. A matching mouthful of bubbles rushed over Teddy's face from Lucas's loud, throaty cackles as their legs kicked hard to get to the surface.

Their heads popped out at the same time, water flying off of Teddy's hair and spraying from Lucas's mouth. They both panted between uncontrollable bursts of babbled amusement. Lucas forced out, "But your penis!" and sent Teddy into harder, raspier laughs. They paddled to a more shallow section, their toes brushing sand.

Teddy wrapped his arms around Lucas's lower back, pulling him closer to his body. Lucas's legs hugged Teddy's thighs as he draped his arms on Teddy's shoulders. The water lapped against their chests. Quiet, dripping sounds mixed in with the cheerful calls of birds perched around them.

"My hero," Teddy murmured with a slow smile.

"Yeah, right. Your penis-protecting hero."

"So, I've been thinking."

"Scary."

Teddy pinched Lucas's bum and Lucas squirmed against him.

"Yes?" Lucas grinned, giving his hair a gentle tug. Teddy's eyes fluttered, his face softening. "What have you been thinking?"

Sunlight illuminated Teddy's eyes to a near golden green compared to the deep tan that had settled over his skin. "You're not so much a wolf."

Lucas chuckled, letting his fingers loosen in Teddy's hair.

"Oh no?"

Teddy shook his head. "Nope. I'm thinking…." He studied Lucas's mouth, wet and pink and panting. "More lion than wolf."

Lucas's brows arched. "Lion?" He touched his own chest. "Me? I'm too small to be a lion."

"Yeah. Lion. For sure. And you're not small," Teddy said on a quiet laugh. "You're… compact. Efficient."

Lucas smiled but looked away. "I dunno about that."

"I do. You're the lion. King of the jungle without even trying. It makes sense. You're a natural leader. Strong. Courageous." Teddy's hand flattened on the small of Lucas's back, rubbing soothing, wide circles. "You're not the wolf. I was wrong. My mistake."

"And what are you, then?" Lucas looked back to him, amused, stroking Teddy's wet hair off the side of his face. "The nightingale perched on the lion's head?"

The skin beside Teddy's eyes crinkled, his dimple deepening. "I'd quite like that. Could snooze in your mane. Get to travel in style with the king."

"Singing your pretty little nightingale songs and keeping an eye out for danger."

"Mm-hmm. We could be jungle travel buddies."

Lucas dropped his gaze. His hand fell from Teddy's hair into the water.

Teddy's brows twitched together. "What is it?"

"Nothing."

"You look sad."

"I'm not sad."

"But are you happy?"

"Yeah, I am." Lucas swallowed. His voice was not quite as rough as he repeated, "I am. Happy. Happier than I've been in a long, long time."

"Then why the long face?"

Lucas put some space between them, pushing his body backward toward the deeper water. "Just feel a bit foolish, is all."

Teddy swam after him, confusion wrinkling his forehead. "Why?"

"Because… because…."

Teddy's arms looped around Lucas's waist, guiding him to the shallow water. Lucas said nothing, allowing Teddy to move him until his back bumped the stone wall beneath the cliffs. Both were able to stand on the sandy bottom with the water at nipple height.

"Because what?" Teddy tilted Lucas's chin up. Water dripped off his fingers to plunk into the cove. "What is it?"

"Because you were right."

"About you being the wolf?"

The right side of his Lucas's mouth twitched up. "No. Not that. You're the animal expert."

"Then what is it? You look so… serious."

Lucas licked his lips, then dragged his teeth over the corner of his mouth. He squinted at something over Teddy's shoulder. "You told me once that a life is a long time to spend alone."

"At the gala," Teddy said. "I remember."

"Despite every bit of mental gymnastics I've attempted to deny that statement, to prove that it was nonsense, you were right. One hundred percent." Water dripped down Teddy's temples to pool at his collarbones, and his eyes widened. "Being with you for even one day, for one bloody *hour*, has only made that more crystal clear to me. You were right." Lucas's voice softened but his jawline was tense. "I was wrong and you were right. I can admit when I've made a mistake. You may think I'm a lion, but sometimes the king of the jungle doesn't want to be king, no matter what he tells himself."

The waterfall crashed against the cove in the background. Teddy curled his palms over Lucas's biceps, soothing up to his wet shoulders. He thumbed both sides of the base of his neck.

"Okay," Teddy said slowly, concern clouding his gaze. "So, what's the problem?" He rubbed lower on Lucas's arms, dipping underwater to squeeze his wrists. "That's what the nightingale is for. To keep the lion company."

Distress caused Lucas's eyes to squint even tighter. "But in the wild, the nightingale would fly away. Or the lion would eat the nightingale. Because he's a lion. That's just the way it is."

Teddy smiled crookedly. "Not this lion. And not this nightingale."

"But… I…." Lucas watched Teddy come closer until they kissed, plush and wet and openmouthed. Teddy's touch crawled around his back to pull him closer. Lucas's eyes fell shut as he breathed, "We…."

Teddy kissed him again, longer and hotter, the fizzies in the back of Lucas's brain nearly overpowering the crushing volume of the waterfall pounding against the cove's water.

"We what? What, Lucas?"

Lucas's shoulders shook, his head trembling ever so slightly. His mouth opened for a split second. A shallow breath brushed over Teddy's and his fingertips trembled on the fronts of Teddy's hips.

"I don't want to be alone anymore," Lucas whispered.

Teddy's eyes lit and grew heavy with sadness at the same time. He dug his fingers into Lucas's lower back.

"Lucas—"

"I don't want to be alone because I want to be with you," Lucas said, his eyes boring into Teddy's face. He flicked one hand in the air and droplets soared off his fingertips before he replaced his touch on either side of Teddy's neck. "I want to be with you. I never thought I'd want that, that I'd want to be with another person for more than a fuck, but I think… I think I just…." His brows pinched, a tiny wrinkle popping on his forehead. "I told myself for so long that I didn't need another person to be happy, that I missed the point completely. It's not a question of happy versus unhappy. It's a question of happy versus—" He studied Teddy for a beat, confused. "—something so beyond happy that I don't even know how to describe it, but it's you."

"Th-that's how you feel with me?" Teddy was unable to keep his voice even as excitement ran through his shaky words. His hands tightened on Lucas's arse. "Is it?"

"It is," Lucas said with boyish innocence, shrugging with water sloshing around his sides. "And I don't care if you're playing me. I really don't." He gently twirled the wet curls at the base of Teddy's neck. "I don't care if we're playing pretend, as long as it means I get to be with you, even if only until the end of the trip. And that is why I feel foolish. Not only because I was wrong, but because I've only known you for days, for *days*, and I'm done for already.

"I know that I could be completely off. I know that you could be lying to me through your teeth. I know that you're an incredible actor when you want to be, and you could be playing a big, amusing game where you'll go off after the trip and laugh about that arsehole Lucas Thompson with your personal consultant friends, but I don't care. I don't." Lucas widened his eyes and let out another choppy laugh. "And that's madness. Madness! That's absolute insanity. I'm aware of all that, but I don't fucking care. Truly. I just want to be with you."

TEDDY NUZZLED their noses together and Lucas grasped at the back of his hair.

"You stubborn, lovely, silly man," Teddy whispered as their lips brushed. Teddy could sense Lucas staring at him, could feel the tension running through Lucas's lean limbs. He hugged Lucas tighter, curling his arms around the small of Lucas's back, and pressed his face to the side of his neck. Lucas's fingers clasped on the back of his own neck. "Took you long enough." Teddy kissed his collarbone. "So smart you're actually stupid sometimes."

Lucas stiffened. "And what the hell is that supposed to mean? We've only been here five bloody days!"

Teddy pulled his head back. He shook his head, and his eyes were soft and fond. "I'm not pretending. Or lying. Or playing a game."

Lucas's throat bobbed. Teddy kissed his hammering pulse point. "You're not?"

Teddy brought their eyes level. He held his gaze for a beat. "No. And you know I'm not. You, of all people, can spot a liar a mile away. I'm not lying." He touched the center of Lucas's chest. "You know it." He gestured to himself. "I know it. We both know it." Lucas ran his tongue over the front of his teeth and flitted his eyes away. Teddy guided his face up with a gentle palm to his jawline. "I'm not going anywhere, love. I'm not disappearing. I'm here. I'm with you."

"And…." Lucas's mouth tightened to a straight line for a moment, blinking faster. "You want…."

Teddy started to smile. "You, of course."

Lucas's right brow quirked. "As a… travel buddy?"

"As whatever you want me to be, if it means getting to be with you."

Lucas's legs tightened around Teddy's thighs underwater. "I don't want to be just your travel buddy."

The blazing blue of his stare, intense yet still gentle, held Teddy in place. Teddy's breath caught in his chest. "I was hoping you'd say that."

"You were?"

Teddy nodded and started to reply, but Lucas sucked on his lips before he could get any words out. Teddy's eyes fell shut and his hands slid up Lucas's wet skin. Lucas's fingers clenched in the back of his hair. Both moaned and tilted their heads, deepening their tongue-heavy kiss.

"Who knew not lying to someone would feel so good?" Lucas whispered. "Like, so, so fucking good."

Teddy kissed him again. Water dripped off their hands onto whatever skin they touched above the surface. "Such romantic words. But… I know exactly what you mean."

"Do you, Theodore Bennet?"

Teddy's smile went shy, and he pressed his face into Lucas's neck, his cock twitching against Lucas's thigh. They spun in a circle. Lucas guided Teddy's back against the rocks as they kissed, their cocks bumping together. Lucas flattened his hands on Teddy's arse and swiveled against him.

"Told you you'd be humping my legs," Teddy whispered.

Lucas rolled his eyes as he went in for another kiss. "I'm not humping your legs."

"You can, if you'd like."

They both snuffled as they kissed. Lucas's hands slid down the sides of Teddy's hips to rest on his arse.

"I'd rather hump another part of you, if we're being honest."

"Oh, yeah?" Teddy dragged one soft fingertip down the front of Lucas's throat. He pulled backward as Lucas leaned forward. "Which part would that be?"

Bashfulness softened Lucas's eyes, causing him to muffle a quiet snort against Teddy's jawline.

"Are you actually shy?" Teddy asked amusedly, grinding against him a touch harder. "Buck naked and hard in the middle of nowhere, yet you're shy?"

"I don't want to take advantage of you."

Teddy's brows shot up sky-high, and his mouth pursed in shock, not in preparation for kissing. "Are you serious?"

"I don't." Lucas shook his head. "I like you. I respect you. I don't want to… I don't want you to feel like we have to do anything you're not comfortable with, just because we're here on this trip and…."

Teddy gripped Lucas's right hand and pressed it to his cock, hard and thick and straining up against his lower abs. Lucas's jawline tensed as he squeezed the fleshy base. Teddy guided his hand in a stroke and hissed, warm water enveloping his cock as his foreskin slid down his length.

"I'm very comfortable," Teddy murmured deeply. "You have my full consent."

Lucas's eyes did a slow wander up to meet his gaze. He brushed his left fingers against Teddy's lower back. Teddy's brows twitched higher as

Lucas's fingers touched the top of his arse, teasing along the seam of his cheeks. "And here?"

Teddy's head lolled sideways, his mouth coming closer until Lucas kissed him. Teddy's upper lip curled as Lucas bit at him. "So, so comfortable," Teddy exhaled. Their lips fitted together and their body temperatures skyrocketed as tingles exploded over every inch of their bare skin. "I want *everything* with you."

Lucas kissed him harder and guided Teddy's mouth open wider. Their tongues slid together, and Lucas's hands tightened on Teddy's arse. He gripped his cheeks and spread them slightly, his fingers pressing just beside his rim. Their cocks swiveled together, hip bones bumping. Teddy's hands cradled the back of Lucas's neck as they kissed. The water lapped against their bodies. Teddy's hand tightened in the back of Lucas's wet hair as Lucas's hot breaths panted against Teddy's firm, confident kisses.

A foghorn blared through the air. Both continued their deep, frantic kisses until the horn sounded again, louder and longer.

Lucas's eyes opened to slits. "Oh," he said, as Teddy's kiss slipped off his mouth. "Uh. Hi."

Teddy tilted his head backward.

"Hello," Teddy said as he and Lucas both turned to face the shoreline.

"Hello, boys," Ezra said from his spot near their soggy swim trunks, with the foghorn grasped in his hand and a small smirk on his face. "Did you enjoy… the cliffs?"

"Yes." Lucas nodded firmly. He tried to move his hands over his groin with as much discreetness as possible, while Teddy stood with his hands on his hips. "Very much."

"Wonderful." Ezra's smirk broke into a toothy grin. "I'm sorry to interrupt, but you said you wanted to be back to the resort by dinner." He thumbed over his shoulder. "We'd best be getting back."

"Right." Lucas cleared his throat, and Teddy turned back to him. A quick smile was shared between them. "Very true. All right."

Ezra lifted their trunks with pinched fingers and tossed them into the water.

"I'll give you your privacy," he said, his voice trembling with mischief. He picked up the waterproof camera. "See you back at the boat."

Chapter NINETEEN

BOTH WERE quiet for the boat ride back to port, with a fresh white towel wrapped around their shoulders and the sun warming their bare chests. They got out of the boat and into Ezra's ancient blue truck, which bumped over the unsurfaced roads for the drive to Flamingo Cove.

Lucas paid Ezra the agreed-upon fee, plus a generous tip, before they hopped out of his truck in front of the main house. Compared to the well-dressed staff, Teddy and Lucas looked like two mermen experiencing their first day with legs. Their hair was still damp and standing in wild, fluffy peaks. Seawater was drying on their skin with a slightly salty texture, and they had looped the towels around the backs of their necks. Both wore only swim trunks and sunglasses, their other belongings tucked into a backpack hanging off of Teddy's shoulders.

Guests were visible on the beach and at the pools as they walked back toward their room, but neither paid any attention to anything besides the gentle grip of their hands between them. Teddy kept his face forward as he moved his eyes down and to the right, watching their linked fingers sway forward and back.

"This was the best day I've had in… in a very, very long time," he whispered. Lucas pressed a kiss to the top of Teddy's wrist, nudging his nose against his knuckles. Teddy grinned at the sand. Their shoulders bumped. "Thank you. For everything."

Lucas rubbed his thumb over Teddy's knuckles. Their hands swayed between them as they both kept their eyes on the sand. "Me too. Thank you for being here. With me. It's… it's been amazing." He glanced at Teddy and found he was looking at him. Both smiled, a zip of nerves whipping between them. The setting sun gifted them with a rosy glow. "So, thank you."

Teddy looked down at their bare feet padding over the white sand. "You're only thanking me because we won Zill-ympics."

Lucas laughed, bumping his shoulder into Teddy's. "Yeah, right." He squeezed Teddy's hand. "No thanks to you and your giraffe legs."

"Oi! My giraffe legs are part of why we won!"

"You dropped your egg so many times in the egg race, I'm surprised there aren't scrambled eggs on the sand right now."

"None of my eggs broke, thank you very much," Teddy said, pulling Lucas against his body and digging his fingers into his side.

Lucas tried his best to remain quiet but couldn't help a small chuckle from escaping as he pushed his prodding finger away.

"C'mere," Lucas said through his laughter. He thumbed backward. "Hop on." Teddy grinned and draped his arms over Lucas's shoulders, carefully settling on top of him, with his chest to Lucas's back. Lucas slid his palms under Teddy's knees and hitched him up. Teddy exhaled a comfortable sigh into his salt-scented hair. Lucas smirked over his shoulder. "I'll give those gorgeous giraffe legs a rest."

Teddy said nothing, hiding his happy sigh in Lucas's damp hair. He smoothed his hand over Lucas's pecs, warm skin and soft hair tickling his palm as he bounced. He stared at the sun as it sank below the ocean. The sky was a mess of colors from deepest red to softest violet, all combining in one wide gradient that led to the hard line of the horizon.

Teddy dragged his eyes away from the setting sun to focus on Lucas's jawline. Even after spending the entire day underwater or in the blazing sun, a small smear of sunscreen was stuck in the dip between Lucas's earlobe and jawline. The coconut scent mixed with salt water and sweat. Teddy was unable to stop himself as he pressed his nose to the spot.

Lucas's hands tightened ever so slightly, cool air rushed beneath his ear, and Teddy hugged his chest tighter. A smile slowly spread over Lucas's face as Teddy brushed a light, teasing kiss to the curve of his neck.

They got back to their room. Teddy wiggled his bum once they were on the porch and Lucas lowered him to the ground. Teddy swung the backpack forward, one strap slipping off his shoulder. Lucas unzipped it and searched for his key card, grinning at the feeling of tiny kisses smattering both of his cheeks while he searched. He retrieved the key and slid it into the slot. The lock clicked and both stepped inside. Teddy walked farther into the suite.

"I'm so glad we left the air conditioner on," Teddy said, tipping his head back. "Heaven after a day in the sun."

Lucas closed the door and locked it, then tossed his sunglasses on the chest of drawers. "Are those elephants on the bed?"

Teddy tilted his head, reaching out to pet one of the towel animals. "Cynthia is truly an artist."

"I wonder what cleaning products they use that get the place smelling like this." Lucas took his backpack off of Teddy's shoulder. He dropped their belongings next to the door, a small pile of sand sliding out from the bottom of the backpack. "It's, like, clean but not sterilized clean. Naturally clean. You know what I mean?"

"Yeah, you should invest in it for your own place. It masks your natural stink pretty well."

"My natural stink?" Lucas gripped the back of Teddy's swim trunks and pulled on his waistband, letting it snap against his skin. "Excuse me, Theodore." He gripped both of his hips. Teddy turned toward him and gently slapped his chest, and they both laughed. "You just smelled me, you utter hypocrite."

Teddy laughed louder and hugged himself, and Lucas's fingers prodded up his sides. "Hey! This is—This—I normally charge quite a lot of money for this type of—Ah!" Teddy yelped and crumpled inward with giggles, Lucas's fingers digging in at birdcage height. He fell back onto their tightly made bed. Lucas landed on top of him and propelled their towel animals off the side of the mattress. "The elephants!" Teddy squirmed and howled. His heels dug into the duvet as Lucas blew a raspberry beneath his ear. "We're going to get the bed all sandy, you—" He laughed heartily for a long beat, Lucas now blowing on the front of his throat. "You barbarian!"

"Yeah, yeah." Lucas chuckled and softened his prods. Teddy panted quickly while grinning up at him. Lucas brushed a wild curl out of Teddy's eyes, Teddy's breaths shuddering over his face. Lucas's fingers lingered in Teddy's hair, and his thumb rubbed over Teddy's temple. Teddy's eyes crinkled at the corners. "Sorry," Lucas chuckled to himself and pulled back. "I'm probably squishing you. And I smell like a sweaty crab, I'm sure."

Teddy's fingers looped in the front of Lucas's swim trunks to hold him in place. "You're fine just like this."

Lucas smiled and ducked away. Teddy tilted his head to peer up at him, open and gentle.

"You're right, though," Lucas said softly. He smiled wider for a moment as Teddy's smile grew. "We're both carrying about half the beach between us. Showers would be a good idea."

Teddy scratched his own hair, his bicep clenching with the motion and causing the hollow of his underarm to deepen. "Very true. Do you mind if I shower first?" Teddy asked. "I feel like I've got more sand than hair, at the moment. I need a deep scrub."

"Yeah, sure, of course." Lucas sat back on his heels, brushing his hands over his thighs. "I'll keep myself busy." Teddy dropped his eyes to Lucas's groin, grinning lasciviously and arching his brows. Lucas's jaw dropped, his hand subconsciously moving over his middle. "Not—not like that. I didn't mean like that. I meant I'd read or something. Maybe I'll go find the diving guy to thank him for hooking us up with Ezra."

"Sure," Teddy drawled, throwing in an exaggerated wink. "Enjoy your reading." Lucas gently shoved his shoulder and Teddy laughed, falling on his back. Teddy rolled off the bed and went toward the en-suite. He paused in the doorway and turned, gripping the arch. "Um, unless…." His knee bent inward. "Unless you wanted to join me?"

Lucas felt his cheeks heat as he pulled a fresh white tee over his head. He brought his head through the neckhole and turned to face Teddy.

"Um, while that is very tempting—" Lucas swallowed, biting his bottom lip and smiling, "—I… I think I've got sand and seaweed lodged in places on my body that are biologically not supposed to have sand and seaweed inside them." Teddy's answering smile was relieved, his laugh quiet. Lucas's right arm looped through his sleeve. "I don't anticipate my shower tasks to be particularly sexy this time around, so maybe it's best if we take turns?"

"Okay. Yeah. Of course." Teddy's eyes sparkled as he pushed off the doorframe to drop his shorts. Lucas strained to maintain eye contact. "This time around."

HE TURNED away and Lucas exhaled, falling back onto the mattress, sand be damned. Lucas pulled himself together and went searching for the resort's resident dive master. He extended his thanks, and they had a quick chat about other dive spots nearby. He stopped at the main house to use the restroom on his way back to their bungalow.

When he walked into the room, Teddy was pulling on short white boxers. The soft, thin material inched up over his arse until it covered the tan line running along his arched lower back. Teddy turned toward him, his long torso stretching. His cheeks were ruddy and shiny, as if he'd scrubbed himself hard with soap. His towel-dried hair brushed over the tops of his shoulders, his smile shy.

"Hi."

"Hey," Lucas said, kicking off his flip-flops. He opened the door to place them outside. He shut the door. "Good shower?"

Teddy nodded. "Very good."

Lucas smiled and said, "Nice," as he went toward the en-suite. "Um." He knocked his fist on the doorframe. Teddy-scented steam pulled his body backward. "Can you let me know if I'm in there more than, like, ten minutes? I don't want to make us late for dinner."

Teddy sat on the edge of the bed and nodded. "Yeah, sure."

"Cool, thanks."

When Lucas emerged from the shower, he found Teddy was still sitting on the edge of the bed in nothing but his boxers. His knees bobbed in and out and he clasped his hands between his thighs. Teddy looked up at him and Lucas stopped moving, his hand tightening on the knot of his white towel. Teddy rose to his full height and stepped closer, his mouth moving without sound. Lucas glanced up at him through his wet lashes. His chest shuddered with a breath he didn't realize he was holding in.

Teddy said, "Luke," at the same time as Lucas said, "Teddy, I—"

Both glanced at each other before looking at the floor. Their bodies involuntarily swayed forward on the balls of their feet. Sweat beaded on Teddy's upper lip despite the air conditioner pumping cold air into the room. The inside of Lucas's stomach trembled involuntarily.

"What were you, um—" Teddy swallowed and scratched behind his ear, making his bicep flex. "—going to say?"

"I was…. I…." Lucas looked up at him. Teddy's eyes, so round and large, came closer. Their chests rose and fell with a faster, more staccato tempo. "Teddy, I…."

"Yeah?" Teddy exhaled, taking one step forward.

Lucas took a step forward, reaching out. He brushed Teddy's bare hip then dropped his hands to his sides, heat burning on the pads of his curled fingers. "I—"

"Please, just say it." Teddy's voice was its usual deep, honeyed drawl, but an undercurrent of begging caused the pitch to rise slightly. "Please, Lucas."

"I don't want…." Lucas stared at the nightingale inked into Teddy's smooth skin and imagined it taking flight right off his balmy shoulder. "I want…."

Teddy touched the top of Lucas's hand, lifting it and placing it on his hip. Lucas's fingers melded around Teddy's curves, with Teddy's hands flat on either side of Lucas's neck. Teddy whispered, "What do you want?" into Lucas's hair. Their chests were close enough to feel each other's body heat.

"I want you," Lucas said. His voice sounded strangled as he dug into the plump, hot flesh. "Fuck," he breathed. Teddy's mouth gently guided his lips open. "I want you so fucking much."

Teddy pressed his lips to Lucas's mouth, whispering, "Fuck, yes, please." His body trembled for the next plush kiss. Lucas wrapped his arms tight around his lower back and pulled their bodies flush. "Take me. Take me. Please, please, please." Lucas walked him backward to the bed. They sucked kisses, and their hands seared whatever skin they could touch. "Fucking *take me*. Please."

"You're sure?" Lucas tried to peer at him as they kissed. The quick, increasingly frantic presses of their lips got in the way. He squeezed Teddy's hips. "I don't want to make you uncomfortable."

"Do you think looking at you and sharing a bed with you and fucking smelling you for the past five days has been comfortable? My balls are practically purple, if they're even still attached to my body."

Lucas smiled into their kiss with Teddy cradling his face. "What about the contract? No sex, remember?"

Teddy sat on the end of the bed and pulled Lucas closer by the hips, giving his thick curves a squeeze. Lucas tilted his head down to kiss him. Teddy walked his fingers around his lower back. They pressed their lips together again, harder, their kisses growing rough and sloppy.

"Contract schmontract," Teddy breathed. "You and I both know there are loopholes. I put them there for a reason, and you let them slide for a reason." A sneaky, knowing look bloomed over Lucas's face. Teddy chuckled, scooting farther back on the bed as Lucas fit between his spread legs. "I'll beg you all night if that's what you want." He kissed the middle of Lucas's chest, dragging his nose over the damp, clean hair curling between his pecs. "I want you." His thumbs pushed Lucas's towel off his hips as he kissed lower into the darkened hair above Lucas's navel. "I'll do whatever you want."

Lucas put his knee on the bed and his hand flat on Teddy's cheek. He bent over and slotted their mouths together, sucking gently on Teddy's lower lip before breaking the kiss.

"I want to do what pleases you," Lucas said, tucking a wet curl behind Teddy's ear. He traced down the side of Teddy's neck while kissing him even more softly. "I don't want you to have to beg for anything." Their lips barely brushed, nothing more than a quick purse and press. "I want to pleasure you."

Teddy blinked up at him, and his mouth popped open. Lucas guided him onto his back. Lucas planted slow, deliberate kisses from beneath his ear down to his collarbone, goose bumps rising on every inch of skin he touched.

"I… I…." Teddy sucked air into his lungs. "I…."

His stomach muscles trembled inward from the waistband of his boxers. Lucas's hands smoothed up and down his ribs, teasing touches tracing down the center of Teddy's abs until he reached his navel. Teddy's stomach hollowed away from his touch, causing his hip bones to press out.

"What do you like?" Lucas asked, brushing his mouth over Teddy's right nipple. "Whatever you want." He kissed the center of Teddy's chest and walked his fingers down the front of Teddy's shorts. He nipped at his left nipple, tonguing over the dark skin. "I want to make you feel good."

Teddy shuddered. "I want you to fuck me."

Lucas smiled against his skin and tilted his head up. He let his lips drag over Teddy's wet nipple, their gazes locked. He bit down and Teddy squinted. "Was hoping you'd say that."

Lucas's hands seemed to hone in on wherever Teddy liked to be touched with the exact pressure and sensation he preferred, even if Teddy could do nothing but release tiny gasps and sighs between nonwords.

Thumbs light over his nipples. A bit of a rougher, handsier grip on his hips and the meat of his arse. Fingers soft on the sides of his neck while he was being kissed. Nails digging into his scalp ever so slightly when their kisses grew more tongue heavy. Smooth palms soothing up and down his inner thighs. Confident touches ghosting up the legs of his boxers without actually taking them off, then barely ghosting over his tented fly in passing, the touch light enough to get him to lift his hips up but never firm enough for real contact.

"Did you forget what you like?" Lucas chuckled, opening his mouth on the inner point of Teddy's collarbone. He kissed lower, pinching his nipples and rolling them between his fingers. "Figured you'd rattle off an itemized list."

"I…." Teddy blinked up at the ceiling as Lucas's kisses moved to the top of his abs. His eyes fluttered closed. Lucas's hot tongue joined in for each slow, deep kiss, dotting his kisses side to side. "I like…."

Lucas peeled his boxers down his hips, and Teddy's cock sprang upward to slap his flat stomach. Lucas tossed them to the floor. "Why'd you even put pants on?"

"I don't know."

"You don't know what you like or you don't know why you put pants on?"

"B-both? Bo—Oh—" Teddy's head fell back on the bed as Lucas's mouth sucked on the tip of his cock. "Both," Teddy exhaled, bending his legs at the knee and planting his feet flat on the bed. "Luke, you don't have to—"

Lucas's mouth popped off. His palms were firm on Teddy's hip bones. "I want to. Been wanting to do it from the first second I met you." His tongue traced over his bottom lip. "Wanted to swallow you whole in the backseat of that car."

LUCAS STARTED sucking his cock again. Teddy was hypnotized by the rise and fall of his messy hair and the flex of his upper back.

"You're so full of shit," Teddy blurted out breathily. He felt Lucas snuffling as he sucked. His eyes clenched shut for a beat, his mouth widening and his whole body shuddering as tingles surged out from the center of Teddy's groin. "You couldn't stand me."

Lucas wetly popped off. "I'm serious," he chuckled, kissing down Teddy's shaft and massaging the base of his cock, squeezing his foreskin. "You were the most obnoxiously smug person I'd ever met, but I spent the entire rest of the day trying to remember exactly how you smelled." He sucked the lightly haired crease of Teddy's thigh. "Trying not to get hard in the middle of a board meeting, thinking about the smell of your skin. Trying not to lick your fucking business card just to see what your fingers tasted like."

Teddy smiled despite the waves of heat rapidly swirling through his body. "You filthy boy. I stank of sweat and day-old cologne."

Lucas inhaled deeply, his nose pressed to Teddy's groin. "You smelled like the sun. Like warm honey. You smelled like sex." Lucas scrunched his nose to take a longer breath. "You smell so fucking good. Your sweat's gonna be the death of me."

He started to suckle again. Teddy's hips twitched as he exhaled a soft, pleased sigh. Lucas's hands rubbed up his inner thighs, digging his fingers into the skin on the fronts of his hips and dragging lower. Teddy bucked up into his mouth and clenched the duvet.

"I'm—" Teddy gasped and arched his lower back. "Lucas, I—"

Lucas pulled off, then rubbed soothing circles on Teddy's lower belly. He got up to his knees and went toward the edge of the bed. Teddy's hand shot out, holding him in place.

"I've got it covered," Teddy said. He reached out with his other hand into his bedside table.

He pulled out what looked to be a thick black wallet. It opened up like an accordion file you would use to save receipts. He glanced at Lucas's half-hard cock before flicking through the sections of the wallet with quick fingertips. He pulled out three condoms covered in shimmering gold wrappers and tossed them on the bed, and then retrieved three travel packets of lube.

Lucas took one of the condoms, ripping it open. Teddy closed the wallet with a snap and dropped it back in his bedside table drawer. He looked back to Lucas, a packet in each hand.

"What?" Teddy asked.

"You're organized," Lucas said, sounding impressed. "And optimistic."

The sound of the wrapper tearing made Teddy's hands speed up in opening one of the lube packets. "Organization and preparation are key. Besides, I'm a glass-half-full kind of guy."

Teddy picked up Lucas's fallen towel and spread it out on the bed, moving higher on the mattress. He lay on his back and opened his legs, then squirted lube onto two of his fingers and pressed them against his arse. He slid his heels up the bed to almost touch the back of his thighs. He exhaled slowly, tipping his head back and sinking his fingers inside.

"Fuck," Teddy whispered, curling his slippery fingers. He could hear Lucas echo the word and felt Lucas's eyes blazing into his skin. "Been fucking dreaming of this."

LUCAS FOCUSED on the in-and-out motion of Teddy's fingers. A minuscule shudder ran up Teddy's stomach muscles, and goose bumps prickled around his hardened nipples. Lucas took the lube out of Teddy's hand and knocked his fingers away. He sucked Teddy's cock into his mouth with a wet, desperate sound. He pressed his index finger inside of Teddy. Teddy cried out weakly, spreading his legs wider, and Lucas added another finger, rotating his wrist to press against the outside of Teddy's arsehole.

"Fuck me, you're totally hairless here," Lucas murmured, pulling his fingers out to tease around Teddy's tight entrance. "Holy fuck. That's…." He spread more lube around Teddy's arsehole, the rosy skin glistening and smooth, sweat darkening the sparse hair dusting the creases of his thighs. Lucas breathed, "Fuck me," and eased two fingers back inside. "Why is that so hot to me?"

"I just maintained my usual prep routine." Teddy pinched his right nipple, sweat glistening on the hollow of his throat. "And I—I sort of like how it feels when I'm smooth."

Lucas dipped his face lower and sucked Teddy's heavy balls into his mouth, one by one, his fingers only about an inch inside him. Teddy's hips squirmed down, and he wrapped his hand around his own cock. Lucas grunted and sucked harder on his left ball, pressing his tongue onto the soft flesh and swirling his licks. His fingers pressed deeper inside, rubbing at Teddy's prostate.

Teddy's squirms went faster, and his heels slipped on the mattress as he cried out, "Fuck!"

Lucas lifted his mouth from Teddy's balls and eased the teasing circles of his fingertips. "Gonna have to eat you out later."

"Okay," Teddy exhaled, nodding fast. "Whatever you want."

LUCAS CHUCKLED lowly and licked up the underside of Teddy's cock, then swallowed him from root to tip. He could only manage a few tight, wet sucks and pumps of his fingers before Teddy's throaty, choked-off sounds made his own cock throb against the mattress. The smell of Teddy's skin, soapy yet spicy, sank into his nostrils. He gasped out, "Teddy, are you—"

"Please," Teddy whimpered, grabbing Lucas's shoulders and pulling upward. "Please, fuck me." He took a pillow from his side of the bed and shoved it down under his arse, his lower back arching so he could stuff it underneath. "I'm dying here."

Lucas crawled up his body and guided Teddy's hands up above Teddy's head. The tip of Lucas's cock slid over the slickness of Teddy's opening. Teddy's arse lifted slightly to meet Lucas's hips, and Lucas dug his feet into the mattress and pressed forward.

Both exhaled long, low, guttural sounds into each other's open mouths as Lucas entered him, their hands squeezing and their gazes locked. Lucas's head shuddered and fell forward, resting on Teddy's temple. Stars exploded behind his eyes and left a trail of flaming stardust over his entire body. Pleasure and heat and wanting all swirled within his stomach and throbbed in his bones. Teddy tightened his grip on Lucas's cock for the next thrust, and both barked throatily. Teddy's sound was higher than Lucas's gruff sob.

Lucas's hips snapped backward and forward once. Teddy whimpered a louder sound and tipped his head back.

"Oh my God," Teddy gasped out, another thrust pulling an involuntary, high sound from him. Lucas's low moans vibrated against his jawline. "Lucas—"

"Yeah. F-fuck."

"You're so hard and—" Teddy's eyes darted side to side. Lucas thrust and Teddy's eyes rolled back in his head. "Thick—"

Lucas's hips ground slower against him, both fumbling together to suck kisses as their bodies moved in unison. Their joined hands squeezed in time with their thrusts.

"I can hear him," Lucas whispered, searing his lips to Teddy's panting mouth. He pulled away to breathe before slamming his cock deeper inside Teddy's lush body. Teddy wailed and bucked against him. Lucas shuddered out, "I can f-fucking h-hear him. Or her. Them."

"Wh-who?"

Lucas's damp fringe fell in his eyes and brushed over Teddy's forehead.

"God. The meaning of life," Lucas said, his voice tight. "Oh my God." He clenched his eyes shut. "I can—I can fucking hear it."

TEDDY WOULD have laughed, but his lungs pushed out a puff of pained breath instead. "What's the—What's the meaning of life?"

Lucas's head fell forward. He made a choked-off sound, and their foreheads pressed together. "This," he whispered, his voice cracking. He squeezed Teddy's hands and ground into him, slow and deep. Teddy's wail was muffled by Lucas's mouth, and his legs hugged Lucas tighter. "Y-you. Fuck, Teddy, you are."

Teddy tried to lift his legs on top of Lucas's shoulders, but his ankles were trembling without his control. His feet wobbled, sweat slippery on his inner thighs. "I—I shouldn't just lie here. Need to—Need to—"

"Are you fucking insane?" Lucas released one hand to grip behind Teddy's leg, hoisting his left ankle on top of his shoulder. He leaned down with his weight on the back of Teddy's leg to thrust. Teddy's leg stretched and burned, and both hissed through their teeth. Teddy's toes curled as his leg trembled. "You're amazing, just as you are."

"J-Jack McQueen is hot and confident and knows exactly what to do, but Teddy Bennet is—I'm—" Teddy bucked up, rubbing the sticky tip of his cock against Lucas's belly. He turned his face away. "My palms are sweaty and I make embarrassing noises and I can't stop shaking."

"Teddy is gorgeous," Lucas spoke over him, cradling the side of his neck. "Teddy is beautiful. And smart." He kissed Teddy's nose. Teddy's breath wheezed out of his throat. "Teddy is fucking incredible. A treasure."

"Lucas," Teddy whined, shivering. Lucas sped up his thrusts, sucking beneath Teddy's jawline. "Fuck, Luke!"

"You like that," Lucas stated. Warm breath brushed Teddy's panting mouth. "You like it when I say your name. Your real name." Lucas's tongue dipped into Teddy's mouth as Teddy whimpered, then Lucas looked him in the eye and whispered, "Theodore."

Teddy's eyes clenched and his head dropped back. His body fluttered so tightly around Lucas's cock it bordered on painful. Lucas sped up his thrusts and brought his mouth to Teddy's ear, breathily chanting, "Teddy," or, "Theodore," with each thrust. Teddy's thighs hugged Lucas's hips extra tight whenever his full name fell from Lucas's lips. His entire body arched and he grasped to hold Lucas's arse in place.

"Oh, fuck," Teddy gasped, his eyes widening, "I'm gonna come."

Lucas ran his fingers through Teddy's hair and gripped the back, curls looped around his fingers, his other hand slipping between their bodies. He gave Teddy one quick, tight stroke, and Teddy cried out nonsense, his fingernails digging into Lucas's lower back and his long toes curling.

"C'mon, come for me, love," Lucas whispered, jerking him slower, thumbing under his head. Teddy's fingernails dug into Lucas's arse, and a high moan ripped from his throat. "Come for me. Fuck, you're so beautiful. Teddy.

Oh—" Lucas's head dropped down, his hips speeding up and his feet cramping on the mattress. "Fuck me, Teddy. Jesus Christ!"

Teddy's body fluttered around Lucas's cock. His hips humped to meet his thrusts without any control.

"Please, Lucas, I—I'm gonna come too fast! Fuck." Teddy's head tipped back. Lucas kissed frantically and sloppily over the front of his throat. "You're so fucking hard. How are you so h-hard?"

"Fucking come. P-please," Lucas panted as sweat dripped down his spine from the back of his hairline. "Been wanting this forever. Gonna—" His jaw locked open and he squinted at Teddy's shining, flushed face. Lucas gasped out, "I—"

Teddy held Lucas's face with one hand, his other guiding his arse faster as Lucas's balls slapped loudly against him. Lucas's motions became erratic. He drove faster and faster into Teddy. Teddy tongued into his mouth, and Lucas's fingers clenched in his hair. A muffled, low shout vibrated against Teddy's lips as he spilled inside the condom. Teddy's cock spurted over Lucas's fist as Lucas shuddered and twitched, squeezing Teddy's dripping head tight enough for Teddy to sob out, "Fuck." They kissed hard, both breathing unevenly and shallowly through their noses.

"Fuck," Lucas echoed, sounding half there as his hips started to slow. "Fuck."

They panted for what felt like hours, and their eyes locked. A sense of awe was transmitted by their wide eyes and weak breaths. Teddy cradled the back of Lucas's head. Lucas nibbled small, exhausted kisses to Teddy's trembling mouth, as he stroked the side of his sweating neck. Teddy groaned and hugged him with his thighs.

"Y'all right?" Lucas rasped.

"I'm amazing."

Lucas lifted to peer down at him. Teddy's sweat-dappled cheeks were round, with a soft, fond smile, his mouth kiss swollen as he panted, his eyes glowing mint green.

"You were amazing," Teddy said softer, his fondness growing. "Not… not that I had any serious doubts, but…." He shifted his hips slightly. Lucas lowered his face to Teddy's neck. "That was… that was incredible. You've got, like, the most perfect thickness I've ever had." Teddy laughed and Lucas started chuckling against his skin. "And you stay so fucking hard the whole time. Jesus Christ. S'like you've got superstrength or something. Super cock."

Lucas lifted his face. His fingertips still trembled slightly, but he stroked Teddy's cheek, cradling his jawline. "You're…."

Teddy arched his eyebrows. "I'm?"

"I don't even know a word to describe what I'm trying to say."

"Amazing? Best shag ever? Flamingo?"

Lucas shook his head and snorted, Teddy's body vibrating around his softening cock. Lucas gripped the base of his cock and swiveled his hips, gently pulling out. "Yes. All of those things." Mischief lit Lucas's face as he and Teddy shared a warm look. "I didn't think you'd be so chatty after a shag. You can barely string a sentence together without stumbling over yourself when you're not lost in an orgasmic haze."

"Well, no, not normally," Teddy said, conversational despite his words slurring together. He stroked up Lucas's lower back, the pads of his fingers picking up on the raised half-moons scattered over the sweaty skin. He kissed Lucas's chin. "You were exceptional. Orgasmic haze, indeed."

Lucas chuckled and lowered his gaze. "Well, now you know."

"Know what?"

Lucas dropped the tied-off condom over the side of the bed, making a mental note to walk carefully when he next got up. Teddy's body pressed against his back and a heavy, muscled arm slid over his stomach.

"Chatty and cuddly." Lucas settled on his side and the bed sagged under their weight. Teddy's foot slid between his ankles. "Noted. Not much of a surprise, though."

"What did you mean? What do I know now?"

Lucas stiffened for a moment and stared straight ahead, his feet frozen midrub against Teddy's fuzzy ankle.

"Erm. It's nothing. Just…." He chuckled quietly, watching Teddy's fingertips stroke lazy, uneven circles over the center of his chest. "You know my thing now."

Teddy's fingers slowed. He moved an inch backward and curled his warm palm around Lucas's shoulder. He guided him onto his back, his hand smoothing to the front of his opposite shoulder.

"What thing?"

"My so-called kink," Lucas said with a small smile, giving the word *kink* extra crisp diction. "What you've been so curious about."

Teddy lifted himself up on his forearm. "What?"

"My kink is not lingerie or high heels or spanking or pissing in each other's mouths or whatever other scenarios you threw at the wall to see which one stuck. Mine is…." Lucas shuttered his gaze, even though they were both still staring at each other. Teddy blinked once, his open mouth twitching silently. "Mine is being with someone I actually care about. That's what… that's what gets me going the most, I guess." He pasted on a smile, looking up at the ceiling and ignoring Teddy's puppy-dog eyes. "There you have it. That's it. Intimacy. That's my nonexistent kink. The joke's on me. I'm vanilla." He swallowed, pushing out a gruff sound. "Thrilling, I know."

He turned toward the edge of the bed, but Teddy's hand stopped him.

"Lucas—"

Lucas flattened one palm in the air. "Look, I know it's stupid, all right? I don't need to hear it from you too. I think it enough for the both of us."

Both of Teddy's hands gripped Lucas's shoulders to push him onto his back. Teddy's leg swung over his groin with graceful ease, pinning him to the mussed mattress. "Lucas, that's… that's not stupid. Not at all." He leaned down and softly kissed him. Lucas exhaled out of his nostrils with their lips joined. Teddy thumbed his cheekbones as they kissed, their heads shifting. "That's lovely," Teddy whispered, stroking beneath Lucas's eyes. He smiled wider and pecked him, gentle and quick. "That's sweet. Surprising."

"Sweet doesn't get guys hard."

"Sweet gets you hard," Teddy said, curling his hand around Lucas's cock. His grip was loose enough so as not to cause discomfort so soon after sex, but present enough for Lucas to feel each pad of his fingers as he teased him. Lucas's brows twitched and his jaw jutted forward. "Sweet got me hard." Teddy tightened his fingers one by one. "You got so, so fucking hard you made me shoot up against my own neck. Fuck, you made me go fucking crazy. Did you hear the noises I was making? You don't fuck sweet, love. You fuck hard. The sweetness is just an added, surprise bonus."

Lucas narrowed his eyes and smirked. "Are you using a pseudo-hustler voice on me?"

Teddy grinned crookedly. "Maybe." He pulled his body up. His hand was still anchored to Lucas's cock, but the muscles of his torso stretched and bulged, and come dried along the middle of his body. He let his head fall to the side; his hair fanned out over the black heart on his tattooed shoulder. He flickered his tongue over the corner of his mouth. "Do you like it?"

Lucas held his stare for a moment. "Is this your way of bringing Jack out to play?"

"Well, you haven't gotten the full package yet," Teddy said in a low drawl. His grin simmered into a flirtier smirk. "Might as well see what all the fuss is about."

He leaned down, kissing Lucas's stomach with their eyes locked. He pushed his palms up Lucas's ribs until he reached his neck, letting his mouth linger in front of Lucas's lips. Lucas thumbed over Teddy's bottom lip. Teddy sucked the pad of his thumb with soft, gentle pressure.

Lucas fanned his fingers, dragging each one over Teddy's mouth as it curved upward. He nibbled the tip of Lucas's middle finger, letting his teeth pinch the very end. He kissed the sore spot and their gazes flickered together.

"We're going to miss dinner." Lucas pulled Teddy's bottom lip down with his thumb. "And possibly breakfast."

"Oh, right, uh, sorry," Teddy said, his normal voice peeking through. His hips shifted, his hand moving to drop from Lucas's cock. "Do you want to go?"

Lucas rolled Teddy onto his back and pinned him in place with his thigh, and Teddy gasped as Lucas sucked on his neck.

"That's what room service is for, love. Now." Lucas ground against him, cradling Teddy's jawline as their lips sucked. He rolled them again, settling on his back with his hands behind his head. His meaty biceps rounded on his otherwise lean arms. "Let's see what Jack McQueen can do."

Teddy sat up. His thighs hugged Lucas's hips and his shins were flat on the bed. He tilted his head side to side and clasped his fingers, extending his arms in front of his body. Lucas grinned as Teddy reached for another packet of lube.

Chapter TWENTY

"LET'S GET a fan like that one."

"That one?"

"Mm-hmm."

Zamir rolled off Cillian and onto his back. They both panted deliriously. The back of Cillian's hand landed on the center of his sweaty, shining chest. Zamir's right arm looped around Cillian's shoulders.

"Dunno if it'd go in our place," Zamir said, squinting and tilting his head. "It's pretty bambooish. Our room is more of a turquoise and hemp aesthetic."

Cillian looked from Zamir's face up to the ceiling, tilting his head in the same direction. He gestured up at the lazily swirling fan.

"But then whenever we see it, it'll make us think of being here. Our happy place with all our happy people!"

Zamir grinned and wrapped both of his hands around Cillian's hand, kissing his knuckles. "I think it's a wonderful idea, my love."

Cillian giggled and rolled onto his stomach, nuzzling his nose against the front of Zamir's shoulder. "We could even decorate an entire wing like this place. All beachy and tropical, you know?"

"Another wonderful idea."

"You're such a sweet-talker," Cillian chuckled, his fingers ghosting over Zamir's ribs. He rolled on top. The sheets bunched around their waists. "You do know I'll still marry you even if you don't approve of a new fan in our bedroom, right?"

"Well, that's a relief."

"Cheeky!"

Zamir slid his hands down Cillian's lower back. His fingers sank into Cillian's arsecheeks. He switched their positions and straddled Cillian. Cillian's legs straightened to stretch toward the end of the bed. Zamir's face lowered to mouth over his fuzzy chest, and Cillian's fingers tightened in the back of his hair. Zamir snuffled as he kissed between his nipples.

"What's up, babe?"

"What's up?" Cillian asked, stroking through Zamir's thick hair. "What's up with what?"

"You made a funny sound."

Cillian scanned side to side as Zamir kissed lower on his chest. "Did I?"

They both slowed their movements. Their hands were gentler as they kissed and touched. A quiet cry sounded in the room and Cillian snorted. His breath rushed over Zamir's hair and fluttered the dark, messy strands.

"Okay, love, that was you this time."

"Me? What are you…."

Their brows rose in unison as their eyes arched toward the open glass door that led to their private pool. The pool was separated from the other bungalows by distance and a tall fence around the perimeter of their property, but sounds from nearby guests occasionally could be heard if they left their windows open.

Zamir asked, "Is that…."

Cillian's hand flattened over his own mouth and uncontrollable laughter snorted out of his nose. "Oh my God, is that *Luke*? And *Teddy*?"

The ecstatic, deep sounds grew louder through their open windows.

"Yeah, Jesus Christ, no wonder they skipped dinner," Zamir said on a laugh and laid his hand flat on his own cheek. His expression was scandalized. He covered his mouth. Both he and Cillian shuddered giggles while the sex soundtrack boomed. "They were so quiet this whole week! Is it a full moon or something?"

Cillian slapped the headboard with both hands. "Fuck yeah, Luke!" he shouted at the top of his lungs, banging the headboard louder. "Get it, bro!"

Zamir clapped his hand over Cillian's mouth and laughed so hard his stomach pushed the sheets down to the base of his cock. "Oh my God, shh, he's going to kill you! Shhh!"

Cillian's tongue licked Zamir's palm. Zamir lifted his hand and laced it in Cillian's hair.

"Whatever." Cillian spread his legs to wrap them around Zamir's thighs. "Sounds like he either didn't hear us, or he doesn't seem to care."

"We can barely hear them, anyway," Zamir said. Cillian kissed him between words. "It's like listening to two ghosts fuck."

"Teddy's a hot piece. I don't blame him."

"He really is." Zamir's mouth pursed, then fell at the corners as his brows furrowed. "Huh. They're… really going at it. I think Luke just came, for what it's worth." A pained, high whimper cut through the air, followed by another loud moan. "I guess that was Teddy." Cillian flipped Zamir onto his back with ease, grinning wickedly and pinning his wrists above his head. Zamir chuckled. "What?"

"Are you jealous?" Cillian asked, practically singing his question.

Zamir bent his legs. "Are you insane?"

Cillian flattened his hands on Zamir's smooth stomach, grinding his hips in a small circle.

"An old lover finding comfort in the arms of another man?" He ground down again. "That's juicy shit, love."

"We're about to get married," Zamir said on a rasped chuckle. He laced their fingers together. "I love you. I don't care if Luke is getting some. I'm very happy for him and Teddy."

"Did he make those noises when you two were together?"

Zamir's head rolled backward toward the sounds. "No," he said, slower. Cillian kissed up his neck, nibbling the fleshy softness beneath his jawline. "Not necessarily those exact noises."

"Oooh," Cillian said, laughing. "Very interesting."

Zamir snorted and rolled Cillian onto his back, the sheets bunching around their thighs.

"We were kids, Luke and I. You know we were each other's firsts. We barely knew what we were doing for the first year. I don't think we even knew what lube was the first time we tried anything."

"Fucking *ouch*."

"It was fine, though." Zamir ran his fingers through the front of Cillian's wild blond hair. Thoughtfully, he said, "The sex got to be pretty great, actually. Luke doesn't like being bad at things for long."

"I've always wondered if he's hung. He seems like he is."

Zamir tilted his head, dropping kisses on Cillian's collarbone. "He's a very nice size when he's hard, but he's got, like, surprising thickness on top of that. If there was a perfect thickness, he's got it. That was always my favorite part."

"Mmm." Cillian reached between Zamir's legs, gripping his cock. "Tell me more." He bit Zamir's earlobe. "I'm chubbing up."

Zamir pulled away, snorting. "I'm not telling you anything else about Lucas's cock. And, please, please, please stop saying *chubbing up*. That's, like, the least arousing of dirty talk."

Cillian's eyes were innocent and curious. "What about his balls? Can we talk balls? He seems like he'd have petite balls. Like two little strawberries or summat."

Zamir laughed and squirmed his hips. Cillian eased him onto his side. "They were fine balls that did not resemble strawberries. They were balls."

"I dunno, man," Cillian teased, stretching his arms up. He propped his hands behind his head, grinning. "Sounds like I've got some competition." He wiggled his eyebrows. "Old love dies hard, you know?"

"I obviously loved him then, and I love him now, it just—" He gestured between them. "—wasn't like this. And not like what I guess he has with Teddy.

It was different. We loved each other, but we weren't in love with each other. You know what I mean?"

All traces of teasing disappeared from Cillian's face. "I do, petal. I do."

LUCAS FELL onto his back, gasping for breath and his eyes wide. His ears were ringing. Teddy's equally heavy breaths pinged through the high frequency sounding between his ears.

"Oh my God," Lucas whispered. His feet flexed and his hands trembled uncontrollably. Even his toes were shaking. A dull, throbbing pleasure was trapped in his bones and vibrating through every inch of him. "Holy fuck," he panted, staring at the ceiling in complete, slack-jawed shock. Sweat poured down the front of his throat and pooled beneath his Adam's apple as Teddy's fingers stroked over the drenched center of his chest. "Jesus. Jesus Christ on a cross. Jesus, Mary and Joseph. Holy God."

"The gang's all here, hm?"

Lucas could not manage a turn of his head, but his eyes rolled toward Teddy's murmuring voice, satisfaction dripping from his every word. "I feel like I'm still coming," he rasped. Teddy grinned at him, his sweaty, wild hair covering half of his shining face. "How do I feel like I'm still coming?"

Teddy reached out and cupped Lucas's cheek. Their lips sucked for a long, languorous beat. He pulled back half an inch only to surge forward again, pressing a touch harder to tease their tongues together. Lucas moaned weakly. His fingers twitched as Teddy tongued him and uneven breaths puffed out of his nostrils. Teddy smoothed Lucas's hair off his forehead, kissing him more softly and thumbing his cheekbone. "It's a good look on you."

Lucas stared at him as if Teddy had switched languages midconversation. "What?"

"Satisfaction."

"Take it easy, Baby Mick. Take it easy. No need to plug one of your hits. You already got me in the sack."

Teddy chuckled and moved closer. His left leg slid over Lucas's thigh. He cradled Lucas's cheek, his gaze moving up and down his face as he leaned closer. Lucas's eyes fell shut before they kissed with a soft moan shared between them.

"I mean it," Teddy whispered, tracing the thin skin beside his eye. "You look like a teenager right now. More relaxed than after we got massages."

Lucas blew a breath out. "I wish I'd been having sex like that when I was a teenager." Teddy started to chuckle, and Lucas laughed as he said, "Maybe I wouldn't be such a pain in the arse in present day."

Teddy's giggles tapered off as he now touched the peak of Lucas's cheekbone. "You're not a pain in the arse."

Lucas blinked at him, his long lashes fluttering. "I'm not?"

Teddy shook his head. "No." Teddy stroked Lucas's collarbone with two fingertips. "Not at all."

"You're sure about that?"

"I'm sure." Teddy's eyes narrowed ever so slightly. "I'm very smart, you know."

Lucas's chest bounced as he hummed, low and slow and delighted. He nodded. "You are. That's very true."

TEDDY'S FINGERS walked lower, tapping over the soft flesh of Lucas's stomach as Lucas watched their journey. Teddy lowered his face to rest his cheek on Lucas's shoulder, starting to grin.

"What?" Lucas asked, tangling their fingers. He turned onto his side and slid his arm over Teddy's waist, his other curled between them. "What is it?"

Teddy thumbed Lucas's knuckles. "Rupert Street. 59 Rupert Street. In Soho." He nibbled his bottom lip, able to see realization click into place behind Lucas's eyes. "That's where I live. The code to the building is 2625, which spells out the word *cock*, though I'm not sure if the building owner did that on purpose or if it's a happy coincidence."

Their fingers slid together.

"Is that so?"

"It is. Apartment three."

"Are you going to invite me over for tea?"

"Of course," Teddy said, his eyes widening for a split second. "Tea." He kissed Lucas and they both smiled into the soft peck. "The D." He tried kissing him again, but both were laughing too loudly to get their mouths together. "All sorts of things."

THAT NIGHT, all sorts of things meant ordering room service at nearly midnight and a round of blowjobs in the outdoor shower, complete with eating fresh fruit and chugging ice-cold beers in the shower once they were finished sucking each other off.

"I'm so happy we finally had sex," Teddy said, bent over with his head between his legs. He rubbed his towel over the back of his hair, watching Lucas's legs lift up and down as he dried himself. "Now we can properly enjoy the rest of our time here."

"It's day five of the trip. We've been kissing constantly, we saw each other naked on day two, and we jerked each other off on day three. We're not exactly in a seminary."

Teddy flopped his hair back and stood up with sleepy eyes, drops of water still lingering between his pecs and around his navel. "That's true." He tilted his head and dried his hair, smiling crookedly. "I guess I just like getting fucked by you."

Lucas's towel dropped from his fingers. "Jesus Christ."

"Here we go with the religious talk again."

Lucas bent over to pick up his towel and a gentle slap landed on his left arsecheek. He laughed as Teddy strode past him, naked save for the towel looped around the back of his neck. Lucas heard his phone vibrate and glanced at the screen. A text from Lane arrived.

reminder: mum sleeps with the windows open. the woman who birthed you just heard you ask Teddy to come on your face. sweet dreams :)))

"Whoops," Lucas said under his breath.

They met in the en-suite. Lucas set up his toothbrush as Teddy got foam going in his mouth.

"Do you ever top?" Lucas asked, squirting toothpaste on his brush.

"Um." Toothpaste dribbled down Teddy's chin as he bent forward toward the sink. "Usually, yeah."

Lucas scrubbed his teeth for a moment, watching Teddy cup water from beneath the faucet and suck it into his mouth. "Usually?"

Teddy nodded, sloshing water from cheek to cheek. He spit. "Yeah." He dried his mouth with a fresh white hand towel. "That was usually what clients wanted if they were into anal. I guess there's a shortage of tops out there. Or maybe they wanted someone who knew what he was doing." He glanced at Lucas's groin in the mirror. "You could make a killing."

"But you're such an outrageous bottom."

Teddy laughed and dropped his towel on the countertop. "An outrageous bottom? Cheers. Not sure if I've been described as an outrageous bottom before, but I'll take it."

"I meant it in only the most complimentary way."

"I'm sure." Teddy reached for his first face product, glancing at Lucas with a small smile. "Are you asking all these questions because you would like to be fucked?"

Lucas snorted, his lashes fluttering. "Obviously."

"All right, then." Teddy knocked his right fist on the countertop. "Add it to the itinerary."

Lucas sucked a dribble of toothpaste back into his mouth, his fingers fumbling to wipe his chin. Teddy grinned at him in the mirror.

They finished up their en-suite tasks and moved into the bedroom. Lucas pulled down the covers on both sides of the bed, eying some sweat-darkened patches on the duvet. He gestured toward the spots. "I hope Cynthia won't be scandalized."

Teddy sat down with one leg crooked on the bed, his other touching the floor. The lights clicked off, stripes of moonlight shining on the bed. "She's been changing Zill's sheets," Teddy said, rubbing his ankle. "I'm sure she's seen enough lube to be numb to it by now."

"Ew, gross," Lucas chuckled quietly, resting one knee on the bed. He fingered the waistband of his loose black boxers as Teddy beamed up at him. His eyes darted to Teddy's middle for a split second. "So, you, uh, really do sleep naked."

Teddy looked down at himself to confirm that, yes, his cock was resting comfortably on top of the 1500-thread-count sheets. "Oh, yeah. Is that a problem?" He started to stand. "I can put on—"

"No, no. It's fine." Lucas looped his thumbs inside his waistband and pushed his boxers to the floor. The soft whoosh of fabric coincided with a bright smile lighting Teddy's face. Lucas waved one hand in lazy circles in the air, climbing into bed. "When in Rome, I suppose."

TEDDY MOVED closer to the middle, and Lucas pressed up against his front. The bed bounced beneath them, then settled. The expensive mattress cradled every inch of their closely cuddled bodies. Teddy watched Lucas's hand reach out. Gentle fingertips dragged from the top of his shoulder down his side and ended at the curve of his hip.

Lucas's voice seemed to be only half there as he said, "It's nice." His eyes focused on his own fingers as they traveled over Teddy's delicate ribs. Teddy nuzzled his cheek against his pillow.

"What is?"

"Having someone next to me," Lucas said, sounding even more secretive. "Someone warm and soft. And real." He touched Teddy's stomach, tracing around his lowest abs. "Sounds silly, I'm sure, but… it's been a while." Teddy said nothing, sneaking glances at Lucas's dreamy face as curious fingers touched all over his torso. "You have the softest skin I've ever felt," Lucas whispered, petting the very center of his chest with two fingertips. "Was one of the first things I noticed about you. Made me feel weak in the knees."

"What was the first thing?"

Lucas smiled slowly, letting his fingers travel around Teddy's nightingale. He kept his eyes on Teddy's chest. "Your annoying, sexy voice."

Teddy walked his fingers over Lucas's hip, flattening his hand on the small of his back. "I noticed your arse first," he said. Lucas's brows shot up, and Teddy grinned. "What? You sat down in the car like a proud turkey, big bum first. It was the first part of you I saw."

"How romantic," Lucas said, laughing as he spoke. "We should tell that story at our wedding. Love at first arse." Teddy's chuckles quieted, but his face warmed. Lucas blanched, frozen in place. "I—I meant that, um, as, uh," Lucas blabbered. "I didn't mean to, like, uh—"

"It's okay," Teddy said over him. His voice was low in pitch and soft in volume. Lucas blinked at him as Teddy squeezed Lucas's hip with gentle pressure. His dimple deepened and he moved closer. "You're right. It's a good story. And"—he joined their lips—"it's the truth."

Lucas's brows weakly twitched higher. Teddy kissed him again and cradled his lower back.

"I like the truth," Lucas breathed. Their lips brushed. "A lot. Fucking love it, actually."

"Me too. And I like…." Teddy paused, drawing circles on the base of Lucas's spine with his thumb. "I like this too. Having you next to me. It's…." His smile faltered for a moment while Lucas stared at him with his full attention. "It's been a long time for me too." He looked down at the mattress. "You know what I mean."

"I do."

Lucas tucked Teddy's hair behind his ear, smoothing his hand down the back of his neck, and Teddy looked up, his smile returning.

Teddy turned onto his back as Lucas pulled the covers higher. Teddy's hand cradled the back of Lucas's head to guide him down. Lucas smiled against his lips, his hand sliding up Teddy's side to squeeze his bicep. Teddy pursed his lips for another small kiss. Lucas's breath stuttered out of his nose. Teddy kissed Lucas's cheek, then smiled, rolling onto his side with his back to Lucas. Lucas snuggled up behind him, burying his face in Teddy's hair, both of his arms hugging Teddy to his chest.

"Night, fluffy-bum."

Lucas groaned through his nose with Teddy vibrating in his arms, his poorly muffled laughter brushing over his pillow.

"Night, honey bunch," Lucas replied. He smoothed his palm over the center of Teddy's chest. "Sugar pie, honey bunch."

Teddy gripped Lucas's forearm and hitched it higher on his chest, resting Lucas's arm almost around his neck. "I like that nickname," he whispered, brushing his toes over the bony tops of Lucas's feet. "Sugar pie, as well."

There was a pause, then Lucas said in a quiet, resigned voice, "I suppose I have… softened a bit when you use fluffy-bum." Teddy started to giggle, and Lucas stuck one finger out. "But only in private."

Teddy dragged his fingers over Lucas's wrist.

"Of course. Scout's honor." Teddy stared out the window at the moon, so bright and round it was as if it were sitting propped on their porch. He smiled faintly and rubbed his lips against Lucas's forearm. "I can't wait for tomorrow."

Lucas inhaled through his nose. When he spoke, his voice was already deepened by sleep. "Why?" he asked. "What's tomorrow?"

"I don't know, but every day with you gets better and better."

Lucas traced Teddy's middle knuckle and shuffled his legs under the blankets. "Even yesterday?"

Teddy nodded. His freshly washed hair brushed over Lucas's nose. "Even yesterday."

Lucas lifted himself high enough to press his lips to the back of Teddy's jawline. Teddy smiled with his eyes shut and Lucas tightened his arm, nuzzling his face against the back of Teddy's neck.

Chapter TWENTY-ONE

Thursday, April 30

SUNLIGHT HAD barely filled the room before Teddy's eyes opened. His long lashes slowly shimmered to look around the bright, airy space. The back of his head pressed deeper into his pillow. He turned his head to the right and smiled. Lucas's cheek rested against his shoulder. With an arm looped around his middle, his fingertips twitched in sleep.

"Hello there," Teddy whispered, so softly his breath didn't even ruffle Lucas's hair.

He watched Lucas sleep for a moment, hypnotized by the gentle exhalations out of Lucas's mouth, then placed his fingers around the top of Lucas's wrist and slowly, ever so slowly, lifted his arm off his torso. He replaced his own weight with a pillow and slid sideways, never looking away from Lucas's sleeping face. His tiptoed naked to the en-suite and pulled the door shut before turning on the sink to begin his morning-after routine.

First came toilet-related activities, which were dispensed with quickly and efficiently. Teddy washed his hands and dried them before pulling a candle out from under the sink and placing it on top of the toilet tank. The lemon candle was not his favorite scent, but it was his go-to for restrooms while traveling. He lit two matches and allowed them to burn for a few seconds, then blew them out and did a slow lap around the room.

Using a warm, soapy washcloth, he did a quick cleanup of his sweatier parts. A spritz of deodorant here and a cloud of cologne there mixed in with the lemon-scented bathroom. He set up his toothbrush and got foam going in his mouth. Teddy bent over and spit into the sink. He stuck his mouth under the faucet to suck water for a moment, then spit that out and dabbed the back of his hand on his lips.

He took a step back and lifted his arms above his head to slowly spin in front of the mirror. His eyes were focused yet moved quickly as he scanned his entire body. He dragged a small comb through the fine hair below his navel and under his arms. He used tweezers to snag two hairs that had sprouted a few inches below his right underarm. Teddy swapped his tweezers for lube. He squirted enough onto his fingers to get himself wet and stretched, yawning as he bent over the sink and fingered himself.

He washed his hands thoroughly and splashed cold water on his face, wiping any lingering sleep crust out of his eyes. His morning skincare routine was fairly basic; a cleanser and a light moisturizer.

Teddy looked in the mirror, tilted his head back, and flared his nostrils. He rooted around his toiletry bag and pulled out a tiny scissor, angling his face in the mirror and snipping inside his right nostril.

He rinsed the scissor and placed it back in his bag. He ran a hairbrush through his hair, the knotted bits in the back making him grit his teeth. He bent over and ruffled his hands through the back of his hair. He flipped his head backward for a fluff and pinched the ends of his curls. He twirled them around his fingers, dropped his head back, and ran his fingers through his hair, then smoothed it off his forehead and parted it to the left. A few finger scrunches at the scalp gave his part some volume.

He dabbed on under-eye cream and cocoa butter lip balm, blotting his mouth to take off most of the balm and leave a hint of creamy sweetness. A dollop of thin, unscented body oil spread over his torso and outer arms was just enough to make his skin feel soft and look a bit tawny.

He dunked his hands in the sink for one final, soapy wash. The air conditioner vent in the en-suite was above the toilet. He walked over to the stream of cool air, held his arms above his head, and let the air hit his front and back.

One more look in the mirror involved another slow spin. He bent and spread his cheeks apart for one last check, then blew out the candle and fanned the smoke around the room. He finished by tucking the candle under the sink and turning off the faucet.

He silently tiptoed back to bed less than five minutes since he'd left Lucas asleep. He had his routine down to a science.

He lay on his side and slid his feet under the duvet. Lucas was still asleep on his stomach. Teddy lifted Lucas's wrist and inserted himself in place of the pillow, nudging the back of his head sideways and scooting his bum over until his thigh was pressed to Lucas's knee. He tilted the top of his head toward Lucas and gave the front of his hair one more finger comb before relaxing his arms over his head at artfully bent angles.

Teddy cleared his throat quietly and nudged his toes against Lucas's ankle.

Lucas inhaled through his nose. His arm slid sideways to loop tighter around Teddy's stomach. He nestled his face on top of his shoulder. Teddy shut his eyes, curling his right arm around Lucas's shoulders and cuddling Lucas on top of his chest. The room was blissful, sunny, and quiet for a moment.

"That was quite a song and dance routine in there."

Teddy looked sideways. Lucas's eyes were closed, but his lips were curled in a tiny smile.

"You were awake?"

"I was."

"Psh. And here I was trying to be sexy for you. A waste of perfectly good body oil."

Lucas chuckled low in his throat, smoothing his hand up Teddy's side. "You are sexy." He adjusted his cheek on Teddy's chest, nuzzling closer to his collarbone, then smoothed his palm up Teddy's abs. "You don't have to do anything special for me. We've been sleeping in the same bed together for almost a week. You didn't primp those mornings."

"There wasn't a chance of you sniffing around those mornings."

"I'd happily sniff you preprimp. Any day of the week."

Teddy laughed. "Yeah, right," and turned onto his side.

Lucas propped his head on his hand, running his fingertips up and down the center of Teddy's chest.

"I'm serious, love," Lucas said, drawing soft circles between his pecs. "I want it all, morning breath and sweaty cuddles and everything." Teddy smiled as he looped his leg over Lucas's thigh. "If you feel more comfortable doing your whole prep routine, then, by all means, go for it."

"It's not so much a comfort thing. More like a habit."

"How about tomorrow you skip the routine?" Lucas circled his navel with soft fingertips. "I promise I'll make it worth your while."

Teddy thought for a moment, humming. As he thought, Lucas snuggled up closer, one hand cradling his cheek to press their closed lips together. Teddy smiled into the chaste kiss. Lucas inched his hands around his body toward his arse.

"I, however, will not subject you to my rank mouth right now," Lucas said, angling Teddy's hips and guiding him onto his stomach. Teddy gave him a bemused smirk before turning his head, resting his cheek on his pillow. "Well—" Lucas kissed the back of his shoulder, hands smoothing down over Teddy's cheeks. "—that's not entirely true."

"What do you mean?"

"While I don't have a preference about how you prep—" Lucas kissed between his shoulder blades, his skin still warm from sleep. "—I still can appreciate your hard work and perfect preparation." He kissed down the small of Teddy's back. Teddy's breath stuttered against his pillow. "You sore?"

"A little."

Lucas nosed lower, and eased Teddy's cheeks apart with his thumbs. "How sore?"

"Sore in the best way." Teddy spread his legs a touch, pressing his inner thighs to the mattress. "I'm fine."

Lucas's tongue teased the cleft of his arse. A shiver ran up the backs of Teddy's legs. Lucas whispered, "Gonna eat you out for a while. That good with you?"

"Y-yeah, yes, of—" Teddy's hips snapped backward. His eyes fluttered shut. Lucas held his hips and lifted him slightly, sliding his tongue between Teddy's cheeks. Teddy exhaled and said, "Of course," as he smiled.

"DUNNO IF I want an omelet today." Teddy placed his menu on the table. "Gonna go big." He stretched his arms above his head, and his bright yellow floral-print shirt rode up on his stomach. His voice was strained as he listed, "Pancakes, bacon and eggs, the works."

Lucas put his menu on his placemat. "Mmm, sounds good. I'm famished."

"Famished? You two? No," Lane scoffed, bouncing a snoozing Maggie on her knee. "Whatever did you do last night that would make you hungry?"

The other members of the breakfast table all snorted or chuckled behind their menus. Teddy ducked his face down, incredibly interested in the tiny white porcelain pitcher of milk resting beside his teacup.

"Dunno. I had a lovely snack before breakfast, but I'm still a bit hungry." Lucas petted Teddy's thigh and smiled at his sister. "May need another snack before dance lessons or I might not make it through."

"I love snacks," Maggie mumbled.

"As do I," Lucas replied.

"We get it." Lane rolled her eyes. "You're both ravenous." She held her hands over Maggie's ears and whispered, "For each other's cock."

"Elena!" Jo laughed, causing John to snort into his tea. She pointed from Lane to Lucas. "Jesus Christ, the two of you." She reached out and smoothed her hand over Marcy's hair. "How did you two turn out so filthy and my dear Marcy is so normal?"

Marcy smiled as best she could, a hangover pinching the corners of her mouth. She had on large black sunglasses and an oversized Flamingo Cove white polo with black bikini bottoms. Jo pulled her hand away from Marcy's hair. A few blades of grass were looped between her fingers. Jo's brows furrowed. "What's all this from?"

Marcy ran her hand through her hair. Grass fluttered down to her shoulders. “Oh, right,” she said slowly in her deep, raspy voice, nodding. She gave Jo an innocent shrug. “I had snacks on the golf course last night.” She refocused on her menu and sat up straighter. “Two snacks, actually.”

“FLOAT! FLOAT, my little waterlilies! I said float!” Chevy, Flamingo Cove’s resident dance instructor, gripped Zamir’s wrists and extended his arms straighter. “Zamir, watch those spaghetti arms! Leslie—”

“Chessie, sir.”

“Whatever. Your form is impeccable! Impeccable!”

Lucas muffled his snort against the top of Teddy’s shoulder as they attempted to float across the dance floor along with eleven other couples. He glanced at Lane, who was dragging Dean as best she could, and Marcy, who had yet to actually attempt a ballroom dance move, instead slow dancing with one of Zamir’s cousins off to the side. Some of the other couples took the lesson seriously and with proper posture. Most were humoring the grooms-to-be. Cillian was especially serious about getting his moves right.

Teddy’s mouth brushed Lucas’s ear. “Are we really having dance lessons to the soundtrack of *Dirty Dancing*?”

“Appears so,” Lucas whispered back. Teddy dipped him. They both started to snicker, then got serious as Chevy swirled past them. “First we had pottery, now dance lessons. We’re making the Patrick Swayze rounds.”

“We should go back to the cove and practice lifts.”

Lucas smiled wider than he thought was possible and hugged Teddy tighter. Teddy’s warm palm rubbed up the back of his tee.

“What is this form?” Chevy said, coming between them. He guided them apart and pulled Teddy’s arms straight, boosting Lucas’s back up by lifting his arse. Lucas’s eyes bulged and Teddy snorted before Chevy fixed him with a stare. They both furrowed their brows to appear serious. “We’re learning a foxtrot, darlings, not”—his upper lip snarled—“a rumba.”

He turned away from them, his green silk scarf slapping Lucas in the face.

Teddy whispered, “God forbid we learn a rumba.”

“I know. Filthy, filthy rumba.”

Teddy checked for their instructor and took a step closer as Lucas’s arms relaxed to lie atop his shoulders. They gently spun away from the group. Teddy ducked his head down as Lucas lifted himself on the balls of his feet. They kissed, soft and sweet, bodies swaying together.

Teddy whispered, "I can't get enough of you," before they kissed again and the tip of Lucas's tongue traced the seam of his mouth. Teddy tightened his hold around Lucas's lower back, their groins brushing together. "I wanna go rumba in our room, to be honest."

"Rumba in our room-ba?"

Teddy cackled, then pressed his face to Lucas's neck, stroking the back of his hair. "You're starting to make jokes like me. You're in trouble, Luke."

"Dear God," Lucas gasped, widening his eyes. "The island heat has gotten to my brain."

"All right, buttercups, all right," Chevy said, clapping his hands above his head. "Let's gather in the center. It's time to learn the moves for your wedding dance."

There were some murmurs of confusion until Cillian explained. "We want everyone to learn the same dance! So at the reception we can all surprise the other guests!" He bounced up and down while Zamir stood calmly at his side. "Like a flash mob!"

A few more members of the wedding party came in at the last minute, fattening the group up to thirty-four.

"Anyone else?" Chevy asked, sticking his head into the hallway.

"We're coming!" Albert and Anna hurried into the room. Their comfortable travel clothes were coordinated around the colors magenta and white, as if they knew the official color scheme of Flamingo Cove. Lucas smiled wide and waved at Albert and Anna. Cillian and Zamir ran to greet them at the door.

"So sorry we're late," Albert said, his words muffled by Zill's combined megahug. "Our ferry was slower than anticipated. Hello, everyone!"

"Welcome, welcome, lovely to see you, all right, get a move on," Chevy said, prying Albert from Zamir and Cillian's arms. He shooed Albert and Anna to one of the rows, placing them beside Lucas and Teddy. "Now." Chevy clapped his hands twice above his head. "Let us begin!"

"Hey, mate," Lucas whispered, holding his hand out. He and Albert bumped fists. Anna waved from beside him. "Glad you're here."

"Us too," Albert whispered. He smiled at Teddy and waved. "Hey, Jack! You having fun so far? This is a big, fun bunch, yeah?"

Lucas and Teddy both froze in place, but the song "My Type" by Saint Motel started to boom from the sound system before Teddy could reply. Lucas noticed Zamir lean back to glance at them.

"Who's Jack?" Zamir asked curiously.

"All right, everyone," Chevy said, "feel the beat. Feel the rhythm. Clap for me." He swirled his hands in the air in front of his face as brass brought in the introduction. The group clapped to the beat. "We shall step left for four counts, then right for four counts, then pound our right feet on the floor four times. Ready? Of course you're ready!"

"Did he say four as in the number or, like, for spelled *f-o-r*? Floor? Four?" Dean hissed to Lane.

"Just follow the moves," Lane said, gripping his hand. "Pretend it's the Electric Slide."

Dean nodded and shook out his shoulders, kicking one leg in front of himself. "I fucking love the Electric Slide."

"Now, let's have the first three rows form a circle, with the other three rows forming a circle around them," Chevy said, tugging people by their shirts to place them. "Circles, people! Circles inside of circles! Now, turn toward each other. Turn, I said!"

In the movement to get into position, Lucas lost Teddy, though he looked from Teddy to Albert every few seconds. Jo and John came between them, with Zamir and Cillian facing Teddy and Albert from the inner circle.

"Nice form, Taz," Cillian said, winking at Teddy. Both swayed their hips side to side as per Chevy's instruction. "Get those Jagger hips moving."

"Who's Taz?" Albert asked.

"Teddy," Cillian chuckled, "duh."

Albert blinked at Teddy once, and the entire group waved their hands above their head.

"Jack?"

Zamir glanced at Lucas, but Chevy shouted, "Spin, inner circle, spin!" which gave Teddy and Albert the chance to move away from Zamir's curious stare. Teddy strained his neck to find Lucas.

The group started a chicken dance sort of elbow movement

"Who's Jack?" Jo asked. She looked baffled at Teddy. "Jack? No." She shook her head. "Teddy." She and John started the macarena, Jo repeating, "Teddy," and nodding at Albert. "Teddy Bennet."

"Jack McQueen," Albert said, his face scrunched. He glanced at Lucas, who was receiving an even more distressed stare from Teddy. "Right? Apologies, sir, I'll have to reorder your address book if I'm mistaken."

"Why do you keep calling him Jack?" Zamir asked Albert, despite the shift in the circle. He looked between Teddy and Lucas. "Who's Jack?"

Albert started to say, "Jack is—"

"It's a nickname." Lucas switched places with Lane. He did the cha-cha as Teddy mirrored him. "I said he looked like Captain Jack Sparrow when we first met."

"On Halloween," Teddy said, sounding relieved. "Though I wasn't technically in costume."

The group all nodded as they cha-chaed, most making quiet *aww* sounds.

"That's adorable," Jo chuckled, squeezing Teddy's bicep. "I'm shocked you gave him a chance after receiving such cheekiness."

"I liked it," Teddy said as Lucas grinned. "I believe he called me 'the ghost of Mick Jagger's youth' as well."

The surrounding dancers all laughed loudly, Teddy included.

"But you were in LA on Halloween this past year," Albert said to Lucas, his look of confusion growing. His mental address book pages no doubt flurried behind his eyes, and he and Anna performed a graceful waltz as per Chevy's instructions. Albert tilted his head. "Weren't you? The Klein-Gross merger?"

Teddy said, "As was I. In LA, I mean. I was there for—" He glanced at Lucas, who did nothing but continue dancing with wide eyes. "—a convention."

"For what?" Zamir asked as he was dipped by Cillian.

"Photography," Lucas and Teddy said at the same time. Teddy's eyes shimmered with amusement despite the layer of stress sweat forming on Lucas's forehead.

Albert wiped sweat off his brow. "But… I thought you said they kept you all in the conference room the entire time?"

"We met in a cab," Lucas said. He and Teddy were now facing each other. Teddy's full smile emerged as he reached for Lucas's hips. "We were battling it out for the same car."

"Oh, that's right," Lane said, nodding. She and Dean were doing the Electric Slide. "Teddy mentioned that. The cab thing."

Chevy stomped his foot on the wood floor and clapped his hands. "I'm sorry, are we interrupting your social hour?" he asked, with one hand on his hip, the other flared in the air. "I thought we were here to dance? Get dancing, people!"

Chapter TWENTY-TWO

"FUCK, YOU were so good at dodgeball."

Lucas tilted his head as Teddy kissed toward his collarbone. "I was all right." He held Teddy around his lower back. "You're such a good dancer."

"I think you're better than I am."

"No way."

Teddy walked Lucas backward as his hands slid up the bottom of Lucas's white V-neck. He lay on top of Lucas as Lucas sprawled on his back, their motions smooth when compared to the frantic presses of their lips. Lucas unbuckled his belt and pulled at the leather.

"Wait," Teddy breathed, placing his hand over Lucas's. His smile went crooked. "I wanna touch you for a bit."

Lucas held his hands out. "Have at it. Figured the whole, uh, no pants thing would help with any touching."

Teddy kissed the lowest point of his V-neck, tugging the neckline to the side to bite a kiss on his pec. He rubbed the crotch of Lucas's tight khaki shorts. Lucas felt himself stir. All their kissing and petting from the tipsy walk back to their bungalow rushed directly to his cock. He watched Teddy's eyes widen slightly, and he cupped a hand around the growing bulge pressing the material of Lucas's fly outward.

Teddy glanced at him mischievously. "I like to watch this part."

"The—" Lucas's breath caught, and Teddy's hand tightened while he sucked gently on Lucas's nipple, his tongue dampening the thin fabric. "The what part?"

"How it moves," Teddy whispered, kissing up to his neck. He laved his tongue over his pulse point. Lucas's cock hardened even more under his hand. The material tented and took on the thick shape growing down his inner thigh. "How it sort of twitches a bit in your pants."

Lucas could feel himself throbbing. His heart pounded in the same rhythm as his eyes fluttered shut. "Okay."

Teddy chuckled lowly and pulled down the zip of Lucas's trousers. "Weird?"

"No. Not at all. I just didn't realize how hot I'd get from someone fondling me through my khakis."

Teddy eased Lucas's khakis and boxer briefs down at once, leaving him in only his tee. He pulled the material over his ankles.

"Do you think you'll get hot when I fuck you?"

Lucas whipped his tee off. "I believe so, yes."

Teddy grinned and swatted Lucas's tee away from his face, crawling closer. Lucas reached out and snagged the collar of his open button-down, which was sheer and floral. He spread his legs and pulled Teddy onto his body.

"Get those silly trousers off," Lucas said, pushing the shirt off his broad shoulders.

Teddy hummed into their kisses, reaching down to unbutton his jeans. "You said my arse looked good in them."

"Your arse looks good in anything, but looks especially good when you have on no trousers at all."

Teddy shimmied his hips, and Lucas pushed his trousers low on the backs of his thighs. The jeans got caught on one of Teddy's ankle boots. Lucas dotted kisses over his upper back as Teddy chuckled breathily and struggled to get his boot off. When both boots and his jeans hit the floor, Lucas rolled away from him, searching through the bedside table.

"Like a bloody Rolodex," Lucas murmured to himself, flipping through the variety of condoms and lubes. "All the colors of the rainbow."

"Flavors too." Teddy reached over Lucas's shoulder and plucked a packet of lube out of one of the pockets.

"Not banana?" Lucas asked, taking two condoms out. "Shocking."

"Not tonight." Teddy moved lower on the bed, holding both sides of Lucas's hips. He kissed the lowest point on his spine. "Tonight, I think you're gonna taste like cola."

Lucas squeezed the packet of condoms. Teddy's hot breaths panted lower, between his cheeks. The hair on his lower back stood up straight. "Babe, just because I did it to you, doesn't mean you have to do it to me."

"But I want to." Teddy kissed his right cheek, nosing the plump curve and kissing closer to the center of his body. "This arse was put on this planet to be eaten." His hands smoothed up Lucas's ribs, sinking down to gently squeeze his hips. "May I?"

"I mean, yeah, sure, of course," Lucas blurted out, his body going limp. "If you… if you want, of course. Yeah."

"Of course. Yeah. Of course."

"Shut up," Lucas laughed. Teddy punctuated each repetition with a kiss closer to his entrance. "Oh, do you—Should I go prep? Is that what you're used to? What do you like?"

Teddy chuckled lowly and drizzled lube between Lucas's cheeks. The muscles of Lucas's arse flexed as he spread his legs wider.

"Nah," Teddy said, dragging his thumb down Lucas's crack from the very top to the back of his balls. Lucas's pale pink skin glistened, and his opening winked each time Teddy smoothed his slick thumb over it. "You're clean. I want you just like this."

"But with hair and all?"

Teddy leaned down, blowing cool air over Lucas's arsehole before he laved a slow line with the flat of his tongue. Lucas's legs shifted on the bed, and his quiet gasp was nearly drowned out by Teddy's wet, slurped lick.

"Especially hair and all," Teddy murmured, thumbs spreading his cheeks wider. "Fuck." He licked quickly two times. "You feel so good under my tongue. So fucking hot."

He gripped both of Lucas's arsecheeks and squeezed, massaging the thick muscles as he pressed his face between his cheeks. Lucas's eyes widened and he stared at the headboard. Shadows from the ceiling fan rotated in and out of his hazy line of vision as he pushed out quiet, breathy whimpers beyond his control.

Teddy licked and sucked and nibbled, exhaling huffed, hungry sounds every few motions. Drool pooled below Lucas's balls on the duvet, Lucas squirming every few licks.

"Are you going to finger me or what?"

Teddy stifled a laugh and pushed the tip of his tongue inside Lucas, prompting another high sigh and squirm. He licked his mouth, letting his tongue brush over Lucas's twitching entrance. "Do you want me to?"

Lucas looked over his shoulder, fresh sweat glistening between his shoulder blades. "You could do this to me for hours and I'd be ecstatic, but I also want to get fucked tonight. Want you."

Teddy kissed his lower back and lifted himself, reaching out for a condom. "Hours, hm?"

"Days."

"Now we're talking."

Lucas pulled himself up higher on the bed. Teddy's fingers lightly touched over the backs of his knees.

"You wanna be on your front?"

"Yeah."

Teddy kissed up the center of his spine, and Lucas arched his back beneath him. "You're not gonna let me see your pretty face when you come?"

"I haven't bottomed in a while and you're enormous. It'll be better on my front this time."

Teddy hummed and smoothed his hands up to Lucas's shoulder blades. "Can you roll over for a minute? Just a minute, please."

Lucas rolled onto his back, bouncing closer to Teddy's knees. He grabbed a pillow and went to put it under his back. Teddy took the pillow from him and tossed it at the end of the bed.

Lucas chuckled. "What?"

Teddy got between his legs, one hand flat on the front of Lucas's shoulder, the other sliding up his inner thigh. His slippery fingers slid between his cheeks, and the top of his hand nudged Lucas's balls. He kissed Lucas's nipple, kissing to his right with slow, deliberate presses of his lips, letting his mouth drag through his soft chest hair. He pushed his middle finger inside him as he sucked his nipple into his mouth. Lucas's chest swelled and his arse arched lower.

"Fuck," Lucas said, digging his heels into the bed. He squirmed, but Teddy's finger only pressed firmer, locating his prostate and teasing at the sensitive bump. Teddy made another hungry sound as he sucked the center of Lucas's chest. Lucas repeated, "Fuck," in a softer, higher voice, hypnotized by the graceful fall of Teddy's waves over his eyes.

Two of Teddy's long fingers entered him, gentle but with firm enough pressure to pull a low, clucked groan from Lucas's throat. Lucas stared up at the ceiling as he breathed quicker. Teddy brought their faces level and flattened one leg on top of Lucas's spread thighs, his fingers still pumping in and out of him, his cock throbbing against Lucas's hip.

Lucas turned his head, exhaling a weak sound that was cut off by Teddy's mouth, and laced his free hand in the back of Lucas's sweaty hair. Teddy's fingers barely teased over the flesh of Lucas's balls to drag up his cock, tiptoeing around his dripping head. The lightest brush over Lucas's slit made Lucas shiver and shift his legs under Teddy's weight.

Teddy brought his fingers back between his cheeks, giving him a hint of two fingertips before he walked them to his balls. Lucas squirmed, making an audible sound of frustration that Teddy caught on his tongue. The cola was sticky-sweet between their kisses.

"Where do you want me to touch you?" Teddy murmured, deep and slow, his eyes scanning over Lucas's face. Lucas felt as if he were falling backward into the very stuffing of their mattress, but Teddy's eyes, kind and relentless and calm, held him in place above the soft surface. "Here?" Teddy kissed him as he gave him one loose stroke. Lucas's lower abs twitched. Teddy palmed his balls, massaging them in his hand, letting his mouth linger a breath away from Lucas's. "Or here?"

Lucas reached between his legs and gripped Teddy's wrist, guiding his hand lower until their fingers slid between his slippery cheeks.

"Fucking here," Lucas said. Teddy's tongue teased into his mouth. Lucas tilted his head as Teddy bit his bottom lip and pressed two fingers inside. Lucas cried out and bucked upward, Teddy tightening his hand in his hair and kissing him again. "Fuck yes, love."

Teddy pulled back an inch to breathe hot and fast over Lucas's mouth while his fingers sped up. Lucas lifted his face and their lips tangled together. Teddy moaned quietly into their kiss as Lucas's arse clenched around his wet fingers.

Lucas broke their kiss and looked at Teddy, his eyes heavy. Teddy shifted his leg enough to let Lucas turn over onto his stomach. Teddy kissed down his back, gripping his hips and pulling his arse in the air. He placed a pillow under Lucas's groin. Teddy rolled the condom on with practiced ease, and he squeezed the rest of the lube on his cock, giving himself a few quick strokes before smearing the rest of the slickness on Lucas's opening.

He enveloped Lucas from behind. The tip of his cock bumped against Lucas's entrance. Lucas made a quiet, whimpering sound into his own forearm. Teddy wrapped one arm around Lucas, from the top of his shoulders to his chest. He looped his other arm up from his lowest ribs until his hands rested on Lucas's chest.

Teddy kissed behind Lucas's ear and ground against him, the head of his cock pressing inside.

"A-ah," Lucas cried out deeply, his head falling forward with his eyes shut.

TEDDY SQUEEZED him tighter, making a small circle with his hips to thrust again. Lucas clenched his teeth, breathing fast through his nostrils. Their erratic breaths and the dull rub of sweaty skin against sheets were the only sounds in the moonlit room. Teddy kissed the back of his neck, flattening his hands to rub soothing strokes over his chest and stomach. Lucas gripped the top of Teddy's hand.

"One… one second," Lucas whispered, out of breath. He swallowed and squeezed Teddy's hand. "Just a second. Just need to adjust."

"Y'all right?" Teddy kissed his cheek, angling his face to kiss along his sweating jawline. "Is it too much? You're tight. Like—" He looked down to where they were joined, only about two inches of his cock inside of Lucas. "—really tight. I don't want to hurt you."

"It's fine. It's perfect. I just—" Lucas tilted his left hip a touch lower than his right, digging his feet into the bed. "I need to move. To change position a bit." He arched his lower back and tightened around the head of Teddy's cock, exhaling smoothly and relaxing his upper body on the bed. "I'm fine."

"Want more lube? I highly recommend the grape flavor when mixed with cola."

Lucas snorted while Teddy chuckled against the back of his neck. "No, I'm plenty lubed up, thanks."

"We could always borrow some from Zill."

That pulled a louder laugh from Lucas. Teddy kissed his ear and started to thrust again, able to feel Lucas trembling around his cock. A broken moan interrupted Lucas's laughter. Teddy kissed down his neck as his hips gently slapped Lucas's plump arse.

Teddy sucked Lucas's neck. "Better?" he exhaled. Teddy's mouth followed the motion of Lucas's nod to continue kissing him. He cupped both of Lucas's arsecheeks, his fingertips digging into the thick muscles. "Fuck, your arse is so fucking good. You're sure you're, *ungh*—" He sucked the salty skin behind Lucas's ear. "Better?"

"Much."

"Good."

Lucas placed his hands flat on the bed and arched his back. "I'm gonna get on my hands and knees. Will be even better."

Teddy sat back on his heels, bracing himself on either side of Lucas's hips. His cock slipped out of Lucas's arse. Lucas crawled higher on the mattress and gripped the headboard, one hand lowering to the mattress to hold his body up. He glanced over his shoulder and smiled, dark fringe falling in his eyes.

"Come on, then."

Teddy came up behind him; Lucas bent forward and dug the balls of his feet into the mattress.

"I'm making an executive decision." Teddy opened the bedside table drawer. Lucas's brow furrowed as Teddy retrieved a small purple packet of lube. He dropped a clear dollop onto Lucas's arsehole, smoothing his thumb around the inside of his rim. "It'll help."

"We're going to have to call room service for fresh pillows and linens. Wow, that really smells like grape."

"Or we could sleep outside tonight."

LUCAS SMILED, able to imagine the dreaminess written all over his own face even without looking in a mirror. Teddy's blazing heat enveloped him from behind, resuming his position in an all-encompassing bear hug. Lucas let out a long, low groan and arched his lower back. Teddy pressed inside him so firm and hard and thick that the insides of Lucas's throat felt swollen. Teddy's hand wrapped around his cock, Lucas pushing himself backward to meet each slow grind.

"Oh, fuck yes," Teddy whispered, resting his forehead on the back of Lucas's shoulder. He breathed, "Fuck. That's so good. M-much better."

Lucas tilted his head and reached behind himself, gripping the back of Teddy's hair. He guided him closer and sucked a kiss to his mouth. Teddy pushed forward and Lucas pushed back. Low, quiet moans bounced into each other's mouths.

The change in position got the best of them in a matter of minutes. Teddy's hips stuttered and he dug his fingernails in the sides of Lucas's arse. Lucas pushed back with both hands on the headboard.

"Fucking pound into me, love," Lucas panted as he shuddered. His lower back muscles fluttered and clenched beneath the layer of sweat shining over his body. "Fucking yes, Teddy, so fucking hard. God, you're so big, J-Jesus, *fuck*."

Teddy groaned and buried his face in Lucas's neck as he came. He shot hot into his condom, his trembling mouth drooling on Lucas's skin.

"Oh God," Teddy rasped. Nonsense words were forced out of his mouth as come pulsed out of his body and he slid his mouth over the sweaty skin of Lucas's upper back. "Fuck, Lucas, shit," he babbled, his hips hiccuping as he thrust. "I n-never come first, fucking hell. You feel so fucking good, love, so fucking—Fuck—"

The sound of Teddy's wrecked voice made Lucas whimper louder, his body shaking and his arms aching. Teddy pulled out and got down onto his belly, gripping Lucas's cheeks and spreading him open.

Lucas's arms gave out and he flattened on his stomach. Teddy's face was between his cheeks before he could even breathe. Lucas gasped out a rough, choppy grunt, and bent his right leg. Teddy's hair tickled the bottom curves of his arse.

"Teddy—"

Teddy hummed deeply and slithered his tongue inside of Lucas's loosened, sore muscles, and jerked him with quick, tight motions. Lucas made a sobbing sound, sliding his feet on top of the duvet and bucking his hips backward.

"Teddy," he moaned louder, digging his fingers and toes into the bed. "Oh, God, fuck—Teddy—"

Teddy's hums deepened to growled sucks. His right hand worked over Lucas's cock, two of his fingers massaging Lucas's prostate in time with his wanks.

"Oh God," Lucas gasped, spurting over Teddy's fist. A dull pain clenched within his brain for a split second, only to release a shower of tingling, burning pleasure deep enough to melt his skin off his bones. "Oh fuck, holy—holy fuck!"

Teddy moaned along with him, licking and prodding with his tongue as Lucas shuddered and shook, come dripping down his knuckles.

Lucas exhaled, "Oh," and shuddered before his body went limp. His shoulder blades popped with each quick breath. He repeated, "Oh," softer, his arse clenching around Teddy's tongue.

Teddy gave him one more slow lick, and Lucas whimpered quietly. He rubbed his palms over Lucas's arsecheeks, squeezing his hips and kissing up until he reached the small of his back.

"Teddy."

"Hmm?"

Lucas looked over his shoulder. Teddy smiled lasciviously at him, his mouth shining as if he'd coated himself in grape-flavored lip gloss.

"I might have to marry you, Theodore."

Teddy's pleasure only grew, tongue darting out the right corner of his mouth. "Is that so?"

Lucas flopped into the pile of sweaty pillows. "Fucking hell. You fucking go for it, don't you? Like, really, really go for it."

"I do try my best."

"This bed is destroyed. It's a mess."

Teddy flopped onto his back and tucked his arms behind his head. His bum must have hit something damp and he shifted his hips. "It sort of is."

Lucas picked up on the sharp, metallic smell of Teddy's sweat. "We're gross."

"I like us gross," Teddy said, unbothered.

Lucas's lashes brushed the pillow beneath his face, and his gaze scanned Teddy's sprawled, relaxed body. He smiled, half his face hidden by pillow. "I like us as an *us*."

Teddy turned his head and grinned, rolling his ankle to bump their toes together. "I do too."

Lucas lifted himself on his forearm and wiggled closer. He dropped down half on top of Teddy's body, nuzzling under his arm. The strong smell of fresh sweat was even more potent from his position, but he couldn't stop rubbing his face against Teddy's skin. Teddy wrapped his opposite arm around Lucas's back, thumbing between his shoulder blades.

"I suppose we could just sleep without the duvet tonight," Lucas said, nuzzling closer. "And tip Cynthia heavily tomorrow before we beg her to firebomb it."

"We could. Or," Teddy drawled, dragging his thumb down his lower back. "We could shower and then have a sleepover on the beach."

"Hippie," Lucas said as Teddy chuckled quietly. Lucas kissed the front of his shoulder. "That sounds like a lovely idea. Although, might I suggest a swim instead of a shower?"

"Yes, please," Teddy's voice was tight as he stretched his legs. "Love that idea. Extra points if we skinny dip."

"Of course we'll be skinny dipping. Might as well get our outdoor antics in. Once we're back in London, I'm not sure how many outdoor activities we'll get into. The weather isn't as forgiving of nudity."

"You could fuck me on your balcony. Blankets do exist, you know."

"God, you're so clever. Getting me hard again so fast. C'mere, love."

Chapter TWENTY-THREE

Friday, May 1

THE SUNRISE spread over their sleeping bodies without any limitations of windows or curtains or blinds. Lucas opened his eyes first and blinked slowly. His nose was full of crunchy, salt-scented hairs. He tightened his arm around Teddy's waist. Teddy hummed as he inhaled, his sandy feet brushing Lucas's ankles.

The night before, they had decided that their duvet was filthy enough that a night on the sand wouldn't do much more harm. They'd grabbed their coconut-scented beach blanket to lie on and two pillows, plus a few beach towels. They had a swim and splashed around beneath the full moon. Humid, starlit air clung to their skin as they kissed and touched each other, the chest-deep water warm enough for a bathtub.

Now bathed in sunlight, Lucas gently brushed sand off Teddy's bare shoulder and kissed the base of his neck. Teddy inhaled again and shifted backward. Lucas's thumbs rubbed the lowest part of his hairline, the baby-soft hair, which pulled purrs from Teddy. Teddy did not disappoint, exhaling pleased, deep hums as Lucas stroked the spot.

"Open your eyes, honey bunch," Lucas whispered, smoothing his hand over Teddy's chest. He peered at the view with his chin pillowed on Teddy's warm skin. "You'll love the colors."

Teddy's sleepy eyes cracked open for a handful of tiny blinks. A wild gradient of oranges and reds and pinks and even purples stretched above the calm blue horizon.

"S'beautiful," he mumbled, his voice low and scratchy. Lucas hitched the duvet up to their necks, replacing his arm around Teddy's middle. "You're beautiful."

"You can't even see me," Lucas said, smiling against his neck.

Teddy rubbed their feet together. "I just know."

Lucas smiled wider, letting his eyes fall shut. He felt Teddy shifting in his arms to spin around. Sand brushed over his skin despite their best efforts to keep their blanket free of it. Teddy tucked his face into the space between Lucas's neck and shoulder. Lucas ran his fingers through the front of Teddy's hair, smoothing it down until he cradled the back of his neck. He kissed his forehead.

"You're beautiful," Lucas said softly, then kissed his brow. "So beautiful."

Teddy's tiny blinks were directed up at his face. "You got your wish. I'm dirty and sweaty and squinty and my hair's a mess and I haven't moisturized yet." Teddy licked his own mouth and wrinkled his nose. "And I taste bad. Like, really bad."

Lucas's eyes crinkled, and his hand was soft on Teddy's cheek. "Still beautiful. More than most could ever wish to be."

Teddy walked his fingers up Lucas's side. "And you said you weren't sweet."

Lucas's cheeks heated. "I know. You keep proving me wrong."

"I have a knack for it."

"You do."

"I… I'm… I love you," Teddy said, surprised yet calm. "I'm in love with you. I wanted to say it because I've been thinking it, and I want to be honest with you, even if you think I'm crazy for falling in love with you so fast. But I did. Fall in love with you, I mean. And that's that."

Lucas smiled, tugging a springy curl near Teddy's right ear. "I love you too," he said simply. Quietly. Teddy exhaled a high sound. His face flushed and his eyes curved happily. Lucas cradled his cheek. "And I am so, so in love with you. Crazy fast or not. It doesn't matter because it's true. I rather like telling the truth. So there you have it."

Teddy tilted his forehead forward as their smiles widened. He dug his fingers into Lucas's upper back.

"You love me?" he asked, excitement raising his tone. "You do?"

"I love you," Lucas chuckled quietly. "I do."

Teddy's eyes rivaled the blazing sun behind his shoulder. "You're certain?"

"I'm very certain. I'm not much for hemming and hawing. When I know I like something, I like something."

"You said you moved fast in business but not in relationships."

Lucas blew air out and waved his hand between them. "What the fuck did I know? I was a fool. I didn't know you and I hadn't… I hadn't yet tried to let you get to know me. I…. Do you feel like you know me?"

"Of course." Teddy snuggled closer, resting his head on a pillow. "You know how I said I read about you for research for the gala?"

"Yeah?"

"When I saw you worked for the same company as Mr. Carson, I… had a minor heart attack, but then I hoped—I prayed—that I'd get to see you that night. That I'd get to talk to you. And I'm not usually the praying type."

Lucas's fingertips trailed down the center of Teddy's chest. "But I was wretched to you when we met in the car. I was a brat."

"Not really. I was a dick to you too."

"Were you?"

"I thought so. I was cranky from work."

"Why did you want to see me again?"

"Because you treated me like a normal person, even when you found out what I did. You didn't pity me. You didn't judge. And you didn't handle me with kid gloves. You teased me a bit and made me laugh, and you were so, so quick. I loved that." Teddy thumbed Lucas's cheekbone. "You were also so hot in that suit that you helped me through a rather dull client that week."

"Oh my God," Lucas laughed, nudging his fingers against Teddy's navel. Teddy giggled and shifted his hips. "That's bizarre."

"But more importantly—" Teddy slid his hand down the front of Lucas's neck. "—I think I just got the vibe that you were good. That you had a good heart, even if you didn't think so."

"There is no way you got that from our first meeting. And then how I behaved at the gala? Nope. No way."

"I did. I could tell from how you spoke to your mum. How you talked to the driver. How you looked when you listened to your messages. Your reaction when I made a jab about the wedding." Teddy tapped his thumb on the center of Lucas's chest. "Perceptive, remember?"

Lucas rolled Teddy onto his back, lying on top of him. He cupped his face. Teddy lifted his head enough for a firm, closemouthed kiss.

"So." Lucas kissed his chin. "What now?"

"I think it's a little early for breakfast, but we could check the kitchen to see if they've got some fruit or something. I'm hungry too."

Lucas chuckled quietly. "No, like, when we leave here. What's next?"

"Oh."

Lucas's eyes widened. "Obviously, I want to be with you, but… but only if you want to be with me. Obviously."

"Of course I want to be with you." Teddy's forehead wrinkled. "More than anything. The nightingale and the lion, remember?"

Lucas watched Teddy trace circles on the bare, unmarked skin over his heart.

"Does this mean I need to get a lion tattoo?"

"Oh, yes, please! I can help you pick the spot."

Lucas laughed as Teddy squeezed his bum. "I want you to take the lead in terms of what we tell people," Lucas said, seriousness adding depth to his soft, raspy voice. "Like, about us. About what you do." Discomfort flickered on Teddy's face, the flicker lasting a second too long for Lucas to miss it. "We don't have to tell anyone, if you don't want to. It's whatever you want."

"Not everyone is as open-minded as you are, love. Like… what if we tell Lane and then she thinks I'm some sort of pervert? And doesn't want me around Maggie?"

Lucas's face scrunched. "Lane would never do that."

"I'm not specifically talking about Lane, I just meant, like, you know." Teddy swirled his hand in the air. "That situation. People not wanting to be around me because of what I did for a living. And what about you? You want people knowing you were with an escort?"

"You haven't been an escort for the trip and we weren't together when you were working. You were never an escort for me."

"But you want other people, colleagues and friends and family members, to know that your boyfriend had sex with people for money?"

"You said it was mostly escorting and not all sex."

Teddy rolled onto his side, leaning his weight on his forearm. "I know, and that's the truth, but it doesn't erase the fact that I have exchanged money for sex. Do you think your boss will be so open? Potential clients?"

Lucas propped himself up. "My boss, and the majority of my clients, would burst into flames upon entering a religious structure of any kind. They've got enough skeletons in their closets to walk a fashion designer's runway show. They can pretend to be perfect, but they're not. Far from it. No one is."

"And you don't care if people know about my past?"

"I don't know why it would be any of their business, to be honest. My mum and family will continue to worm their way into whatever aspect of our lives they can manage, but that doesn't mean I'm going to share every private detail between us with the world. Things between us will remain between us. And, like I said, the ball is in your court. I'm not going to tell anyone anything, and you don't have to tell anyone anything, but the power is with you."

Teddy smiled crookedly, brushing his fingers over Lucas's lower belly. "How'd you get to be so gentlemanly?"

"I have no idea. This is all new to me. I was a right tit before you."

They both laughed. Teddy shook his head. "That's not true at all. Your family and friends practically kiss the ground you walk on."

Lucas shrugged, watching Teddy's fingers travel over his soft abs, his fingertips gently poking at the small layer of pudge sticking out from his baggy athletic shorts.

"I try to believe I'm someone who thinks rationally and logically," Lucas said, wrapping his foot around Teddy's ankle. Teddy's eyes moved up to his face, as he still stroked his navel. "I'd never ask another person to change their life for me, to change their job for me, especially not immediately upon starting a relationship. I'm only wondering how… how is this going to work, um, physically? If you…."

Lucas dropped his gaze. "Are you… like… with other guys. Are you going to be with other guys for work the minute we get back to London?" He held one palm out, bringing their eyes level. "I don't want you to lose any money or mess with your schedule and I don't want to pressure you. I trust you. I trust that you can keep your work separate. But my only concern is if you have clients who know me, and then… then it might seem like we're not really real, you know? I don't care if people know what you do, if that's what you want to put out there. I don't care what anyone thinks of me. But I don't want to confuse people, you know what I mean?"

Teddy smiled slowly, as if he were savoring a delicious secret blooming in his chest. He dragged his fingers in a circle around Lucas's left nipple, walking his fingertips through his chest hair.

"You haven't checked your phone lately, have you?"

"No, why?" Lucas asked. When Teddy said nothing and let out a quiet, amused snort, Lucas's brows pinched. "What? What is it? What's so funny?"

"I e-mailed my client list on Tuesday night. You're on the general list, so you should have gotten it. BCCed, of course."

"Tuesday? As in, three days ago Tuesday?"

"Mm-hmm."

"And? What'd you say?"

"That…" Teddy held the word out. His face threatened to burst, he looked so happy. "I've retired."

A barked laugh rattled out of Lucas's throat. "Wh-what?"

Teddy grinned with crinkled eyes. "I said that I loved spending time with them through the years—and that they're all lovely, generous men—but that the time has come for me to move on. All current deposits will be refunded upon my return from holiday. My records will be destroyed in thirty days, unless they request receipts. I'll be following up with personal good-bye e-mails once I'm back, and then will probably end up meeting a couple face to face to say good-bye. No sex."

"Again: What?"

Teddy snapped his fingers. "Oh! And I referred them to a mate of mine. Nick. The one who supervised me when I was tied up. He was very excited to inherit potential clients from my list."

Lucas rolled Teddy onto his back. The duvet clung tight around his arse.

"Congratulations to Nick for inheriting a well-organized gold mine. But, are you serious? You retired? Just like that?" Lucas propped himself up on both hands. "Isn't that…. Is that normal? In your field?"

"I'm not sure if there are many normal things about my field. It was time for me to bow out. It's been time for a while. My clients were all mostly so sweet that it didn't feel like work, but I'm burned out. I'm tired of having to do all the security and paperwork and, uh, sex with strangers." His voice broke into laughter for his last few words, and Lucas laughed along with him. "I was just being—" He wrinkled his nose. "—greedy. And lazy. I've known I should get out for a long time, but it was so easy and paid so well. I needed a push, that's all."

"But it's, like, your empire. Your career. And I—I didn't mean to push you."

"It's not a career that fits with the life I want, though, and you didn't push me. Not at all. Seeing what life with you could be like, even after only a few days, it all became very clear to me. That was the push I needed. For every pottery class I take to try and keep my work-life balance even, it's worthless. Pottery is not, and will never be, you."

Lucas grasped Teddy's face in his hands. "Holy fuck, Teddy!" he cackled, loud and ecstatic. Teddy giggled just as ecstatically with him. "This is—That's—that's amazing! You can be a photographer or a pirate or Mick Jagger or whatever you want!"

Teddy pulled him down and their dry lips mashed together. Even sour breath could not hinder them. Their giggles were the only things breaking up their long, tender kisses.

"Oh, hey! Are you guys joining us for Sunrise Tai Chi? That's magical, mates! Magical!"

Teddy and Lucas looked to the right while still kissing. Cillian waved cheerily, wearing nothing but a small white loincloth and a white headband. Their lips slipped apart.

"Oh, um, no," Lucas said, shaking his head. Teddy pulled the duvet higher on their bare chests. "We weren't planning on it."

Zamir came up behind Cillian and slung his arm around his shoulders.

"Highly recommend it. Really gets the energy flowing first thing in the morning." Cillian pointed between them. "Did you two sleep outside last night?"

"Uh, yeah." Bashfulness deepened Teddy's voice. He and Lucas shared a smile. "We did."

"Aw," Cillian and Zamir drawled together as they hugged each other.

TEDDY WENT to his bag of rented clubs and hummed as he pulled a face. He located his seven iron and pulled it out.

"Seven, not nine?" Cillian asked from the cart. "A risk taker. I like it."

"Lucky number seven," Teddy said, grinning. He walked up to his ball and lined up his hips, gripping the soft leather handle. Cillian appeared beside him, holding out a fresh beer. Teddy took the can from him and smirked, holding it up to clink against Cillian's can. "Cheers, mate."

Cillian tipped his head back. They both chugged as fast as they could.

"Drunk golf is the best golf," Cillian declared, crushing his empty can in his hand. Teddy finished up his beer, gasping for air. Cillian took his can from him. "It's why our scores are always so magical."

"We're keeping score?" Chessie asked from the cart, balancing a club on his chin.

Their cart driver chuckled as he turned a page of his sports magazine. Another cart pulled up beside theirs. Lucas, Albert, and Zamir poured out of it.

Cillian tossed his putter in the air and ran toward the cart. "My love!"

Where Cillian was dressed in his most professional array of golf clothes, Zamir refused to wear pleated trousers. Instead, he golfed in his orange bathing suit, white trainers, and a tank top with the word "Namaste" printed on it in the shape of a rainbow.

Lucas stretched his arms over his head. His baby blue polo rose on his stomach. Teddy gazed at him, then looked toward Albert, who was wandering toward a pond in the distance. Lucas came up to him and Teddy ducked down to peck his cheek. Lucas bumped his forehead against Teddy's neck.

"Having fun?" he asked, rubbing the small of Teddy's back. He smiled fondly. "Only you would own a purple golf shirt. I love it."

"Yeah, it's been fun."

"How's your game going?"

Teddy pursed his lips as he nodded, his hands on his hips. "No idea. Cillian makes us drink a beer every time we change clubs. I'm not even sure what hole we're on."

Lucas snorted and snapped the front of Teddy's black athletic headband. "You're so sporty looking. Meanwhile, I look like I'm starring in a porno that takes place on a golf course in these white trousers."

"Ooh, tell me more about this porno."

Lucas chuckled and slapped Teddy's hand away from his arse. "Oi. It's not my fault these golf trousers are so tight."

"Clearly, my next job should be to design golf attire meant for those of us who are more"—he squeezed Lucas's arsecheek—"well-endowed than others."

"Oi! Cheeky!"

"Switch!" Zamir cried, hopping into Cillian's cart.

Teddy and Lucas broke into a jog and went to get into the other cart together, but Albert took one of the last two seats. He stared at them in a daze. Lucas jumped into the other seat and blinked innocently at Teddy. He slid his arm around Albert's shoulders.

"Where are we?" Albert asked in a hushed whisper.

"See you at the next hole, love," Lucas said to Teddy.

TEDDY WENT to the other cart and sat next to Zamir, who hugged Teddy's face to his chest. Zamir petted his hair, letting out a soft sigh as the cart began to move. Teddy chuckled quietly.

"I'm so glad you're here," Zamir said in a hushed whisper. Teddy sat up straight as Zamir continued to stroke his hair. "The spirits are glad you're here. The island is glad you're here."

Teddy adjusted his headband. "Me too."

"And with Luke. You're a blessing." Zamir pressed his palms together and bowed his head. "A true blessing." His long lashes fluttered open. "It's great that you mellow him out. You're exactly what he needs. He's acting his age, you know?" He squeezed Teddy's shoulder. "It's magical, mate, truly magical."

Teddy continued to smile, but the corners of his mouth pinched as the cart bumped over the course's path. "You say that like there's something wrong with the way he is when he's not around me."

"No, no, not like that!" Zamir shook his head, holding his palms out. "Not at all. I just meant…." He thought for a moment with his fingertips steepled. "He's always so serious. Always working so much. Always so stressed. It's nice to see him having fun and being normal."

"Lucas doesn't need me or anyone to"—Teddy lifted his fingers for air quotes—"'mellow him out' or be normal. He works hard to make a living for himself and, yeah, sometimes he gets stressed, but that's what happens when you have a job, no matter what job it is."

A spark of shock fizzled over Zamir's face. His head recoiled on his neck. "What's that supposed to mean?"

"It means that he has a job and wants to support himself and his family. That's all it means."

A beat passed.

"Sounds like an implication to me."

Teddy's brows arched over his black Ray-Bans. "An implication of what?"

Zamir's jawline set. "Just because Cillian's got money and I'm an artist doesn't mean we don't have stress and problems. We have them just like everyone else."

"I didn't say you don't have problems. I'm just saying, as someone who doesn't work in the corporate environment, I have no idea what kind of stress Lucas is under, because I have no experience in that world."

"And what is it that you do again?"

"I'm a photographer."

"Are you?" Zamir's voice was airy and higher than usual.

"I am," Teddy said, a touch firmer.

"Huh. I don't think I've seen you take a single photo since you've been here."

"I'm on vacation. I'm not at work."

"Is that so?"

Teddy's hand wrapped around the roof's support pole. "And what's that supposed to mean?"

Zamir crossed his arms over his chest and looked out at the grassy green, flicking his sunglasses down to his eyes. "Nothing, man, nothing. Implications, right? Implications. They tend to happen when some guy shows up, out of nowhere, and is attached at the hip of my best mate."

"Mates, chill out," Chessie said from the front of the cart. "Have another beer."

Zamir and Teddy were silent, both sitting and staring out at the distance. Teddy spoke first.

"I know I'm new. I know my time with Lucas is a fraction of a fraction of a fraction of the time you've had with him. I get it. And that's why I'll tell you that if you have questions about me, to please just ask me. You're the most important friend Lucas has ever had, or will ever have, and I want him to be happy as much as you do. He won't be happy if we don't get along."

"But we do get along," Zamir said quickly, turning to face him. Teddy raised his eyebrows with his mouth set in a tight line. Zamir flattened his hands on top of Teddy's shoulders. "We do! I like you. I really, really like you. Everyone loves you! I… I guess I'm just protective of him and want to make sure he's in good hands. I don't care about details, as long as you make my best friend happy now and in the future."

"How beautiful," Chessie said, he and the driver snickering.

Teddy exhaled a shaky breath, looking out to the grassy hills. "Good."

"Good," Zamir repeated, nodding once. He held his hand out. Teddy went for a shake, but Zamir flattened his hand on Teddy's heart, leaning their foreheads together. A low, growled hum came from Zamir's throat. He droned, "Namaste and love."

The cart stopped and Teddy repeated, "Namaste and love," while looking around. Everyone else was busy with their clubs and drinks, save for Albert, who was sitting silently in the golf cart.

"Namaste and love," Zamir whispered ever so softly, petting the back of Teddy's hair.

Teddy lowered his voice to say, "Namaste and love," which seemed to pacify Zamir, who planted a wet kiss on his forehead.

"We're soul brothers," Zamir declared, hopping out of the cart. He pressed his palms together and bowed toward Teddy, whispering, "Soul brothers."

ACROSS THE way, Lucas went to his cart and rifled through a golf bag. He looked at Albert and prodded the center of his chest with his club handle. "Y'all right, mate? You were silent for the ride over."

Albert blinked at him. "Can you hear music?"

"What?"

"I hear music," Albert said to a shaky melody, gripping the center of Lucas's shirt. "Let's close our eyes." His voice dropped to murmur nonsense words to a beat, then whispered, "Feel it."

Lucas listened to Albert's slightly off-key singing. "Albert, is that…. Is that the *Flashdance* song you always listen to at work?"

"I have to dance!" Albert cried. "It's all I am!"

Lucas burst out laughing and held his hand over Albert's mouth, glancing around at the other curious golfers. "Jesus, mate, what's gotten into you? The heat or something?"

Albert grasped both of Lucas's hands, and his big brown eyes blinked widely up at him.

"Zamir and Cillian gave me a cookie."

"A cookie?"

"Zamir said it was a special wedding cookie, but it tasted like chocolate chip to me."

"A special wedding. Chocolate chip...." Lucas trailed off. Realization dawned on him in a burst of high laughter. "Oh shit, man." He patted Albert's cheek, laughing even louder. "You're high as fuck right now. Congratulations."

"No, I'm not. You're my boss. No, I'm not. You're my boss. No, I'm not," Albert said in a completely professional tone of voice, sitting up straight. "I'm... I'm...." He spread his arms and took off across the grass, singing, "Let's dance!"

Lucas tried to control his amusement. Zamir walked up to him with a guilty smirk.

"I always thought he'd be a fun high," Zamir chuckled, bumping their hips together. "I told him it was a special cookie. He had to know, right?"

They watched Albert do an array of cartwheels, ending by cartwheeling into a decorative pond half the size of the resort's swimming pool. Teddy and Cillian ran after him, and Teddy waded into the water to pluck him out.

"Maybe not," Lucas said simply.

"Teddy the hero," Zamir said. Lucas snorted. Zamir squeezed his shoulder, pulling him into a half hug. "He's, like, totally in love with you. You know that, right?"

Lucas grinned as he watched Teddy haul Albert over his shoulder and away from a stone frog that spouted water out of its mouth. "Yeah," he said, not even trying to mask the fondness seeping through the single word. "I know."

"I guess he was your type all along. You just didn't know it."

Lucas turned toward Zamir, whose arm was still looped over his shoulder. "What do you mean?"

"Well, he's different from who you usually date. Lookswise. Personalitywise. He's nothing like anyone you've ever been with, at least to my knowledge."

"So?"

"It's interesting, is all."

Lucas pushed his sunglasses into his hair, his eyes serious. "Just because he's different doesn't mean I didn't care about the other people I was with."

Zamir patted his chest. "I know, man, I know. I'm not talking about us. I'm not talking about anyone in particular. Don't let Teddy see you serious, though. He'll get all tiger boyfriendy."

"Tiger boyfriendy?" Lucas asked, sounding truly baffled.

"Never mind," Zamir laughed, pulling Lucas to his side. They walked toward the pond, where Cillian was now swimming around the spouting frog, golf gear and all. "I just said to Teddy that it's nice to see you having fun, to not be so serious, and he jumped to defend your honor, work stress and all."

Lucas frowned, crossing his arms over his chest.

"I didn't ask him to defend my honor."

"I don't think you had to." Zamir watched Cillian jump on Teddy's back, propelling both into the pond while Albert did the backstroke around the frog. "You might not have wanted a white knight, but you've got one." He patted between Lucas's shoulder blades. "It's a good thing, mate. I'd have accepted no less from your boyfriend."

"Wait. Did you…" Lucas narrowed his eyes, starting to smile. "Grill him?"

Zamir smirked. "A bit." Lucas guffawed and Zamir held his hands up. "What? I've got to! He's your boyfriend. I've got to be sure he's the best."

Lucas gripped Zamir's tank, marching toward the pond. "All right."

"Oi, what's this?" Zamir dug his heels into the plush grass.

"I'm trying not to be so serious."

Lucas threw him into the pond, Zamir cackling "Luke!" before he hit the water. Cillian jumped on Zamir's shoulders as Albert and Chessie climbed the frog statue. Teddy came up behind Lucas and lifted him over his shoulder. Lucas slapped his hands on Teddy's wet bum, laughing before he was dunked into the murky water.

"S'JUST A little nap." Lucas pulled the duvet up higher. "To recharge."

"Mmm."

"Golf's exhausting."

"Mmm," Teddy hummed, lower.

Lucas tucked his face in the crook of Teddy's neck, tightening his hold around his middle. They breathed in together, air conditioning brushing over their bare shoulders.

"We're totally going to make it to dinner."

Teddy murmured, "Totally."

Lucas was already snoring.

Chapter TWENTY-FOUR

"I LOVE strippers!" Cillian's voice cut through the throbbing dance music like a trumpet being played in the middle of the luxury club. A muscled, well-oiled brunet ground backward against his groin. The stripper's metallic gold thong shimmered between his plump arsecheeks. "They're pure joy." Cillian raised the roof as the stripper gyrated on him. "Poetry in motion!"

Zamir was sitting next to him, wearing an array of plastic penis necklaces looped around his neck, a wiry blond stripper sitting on his lap and feeding him strawberries. Cillian rolled his head along the plush sofa and grinned. A crown of plastic penises perched crookedly on his wild hair.

"God, you look so fucking hot right now, Z. Can we take one home? Please?"

"Oh, okay," Zamir relented with a lazy flick of his hand, as if Cillian had asked him to see a movie he didn't care to see. "If you insist."

The upscale club swirled around their group, comfortably seated in a private, roped-off area that overlooked the entire club and stage. Male and female burlesque dancers walked around with mirrored trays of drinks, scantily clad but tastefully put together. Different circus performers did tricks on the stage between stripteases.

Most of the golf crew had come to the club for Zamir and Cillian's combined bachelor party, plus a lot of wives and girlfriends from the wedding group. Albert was attempting to hold an actual conversation with a female burlesque dancer as she demonstrated dance moves for Anna, who sat beside Teddy and Lucas. Some of the older men from their group were off in another area of their section, smoking cigars and clapping enthusiastically for a pair of female fire breathers.

Lucas moved close to Teddy's ear, keeping his eyes on his champagne as he swirled the remnants of bubbles in his glass. "Do you think Buddha would approve of strippers?"

Teddy smiled into his vodka tonic as Lucas softly kissed beneath his ear. He slid his arm around Lucas's shoulders. "Dunno. Maybe? He seems like a liberal-minded fellow. If everyone's having fun and being positive, I don't see why not."

There was a flurry of money and cheers around Cillian and Zamir. Five more glistening male strippers appeared to dance for them. A man with smooth caramel skin, leanly muscled thighs, and hair so blond it was nearly white came up to where Teddy and Lucas were sitting. His body was hairless and shining. His deep tan contrasted with his pale gold booty shorts and knee-high gold combat boots. He quirked an eyebrow at them and ran his fingers over his oiled abs.

"Would either of you care for a dance?"

Teddy thumbed toward Lucas. "His turn."

Lucas gaped at him, spreading his arms in time for the stripper to straddle him. He was hit with a whiff of cologne and a strong wave of bodywash. "Oh, uh." He shifted under the new weight on his lap. "I, um—"

"Just enjoy it, love," Teddy murmured. His low words buzzed over Lucas's skin. He stroked the hair above Lucas's ear. "He's hot, yeah?"

The stripper started to gyrate, his well-sculpted muscles flickering and stretching with each rotation of his narrow hips. The stripper and Teddy exchanged a look. Teddy smirked at him before directing his attention back at Lucas. The stripper ran his hands through Lucas's hair, mussing it into wild peaks. Teddy muffled a laugh with his drink. Lucas smiled tightly and allowed the stripper to place his hands on his arse.

Teddy leaned close and whispered, "You could pretend he's me." He cupped the back of Lucas's neck, thumb teasing over his skin. "Or I could practice on you later." He let his mouth brush Lucas's ear. "Do you like that idea?"

Lucas exhaled a soft, nearly inaudible sound as he tilted his head back. Teddy's fingers stroked over his neck while a golden god ground against him.

There was another section of private booths, smaller and less luxurious, flanking their roped-off area. A loud crash cut through the music, a group of men jumping up amid shouting. The stripper on Lucas's lap continued to dance, slow and masterful, but his eyes darted toward the noise.

Whatever had happened in the section caused two of the managers to rush over and a group of female strippers to hurry out of the area, leaving a group of red-faced, angry businessmen in their wake.

"Watch your wallets," one of Cillian's cousins teased. Most of their group laughed.

Teddy's hand faltered on the back of Lucas's neck, and Lucas glanced his way. He wasn't frowning, but he wasn't smiling, a far-off sort of sadness dampening his eyes as he stared at the retreating female strippers.

"What is it, love?" Lucas asked, squeezing his thigh.

The golden-god stripper looked between them, his hips still moving lazily.

"Nothing," Teddy said.

"Is this weird for you?"

Teddy shook his head. "Nah, it's fine." He met Lucas's gaze. "It's fine. Just silliness. As if those ladies are to blame for drunk, rude clients getting out of hand."

"Those guys are the worst." The stripper kept his sexy face on as he spoke quietly, letting his head roll backward as he ground down. "They come in every month or so. Always make a big scene to try and get free drinks. Terrible tippers." He made a locking-his-lips motion. "But you didn't hear that from me."

Teddy and Lucas nodded. Lucas slipped a few bills into the stripper's waistband. "How about you hop on Baby Mick over here? Rock his world for a bit."

The stripper looked amusedly to Teddy, doing a quick scan up and down. He stood up and straddled Teddy's lap, smoothing his hands up his billowy black-and-white sheer shirt.

"You really do resemble young Mick Jagger." He fingered his unbuttoned shirt collar. "Are you in the industry?"

Lucas snorted into his glass, and Teddy rolled his eyes.

"Formerly."

"Stripper?"

"Escort."

"Ah." An understanding smile warmed his face. "You must be very patient. I could never get a client list going. I'm not nearly polite enough to pretend I care about what these rude fucks have to say for more than a dance."

Teddy and Lucas laughed.

The drinks kept flowing, as did the attractive, nearly naked people coming in and out of their booth to entertain and dance. The women in their group had left the booth to join the dance floor, trying out some of their new dance moves between gulps of champagne. The older men in their group were escorted to a back room that specialized in cigars and brandy. Most of Zamir's and Cillian's younger family members had moved downstairs to gamble, leaving Cillian, Zamir, Teddy, Lucas, and Albert at the booth by themselves, along with an army of friendly strippers.

Cillian and Zamir were flanked on both sides by gorgeous men. A pair of Italian twins sat between them and refilled their champagne flutes each time they took a sip. Albert was puffing on a cigar beside Cillian while chatting with a male stripper about stocks, continuing his trend of holding serious conversations with people in a strip club. Lucas sat beside Zamir. Teddy was half on top of him. They were both unable to stop cackling and spilling champagne as Teddy attempted to grind. A couple of strippers cheered him on.

"You're pretty good at that, Taz," Cillian laughed.

"Yeah, excellent form." Zamir smirked at Lucas's flushed face.

"Hey! Sam has a degree in maths." Albert pointed at the stocky ginger stripper next to him. "Isn't that amazing? He can dance and do maths!"

"Why would you do this if you have a degree?" Cillian asked curiously.

"Maths bored me." Sam shrugged, a hint of an Irish accent lilting in his voice. "I like living in paradise and not going to an office every day. You're only young once, you know?"

"I'd think anything could be better than this," Zamir said, swirling his champagne glass.

Teddy stiffened and slowed on top of Lucas, and Lucas's mouth straightened to a line. Sympathy transmitted from the golden-god stripper to Teddy.

"No offense," Zamir hurried to say, smoothing his hand up the back of the stripper currently sitting on his lap. "You all are excellent at what you do. And I suppose it must be a fun job. Shit, I'm sorry," he said, an apologetic frown darkening his eyes. "I didn't mean it in a bad way. I'm sorry."

"You're fine, love," one of the twins said, pecking Zamir's cheek. "No worries at all."

Teddy smiled down at Lucas's lap. A tinge of sadness tugged at the corners of his mouth. Lucas kissed the front of his throat, lacing his fingers in his hair to scratch the back of his scalp.

The strippers decided to take a break to freshen up and left the five men alone in their booth.

"Shit, was that rude?" Zamir asked. More champagne was poured into his glass and he glugged it down, then squinted thoughtfully. "I didn't mean to be rude to them. They're all so fun. And hot."

"It's all right, babe, it's all right," Cillian said, his words slurring together. "That guy said it was fine. Besides, they're probably used to people saying things like that."

"Doesn't mean you should say them." Albert's eyes widened, and he coughed a smoky breath out, pounding the center of his chest. "Shit, sorry, now I'm being rude."

"Nah, you're right." Cillian swallowed a gulp of champagne straight out of the bottle. "Totally right. Seems like a last resort for a job, but I guess it happens."

Lucas and Teddy made eye contact. A beat passed while they stared at each other. The club's music pounded in their ears, champagne fizzing into their glasses from Albert's generous pour. Teddy smiled, with his lips shut. Lucas squeezed his knee under the table, tilting his head in a small nod.

Teddy lifted his glass of champagne and sipped it, then looked at the other three men at the table.

"I used to escort, myself," he said, conversational and cheerful.

He was met by slack-jawed silence, Cillian, Zamir, and Albert blinking at him in unison with matching flutes of shimmery champagne in each of their hands. Lucas's mouth was pressed to his shoulder. He hugged Teddy tight around his waist. He kissed Teddy's bicep, squeezing his hip. Teddy sipped again, then placed his glass on the table, resting his thumbs on the stem of the glass.

"Sometimes," he continued, just as breezy, "things happen, and in order to survive, you go down roads you could not anticipate. And that was a road I went down for a period of time."

"But…." Albert slowly tilted his head, eyes darting from Lucas to Teddy. "Not anymore?"

Teddy smiled and glanced at Lucas. He shook his head, then directed his attention to Albert.

"Nope. Not since Luke." He laced their fingers together, their joined hands resting against his hip. "I'd rather keep that detail about me between us," he said, softer. "If you all don't mind?"

The other three men nodded, their mouths still open but their eyes returning to a more normal size.

"So," Cillian drawled, swirling his hand in the air, "are you, like, an Avenger in bed? That explains the noises."

WHEN THEY got back to the resort, karaoke was still going strong. Luckily their group was so drunk from the club that even the shrillest of singing could not bring them down.

"Oh, thank God you're back," Lane said, pulling Lucas and Teddy to her table. "Since all the mums were here alone, they've been singing disco songs. Exclusively disco songs. I think we've heard *Last Dance*, like, ten times. Not exactly the last dance."

Teddy chuckled and sat down next to Marcy, and Lucas plopped down beside him. Zamir and Cillian ran toward the DJ, shooting song titles back and forth between them. A group of the mums finished up a song on stage, goblets of red-wine sangria sloshing in their hands. A group of Zamir's younger cousins got on stage, and the twangy strains of some country song played through the speakers.

Lucas stroked Teddy's hair, tucking a curl over his ear. He leaned closer. "You didn't have to tell them."

"I know." Teddy rested his head on Lucas's shoulder. "I wanted to. I wanted them to know something about me. About where I come from. Maybe it'll change their minds about sex workers. Or maybe they'll be less judgmental toward people who work any sort of job that can be unpleasant, sex work or not. I might not be a sex worker anymore, but I'll still support sex workers and their rights whenever I can. And I like the truth. I want your friends—"

"Our friends."

Teddy smiled slowly. "Our friends," he corrected, "to know the truth about me."

Lucas pressed his nose to Teddy's jawline, squeezing his shoulder. "You're noble."

"Nah."

"And brave."

"I dunno about that. Are you—" Teddy ran his fingers up the seam of Lucas's black skinnies. "—are you okay that I told them? It involves you too."

"Of course," Lucas said simply. "I was shocked you would share that so soon, but the fact that you did… that you'd care about changing the minds of others for the better." He pecked Teddy's lips. "That's lovely."

Teddy grinned and buried his face in Lucas's neck.

Jo plopped down at their table and hugged Lucas to her side. "When are you two going to do a duet?" she asked, wiggling in her seat.

Lucas and Teddy grinned, shaking their heads. Teddy stood up and leaned toward a passing waitress, reaching for two glasses of bright red rum punch.

Lucas petted Jo's leg. "Don't hold your breath, Mum."

"Oh, come on," she chided playfully, knocking her fist to Lucas's jawline. "Teddy's given how many star-turning performances on that stage? And you've done none! What a big baby you are!" She slurped her sangria and bopped Lucas's nose with one finger. "Be brave, dear! Be—Oh, Tracy! Praise you!"

She stood up and hurried to a table of the other mums, where Zamir's mother was hoisting a pitcher of fresh sangria into the air. Teddy chuckled as he sat back down and placed a glass of rum punch in front of Lucas. He blinked at the empty space, then looked down. Maggie grinned up at him from where Lucas was sitting.

"Hello there," he said happily, ruffling her hair. Maggie snuggled against his side. "Where'd your uncle go?"

She lifted her hands near her face. "I don't know," she said in a sugary-sweet voice.

Teddy squinted curiously at her, Maggie shimmying her shoulders and kicking her legs under the picnic bench. He faintly registered the DJ announcing, "Next up, someone new to this stage—let's welcome Lucas!"

"Oh my God!" Lane cried.

Teddy's jaw dropped. He blinked wide-eyed at the stage. Lane jumped up from the table and ran toward the stage, other members of the party doing the same.

LUCAS STRODE to the center of the stage and gripped a mic on a stand, his hands visibly shaking around it. Spotlights formed a fan behind his body. He winked at Teddy and brought the mic to his mouth.

"I hate karaoke, but I love Theodore Bennet, so, this is for Teddy." He pointed two fingers toward the crowd. "Oh, and a big thank-you to Albert, the best assistant in the world, for listening to this song every day at work, without which I'd never have learned all the words."

THE CROWD'S wooing cheers and Maggie's cackles barely registered with Teddy, who forgot how to breathe while Lucas smiled at him. Marcy gripped his arm and pulled him up to the stage, where the guests formed a big pit in front of Lucas. Teddy held Maggie's hand and walked up to the stage, bending down to place Maggie on his shoulders.

"Can you see, little love?" he said up to her.

"Yes, big love," Maggie said, hugging his head.

Teddy's dimples popped as the song "I Want To Know What Love Is" by Foreigner started to play, the synth-heavy ballad matching the cool-colored beams of light shooting up around Lucas.

Lucas kept his head down and bobbed to the intro.

"The eighties are the most underrated decade of music!" Albert cried, chocolate chip cookie spilling out of his mouth. He fist-pumped. "Thank you, sir! I love you!"

Lucas exhaled a nervous chuckle and the sound picked up on the mic. His eyes clenched shut and his hands gripped both sides of the mic as he started to sing the first verse.

"Oh, he—he sings," Teddy stuttered out over a short interlude. "He's a tenor."

"I know, crazy, right?" Marcy whispered, cupping her hands to shout, "Yeah, Luke!" at the top of her lungs.

"I'm videoing," Jo hissed over her shoulder, her iPhone poised.

ON STAGE, Lucas tried to breathe evenly, well aware that air needed to go both in and out of his lungs to produce sound. He sang the second verse with his eyes still shut, trying to focus on keeping his voice even. The crowd sang along with every word. He flattened his left hand on his upper belly and took an extra big breath to tackle the bridge. His eyes opened to slits and landed on Teddy's shocked face.

The beams of light exploded out from the stage as the chorus kicked in. The entire crowd shouted the chorus with him, and their voices gave him extra strength to wail. He heard a chorus of voices nearby. His eyes widened.

Male strippers swayed on either side of him, spotlights bouncing off their shimmery metallic shorts. He sang as eight men in booty shorts did basic foot-to-foot sways forward and back, as if they were a barbershop quartet.

Lane and Albert appeared on either end of the stripper backup dancers, both holding mics of their own and mirroring their dance moves. Cillian and Zamir climbed up the front of the stage and went to the sides. The DJ handed them mics.

"What is going on?" Lucas chuckled into his mic during the break before the next verse. The crowd's laughter, including Teddy's loud cackle, carried over the speakers.

He sang through the next verse, his crinkled eyes zoning in on Teddy's face to sing as best he could while uncontrollable, smiley giddiness shook his voice. Lucas snarled his top lip and jutted his chin sideways in his best Billy Idol impression to sing the rest of the bridge with even more confidence than the first time.

Once the chorus kicked in again, Lucas barely had to sing at all. The group of strippers and family members sang loud enough to wake people sleeping on nearby islands. Lane started to riff, taking over the gospel singer's lines from the recording, Cillian and Zamir and Albert riffing their own personal improvisations.

Lucas handed his mic to a stripper—his golden god from earlier—and jumped off the stage, throwing in a quick Johnny Castle finger snap and a bob of his head. The tiny, brief motion was enough for Teddy to notice and grin wildly, rushing up to him and wrapping him in his arms, twirling him on the sand.

"You sounded so beautiful, love," Teddy whispered in his ear. The music was still pounding, and family members all reached out to talk to Lucas, but he heard nothing besides Teddy's raspy whisper. "I-I can't believe you did that. I love you. You're—" He rubbed between Lucas's delicate shoulder blades. "—you're shaking."

"I was nervous," Lucas said in a small voice, pressing his face to Teddy's neck. "I hate karaoke."

"Then why did you do it?"

Lucas cradled the back of Teddy's head, stroking over his hair. "Because I love you. And sometimes the scary stuff turns out to be best."

"Like naked cliff jumping?"

"Like falling in love."

Teddy made a high-pitched, murmured, happy sound and spun Lucas again. He planted Lucas's feet on the ground. "You know what we have to do now, don't you?"

Lucas pulled back and peered at Teddy, smiling but confused.

"What?"

Teddy grinned and turned toward Jo.

"You'd better keep your camera out."

"I CAN'T believe you talked me into this."

"Talked you into it? You walked here completely by your own will and had your shoes off even before me."

"Yeah, well," Lucas mumbled, brushing his bare toes over the smooth plastic below their feet. "When you hold my hand and walk, I just sort of follow."

Teddy giggled and clapped his hands together fast, stepping into a large blue inner tube. His unbuttoned shirt fell to his sides, revealing his scrunched abs. He held his hand out.

"Time to go, love."

Lucas sighed and stepped between Teddy's legs. He sank down onto his lap, his bum to Teddy's groin, with Teddy's legs spread on the outside and Lucas's legs on the inside.

"Come on down already!" Lane yelled amid camera flashes going off. "We have to get our beauty rest for tomorrow!"

Teddy kissed Lucas's neck and jutted his groin up, wrapping his arms around his middle.

"All right," Teddy said as Lucas gripped the sides of the water slide. "Ready?"

Lucas smirked over his shoulder. "Are you?"

"Of course I'm—*Ahhh*!"

Teddy screamed high in his throat as their tube was propelled down the slide, a slide meant for the weight of one person of moderate size, not two fully grown adult men. Teddy's long legs flailed over the edges of the swirly slide. Lucas's bottom-heavy weight in the center of the tube sent them flying faster than anticipated, both hitting the warm water in mere seconds. They popped out to gasp as their clothes weighed them down.

The wedding group cheered as Zamir, Cillian, and Albert jumped into the pool with their clothes on. Dean and Maggie zoomed down the water slide.

"Yes! Finally!" Jo shouted. Teddy and Lucas laughed hysterically. She came closer to the edge of the pool, snapping photos. Lane grabbed Jo's iPhone before Marcy gently pushed their mum into the deep end, her colorful dress puffing up above the surface. Jo squawked and shouted, "You little brat!" while attempting to keep her head above water as she paddled. Lane cannonballed next to her. "I just straightened my hair!"

LUCAS PLACED his white towel on the rack, turned off the en-suite lights, and walked into the bedroom. The bedside table lamps were still lit, but the rest of the room was dark. Teddy had his back propped against the headboard, his iPad grasped in his hands and resting on his bent legs. The duvet tented over his knees.

"Look, it's the bird!" Teddy turned his iPad toward Lucas. A PDF page from a book lit the screen. He pointed to a photo. "The one from the first day. The one with the cute outfit and lipstick. They're called Bananaquit. Isn't it funny that banana is in its name? I love bananas. Crazy how coincidences work, yeah?"

Lucas kneeled on the edge of the bed and crawled up Teddy's body, straddling him on top of the duvet. He cupped Teddy's face with both hands and kissed him. Teddy hummed and dropped his iPad on the bed, and wrapped his arms around Lucas's lower back.

Chapter TWENTY-FIVE

Saturday, May 2

"BODY, MIND, soul, spirit, essence," Zamir said.

"Body, mind, soul, spirit, essence," Cillian repeated, both leaning forward to touch foreheads.

Their families and friends sat completely still while Cillian and Zamir hummed on the same pitch, their flat palms mirroring each other's hand motions in the air. A man sporting an all-white robe, a long white beard, and friendly brown eyes clapped his hands once. He placed one hand on each of their shoulders.

"And your vows?" he asked.

Together, Zamir and Cillian chanted, "Love. Mother Nature. Brother Sun. Moon and stars. Love. Always love."

They joined hands.

"My soul is your soul," they whispered together. "My spirit is your spirit. In this incarnation, the next, and any other after that." They each lifted a glass cylinder of sand, Cillian's sand neon green and Zamir's sand teal. They poured sand into a hollow glass seashell. "One being, one love." Tears streamed down their faces and their smiles were ecstatic. "Namaste and love."

Every other member of the wedding party was either sobbing openly or teary eyed. Even Lucas dabbed beneath his eyelashes with the back of his fingers. Teddy's hand lay warm on the top of his thigh.

"Your two souls are now one," the bearded man said, bowing at them. "Go forth into the world to spread love and joy with whatever you do."

The newly married couple kissed firm and long, Cillian grasping Zamir's face while Zamir dipped Cillian backward. The bearded man whispered, "Namaste and love," before he reached down and unlatched a box.

A rainbow of butterflies flew up into the applauding crowd, swirling around the white canopy. Lucas glanced toward Teddy without turning his head and found Teddy to be looking at him with the same sort of secret amusement, continuing to clap even when a tiny purple butterfly landed on the tip of Teddy's nose.

A STEEL-DRUM-LED ensemble played a mellow, tropical arrangement of "So This is Love" from *Cinderella*. They were performing on the stage usually reserved for karaoke. The entire beach was covered in sheer white linens and tents, and fairy lights twinkled against the starry sky. Lucas and Teddy swayed slowly amid the other couples, nuzzling as their bare feet spun them around the sandy dance floor.

"Aren't you two lovely," Jo said, snapping a photo of them. She took another photo, catching Lucas resting his face on Teddy's shoulder, his eyes shut and his smile relaxed. "Just lovely!"

Neither noticed her presence. The gentle music, all-encompassing humidity of the island, and warmth of each other's skin hypnotized them past the point of noticing someone taking a photo. Food had been served. Drinks had been drunk. People had been bound together for life.

"Your arse looks gorgeous in those," Teddy murmured softly.

Lucas felt Teddy's hand ghost over the swell of his arse, and he pressed his lips to Teddy's exposed collarbone. His thin white shirt was barely buttoned to nipple height.

"You were right, honey bunch."

Teddy patted his bum. "You're already doing this whole relationship thing so well. Masterful."

Lucas chuckled and Teddy hugged him as they swirled around the dance floor.

Chapter TWENTY-SIX

Monday, May 4

LANE HUGGED Teddy tightly to her chest, swaying him in place. "We'll see you soon, yeah?" she whispered. Teddy squeezed her as they hugged. "Maggie's birthday is next month, and it would be amazing if you were there. She'd be so happy."

Teddy tucked his face against her neck and nodded. "Of course." He squeezed her once more and stepped back, cradling the tops of her shoulders. "I wouldn't miss it for the world." He glanced at Lucas, who was midhug with Dean. "We wouldn't miss it for the world."

Lane grinned, her eyes sparkling much like Lucas's. She cupped Teddy's face, thumbing the highest peak of his cheekbone. "I'm so glad he picked you."

Teddy's smile went crooked, and he bent his knee inward. "You said that at the beginning."

"I meant it then, and I mean it even more now."

Lane continued to stroke Teddy's cheek as family members whirled around to say good-bye to everyone they could before the ferries took off.

"I can't even express how glad I am that he picked me." Teddy tucked his hands in his pockets and chuckled breathily. He glanced up at her through his lashes. "Truly. Him and all of you."

Lane lowered her hand to his chest, drumming her fingers against his pec. "So." She cleared her throat, wiping any hint of sentimentality from her face. "We'll see you soon, yes?"

"Yeah, definitely."

"Not just Maggie's birthday, but you and Luke need to come by for dinner. Like, sometime this week?"

"Sounds good. I'll check with Luke."

"Oh!" Lane snapped her fingers. "Or I could come by to help you with your backsplash!"

"Yes! That would be much appreciated. So far I've managed to watch hours of television about doing it, but have yet to buy a single tile." Teddy's laughter was cut off by a firm little person clinging to him. He hitched Maggie up on his hip, and she buried her face in his neck. "You hear that, Mags? We get to play together very soon!"

"Tonight?" she asked, her voice wavering.

"Not tonight, love. You need to recover from our holiday." His eyes were drawn to Lucas's face—Lucas was staring him down as one of his uncles rambled in his ear. "I think we all do. We need a holiday from our holiday."

"Yes, well, some of us have been very busy this holiday," Lane said. Teddy looked at Lane's smug smile and stifled an eye roll. Lane snickered and prodded his side. "Welcome to the family, Captain Jack."

LUCAS GRIPPED the handle of Teddy's suitcase and rolled it over wet concrete. The small wheels bumped over the uneven surface. A driver lifted Lucas's luggage into the boot of a black SUV, water dripping down the tinted glass window.

"Let me help," Teddy said, clutching the collar of his jacket closed and bumping Lucas's hip with his bum. Lucas hoisted his bag into the boot, bumping him back. "You're silly."

"Am not."

Teddy slipped his hand in Lucas's back pocket and walked him to the car door. Lucas climbed inside, and Teddy got in behind him. Teddy brushed his hand over Lucas's damp fringe.

"I'm so glad it rained to greet our return." Teddy buckled himself in. "As if we needed more of a reminder that we're no longer in paradise."

Lucas chuckled. "Just gives us an excuse to go on holiday soon."

"I approve of that way of thinking."

"Especially now that you're a retiree." Lucas laced his fingers in the back of Teddy's hair. They kissed softly. "Lots of free time. You should take up bingo."

"I already have so many ideas of how I want to build my business."

The true excitement radiating from Teddy's voice made Lucas smile wider. He leaned in for a longer, sweeter kiss. Lucas stroked a curl above his ear while Teddy rubbed their noses together.

"I'm very happy for you, love. I can't wait to see what you do."

"Oh!" Teddy lifted his carry-on. "I got you something."

"Me?"

"Yep." Teddy unzipped his bag and stuck his hand inside. "Just need to find it."

Lucas turned to face him, sitting on his bare foot with his shoes left on the floor of the backseat. "What did you get me? And when did you get me anything? When was there time?"

Mischief lit Teddy's eyes, and he lifted his hand. A small plastic bag was clutched in his fist. He placed it in Lucas's hands and bopped him on the knuckles. "For you."

Lucas pulled the bag open, reached inside, and lifted a small plastic rectangle with a printed Union Jack on it.

"Someone in London loves you," he read aloud off the magnet, his voice growing softer as he spoke. He thumbed over the shiny plastic, and the pads of his fingers rubbed on the magnet glued to the back. He looked up and found Teddy's warm, crinkled eyes. "Teddy, thank you. That's…. This is the best gift I've ever gotten."

Teddy smiled crookedly and scoffed, "I find that hard to believe."

"It is. Truly." Lucas nodded and lifted his hand, pressing a long kiss to his knuckles. "It is. Thank you."

Teddy's crooked smile straightened itself out, his face dropping to huff out a bashful laugh. Lucas tucked a wave of hair over his ear.

The driver glanced at them in the mirror. "Sorry to interrupt, sirs, but are we going back to Mr. Thompson's? Just want to plan which route has the least traffic."

Teddy and Lucas looked at each other. A flush crept up both of their necks.

"Um," Lucas said, holding out the sound. "I… I could drop you at yours, if you want, or we… we could both…."

Teddy's gaze flickered down. He looked back to Lucas with arched brows. "Do you want the night alone?"

"Why would I want that?"

"Uh, I dunno. I didn't know if…." Teddy chuckled breathily and shook his head, running his fingers back through his hair. "If you wanted some space or time on your own to… you know. Do alone stuff. Since we just spent the last ten days together, twenty-four hours a day."

Lucas's brows pinched. "I've had plenty of time on my own. Years on my own. If we say we're going to spend the night alone, I'm going to end up calling you at three in the morning and begging you to let me send a car to pick you up and bring you to my place so I can listen to you breathe your tiny breaths and smell your neck when I wake up. So, let's save the cab fare and go out to dinner with that money instead. I'm in the mood for Indian. Or maybe Japanese. Sound good?"

Teddy grinned, slow and wide. "Okay. But"—he held up one finger—"I'm paying. And I think we should go to my place. In addition to having an amazing Indian place down the street, I missed my bed."

"Whatever you say." Lucas thumbed the back of Teddy's neck. "I've got clothes and stuff with me. Oh, but, um." He checked his watch. "We have to make one stop first."

"Sure. What do you need?"

TEDDY DUNKED two teabags into a white teapot and looked down. A red rubber ball bounced between his bare feet. He grinned and kicked the ball toward his living room. A tornado of fur slid between his ankles. Georgie huffed excited breaths out of his wrinkled nose.

The ball was lobbed back into the kitchen. It knocked Teddy in the bum. Georgie ran back to his ankles to chase the bouncing ball. The ball somehow managed to get thrown high enough to reach between Teddy's shoulder blades.

"Oi, you trying to kill us?" Teddy asked, grinning over his shoulder. "He'll sprain something if he tries to jump that high."

Lucas came up beside Teddy. "I think Georgie is more likely to accidentally die of joy." He picked up the ball and threw it into the living room. They watched Georgie run, only to abandon the ball to hump the leg of an armchair. "Or give himself a heart attack midhump."

Teddy chuckled and Lucas reached into the refrigerator. He pulled out a fresh container of milk, took off the top, and dropped a splash into one mug. He poured a bit more in a second mug. Teddy poured tea into the mugs and opened a cabinet next to the sink, grabbing a packet of crisps while Lucas replaced the milk in the refrigerator.

As Georgie ran circles between their feet, Lucas studied the newest magnet on Teddy's refrigerator. Teddy slipped a warm mug of tea into his hand and planted a kiss on the lowest curve of his neck. Lucas turned his head to press their lips together as Teddy's hand slid to his bum. Georgie mounted Teddy's leg, and Lucas and Teddy snuffled laughs as they kissed.

Epilogue

"ALL RIGHT, let's have a big, loud, majestic lion's roar," Teddy said, giving his deep voice extra raspiness. He held his scrunched fingers by his face and demonstrated. "*Roaaarrrr*!"

The set of triplet girls all giggled, high-pitched and hysterical. Their small hands mimicked his position.

"Beautiful." He snapped a handful of photos. The warm spring breeze blew through his short-sleeved button-down—black with flamingos printed on it. His black skinnies were rolled up his to ankles and his feet bare. "One more roar. C'mon, I can't hear you!"

"*Roaaarrrr*!"

"That's it," Teddy cheered over them, snapping more pictures. "You girls look lovely."

"We're lovely lions," one said. Her puffy purple hat was falling into her eyes.

Teddy ran in front of his tripod and adjusted her hat, tilting her sister's blue hat on her head of soft blonde hair. He bopped the pink hat of the third sister for good luck, earning a chorus of giggles.

"There we are," he said, running back around the tripod. "Let's see." He checked the viewfinder and scanned through some photos, tilting the camera downward. "We've had lions, bears, tigers." He bent his head around the camera and grinned at them, sliding his black aviators up higher into his long hair. "What else do you girls want to be?" He fanned his fingers out, and excitement shimmered in his voice. "You can be anything you want, anything at all, now that we have the"—he rolled his eyes dramatically—"boring, serious photos done."

"Cows!" the puffy-pink-outfitted sister cried, kicking her legs on the park bench. "*Mooooo*!"

Teddy mooed along with them as he took more photos. They had passed their allotted time, but he didn't have anyone booked directly after them. Sometimes the best photos came when his clients were relaxed and under the impression the shoot was over. He didn't mind an extra few minutes here or there.

He took his camera off the tripod and ran closer to their propped position, then dipped the camera in and out as they mugged up at him. "You girls are perfect. Perfect!"

Their mother, Lucy, chuckled from her place at an adjacent bench. She looked up from her book, watching Teddy run around her daughters to take photos, their giggles growing more and more.

"You're so good with them," she called over to him. Teddy looked away from the girls to smile at Lucy. "Do you babysit?"

"Not professionally, but I've been known to nanny when needed."

"Do you have any of your own?"

"Oh. Uh." He shook his head, snapping a quick photo of the girls trying to climb down from the bench in their puffy dresses. "No. Not yet."

"Are you seeing anyone?"

Teddy's fog lifted, a bright grin stretching over his face. "Yeah, I am. I've been with my boyfriend over a year now." He held each of their tiny hands as their short legs struggled to find the ground. He pointed over his shoulder at a patch of grass bursting with wildflowers. "How about those flowers, girls? What do you think? Wanna have a photoshoot over there?"

They all cried, "Yeah!" and ran to the spot.

He winced toward Lucy. "Sorry in advance for their dresses."

"That's all right." She turned a page of her book. "I learned long ago to buy fabric that can handle grass stains."

A high-pitched voice shouted, "We're ready, Mr. Teddy Bear!"

Teddy turned toward them. He made a loud gasping noise and clutched his chest, pretending to stumble as he walked. The girls giggled on the grass.

"Oh, ladies. Wow. Just wow," he said, starting to snap as he walked closer. They had positioned themselves on their backs, with their heads together among the colorful flowers. "You're making my job so easy! How did you know I was going to ask you to do that?"

A small tan blur came closer in the background of his frame. He glanced up from his camera, tingles swirling inside his stomach.

Lucas followed behind the energetic blur with his arm outstretched from the taut leash linked to Georgie's collar.

"You can let him off," Teddy called, squatting down. He slapped the tops of his thighs. "Come to papa, Georgie Boy!"

The second Lucas unclipped Georgie's leash, the dog came flying across the field. Well, he flew as fast as his little pug legs would allow, which wasn't terribly fast, but he made up for speed in enthusiasm. He barreled into Teddy's legs.

"Hello, my little monster," Teddy said in a grumbly voice, picking Georgie up to cradle him in his arms. He turned Georgie's scrunched, wrinkled face toward the triplets. "Ladies, this is Sir George Harrison Thompson the First, otherwise known as Georgie." He glanced up at Lucas's smiling face as he jogged closer. "He prefers Georgie. Just ask him."

"Mummy, can we play with Georgie?" the triplet in puffy pink asked, already rolling out of formation. "Please?"

Lucy didn't even look up from her book. She flicked her hand toward the grass. "Sure. Have fun, loves."

Georgie preened at the attention from the blonde triplets, wriggling out of Teddy's arms and toward their colorful, puffy dresses. They all started to giggle as Georgie hopped from puffy dress to puffy dress.

"He's good with kids, I promise," Teddy called over his shoulder to Lucy. "I'll keep an eye out."

She turned a page in her book and sipped her iced coffee, swirling her hand toward the sound of her children's chatter. "I'm just so glad Janine referred you," Lucy said, her eyes peeking happily over the top of her book. "We'll have to take birthday pictures every week if you can wrangle the girls to behave like this!"

Teddy smiled and bent over, scrunching his fingers in the rolls of chub on top of Georgie's neck. His referrals were a bit different now than compared to one year ago.

"Hello, beautiful."

He looked up. Lucas beamed down at him, his hands on his hips and his eyes soft. Sunlight shone around Lucas's head, his quiff messy in his now-regular Saturday-morning style. His black skinnies were cuffed at the ankle, a simple white V-neck tee hung loose off his collarbones, and an open black cardigan flared out from his torso. Lucas was happy to alter his personal training schedule when he had a reason to sleep in on weekends, and Teddy was most definitely glad he was the reason for lazy days spent in bed.

Lucas pulled Teddy up from the ground. They wrapped their arms around each other, squeezing tight for one long moment. Georgie ran around their feet.

"Hi," Teddy whispered against Lucas's neck, pressing his lips beneath his ear. He smoothed his hand up Lucas's chest to cradle the front of his throat. Lucas kissed his jawline. "This is a lovely surprise."

Lucas stepped back with a playful smirk. "Someone fed our boy an obscene amount of treats before he left for work, and he was dying to stretch his legs. For digestion purposes, obviously. Plus—" Lucas swung a brown leather messenger bag around his body. "—I saw you left this at home." He reached inside, producing a long black lens. "Didn't know if you needed it today."

"Aw, you didn't have to walk all the way here to give me that." Teddy took the lens, and their fingers brushed. His cheeks pinked, and Lucas shared his rosy expression. "Thank you, though. That was so sweet of you."

"I heard something weird when I picked it up. I hope I didn't break it in my bag."

"Nah, as long as the lens cover is on, I'm sure it's—" Teddy bent over and gave Georgie, who had started to climb his leg, a firm scratch behind the ears. He patted Georgie's pudgy bum, sending the dog back toward the trio of giggling girls. "I doubt you could have done anything harmful to it."

Lucas asked, "Would you mind checking? If I broke it, the least I could do would be to drop it at the shop for you. It's on the way home."

Teddy snorted and shook his head. He bent enough to brush a kiss to the tip of Lucas's nose.

"You're so cute." He held the lens vertical against his chest. "This type of lens is actually pretty sturdy. It's fine, I'm sure." He unscrewed the black lens cover, watching Georgie run from girl to girl. "Look at Georgie right now. He's totally in his element surrounded by…."

There was a tiny, pinged metallic sound against the glass of the lens, the sound pulling Teddy's attention back to it. A simple silver ring shone under the afternoon sun, the glass lens glinting below the perfect metal band.

Teddy looked forward with frantic, enormous eyes, but found Lucas was no longer standing in front of him. He opened his mouth to call out for him.

"Ahem" came from below.

Teddy looked down and exhaled a choppy laugh, tears of shock prickling his eyes.

Lucas smiled up at him with crinkled eyes, one knee pressed to the grass in a kneeling position. He plucked the ring off Teddy's lens, pinching it between his thumb and pointer finger.

"What is—what—" Teddy's lungs struggled to balance words and airflow. His head shook side to side without his control, his hand clutched to his chest. He laughed out, "What—"

He looked behind Lucas. They weren't alone.

There was an army of overjoyed, buzzing family members flanking Lucas on all sides. Jo trembled and bubbled happy tears, with her iPhone poised, while kneeling next to Lane. Lane held an iPad in her arms with Marcy's face Skyping on the screen, while Dean grinned and held Lane from behind.

Cillian and Zamir, already crying, embraced on either side of Albert with their arms wrapped around him. Albert was taking a video on his own phone while tears glistened in his warm brown eyes. A purple tie broke up his professional ensemble, even on the weekend. Maggie was sitting next to Lucas on the grass in a flamingo-and-watermelon-patterned sundress, grinning and holding Georgie, who now sported a black bow tie.

"We're all sort of a package deal, I suppose," Lucas said softly, spinning the ring and lifting it. "And, despite my pleas to keep this a private moment between us—" He sighed, his eyes crinkling with playful annoyance. "—everyone sort of arrived this morning and congregated near the park."

"Oh, pishposh." Jo scoffed and gently slapped the back of Lucas's head. "He's been ring shopping for months."

"I have not," Lucas insisted, though his smile said otherwise.

Lane butted in. "We've all known this was coming."

"You did?" Teddy asked. His watery eyes glanced from Jo to Lane to Lucas. "You… you want to marry me?"

"Yes! He does!" Maggie shouted, bouncing in place. "We all do!"

Teddy and Lucas laughed.

Lucas reached up and thumbed tears from under Teddy's eyes. Teddy smoothed Maggie's wild curls and scratched between Georgie's ears. The dog panted excitedly. He got down to his knees, bending the soft grass under his weight. He grasped Lucas's ring-holding hand with both of his, cradling their joined hands to his chest. He pressed his face to Lucas's neck. Lucas's free arm looped around the small of his back.

"Marry me, love," Lucas whispered. "Please?"

His voice was the only thing Teddy could hear, even with the chorus of ecstatic people behind him.

"Yes," Teddy whispered back.

Lucas smoothly slipped the ring onto his finger, then wrapped him in his arms. Their family applauded and cheered behind them.

"Yes," Teddy laughed wetly, kissing Lucas's jawline. "Yes!" Their lips connected, uncontrollable smiles breaking up their kisses. "A thousand times yes!"

"I'll call Flamingo Cove!" Cillian exclaimed over the cheers, clapping loud enough to startle a family of tiny white birds out of a nearby tree. "We've got another wedding to plan!"

Suggested Soundtrack

I tend to visualize scenes in a cinematic sort of way, and I often listen to playlists with certain tracks in minds for specific scenes. I've included a suggested soundtrack for *Escapade*, which goes along with any of the songs mentioned within the story itself. The songs are in no way needed to enjoy the story, but I've found that music can usually enhance the experience, whether that be something in the lyrics, the tempo, the driving beat, or the overall energy of the song.

I included a lot of popular songs from the eighties because I felt that era of pop music most fitted *Escapade*: Sexy, fun, luxurious, a bit silly, and adventurous.

Chapter One

1. DURAN DURAN, "HUNGRY LIKE THE WOLF."

I envisioned this song playing right after Lucas secured the deal with Acker-Jones. I thought this was a perfect song to set the tone for the story, since it's a tropical-sounding pop tune that made me think of going on holiday on a yacht. It also went along with the wolf imagery used for Lucas's character throughout.

2. DEPECHE MODE, "PERSONAL JESUS."

This song screamed Jack McQueen to me and felt like his perfect character entrance song in the cab. The sexy slapped rhythm, the low-droned singing that matched his voice, the dark vibe that matched his attire, and the mirroring between Personal Consultant and "Personal Jesus" all seemed too perfect to pass up.

Chapter Three

3. JANET JACKSON, "NASTY."

The first of three Janet Jackson songs on the soundtrack. I am a huge Janet fan and felt like her songs all fit pretty much perfectly into the *Escapade* universe. This song was placed during Jack's shower. In addition to having a great beat that went well with his list of tasks, it was also a small lyrical joke, since Jack is taking care of some heavy duty primping (to make himself less of a nasty boy). Plus, in his profession, he likely came in contact with some nasty boys himself.

Chapter Four

4. MUSE, "DEAD INSIDE."

This song reminded me of the Depeche Mode song from earlier, and I liked that both of Jack and Lucas's meetings were accompanied by synthy, but still crunchy, rock songs that were a bit darker and heavier than the other pop tracks. The lyrics worked for the gala scene because they describe people playing characters, which both Jack and Lucas accuse each other of doing.

Chapter Seven

5. INXS, "Need You Tonight."

This song, to me, is super sexy yet still playful, mysterious, and fun, all of which are very much *Escapade*. I thought it was a good match for Jack's coaxing of Lucas to relax and get comfortable kissing him, along with the extended kissing scene once they get going.

Chapter Eight

6. The Rolling Stones, "Start Me Up."

All the Baby Mick jokes needed a Rolling Stones song on the soundtrack, and this song was similar to INXS in that it was hot but still playful, never creepy or overdone. I imagined this during their kissing scene in Lucas's office, and specifically envisioned it starting when Jack kisses Lucas's neck and gets him going (starts him up).

Chapter Nine

7. Rhoda Williams & Ilene Woods, "Oh, Sing Sweet Nightingale" from Cinderella, (Disney version).

This is the song Lucas hears when he observes Jack sleeping in the guest room. Along with the overall hints at *Cinderella* throughout the story, Jack has a nightingale tattoo on his chest and, as he explained, mirrors the nightingale with his career.

Chapter Ten

8. Janet Jackson, "Escapade."

The second Janet song, and possibly the most perfect for the story. I placed this song at the very start of the airport scene, almost like a signal that the holiday is beginning after the long buildup of them getting together. The tropical vibe and lyrics about getting away were a natural fit.

Chapter Twelve

9. Madonna, "Open Your Heart."

The first karaoke song Teddy sings with Lane. I felt the lyrics worked really well as they hint to the fact that Teddy already knows he and Lucas are falling for each other, and structurally it worked for a quick round of choreography created by Lane and Teddy.

Chapter Fourteen

10. Van Halen, "Jump."

This song played during the Zill-ympics, specifically the Final Countdown. I love movie montages with slightly cheesy songs, and this one seemed to work for the big athletic event in the story.

Chapter Sixteen

11. Depeche Mode, "Precious."

A second Depeche Mode song. This time, instead of the band being used to introduce Jack McQueen, a different type of song is used to symbolize the pain Teddy feels when being faced with Jack McQueen while with Lucas. I imagined this song starting up as Teddy leaves the pool.

Chapter Seventeen

12. The Beatles, "Here Comes the Sun." (Composed by George Harrison.)

As mentioned in Georgie's introduction, he was named after George Harrison due to this song playing on the car radio when he was taken home. Lucas also mentions that Georgie sounded like he was talking over the song when he was distressed. I imagined this song playing during Lucas's bedtime story to soothe Teddy, since Lucas tends to be the unofficial soothing person (bedtime story for Maggie, his love of Georgie, and now with Teddy), even if he would never admit it. This song is so beautiful but also so simple that it almost sounds like a lullaby. It seemed to work for such an emotional moment.

Chapter Eighteen

13. a-ha, "Take on Me."

Back to the eighties, this bubbly song was what I imagined during their scuba scene…

14. Baltimora, "Tarzan Boy."

…And this was the song during cliff jumping. Another homage to eighties movie montages.

Chapter Nineteen

15. Madonna, "Like a Virgin."

I imagined this song starting up when Lucas guides Teddy onto the bed for their first sex scene. Neither are virgins, but I felt it was suited for Teddy especially, since he's feeling very new and different and excited with Lucas compared to anyone else. I also loved the tempo of the song and felt it worked well with the building pleasure of the scene.

16. Blondie, "Rapture."

I imagined this song playing when Lucas falls onto his back after Teddy gave him the Jack McQueen experience. Total relaxation and afterglow.

Chapter Twenty-One

17. Eric Carmen, "Hungry Eyes."

This was for the dance scene, and obviously hints to the iconic *Dirty Dancing*, which they make a few jokes about throughout the story.

Chapter Twenty-Four

18. Foreigner, "I Want to Know What Love Is."

Lucas's karaoke song after the strip club. I wanted to give him something the crowd could sing along to, while also giving him as much of a love song as I could without it being a slow ballad. This is one of my favorite power ballads, and the lyrics about finally finding love seemed perfect for Lucas to sing to Teddy.

Chapter Twenty-Seven

19. Janet Jackson, "Love Will Never Do (Without You)."

The final Janet song in the soundtrack for when they're back home. I imagined this playing when Lucas and Teddy are making tea and Georgie is running around the kitchen. I thought it would be a perfect song for end credits if it were a film, since it has a hopeful, fun, upbeat sound for their happy ending.

Chapter Twenty-Eight (Epilogue)

20. Lionel Richie, "All Night Long (All Night)."

I imagined this song playing when the ring is revealed to the camera lens. I don't know many people who hate this song. It just screams "fun, eighties, group number" to me. If a DJ plays it, people will probably sing and dance. The tropical sound worked well with the story, and I thought it was a fun way to close out the epilogue while hinting that their happiness will only continue.

DOLCE is a twentysomething New Yorker who loves iced coffee, laughs loudly, lives for naps in air conditioning, and choreographs dance moves in the shower. Trained as a classical musician, Dolce found a different part of herself through rock and pop music, which led to her interest in writing.

Dolce is on a lifelong journey to find new brunch spots or restaurants that serve breakfast all day, but is eternally loyal to her favorite diner. She is almost always dressed incorrectly for whatever the current weather is and has a knack for selecting accessories that disintegrate within a week of use.

When not working or writing, Dolce is probably at a copy machine organizing materials; school supplies are gold. She is very slow at replying to online comments, but reads them all and can often be found in her car between gigs, clutching her face over whatever sweet words readers share with her that brighten her day.

A *Real Housewives and Law & Order: SVU* Scholar, Dolce spends an unknown amount of hours each week marathoning episodes she's definitely seen before, wondering when the day will come that she can afford to get a professional blowout every other day. She hopes that day is soon.

Tumblr: haydolce.tumblr.com
Email: dolce@dolcewrites.com

Also from Dreamspinner Press

www.dreamspinnerpress.com

Also from Dreamspinner Press

www.dreamspinnerpress.com

Also from Dreamspinner Press

www.dreamspinnerpress.com

Also from Dreamspinner Press

www.dreamspinnerpress.com